# MY FATHER'S GOD

GWAMBI TETRALOGY
BOOK THREE

A. C. WILSON

*My Father's God*, volume 3 in the *Gwambi Tetralogy* by A. C. Wilson

Copyright © 2025 A. C. Wilson



Interior illustrations by Shelby Elizabeth

Cover by Kirk DouPonce

ISBNs:
978-1-959666-88-2 (paperback)
978-1-959666-89-9 (ebook)

Published by:
**Wise Path Books**
a division of To A Finish LLC
12407 N MoPac Expy #250
Austin, TX 78758

www.wisepathbooks.com

rev: 10/31/2025

*To Beni:*

*For forcing me to read fantasy.*
*What else are brother's for?*

# CONTENTS

## GWAMBI TETRALOGY

# GWAMBI TETRALOGY

BOOK THREE

The Year 1027 KA
Entwerp City, Llaedhwyth

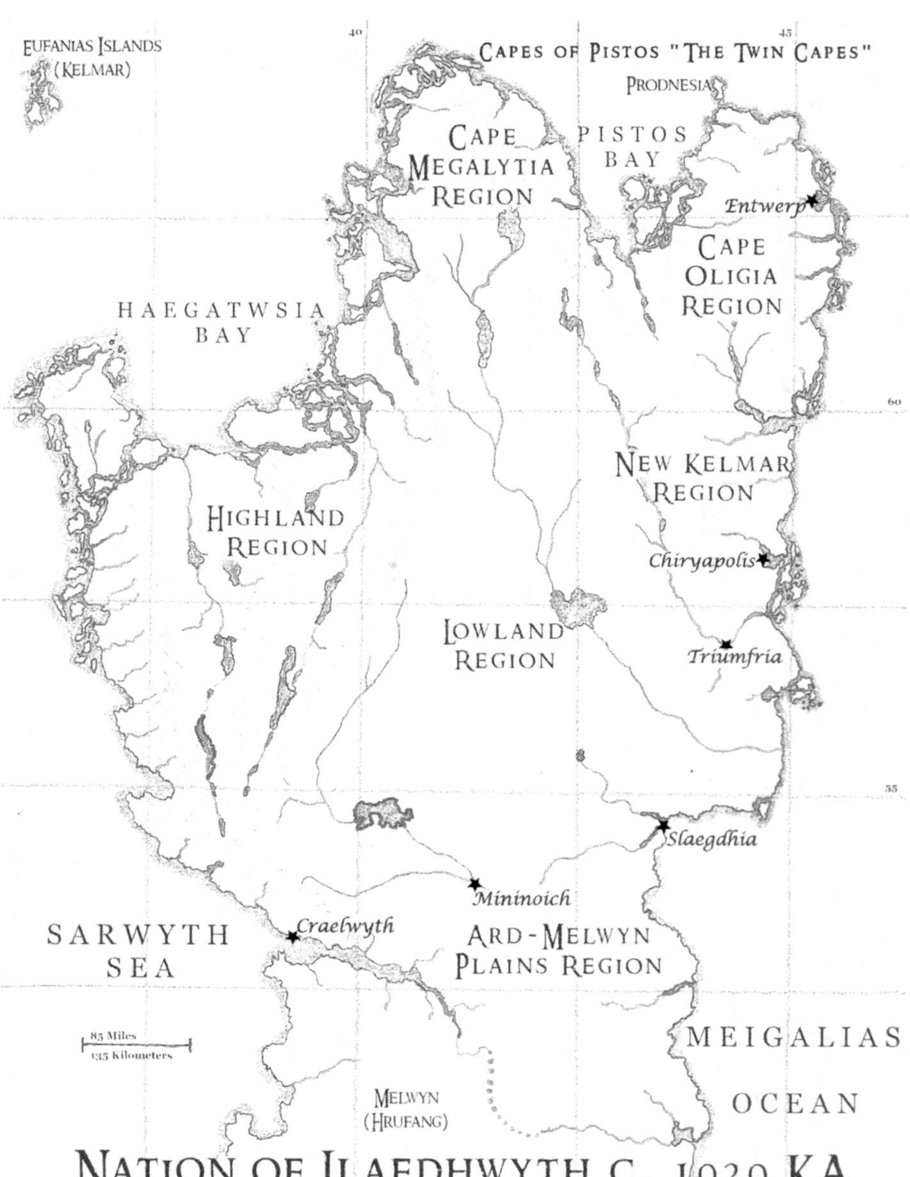


# NATION OF LLAEDHWYTH C. 1020 KA

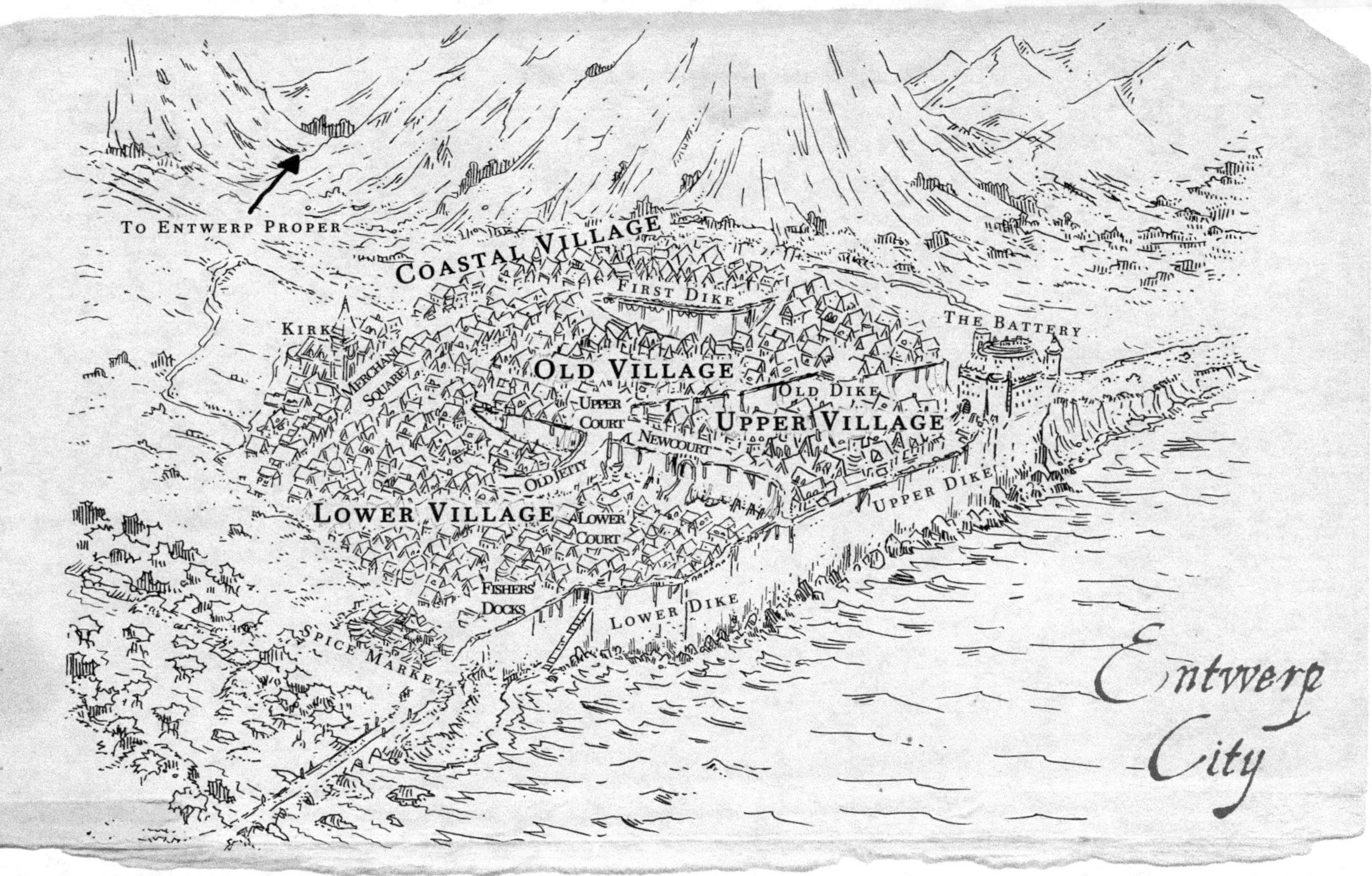

To Entwerp Proper
Coastal Village
First Dike
The Battery
Kirk
Merchant Square
Old Village
Old Dike
Upper Court
Upper Village
New Court
Old Jetty
Lower Village
Lower Court
Upper Dike
Fishers
Docks
Lower Dike
Spice Market
Entwerp City

# PROLOGUE

*E*rnest could feel the coarse wooden match between his fingers, but he could see nothing in the utter blackness. Without the aid of his eyes, every other sense in Ernest's body strained to give him information. The galleon slowly rocking beneath his feet as the stiff night breeze filled its sails, the salty freshness in the air tingling Ernest's nostrils. His ears could clearly make out the groaning of the ship, the sails snapping against the wind, the rigging creaking, and the mournful cry of a far-off night-hawk. Most of all Ernest could hear the hot breathing of Cweel, the Eagle Griffin, just at his side, loud and harsh in the stillness of that night.

Ernest held the match firmly now. He felt in front of him with his other hand, and his fingers touched the wooden side of the stern. Now he only had to strike it. Ernest set the match to the wood, then took a slow, deep breath as he struck the head of the match across the weathered wood of the stern.

The match sparked, sputtered, hissed, and then the flame stabilized; just a small, flickering flame dancing at the end of that match. Ernest looked at the light closely, breathing deeply as he did so. Beside him, he could hear Cweel take in a sudden breath and then let out a quiet chuckle.

This was it.

This insignificant spark of fire would begin the inferno that was to follow. Ernest shook his head. That little flame could hardly banish the darkness two feet from itself — such a small flame, and yet such a deadly purpose.

Ernest heard Cweel let out a low hiss. "What are *you* waiting for?"

Ernest sighed. "Alright then."

He looked down, seeing a gleam of light reflecting off the line of oil on the well-worn deck. Grimacing, Ernest dropped the match — a comet falling through the darkness.

The flame had no sooner tasted of the oil than it leapt up in a blaze, streaking across the deck like a devouring lion and curling up the masts and rigging with the fury and revelry of hell.

Ernest trembled all over as he surveyed the scene which the fire brought to light. The grisly corpses of his crew members lay strewn across the entire deck, left where Longfinch and his pirates had cut them down. The air filled steadily with the putrid smell of cremation.

Ernest felt sick, his gut rising inside of him. How had it come to this?

Suddenly, he heard a metallic clink just at his feet. He looked down to see Cweel locking a chain around his ankle.

"What's this!" Ernest cried in horror. "Longfinch do'edn't say anything about a chain. How am I supposed to get off this ship?"

Cweel snickered devilishly. "No, he *didn't*, did he?"

"Absolutely not!" Ernest replied, shaking his head emphatically. "He only sayed I haved to steer this fire-ship to the battery; that's all what he sayed."

Cweel snickered again. "Well then, *this* is to make sure that *you* do just that."

Cweel leapt into the air, beating his wings and cackling. As he rose from the deck, the smoke curled about the Eagle Griffin. He twisted and whirled just above the hungry flames like a demon cavorting above the fires of hell.

Ernest was in a panic now. He pulled on the chain, but it held fast to the helm. He kicked out and tried to shake his shackles loose, but the chain still held.

"How am I supposed to get off on this ship?" Ernest cried. "Longfinch sayed that he'd let me live if'n I bringed this ship to the battery."

Cweel laughed again, fluttering back towards Ernest and hovering just before him. The Griffin's wing-strokes beat back the smoke and fanned the flames into new fury all around him. "Of course, that *is* what he said."

"Then how am I to get off and get away?" Ernest asked desperately.

Cweel waved a key in his fore-claws. "*I* will unlock the chain if *you* bring the ship safely to dock."

Cweel snickered again, beating his wings heavily. He soared into the air, cutting a quick circle around the flaming mainmast before flying directly over Ernest again.

"A *word* of advice," the Eagle Griffin cried, hovering like a phantom in the smoke. "Guide her well and guide her *quickly*. *You* would not want her to *explode* before you reached the docks, now would you?"

The Griffin cackled again and sped away through the air, heading back to Longfinch's man-o-war.

Ernest watched Cweel go. He looked long and hard at the twinkling lights on board the man-o-war as it kept its distance behind the fire-ship. Ernest's heart pounded in his chest, and he swallowed. He turned back to the galleon again, surveying the flaming deck strewn with his comrades' bodies.

He shook his leg, hearing the chain rattle against the deck. Would Cweel really come back for him? Or was he condemned to death when the flames reached the ammunition charges?

Ernest set his jaw firmly, gripping the wheel of the helm before him. There was really nothing else he could do. He had to submit and do all that he was told. He would prove to Longfinch that his life was worth saving.

Looking through the flames, he could see the little village of Entwerp Coastal stretched out on the other side of the bay. House lights flickered cheerily above the city's dikes. Ernest's heart grew heavy at the sight of them. Lexi was in one of those houses. He was about to destroy *her* home.

Ernest felt like groaning. This blazing ship he piloted was no more than a match. It was nothing to be compared with the flame of violence that would soon consume that peaceful town.

1

# APOSTLE

It wasn't a dream. Not precisely. Of course, Clerans was asleep, and the images running through his head were very like dreaming. The problem was that they really happened.

The young striker stared at Clerans, blood leaking from the gruesome bullet hole in his side. "My mother. Tell my mother..."

"I do no know yer mother," Clerans was sobbing, and he was cradling the man in his arms, as the life left him.

"Come along, lads, let's clean this up." And the spokesman waved his hand dismissively, as his cronies fired point blank into the strikers — the strikers who were actually trying to change things for good.

And the one-armed striker was collapsing wetly against Clerans, grabbing at his coat sleeve.

"Get that letter out o' here, younker."

He had taken the bullet that should have blown a hole through Clerans instead.

And then there was Governor Braedhwyc, wiping puss from

his leaky eye as he strode past the dying remnants of a group of strikers.

"Shoot them on sight!"

"They are strikers, Clerans." Sheriff Laei was looking at him in confusion, and Clerans readjusted the man he carried drooped over his shoulder.

"Does that mean they are no longer people?"

The sheriff looked away, whispering, "I did no teach you that."

"No."

And Clerans was trudging the long, long road to the doctor's house.

"I ha' to learn that the hard way."

---

CLERANS WOKE WITH A SUDDEN START. Tears streamed down his cheeks, and he folded his legs up to his chest, hugging his arms around them. He was trembling all over, his chest heaving, as his throat choked with sobs. It wasn't supposed to be like this. He was supposed to be a soldier, proud of fighting the bad guys and keeping his village safe. Fighting wasn't supposed to be dark and bloody, was it?

He did not know how long he sat there, sobbing into the darkness, before he finally got control of his breathing again. He still clutched his knees to his chest, breathing in great gulps of air. What was he doing? This is what he wanted for his life. He wanted to be a soldier. Didn't he?

In the bed beside him, Robert snorted loudly and rolled onto his back, letting out a long series of snores. Clerans wiped his eyes, took a deep breath. He should be sleeping, too. He desperately needed the sleep. He shuddered involuntarily at the thought. What other memory would he have to relive if he closed his eyes?

Just then, the door cracked slowly open. There was a low light from the room beyond, casting a halo of light around his father's figure.

Clerans stiffened, wiping his eyes again. What time was it?

"Clerans?"

"Ay, Da, what is it?"

His father gave him a foreboding look. "Get dressed, Clerans; the Sheriff is waitin' fer ye in the family room."

Clerans threw aside his sheets and shimmied into his overclothes. His fingers worked out of habit, his mind too exhausted to contemplate what was likely just another training session with the sheriff.

Clerans quickly left his room, leaving his two younger brothers, Robert and Roland, still asleep in their beds. Walking quickly down the hallway, Clerans entered the family room, where he could see his father, his two older brothers Martyn and Laendon, and Sheriff Laei standing silently and ominously before the dying light of the fire.

The sheriff looked up as soon as Clerans entered. "Good. Ye are here."

Clerans looked briefly around. Da, Martyn, and Laendon all had their rifles, and even now Martyn was honing one of his skinning knives. It certainly looked like the sheriff was summoning them to defend the dikes. But they wouldn't all be on duty at once. For a moment, Clerans' heart dropped. The Sheriff must be calling for a complete mobilization of the militia, the very last resort of desperate defense, where everyone above the age of fourteen would be called upon to defend the village (excepting only the women with young children depending on them). But no, that couldn't be right. The village wasn't in danger — certainly not *that* much danger. Clerans was just reeling from his bad dreams. Besides, Sheriff Laei would not come personally if he was calling up a complete mobilization. But then, why was he here? And why was Da strapping his tomahawk to his belt?

Clerans threw a casual salute, trying not to show the anxiety that was coursing through him.

"I need ye to vene with me," the sheriff said.

Clerans nodded. "Ay, sir, an' will I need my weapons?"

The sheriff nodded darkly.

Clerans quickly grabbed his own rifle, knife, and tomahawk, casting a sidelong glance at his Da and brothers. Neither of them was moving. Were they not coming too? Lacing on his boots as quickly as he could, he stepped out the door after the sheriff.

"God be with ye, my son!" his father called out behind him. So they were *not* coming with him. Clerans' heart was racing now, but he forced a roguish smile as he looked over his shoulder at his father and brothers. Then the sheriff swung the door shut behind them.

"Come along, then."

The sheriff now walked off quickly, setting a course directly towards the battery. Clerans took a deep breath of the salty night air to calm himself. For a moment he felt like whistling a fortifying tune as he walked, but one glance at the sheriff's grim demeanor told him he had better be a little more sober. The sheriff was always a bit grim, but there seemed to be something desperate about him tonight.

Clerans licked his lips, quickening his steps so that he could come up level with the sheriff.

"Is it the pirates, then, Sheriff?"

The sheriff nodded. "Ay, Clerans, they ha' returned, I'm afraid."

"Do ye need me at the battery, then?" Clerans asked.

The sheriff shook his head. "There's other work I tain fer ye."

Clerans raised an eyebrow. "That sounds foreboding."

The sheriff cracked a dry smile. "I suppose it does, does no it?"

Just then, a voice called out in the darkness behind them, "Sheriff Laei!"

The sheriff halted abruptly and turned to face the voice. "Ay, here I am."

A young man came rushing down the street towards them. "Governor Braedhwyc ha' legated me back to ye, sir."

"Ay," the sheriff said, stamping his foot on the cobblestones impatiently. "Ay, an' what does he say?"

The youth reached the sheriff now and saluted, panting heavily. "The governor says that he cen no spare ye any more men."

The Sheriff ground his teeth together. "Cede back to the governor, then, and tell him that if I'll cen no tain any more men, the dikes *will* fall, and the pirates *will* sack this entire village."

"Ay," the messenger said, "an' that is jist the eventuality fer why the governor cen no send more men. He wants to tain men left to guard the bank."

The Sheriff growled in frustration. "But they will no get to the bank if I'll cen hold them off *here*. Tell the governor to give me thirty more men — jist thirty — an' I cen hold them off at the dikes with a complete mobilization of the militia."

Clerans' heart skipped a beat. Why was he already contemplating a complete mobilization? No pirate could make it past the battery.

The messenger nodded. "Ay, an' he will only tell ye that then he would tain thirty *fewer* men to guard the bank."

"An' what immediate danger is the bank in, eh?" the sheriff cried.

The messenger wilted a bit, but still continued. "The governor is afraid that the strikers may ceive this opportunity to attack again. He wants all o' his men with him to hold them back should they'll try anything."

The sheriff shook his head. "Confound those strikers!" And he turned on his heels, marching off again towards the battery. "Tell the governor," he called over his shoulder, "that I need *thirty more men*. You tell him that, an' if he'll refuses, cede back an' tell him again!"

The messenger sighed wearily and then ran off.

Clerans rushed after the sheriff, trying to keep pace with him. He had never seen the sheriff so upset before.

"Sheriff?" Clerans asked, "What's goin' on?"

"Coincidence, ha!" Sheriff Laei said, apparently not hearing Clerans' question. "Do you think the pirates and the strikers are a coincidence?" The sheriff shook his head and growled.

"It is the pirates, then? Is that what is happenin'?" Clerans asked.

"Ay," the sheriff replied.

Clerans furrowed his brow. "Then why the concern? Ha' no we driven them off a'fore?"

The sheriff nodded. "Ay — but this is Longfinch we are talkin' about."

"True," Clerans said, "but he tried to attack once already, and he could no even make it past the battery. He never reached the dikes. Why would this time be any different? No pirate ha' ever made it past the power o' the Entwerp Battery!"

The sheriff smiled slightly and looked over at Clerans. "Maybe I jist need some o' yer optimism, Clerans." The sheriff sighed and looked forward again glumly.

"So, what is the concern?" Clerans asked, hurrying to keep up with the sheriff's rapid strides.

"Ha' ye heard o' an fire-ship, Clerans?" the sheriff asked abruptly.

Clerans squinted his eyes as he thought. "Ay... I think so. Is no that a ship that ha' been loaded with charges so that it will explode an' destroy any other ship around it?"

The sheriff nodded. "Ay, that is it."

Just then, they came to the Old Dike Wall, where the sheriff halted. From here they could look out over the rooftops of the town below them (right out over the Upper Dike Wall) and see the bay stretching out before them in the dark night. There was not a sliver of a moon in the sky; only the stars' pinpoints of light tingled in the black canopy above.

The sheriff pointed across the bay. "Ay, *that* is it."

Clerans looked out where the sheriff was pointing and saw a glowing light on the far side of the bay. It flickered and danced like flame, but even from this distance, Clerans could tell it was a ship's outline. At a reasonable distance from this flaming ship, Clerans could see a second ship (the man-o-war he remembered from the first attack) gliding through the water like a hawk on the wing.

The sheriff shook his head and started walking again. "Ay, *that* is a fire-ship."

Clerans hurried after the sheriff. "I see it, sheriff, fer sure I do. But what is the concern? If they'll sail that to the docks, they may cause some damage I s'pose, but they surely cen no breach the dikes, and they certainly cen no damage the battery."

The sheriff shook his head. "Oh no, I fear they'll most certain *may* damage the battery... if no destroy it completely."

Clerans raised his eyebrows in surprise and disbelief. "How would anyone damage the battery? I cen no but think that it is invincible with how well built it is. Its walls are so merri o' thick that–"

The sheriff cut him off. "Ay, it wos very well built, an' ha' stood fer us thus far, but this is *Longfinch* we're dealin' with. He ha' done the impossible many times a'fore now."

"But how?" Clerans asked, still skeptical.

The sheriff shook his head. "When they built that new dike,

the engineers ha' to expose some o' the battery's foundations to tie it into the dike — ye can still see that exposed foundation next to the docks. At high tide, the bay reaches right up to it."

The sheriff paused and looked Clerans in the eye meaningfully, as if trying to impress on him the importance of what he was about to say. "It is spring tide now, and that fire-ship could sail right up to the foundation o' the battery. If Longfinch could blow out those foundation supports, the whole battery would slide into the bay."

Clerans looked at the sheriff in alarm. Could that be true? He had never thought of such a possibility. To be honest, he had never once considered that the battery had any vulnerabilities.

The sheriff sighed. "I ha' seen that weakness fer many years, an' I ha' known that wos how this city would fall. I pray to God that it ha' no vened to that now."

"It cen no be," Clerans broke in. "Those supports are solid granite. Surely a fire-ship could no destroy them."

The sheriff smiled grimly. "Ay, with mere gunpowder, mayhaps ye would be right. But, with dynamite... ay, then they would tain the power to destroy the foundations."

"Dynamite!" Clerans exclaimed. "Where would a pirate get his hands on dynamite? What would make ye think that Longfinch tains–"

The sheriff continued to look Clerans in the face, and his eyes hardened in desperation. "A little research, Clerans. I ha' jist heard from a friend from Slaegdhia that the pirate Longfinch wos last sighted off the coast o' Ciro. He attacked a chemical factory there. Do ye want to make a guess what that chemical factory wos makin' at the time o' the attack?" The sheriff didn't wait for a reply. "Dynamite. That factory was manufacturing dynamite fer the railroads. Ay, an' Longfinch made off with enough sticks o' dynamite to raze this entire village, Entwerp Proper, and Maerybion to boot."

The sheriff shook his head. "Ay, I am afraid he ha' been plannin' this fer a merri long time, an' the chances o' his plan misfirin' now are pretty slim. After all, this is Longfinch we are dealin' with."

Clerans could feel a sense of panic forming in his gut. Did the sheriff really believe they would lose the battery? But if they lost the battery...

Clerans looked out across the bay again to see that second ship (the man-o-war) still moving in slowly behind the fire-ship. If they lost the battery, that ship would certainly land on the dikes. Without enough men to defend the dikes, the village would fall.

Clerans took a deep breath, then faced the sheriff again, allowing the true gravity of the situation to fall on him. "Alright then, sir. What am I to do?"

At that moment, the great alarm bells sounded loud and clear, ringing out dolefully from the mountainside above the battery. In answer, lights sprang up in windows all around Clerans. He could see shadows of people moving around inside the low stone houses. A few moments later, the doors swung open as the sturdy and well-armed men of the village marched off quickly towards the battery.

The sheriff looked around and let out his breath slowly. "Well then, the summons are made."

The sheriff seized Clerans by the shoulder and started walking again at a brisk pace.

"Hurry!" the sheriff said. "We tain merri little time now."

# 2

# A GREAT COMMISSION

The sheriff walked quickly through the streets of the city, marching from the Old Village down into the Upper Village. He took a small alley onto the Broadway, always heading towards the docks, and dragging Clerans along with him. Clerans breathed heavily, practically running to keep pace with the sheriff. Once he had thought that *he* could move quickly through the town while delivering messages for the Beacon Company. Well, he was wrong. The sheriff was certainly putting him to shame.

"Fire ships are merri finicky things," the sheriff was saying. "It is a merri o' an art to load the ship correctly, an' start the fire jist so as to tain the ship explode right when it is supposed to — no before or after."

Clerans nodded. He was trying to listen to the sheriff as best he could, but staying on his feet while he hurried over the uneven cobblestone streets was about all his mind was up for at the moment.

"Ay, but that's no the half o' it," the sheriff continued. "Aimin' the fire-ship at its mark... that is an entire art to itself. Ye cen tie the helm in place an' hope ye aimed the ship right, or ye cen leave a crew member aboard to steer the ship in place. Both tain their own risks."

They now reached the Upper Dike Wall. The sheriff walked quickly along it to the north until he was directly beneath the ominous face of the battery. Clerans looked up at the hundreds of gun ports which peppered the battery's formidable granite face. Already he could hear men inside the battery wheeling the cannons into place and loading them. They were certainly preparing for battle, as usual. So why did the sheriff have him here? What was he to do?

The sheriff now turned, walking down a tiny pier which jutted out from the dike directly beneath the battery. Clerans followed.

"There are only two ways to defeat a fire-ship," Sheriff Laei said. Clerans was now listening fully, waiting to hear his orders.

The sheriff paused and turned to look Clerans fully in the face. "First, we could fire on the ship an' hope that one o' our cannon balls might detonate the charges a'fore the ship reaches us. However, that runs the risk o' no detonating the ship in time. Second, is to send someone to board the fire-ship and steer it away from its target. However, that runs the risk o' killin' whoever boards the ship." The sheriff took a deep sigh and looked at Clerans earnestly.

Clerans took a deep breath. "Am I, then..."

The sheriff placed both his hands on Clerans' shoulders, nodding soberly. "Clerans, ye are the only man I would send to do this. I ha' trained ye, an' I ha' garded ye, an' I know that ye cen do this — if anyone cen! Ye are a merri brave younker, an' ye will no shrink from doin' what needs to be done. The way ye took care o' those pirates in the city the other day wos strong evidence o' that." The sheriff sighed, a look of grief passing over his face. "An' the way you conducted yourself against the strikers was nothing but admirable. I would wish that I'll never ha' to send ye into sich a dangerous situation, but I am confident that ye cen handle yerself."

Clerans saluted, trying to feel confident as he contemplated exactly what the sheriff was sending him to do. "So then, I am to swim to the fire-ship, board it, an' then steer it away from the city?"

The sheriff allowed himself a small smile. "There is a boat fer ye jist behind ye. Otherwise ye tain the gist o' it."

Clerans nodded. "Ay then."

He turned around to see a small boat tied to the pier just behind him. With another deep breath, he stepped into the boat and untied it. So this was his adventure tonight? He would board a flaming ship laced with dynamite, steer it away from the village, and then hopefully get off before it exploded. At least he shouldn't have any well-meaning strikers bleeding out on him. It was simple, with a guilt-free objective — the way it was supposed to be.

"Be careful now," the sheriff said. "There may be pirates on board the fire-ship guardin' it so that no one cen steer it away. Ay, an' if they'll see that *ye* tain command o' the ship, they'll may send out a boatload more o' them to board the fire-ship *themselves* an' steer it *back* on target."

Clerans touched his rifle and nodded. "Ay, sir, I tain my weapons." There was no way he would feel guilty about killing pirates.

"Do ye tain a pistol?"

Clerans shook his head.

"Ay then." The sheriff pulled out his own pistol and tossed it to Clerans. "Ceive mine. It'll may be o' some use fer ye."

Clerans now sat himself down at the stern of the little boat. Grabbing hold of the oars, he rowed away from the little pier, looking over his shoulder now and again to see the bay, with the far-away light of the fire-ship before him.

"If ye'll cen no steer it away," the sheriff called out after him, "fire off both yer guns into the air and then dive overboard. That will be my signal to tell the battery to try an' gun down the fire-ship."

"Ay, sir!" Clerans called back. "We will bring this fire-ship down one way or the other!"

"God be with ye, Clerans!" the sheriff replied. "May He guide yer hands to war."

*Guide my hands to war,* Clerans prayed. *Ay, God, guide my hands.*

Clerans now turned all of his attention to rowing. The bay was relatively calm that night, so he had to do very little navigating around waves. He set his course straight for the fire-ship. Pulling hard against the oars, he dug deep into the water to make every stroke count. In a matter of moments, his little boat was skimming across the surface of the bay; the lights of the village astern, the flame of the fire-ship before him, and the sparkling points of the stars above him reflected in the waters of the bay beneath him.

The fire-ship steadily moved towards him, and he rapidly made his way towards it. Perhaps in another twenty minutes he would reach that flaming ship. Clerans pulled on with the oars, breathing deeply after each stroke, allowing his body to enter the rhythm of his rowing.

So this was it. He was embarking on his first real adventure. He wouldn't let that messy business with the strikers count. No, that hadn't been an adventure at all, only horrifying and needful. Clerans shivered.

No, but this was his very first adventure. He would board that flaming ship, facing dangers on all sides. Of course there were the flames themselves, but then he might have to battle pirates aboard the ship (or pirates *boarding* the ship), and then he must see that he got well clear of the ship before it exploded. Clerans pulled hard against the oars, huffing as he studied the fire-ship over his shoulder.

*The Fire-Ship*

Clearly, he needed to approach it in such a way as not to be seen from the man-o-war coming on just behind. So long as he was in the middle of the dark waters, he suspected he was invisible. However, the closer he came to the fire-ship, the more likely it was that the light of the flames would reveal him to the pirates aboard the man-o-war. He would have to be careful then to stay on this near side of the fire-ship, always allowing the fire-ship to block the man-o-war's view of him.

Clerans took a deep breath. He could do this.

After only a few more minutes of rowing, Clerans was almost to the fire-ship. The flames were roaring furiously, cracking and spitting like demons, but the flame was still confined to the deck, so Clerans, as yet, could not feel the heat of the fire from where he was low down in the water. Still, the air was thick with the smell of burning wood, and an odd smell that reminded Clerans of his Ma's roast pork.

He was now only a few yards from the prow of the burning galleon. Realizing now that he was risking being rammed as the fire-ship plowed through the water, he quickly began rowing his little boat backwards. Though he was more likely to find a way up onto the galleon from the side, he knew he couldn't risk rowing out to the side. Only by staying here (directly in front of the fire-ship) would he be invisible from the man-o-war.

As he rowed frantically (trying to stay ahead of the fire-ship), he scanned the hull of the ship, seeing if he could spot a way to climb up to the deck. To his disappointment, he could see no stray rigging lines or anything of the sort that he might have used. Bother. That would have been too easy, wouldn't it?

Still, he needed to devise some way to climb aboard — and quickly. His arms were wearing out, and there was no way he could keep ahead of the fire-ship much longer. He had to think of a way to climb up on deck.

There! He could see an open gun port just off to the side of the prow. It was a little way up, but Clerans thought that if he were to stand on his little boat and jump, he could grab onto the gun port.

Clerans heaved one last time with his oars, using every bit of strength he could muster. Dropping the oars, he jumped to his feet, wobbling a bit as the boat bucked underneath him. To reassure himself, he touched the shoulder strap of his rifle. It was secure for the jump. This was it. He'd only get one chance at this.

The little boat skimmed ahead of the galleon, but it was slowing down. The fire-ship plowed on, rapidly overtaking the little boat. Clerans watched as the fire-ship closed the short distance between it and his boat. He fixed his eyes on the gun port. Yes, it wasn't too far up. With a good jump, he should easily be able to reach it.

Just as the galleon came up to the little boat, and just a second before they collided, Clerans sprang. As he leapt, the little boat slid out from underneath him, taking away all his momentum. He didn't so much jump as simply pitch forward, face-first. The barnacle-covered side of the ship slammed into him, just before the icy waters of the bay washed around him.

# 3

# FROM THE DEPTHS

*P*ain coursed through his body. Kicking frantically, Clerans fought his way back to the surface. But the ship plowed on, the wake curling around the prow. He gasped for breath, but then the wake sucked him back under the water and threw him against the side of the ship. Again, the ship's hard hull slammed into him. The barnacles on the side of the ship sliced into him, cutting his clothing and lacerating his skin.

Clerans kicked and struggled, trying to get out of the way of the ship, but the curling wake pressed him in close, dragging him across the side of the barnacle-covered hull as if he were a cube of cheese on the grating board. His lungs burned for air, and the harsh saltwater stung in his wounds.

Suddenly, Clerans' hand felt something in the water. He seized it. With sudden violence, his arm caught his total weight, and he stopped sliding across the barnacles. He reached out with his other hand to grab on to whatever he had seized upon. Was it a rope?

He hauled as hard as he could, now fighting against the water that rushed against him. Then his head broke the surface of the water. Clerans gasped deeply of the fresh, salty air. The wake curled around his head, pulling on him as if it were trying to drag him back under the water and slice him to pieces on the barnacles again. Clerans gritted his teeth and hauled harder on the rope, slowly drawing himself out of the foaming wake.

Finally, he pulled himself free of the water. For a moment, he dangled there from the side of the ship on this life-saving rope, trying to rest his aching muscles. He breathed heavily as the water (mingling with blood from his open wounds) ran off of him, dripping into the churning waters below. The salt water stung his fresh cuts terribly. *So that is what keelhauling feels like,* Clerans thought. He sighed. *Thank you, Lord, for this rope.*

Clerans sighed again. This adventure certainly didn't seem to have any romantic, rosy hue about it. He had to focus. He couldn't afford another miscalculation. The village was in danger. His family's lives were at stake. He had to turn this fire-ship away.

*Lord,* he prayed, *give me strength. Guide my hands to war.*

Setting his jaw firmly, Clerans hauled himself up the rope. He reached the gunwale and grabbed hold of it, but here he paused. There was no telling what might await him on deck. He should be ready for anything now. Perhaps there would be some pirates aboard ready to intercept him. At any rate, he had to be prepared. Clerans took a deep breath and then let it out slowly.

With one more pull, he slid over the gunwale onto the deck. Crouching there for a moment, he looked around him. The smoke smarted his eyes and filled his nostrils with a dreadful stench like burning meat. Flames enveloped all the rigging before him. Here and there, he could see spots of deck and gunwales that were burning as well, but the flames had not yet scorched the area of the deck where he crouched; certainly this was another great providence. He seemed to be on the mid-ship on the lowest deck.

He could feel the heat of the flames now, though it wasn't unbearable. (Actually, the fire was drying him out effectively.)

As Clerans surveyed the deck a second time, he recoiled in horror. Piles of corpses lay strewn about in every direction. Many of the bodies were badly mutilated, and several were already succumbing to the greedy flames. Clerans shivered in disgust, bile rising in his stomach. So that was what had smelled like roasting pork. This ship suddenly made him feel uneasy, as if some phantom killer haunted it, lurking even now in the shadows formed by the billowing clouds of black smoke.

However, he could see no imminent threat. Clerans let out a sigh and sat on the deck for a moment, leaning his back against the gunwale. He needed to gather his strength, if only for a moment or two. His arms were aching from his exertion, and he was out of breath (as if his body were still working on a deficit from the breaths he had lost underwater). Clerans groaned lightly. He was already cut up and sore, and this was only the beginning of his adventure. But if he could justify taking a moment to catch his breath, he knew he could not delay long enough to look at his wounds.

There was a loud cracking sound to Clerans' left. He jumped back, snatching at his rifle. To his horror, he felt no rifle on his shoulder. *Llifsa!* He must have lost it in the water. He bit the inside of his cheek in frustration. That rifle had cost him nearly two years' earnings.

Clerans quickly scanned the deck again. It must have been the fire that he had heard; he could see nothing through the flames and smoke. With his rifle gone, Clerans pulled out each of his weapons and looked them over, while he continued to catch his breath.

Yes, he still had Sheriff Laei's pistol, but the sea had ruined the charges (of course). His knife and tomahawk had survived just fine, and his powder horn and bag of shot remained tied to his belt. Clerans carefully opened his powder horn and found, to his satisfaction, that the powder was still dry.

Letting out a deep sigh of relief, he quickly knocked the wet powder from his pistol and reloaded it. He worked as quickly as he could, his heart pounding in his chest. He desperately wished he had time to strip the pistol and oil it, but he had to content himself with the simple change of powder. His lacerated skin was throbbing, and he could feel warm blood running down from his right shoulder, but he forced the pain into the back of his mind. No time to worry about that now.

Standing to his feet, Clerans took a deep breath to relax his body. There! Now he was ready for whatever this ship would throw at him next. He glanced around the deck one last time. But for the bodies everywhere, it looked deserted. Maybe the pirates had sent the fire-ship on its way unmanned. That would make his task easier. He only had to find the helm then, and he could turn the ship from its fatal course.

He looked aft, but couldn't make out much of anything through the thick, black smoke. Certainly, the fire was burning more furiously on that side of the ship. It would be quite difficult to navigate through the flames and get up to the poop-deck, but that was what he had to do.

Clerans took another deep breath (trying not to recoil at the odor of burning flesh), and then he marched towards the aft end of the ship. He would have to be quick now. He had lost a lot of time, as it was. Stepping nimbly over the corpses all along the deck, Clerans weaved his way around the dancing flames. The fire now burned hot against his face, and he was thankful for his wet clothes to keep him from being singed. The smoke burned his eyes, and the filthy smell of the burning corpses stung in his nostrils.

Soon enough, however, he came up to a wall of flames which he could see no way through. *Tar and needles!* There was only one way for it, then. Clerans took a few steps back and rushed forward as quickly as he could. He broke through the flames, coming out on a scorched bit of deck on the other side. Stumbling heavily, his foot broke through the burnt wood of the deck, and he pitched forward onto his face. The deck crumbled beneath him in a shower of charcoal, but (as providence would have it) his chest struck on a floor joist, which still held solid. He gripped tightly to the joist. Clerans could now look through this new hole in the deck to the level below.

Very little fire had reached the lower deck, but, even in the dim light, Clerans could see cannon-shot, merlon spikes, axe heads, and other metal oddities covering the whole lower deck. Clerans drew in his breath sharply. When this fire reached the ammunition charges, the explosion would hurl that metal in all directions like shrapnel from a gigantic grenade.

Just then, Clerans heard a voice calling out over the roaring of the fire, "Who's there?"

Clerans tingled all over in apprehension. He was not alone then. There *were* pirates on this ship. Hurriedly, Clerans scrambled along the floor joist to a more solid section of deck.

"Who's there?" the voice called again.

Clerans stayed crouched low, peering through the smoke and fire to see if he could glimpse the speaker. The fire burned hot against him, and he knew he would have to move soon or be burned. He slowly stood up when the loud report of a gun sounded from very near him. Clerans threw himself flat on the scorched deck again, just as a bullet embedded in the deck not three feet from him.

Clerans scuttled forward, breaking through a screen of smoke to find himself at the base of the poop-deck. There was a wall in front of him, which was still relatively unburned. On both sides of this wall, he could make out the remains of wide staircases rising to the upper deck (both burning wildly). Clerans stood up, flattening himself against this wall.

He guessed the helm rested just above him on the poop-deck. Therefore, the pirate who had shot at him was probably guarding the helm. Sure enough, as he stood there waiting,

Clerans could just make out the sounds of footsteps on the deck above him.

"Who's there?" the pirate called out again.

Clerans peered at the two stairways to the poop-deck. He would have to climb one of them if he were to reach the helm. The stairway on his right seemed almost totally consumed by flames, but the left staircase was not much better off. Still, as he looked at it, he thought he could see a way up the stairway on his left. He would have to jump a few of the steps to avoid falling through the scorched wood, and he'd have to run pretty quickly up the stairway to keep from being scorched himself, but he was pretty sure he could do it. Anyway, he *had* to do it. The safety of the village depended on him.

Once he reached the poop-deck, however, there would be a pirate waiting for him. Clerans snatched up his tomahawk and knife. It was probably better not to have his pistol primed and cocked while running through the flames. Clerans took a deep breath, uttering a prayer before rushing up the steps.

*Lord, guide my hands to war.*

4

## FIRE AND SULFUR

The fire and smoke seemed almost to cut into Clerans' flesh as it swirled around him. In a moment, he reached the stairs and bounded up them, trusting the first two stairs, then leaping the next three, again trusting his weight to the right side of the next step, then the left side of the next two, jumping a few more stairs, and then he was on the deck. The heat of the fire was blistering his cheeks, and steam (or perhaps smoke) rose off his clothing, but he was through the fire now.

Through the curling smoke, a shadowy form materialized before him. Clerans could just see the fire glinting off the barrel of a musket. He threw himself flat on the deck — and not a moment too soon. The musket fired, and wood splinters flecked across his face (stinging like wasps) as the shot hit the deck only inches away from him.

Adrenaline pounded in Clerans' head as he rolled to his feet, still clutching his tomahawk and knife. He threw himself at his opponent with all the force and fury he could muster. The pirate blocked Clerans' first blow with his still-smoking musket barrel, but, as Clerans followed up this strike with a forceful blow of his tomahawk, the pirate gasped in horror and dropped his gun.

"Not you!"

Clerans struck out with his knife, but the pirate quickly backed away, raising his hands to show that he was weaponless.

"Please don't!" the pirate whined. "I do'edn't know what it was *you*."

Clerans paused, regarding the pirate warily, but still holding his weapons at the ready. In the flickering orange light, it was hard to make out the features of his opponent, but Clerans thought he looked familiar. The pirate was a gnome, pitifully scrawny and weak-looking. That couldn't be the same gnome he had captured in the alleyway, could it? Clerans peered closer.

"Are ye...?"

"Yes sir," the scrawny gnome replied, "you've seed me before. You were kind enough to let me live the last time we meeted..."

Clerans' eyes went wide with anger. "Ye villain! So this is wot ye ha' been about, is it? Ye ceived advantage o' our lax judgment on ye, an' ye escaped from the barn. Oh ay, an' then ye kidnapped Haeli again (an' Lord knows wot ye ha' done to her). Now ye are leadin' this attack against the village?" Clerans trailed off, glancing through the fire at the glimmering lights of Entwerp Coastal. What was he doing? He couldn't be wasting time with this shriveling pirate. "Well, an' whatever came o' ye givin' yer word that ye would no hurt a citizen o' Llaedhwyth again?"

The pirate fell to his knees now, sobbing. "Ah no! It isn't like that one bit. Baptize me if'n that's what I've been doing!"

"Ay," Clerans replied, gripping the handle of his tomahawk tighter. A strong disgust filled his stomach as he looked at the pathetic pirate, and he could feel a growing sense of hatred towards him. What a horrid, deceptive, villainous wretch! "Ay, ye'll could use a good baptizing. Now move away a'fore I kill ye, like Martyn said we should from the first."

The pirate flinched. "Ah, but I would if I could, sir. I would for sure!" And he rattled a chain about his ankle.

Clerans looked at the pirate closely and ground his teeth together. For the first time now, he noticed a large chain which tangled all about the helm, holding the wheel in place, and holding to the gnome's ankle. Clerans glanced between the gnome and the musket lying close by.

"Ye expect me to believe you're chained here helpless, when ye had that the whole time to free yerself?"

The pirate frowned in confusion. "What?"

Clerans put his knife and tomahawk back into his belt with a heavy sigh. "Ye tained a gun with ye, and ye did no shoot yer chains? What kind o' act o' flim-flammery is that, then?"

The gnome blinked, blushing hearty. "I could shoot the chain off, couldn't I?" And he chuckled to himself, reaching for his musket.

"None o' that!" Clerans barked, pulling out his pistol and leveling it at the pirate's head. This was taking too much time. He needed to turn this ship about. His heart pounded in his chest as he glanced quickly from the approaching lights of Entwerp, to the chained helm, to the sniveling gnome. He had to break the chain, but then this pirate would be free to attack him.

"Oh, sir!" the pirate whined. "Don't kill me!"

"An' why no?" Clerans asked viciously, focusing all of his attention on the miserable gnome, and trying to ignore the chain around the helm for a moment. "Ye ha' already proven to us that ye cen no be trusted. Ye ha' broken yer word directly by kidnapping Haeli and by piloting this ship to destroy our town. I ha' wasted enough time on ye as it is. I am goin' to kill ye, an' then I am goin' to vert this ship from its course."

The pirate burst into tears, reaching out and clutching Clerans' ankles with his long, filthy fingers. "I had to do it! Longfinch was going to kill me if'n I do'edn't steer the ship!"

"Stop!" And Clerans stomped at the fingers.

The pirate recoiled sharply, clutching his fingers to his chest as if Clerans had actually crushed them. Whimpering, he scooted backwards as far as the chain would allow.

Clerans ground his teeth together, glancing quickly at Entwerp. This was taking too long. He should just shoot the gnome, and then he could turn the ship about without worrying about his filthy fingers stabbing him in the back. Taking a deep breath, Clerans exhaled through his nose as he sighted the pistol at the pirate's head.

"Ye deserve to die," he said coldly. "Ye are a pirate."

The pirate's shoulders drooped, and he let out a shuddering sob. "Sure, and you're probably right. But how could I let Longfinch kill me, if'n I don't even know what that catechizement meaned? What was to happen if'n I died, anyway?"

Clerans set his jaw firmly. Suddenly he thought of that young striker, bleeding to death in his arms. Clerans shoved the thought roughly aside and glared at the pirate. He had made up his mind. Slowly, he leveled the pistol and pulled the trigger. His aim was true. The charge struck the chain that held the gnome's leg, bursting it and throwing broken bits of metal in all directions. At the sound of the shot, the gnome let out a startled cry. Then, shaking all over, he looked at the now-shattered chain and then at Clerans.

"Alright then," Clerans said, grimacing. "I will give ye one more chance. If what ye'll are sayin' is true, then ye'll will prove it. Ye are goin' to help me vert this fire-ship from its course, ay?"

Tears spilled over from the gnome's eyes. "Thank you, sir! And wasn't that what I was just saying? Aren't you the only people what have ever been nice to me?"

Clerans smiled dryly.

As the scrawny gnome scrambled to his feet, Clerans turned his attention back to the helm. He had to turn this ship. He had wasted enough time as it was. The thick chain wrapped all around the helm, locking the wheel in place, keeping it from turning for more than the most minor adjustments. Pulling the free end he had just broken, Clerans began unwinding the chain from about the helm.

Glancing up at the ship, he gasped in dismay. The fire had been all too busy while Clerans was distracted with the pirate, and it now raged over the better part of the ship. The stairs Clerans had only recently ascended were now nothing more than charcoal, and much of the lower decks were scorched through and disintegrating like moth-infested cotton. Here and there, Clerans could see the joists which had once held up the decking, standing out like macabre ribs in the fire's light. Even as Clerans watched, the foremast bowed and collapsed onto the deck, sending up a shower of sparks and cinders.

Clerans' heart raced. If any more of the masts burned through and crashed to the deck, they might just break through to the ammunition charges below. It was only a matter of time before this whole fire-ship exploded. The chain looped and coiled around the helm in a tangled mess, making it hard for Clerans to unravel it. Hurriedly he pulled at the chain, working loop after loop off of the helm. For being tied there by a sailor, this was certainly the messiest knot Clerans had ever seen. He tried to stay calm as he untied the chain, loop by loop, but he knew he had very little time left. If he couldn't turn the ship soon, then the ship would be too near the village to turn effectively. Perhaps he could turn it away from the battery, but then the ship would crash into the dike. Should he simply signal the sheriff to open fire on the galleon? What if he didn't get this chain free in time?

"Alright, Mr. Pirate," Clerans began.

"Ernest, please," the gnome replied apologetically. "I amn't a pirate anymore, sir."

Clerans looked at the gnome carefully and allowed himself

to smile. "Alright then, Mr. Ernest, answer me this: where is the ammunition?"

"Directly below us," the gnome replied, grabbing a loop Clerans had just loosened, and pulling the loose end of the chain through with one long pull, "in the cargo hold."

Clerans nodded. "Right then, we will ha' to move celerly."

After only a few more minutes, Clerans and Ernest pulled the last loop free, and, with a cry of triumph, Clerans flung the chain aside. The helm was his now! He had done it! The ship was his to command! Just at that moment, there was a muffled rumble, as if of thunder, followed by a low whining, a tremendous crack and a groan. A cannonball bounced over the deck a few paces to Clerans' left. Clerans felt suddenly numb. The sheriff must be opening fire on the ship. He hadn't even waited for Clerans' signal. Clearly, Clerans had taken too long. He had to turn the ship right now before the battery fired again.

"Watch out!"

Clerans looked up as Ernest cried. A cannonball had cracked the mainmast, and now it was falling. The huge, flaming mast leaned and sagged. It would fall directly onto the helm.

Time seemed to come to a standstill as Clerans watched. His mind reeled in horror. That mast would fall directly on him, and it would kill him. He had just enough time to step aside, and he would probably survive. However, when that mast landed, it would obliterate the helm — and with it, any chance of turning the ship aside. Could the battery's guns stop the fire-ship then?

But right now (for just a moment longer), the helm was still intact. Clerans had but to reach out his hands and turn the wheel. The ship would turn aside, and his village would be saved. But if he stayed for the moment it would take him to turn the wheel, the mast would certainly crush him when it crushed the helm.

A feeling of resolution flowed through Clerans' veins. He

knew what he had to do. In his mind, he could hear his father reading from the scriptures:

"Greater love has no one than this: that a man lay down his life for his friends."

His life was, after all, only a small price to pay for the lives of the entire village of Entwerp — his family, his friends. There seemed to be a spark of joy at the thought that he could give this little thing for the sake of so many others.

Clerans reached out for the helm. The mast leaned farther and then slowly collapsed towards him in a flaming arch, like the fiery path of a comet. Clerans' fingers had only just touched the wheel of the helm when Ernest bowled into him.

"Look out!" Ernest was yelling, "She's going to touch off the ammunition!"

Clerans and Ernest tumbled to the deck on top of one another. Clerans fought his way back onto his feet, but Ernest seized him again, and then they crashed into the charred gunwale. There was a sickening crunch as the burned wood gave way, and Ernest was yanking on him again.

"No!" Clerans screamed, but then he was falling.

# 5

# WELTER AND WASTE

Clerans splashed into the bay, kicking and fighting. He finally burst back to the frigid surface of the water, boiling mad. Ernest was treading water just beside him.

"Are ye mad! What were ye doin', man!"

"I saved your life!" the gnome replied breathlessly. "You do'edn't see it, but the mainmast was falling, and it would've killed you if'n I hadn't pushed you aside!"

"Do ye think I am blind?" Clerans cried. "O' course I saw that the mast wos fallin'! I could ha' saved the village if ye'll ha' no stopped me!"

Clerans looked up at the fire-ship as it sailed past them. He looked up towards the poop-deck, and his heart sank within him. The mainmast had indeed fallen, but the rigging around the aft mast had caught it before it reached the deck. It now hung poised over the deck, but the helm was still intact.

Despair fell over Clerans. The mast would not have crushed him, and he would have turned the ship aside. But it was too late now. There was no way they could swim after the ship and climb aboard.

"See!" Clerans pointed up at the poop-deck, but he could feel a catch in his throat. He was so frustrated that tears were coming to his eyes. "I would ha' survived! Ye did no save my life, ye coward, ye only condemned the lives o' everyone in the village!"

The gnome turned ghostly pale. "What've I done?" he gasped.

"I knew I outta-should ha' shot ye," Clerans fumed. "See what comes o' letting' ye live?!"

Ernest remained perfectly silent as Clerans tread water furiously beside him.

"I knew I should no ha' trusted ye," Clerans said finally. "After ye broke out o' our barn, and stole Haeli again, and then ye decided to pilot that ship to destroy my village. No wonder ye kept me from turning it."

Clerans could see in Ernest's face that every word cut him to the heart.

"You don't understand," Ernest said with a whimper, "they were going to kill me."

"Last I checked," Clerans replied, still boiling with anger, "the laws o' morality were never waved fer a man's convenience or security."

"You don't understand," the pirate replied, a sudden light of anger appearing in his eyes now. "How could you understand? You can sound all high and mighty and moral, but you don't know what it's like. You and your happy, ideal family what's never turned against you and threatened to kill *you*."

Just then, the guns of the battery opened fire, the thunder booming out over the water as their shots peppered the fire-ship and the surrounding waters. Still, the fire-ship glided slowly forward, unaffected by the guns.

As the echo of the guns died away, Clerans caught Ernest's eye. Tears streamed down the gnome's face.

"Do you think I wanted to do this? Do you think I wanted any on this? Your family was so nice to me — no one's been that kind to me before. Do you really think what I wanted to pilot that ship and hurt them? Anointment! Do you really think what I wanted to escape from your family in the first place, at all, at all? Do'edn't you let me live? Do'edn't you feed me and give me a good place to sleep? Do'edn't you have the most beautiful gnome-maid what I've ever seed? Baptize it! I never wanted any on this!" And he started to weep.

Clerans looked the scrawny gnome over critically. Despite his better judgment, he couldn't help but believe Ernest. With some alarm, he realized he was feeling *sympathy* towards him. If he could grow sympathy for the strikers, then why not for this pirate?

"Ay, then," Clerans said in a level tone, "but ye could jist be sayin' that."

"Is that what you think, then?" Ernest asked bitterly.

"What did ye do to Haeli?" Clerans snapped.

Ernest tread water for a moment. The battery fired again, so that Clerans and Ernest had to wait for a moment before the scrawny gnome replied.

"I do'edn't break out of your barn, and I do'edn't kidnap the little lady. It's not like that at all, at all."

Clerans laughed derisively. "Ye did no, did ye? Ay, then, how are ye here then?"

The pirate shivered all over. "*They* do'ed it — breaking into the barn and recapturing me. They haved the little lady with them already. *I* do'edn't capture her. They do'ed it without me."

Clerans eyed the pirate closely. "Well then, what did you — they — do with Haeli?"

"They taked the key from her," the gnome replied solemnly.

Clerans flinched at this statement. The key? How did this pirate know Haeli had a key on her unless he had actually seen it? As much as he didn't want to admit it, this seemed to give the pirate some credibility.

"They were going to peel her," the pirate said, "but I stopped them. I taked her, and I throwed her off the ship. It was the best what I could do for her, and we were so close to the shore what I'm sure she swimmed there and is safe now."

Again, the battery fired. Clerans glanced up to see the fire-ship slipping ever closer to the battery, the water about it casting back the glow of the blood-bright flames.

"God grant Haeli is safe, then," Clerans whispered, suddenly shivering in the cold water. He hadn't noticed how cold it was until now. A feeling of helplessness came over him as he stared at the dark shape of the battery, illuminated now and then by the flash of cannons vomiting their charges at the fire-ship. He had not turned the ship aside. He had failed.

"What else was I supposed to do?" Ernest muttered, splashing noisily closer to Clerans. There was a hitch in his voice, as if he meant to sob again.

"Silence." Clerans hissed, exhaustion steeling over him.

"What else?" Ernest said. "I'm sorry. Really, I am. I wish I could've done something else — something *more*, like, but..."

"Shut up!" Clerans growled. "I do no want to talk with ye anymore!"

Ernest hiccupped suddenly, but then he moved back a few paces, treading water and glancing between Clerans and the fire-ship. Thankfully, he didn't say another word.

There was nothing to do now but tread water and watch. The fire-ship continued its course, as straight as an arrow, towards the battery. Clerans could hardly bring himself to breathe as he stayed there minute by minute (the freezing waters slowly numbing his body), watching the fire-ship sail on.

The battery fired several more times, but each time with less and less vigor, as the guns showed no effect on the inexorable fire-ship. First one level ceased firing all together, and then the next. The sheriff must be evacuating the battery. Was that really it? Was there nothing else to do?

With a tremendous crash, the fire-ship struck the docks just below the battery. Several of the piers splintered on the impact, and the fire-ship rocked and bucked in the waters of the bay. The main mast now broke free, and the aft mast sheared in half. For a moment the ship sat thus, rocking up and down and spewing thick black smoke and sparks into the air.

Then the fire reached the ammunition.

A great wave swelled up around the explosion, and a pillar of fire and light rose out of the midst of this swell. The little galleon disintegrated, not one board left nailed to another. The nearby piers and the docks all around the fire-ship splintered into a million pieces as the explosion lacerated them with cannon-shot, marlin spikes, rusty axe heads, and other bits of useless metal.

As soon as Clerans saw the explosion (but before the great roar reached his ears), he threw himself under the water, hoping to avoid any pieces of metal or bits of debris that might reach him. He held himself under for the count of ninety before he thrust himself back to the surface for breath. As he gasped for air, the water around him still rocked with the great waves from the explosion, and debris still rained down steadily from the sky.

As soon as he dashed the cold salt water from his eyes, Clerans turned to look at the battery with breathless anticipation. The smoke of the explosion was just beginning to clear, but even through the smoke, it was quite clear: the battery still stood firm.

Clerans could hardly contain his enthusiasm, letting out a cry of victory and raising his fist in the air in his excitement. "Huzza! Ye pirates, is that the best ye'll cen do?"

But no sooner had these words left his mouth than a low groaning noise echoed over the water. He glanced back towards the battery, watching in horror as the stones that formed the foundation of the battery buckled and then disintegrated. With a great roar, the massive stone structure crumbled, sliding into the bay in a great heap of granite, cannons, and smoke.

# 6

# THE VALLEY OF THE SHADOW

Clerans stared in disbelief at the ruins of the battery. How could this be? The battery was that indomitable refuge, that invincible defense, that irresistible protection of the city. How could the battery have fallen, crumbling like a toddler's block house? No, this couldn't be real. This could not be happening. It wasn't supposed to be like this.

A voice suddenly broke through Clerans' thoughts.

"Quickly now, sir!" It was Ernest, that scrawny gnome. "If'n you want to live, ye'd best swim!"

Clerans looked around to see Ernest swimming away as fast as he could with long, desperate strokes. What had startled Ernest? Then Clerans' eyes fell upon the awful form of the man-o-war, now sweeping across the bay towards the village of Entwerp. Clerans' mouth went dry. Those pirates would waste no time then. They were already descending upon his home, hardly giving the people of Entwerp time to recover from the destruction of their battery. They meant to strike hard, and they meant to destroy.

True, that was a good military tactic, but it still made Clerans' blood boil. Those pirates were hell-bent on destroying his village. Who knows how many people (innocent people, mind you) they would slaughter in their attack? Did those pirates really think they could succeed so easily? Not if *he* had anything to do with it!

A fresh wave of energy washed over Clerans, warming his limbs, which were now almost numb from the icy water. Facing back towards the village, Clerans thrust back his arms in a great stroke, propelling himself through the water. He had been swimming in this bay for most of his life, and often in much colder temperatures than this. He would make it to the shore easily enough.

Clerans regarded the pirate man-o-war one last time before focusing all his attention on the village. It would be close, but if he pushed himself, Clerans guessed that he would make it back to Entwerp before the pirates made it to the dikes. Once there, he would join in the village's defense. There was nothing else for it. He had let his village down once already; he would not do it again. If his village would fall to the ravages of these power-crazed pirates, then he would die in its defense!

As Clerans pushed on through the waters of the bay, a dreadful thought came to him. These pirates weren't interested in Entwerp. No, they were really after the Gwambi Treasure (which Miss Ella was so passionately looking for). If they had stolen that key from Haeli, then that must be the reason for their attack. They could now open the Gwambi door in the Pickering's manor, and they were coming back to do just that. For them, Entwerp was only a fence, an obstacle that must be leveled. Captain Longfinch would strike hard and with an aim of complete destruction. Just as they had so directly and so effectively razed the battery, so they would raze the entire village — and every man, woman, and child who dared to resist.

If any pirate possessed the means to level Entwerp Coastal, and enter Entwerp Proper, it was Longfinch. He had already proven his capabilities by destroying the battery — a feat no other pirate could have even dreamed of. It was sure to be a desperate struggle, then. Only by the hand of God — and the stout bravery of the people of Entwerp — would this pirate ship be repulsed.

Clerans set his jaw firmly and swam on, pushing himself as hard as he could. He had to get back to the dikes. He had to be there to defend his home. Clerans prayed fervently now, repeating the same phrase over and over with each stroke of his arms.

"O Lord, defend us! O Lord, protect us! O Lord, defend us! O Lord, protect us!"

After swimming on for several more minutes, Clerans could see the docks at the north end of the village just before him. Two or three of the piers still jutted out into the waters, but these leaned dangerously like branches on a dying tree, their supports shattered, and their boards splintered. No great ship could land here again, and even a tiny fishing boat would hardly dare to tie off on one of these crippled piers. Clerans only hoped that they would still serve him well as a place to climb out of the icy waters and ascend back onto the dikes.

As he neared the pitiful remains of the docks, he heard cannon shots ringing out across the bay, first from the dikes, and then from the man-o-war. He chose not to look back, but pushed forward. With two more strokes, he gained the end of the outermost pier. He quickly grabbed hold of a support (the one which looked to be the least damaged) and hauled himself out of the water. As nimbly as he could, Clerans shimmied up this support post until he reached the top of the pier, and then he scrambled up onto it. The pier swayed slightly under him and groaned. Clerans trembled all over with cold, but he knew he could not wait here and dry off. He would warm up as he ran.

So Clerans took off across the pier, running straight towards the dike at the other end. He stumbled many times as the pier rocked beneath him, and he had to jump over the many splin-tered boards along its length. Once or twice the whole pier groaned and sagged towards the water with the creaking of strained wood, and Clerans was certain that it would collapse under his weight, but the pier held on.

Finally, Clerans reached the dike. He was on solid ground now, but he knew his struggles were not over for the night. The village must be defended. He had no rifle now, but with such weapons as he had, he would gladly protect his home.

Ah, right! But his pistol wasn't loaded! He had best see to that before he rushed headlong into the fight.

Clerans stopped for a moment and then pulled out the pistol Sheriff Laei had given him. His powder horn had again survived the swim, and the gunpowder inside was still quite dry.

As Clerans quickly reloaded his pistol, he looked down the dike wall to the south. The man-o-war had chosen the other end of the village for its attack, coming in for a landing amongst the Fishers' Docks. Those docks were (of course) too low for a great ship like that to land at, but the dike there was low enough for the man-o-war to dock to directly. That, then, would be where the fight would take place. Already he could see the dark forms of the Entwerp militia gathering in the square before the Fishers' Docks. As he watched, red fire spewed from a cannon along the dikes. The man-o-war answered with a broadside, sending flames and cannon shot streaking out from its side and raining death on those defending the dikes.

The dreadful ship now turned, moving in for a landing. Clerans knew they would not stop the man-o-war from making her landing. He would have to hurry now if he wanted to join in defending his home.

Clerans ran as fast as he could now across the dike wall. It was easy going and well-paved. In no time at all, he crossed the Dike Plaza and then descended from the upper dikes onto the lower dikes. He was very close now. Again, the thunder of the dike cannons sounded in his ears, though, this time, they sounded much louder. In front of him, he could now make out the distinct shapes of the Entwerpi militia as they ranged themselves in a crude battle line across the dike, preparing to receive the pirates' attack.

Now Clerans could hear the voice of Sheriff Laei rising loudly and authoritatively through the air. "Stand your ground! Form your line. The line must no break; no on your lives! No pirate ha' ever set foot on the dike walls. Hold them off. They will no land!"

Again, the dike cannons fired. Clerans was rushing past one now. He glanced quickly at the gunning squad as they jumped back and held their hands over their ears while the cannon vomited out its shot at the impending man-o-war. With a start, he recognized Miss Sylfia Collyms, ramrod tucked into her elbow, and black grease streaking her face. Clerans' heart fell. There was only one reason that someone like Miss Sylfia was on a gun crew — the Sheriff had called for complete mobilization. Only the mothers and young children would be exempted.

Clerans chanced a look at the man-o-war now. It was so close that he could see every pirate on deck as they assembled for their attack. The marines formed a line across their deck, many holding boards or else grapnels so that they could cross onto the dike. Behind them, all the sailors and spare gunners ranged themselves like hungry dogs. The cannons on the lower decks were now silent, but the swivel gunners (still working busily) were loading and firing as fast as they could. Clerans guessed there were about two hundred pirates aboard that ship, which was fewer than he had expected for such a large ship, though still more than the number of men and women standing to defend the dikes.

As Clerans looked, one of the swivel guns turned in his direction. He quickly threw himself to the ground behind the ramparts of the dike wall as the swivel blasted fire and lead at the dike. Behind him, Clerans heard a cry of pain. Looking back, he saw the dike cannon, which he had only just passed, now smoking and broken from its housing. The gunning squad, which had only just moments before commanded that cannon, lay scattered across the ground nearby. Most of them were dead, though one or two groaned in agony, having sustained gruesome wounds. Miss Sylvia lay still, one hand draped over her shattered cannon.

Clerans' stomach turned inside of him, and his heart pounded in his head. This was war. This was honest-to-goodness war!

Panic tightened his gut, but he forced himself to remain calm by breathing deeply with his stomach. Hadn't he always wanted to become a captain, or an admiral, or something of that sort? He had always dreamed of fighting in an actual war. Here he was, then. His dreams had come true. He must rise to the occasion now and show what he was truly made of.

At least this wasn't like fighting the strikers. He didn't have to feel guilty about shooting the pirates.

As he scrambled to his feet again and fell in line at the back of the impromptu column of defenders, he again heard the voice of Sheriff Laei above the fusillade of cannon fire:

"May the Almighty God be with you all! May he steel your hearts and guide your hands to war. Fer God, fer home, fer family: stand fast!"

"Amen!" the militia replied with one great shout.

Then Clerans heard another voice rising through the air. He knew that voice all too well: it was his father's. Only then did the weight of the moment fall on Clerans. This was complete mobilization. They had never called for this before. Aside from the mothers and the young children, everyone in the village would be here defending the dikes. Everyone who fought here and died here would be his friends and his neighbors. There were no regulars coming. It was up to them alone.

His father's robust tenor voice rang out loud and clear above the confused explosions and the whine of the cannon balls:

*"O God of armies, now defend*
*Thy people from these wicked men.*
*For we are weak and prone to fall*
*Without Thy aid, O Lord of all!*
*Deliver us in this our need,*
*And show the world Thy majesty!"*

Clerans felt a lump forming in the back of his throat, and he looked carefully at the men and women around him. He recognized all of them, though not all by name. There was the baker from the little shop on Busyway Street; there was Mr. Fflemins, the tailor; there was the man who came to the kirk and sat in the row just behind them.

A chill ran down Clerans' spine.

*"The lions prowl about Thy flock.*
*Apart from Thee, Lord, we are lost.*
*Now in Thy dreadful wrath arise,*
*And cast their wicked schemes aside.*
*Let all their plottings come to naught.*
*Remember us, who Thy blood bought!"*

A desperate desire to find his father filled Clerans. If anything happened to him on this dike, Clerans wanted to see his father one last time. He could hear the general direction from which his father's voice was coming. Surely he could push his way through the crowd. He had to be by his father's side. That would be where his brothers would be, too. If they would fall, they would fall together.

Suddenly, another cannon shot rang through the air, and Clerans heard a loud whining noise. All around Clerans, men fell to the ground, some screaming in pain, while others dropped dead, never to rise again. There was blood on the cobblestone pavement. Clerans trembled all over. It was grapeshot. The pirates would cut them all down where they stood.

Through the thinning crowd, Clerans could now see his father standing straight and tall near the middle of the lines of defense. His eyes were turned towards the skies, and his hands were raised in a petition as he continued to sing. Clerans rushed towards his father, joining with the last verse of the hymn:

> *"Though we are crushed, we are not slain.*
> *Though we are vexed, 'tis not in vain.*
> *For Thou wilt save when we're dismayed,*
> *And Thou, O Lord, wilt give us aid,*
> *We praise Thee, knowing Thou wilt stand,*
> *For us, Thou wilt lay bare Thy hand!"*

# 7

# MARTYRDOM

The man-o-war drifted steadily closer to the dike wall. In a moment, it would be near enough for the pirates to leap the distance.

"To the edge!" the sheriff was crying, still somehow calm through all of this slaughter. "Ready your guns! They *can no* land. They *cen no* set foot on this dike!"

The Entwerpi militia stepped forward now, forming a tight wall all along the ramparts of the dike. Clerans could see his father stepping forward as well, about to join in the front line of battle.

"Da!"

"Clerans!" His father turned, a look of relief spreading across his face. "I am glad to see that ye made it off o' that ship a'fore..." His father swallowed.

Clerans threw a casual salute, trying to smile through the lump that was forming in his throat. "I ha' vened to defend the dike, sir."

His father smiled, though painfully. "Stand in the back, son. Let the elders o' us who ha' seen too many summers as it is fall at the front."

His father rested his hand on Clerans' shoulder for a moment before he snatched up his rifle, taking his place in the line of defenders along the dike wall. Clerans looked on helplessly. Could this really be happening?

Pulling out his pistol in his right hand, he drew his large skinning knife with his left. He was ready for this fight.

Again, he scanned the crowd of defenders, hoping he might glimpse either of his brothers. Unfortunately, the wall of tall militia before him blocked most of his view. All he could see above the dark figures of the Entwerpi militia was the tall mast of the man-o-war towering above them, lit up now and then by cannon-fire. The shrouds and rigging of that ship hung in the air like cruel spiders' webs, a few stringy pirates clinging to them with muskets ready to fire on the militia.

"Fire!" he heard Sheriff Laei call out. Clerans could only barely see the top of the sheriff's white head above the throng of defenders.

A flash of light burst out from before the defenders as they fired the guns *en masse*. Clerans could hear many of the pirates yelling and screaming in pain, but could only guess at what damage the volley had done. His heart pounded in his chest. Oh, if only he could *see* what was going on! If only he could join in!

Another fusillade of gunshots sounded in the close air. In front of him, Clerans saw many of the defenders fall to the ground, many writhing in screams of agony.

"Hold your ground!" the sheriff cried.

But any further orders the sheriff might have given were drowned out as the pirates let out a great shout. Clerans could hear more gunfire and the boom of cannons. The men in front of him surged forward, raising their rifles to their shoulders. Still, Clerans could see almost nothing through the boiling throng of men before him. Thick clouds of gunpowder smoke now lingered in the air, further obscuring Clerans' vision.

He had lost sight of his father. He couldn't make out the

shapes of people's faces anymore. All he could see for certain was the growing number of dead and wounded piling up on the cobblestones.

Clerans trembled all over. His pulse thundered in his ears as bile welled up in his throat. He had to stay calm. He couldn't allow himself to become excited — that might be the death of him if he had to join the fight.

Just then, he heard a shout rising from the pirates. There was a flash of light and a clap like thunder, almost as if some large grenade had gone off right in the midst of the Entwerpi lines. The wall of defenders before Clerans fell back all at once, as if thrown by an irresistible force. Clerans kept his place, standing resolutely as men fell back all about him. Before he knew what was happening, Clerans was standing in the front line of the defense.

Now (at last!) he could see. The first thing that entered his vision was a short and swarthy nymph pirate charging at him across the cobblestones with a drawn sword. Clerans leveled his pistol and shot the man in the head. The pirate collapsed to the ground, finally giving Clerans a full view of the catastrophe before him.

The first thing he saw was the man-o-war, sprawled out like a hideous monster along the dike wall. Many planks and grapnels joined the deck of the man-o-war directly to the dike, and over these planks the whole host of pirates came rushing at once. Many of the pirates at the van of the attack were throwing oblong objects at the militia. These objects exploded in smoke and fire, driving the brave defenders back even more. Was that dynamite?

All around him lay the bodies of the dead and dying; many were pirates, but by far the majority were Llaedhwythi men and women. The dike militia stumbled over these corpses in their hasty retreat. The flashes of gunfire fitfully illuminated the ominous scene, even as the billowing gunpowder smoke obscured it.

A large group of pirates now vaulted onto the dike directly before Clerans, each of them a leering, wicked-looking sailor. Clerans snatched up his tomahawk and drew in a deep breath, releasing it slowly while he consciously relaxed his body. So it had come to this at last. He was about to die.

Just at that moment, a shrill cry rang out over the noise of battle. Clerans looked for the source, and saw a tall, rather wiry man stepping down from one of the planks onto the dike wall. He had very dark features, and he held a long saber in his hand. He wore no hat, but his long, raven-black hair flowed freely about his head.

"Which is! Hold, lads!" the man cried. "Hold, I say, whatever!"

The pirates immediately halted their attack, chuckling together. Sheriff Laei lost no time in this interlude and quickly began barking out orders again. Clerans still could not see the venerable sheriff, but he could hear his calm and strong voice.

"Form your lines, men! Close in the gaps! Reload! Prepare to receive them!"

The dark pirate raised his saber and pointed it at the line of defenders before him. "Which of you is the captain, whatever?"

In answer, Sheriff Laei stepped out of the throng of men, standing grimly and somberly in the dim light. "Is this a parley ye'd tain?" the sheriff asked levelly. "My only words to ye are these: away with you, every one o' ye! Get back on your ship and be away!"

The tall pirate snickered. "Ah, is that it? Which is! My name is Vania Bloodrummer. I have an offer for you, whatever."

"Ay," the sheriff replied. "An' ye ha' heard my offer already. I will tain no other."

The pirate (Vania, as he called himself) smiled sinisterly. "Which is! Let us duel together: you and I. If'n you win, my men will all surrender to you, whatever. And if'n I defeat you, your men must all surrender to me, whatever."

The sheriff raised his eyebrows at this. "An' where is *yer* captain then, pirate? Where is Longfinch, fer ye to make sich an offer?"

Vania chuckled again. "He is awaiting your head."

The pirates let out a taunting jeer at this, and they all took a step nearer.

The sheriff looked at Vania closely for a few minutes. "I will fight ye," he finally said, "an' I will defeat ye, I am certain. Let my men answer fer themselves."

The Entwerpi defenders let out a cheer, standing now in an organized line again.

Vania laughed. "You will fight me? Then where is your sword, whatever?"

Without waiting for a reply, Vania lunged at the sheriff with his saber point. Sheriff Laei seemed ready for this, for he batted the blade aside with the steel bracings that surrounded his right arm, striking out forcefully with his left fist in the same moment. The sheriff caught Vania squarely in the nose, and the pirate stumbled back in some surprise.

Clerans heard the sheriff mutter something under his breath. It was rather muffled and indistinct, but Clerans knew what the sheriff was saying; he was praying.

"Lord, guide my hands to war."

Springing forward with the ferocity of a panther, the sheriff drew out his own sword, using the draw itself as an up-handed slash. Despite his surprise, Vania parried the blow neatly with his own sword. In an instant, Vania regained his balance from the punch, and he stood poised and ready. The sheriff continued his forward movement, striking at Vania with several swift and well-placed cuts. These, too, Vania countered with the air of an expert swordsman before striking out himself at the sheriff.

Clerans watched, hardly daring to breathe. He recognized

every attack the sheriff delivered, though the sheriff executed them with far more skill and dexterity than Clerans could have. Still, Vania held the sheriff at bay, many times throwing the sheriff on the defensive while he took the offensive position in the fight.

Suddenly, Vania drew out a short dirk in his left hand and plunged it at the sheriff. Still, the sheriff remained calm as he threw the blow aside with his sword. Vania took full advantage of this distraction and struck out with his saber again. Sheriff Laei stepped neatly to the side to avoid the blow, Vania's blade passing within an inch of the sheriff's nose. As the sword whizzed past, the sheriff struck down with his left hand, delivering such a blow to Vania's inner elbow that the pirate dropped his own saber.

With expert poise, the sheriff wrapped his arm around Vania's right arm, pressing downward against the back of Vania's shoulder. Clerans couldn't help but smile to himself. He knew the attack well — it was a shoulder lock. Vania would have a deal of time getting out of that. Vania leaned forward in surprise, trying to take the strain off his shoulder, but as he leaned over, the sheriff struck him full in the face with his knee.

The blow threw Vania from his feet, and he landed hard against the cobblestones. Not backing down for a second, the sheriff continued his attack, plunging the tip of his sword at Vania's heart. Vania rolled to the side at the last moment, leaping to his feet and tossing his dirk to his right hand. Vania was breathing heavily and grimacing in pain. Blood was now streaming down from Vania's nose, and he had the ugly beginnings of a black eye, but somehow he was still holding on.

"You're a worthy opponent, sir, whatever," Vania taunted, snapping his fingers in the sheriff's face cheekily.

*The Sheriff Duels Vania*

For a moment, Clerans thought he saw a spark flicker between Vania's fingers and then dart away, but it seemed so absurd that he must have imagined it. At that moment, one of the militia's rifles misfired just behind Sheriff Laei. The shot struck Sheriff Laei in the hip, and he stumbled forward in surprise and agony. That was all Vania was waiting for.

The pirate struck out with his dirk, yet as the sheriff moved to counter it with his sword, Vania caught the sheriff's sword by the hilt-guard with his free hand just before stabbing the sheriff in the wrist with his dirk. The sheriff let out a sharp cry, releasing the hold on his sword. Yet before Vania had even gotten a good grip on the sheriff's sword hilt, Sheriff Laei threw himself forward again, striking out with the bracings on his right hand.

Vania caught the blow head-on with the edge of his dirk, then dealt the sheriff a blow across the chest with his own sword. As Sheriff Laei doubled back, Vania pressed forward, dealing the sheriff two more deep strokes across the stomach. The sheriff collapsed to his knees. Clerans looked on in disbelief. This couldn't be happening.

Vania smiled menacingly at the sheriff. "I don't expect your men to hold up your side of the bargain. No matter, we'll kill them all too, whatever!"

And with that, Vania Bloodrummer plunged the sword through Sheriff Laei's heart.

8

# DOOMSDAY

Clerans stared in shock. His mind seemed numb, unwilling to admit to what his eyes had just seen. Sheriff Laei couldn't have lost this fight. That pirate Vania Bloodrummer couldn't have run the sheriff through with his own sword. That was not how this was supposed to end.

Vania leered over the sheriff, spitting in his face before drawing back his sword. The sheriff's dead body collapsed onto the cobblestones. Now he was just one more dead body amidst the dozens that already lay along the dike wall.

*He is dead. Sheriff Laei is dead. That pirate killed him. Vania Bloodrummer killed Sheriff Laei.*

A sudden wave of anger rushed over Clerans. He clenched his fists and set his jaw firmly. Why was he just standing there? He had a pistol — he would make that blasted pirate pay for this!

Clerans snatched his pistol from his belt, leveled it at Vania, and pulled the trigger. The flint sparked against the striking plate, but that was all.

*Idiot,* Clerans berated himself. His pistol wasn't loaded.

Vania took one step back from the body of Sheriff Laei, letting out a crow like a rooster as he raised Sheriff Laei's bleeding sword over his head.

"Havoc!" Vania cried.

This must have been a predetermined signal, for at that cry, every pirate leveled his musket and fired into the line of dumbfounded militia. Clerans didn't even have time to throw himself to the ground. It all happened so suddenly. All around him Entwerpi men and women crumpled to the ground, many screaming in agony as they clutched horrendous wounds. Clerans looked on the devastation in stunned horror. He knew those people — every one of them. He greeted them in the streets most days. He had delivered letters from the Company to most of the men, and he had danced with many of the young women. How could they all be dead, just like that?

"Havoc!" the pirates now cried, drawing out their swords and rushing over the bodies of dead militiamen.

Clerans looked on at the wall of pirates charging towards him. Somehow, he felt distant. This wasn't really happening. It couldn't be happening. If this was real, it would mean the pirates were going to kill *him*. He couldn't really be about to die, could he?

Just then, his father's voice called out loud and authoritatively above the discordant cries of the charging pirates. "Return fire! Stand, my friends; we cen no falter now!"

Though the line of defense was now quite ragged, the militia members seemed to take heart at this clarion cry. Many men moved now for the first time since the sheriff's death, as if woken from a state of paralysis. Though not in a simultaneous volley, the militia discharged their guns into the ranks of the pirates with lethal accuracy. The pirates stumbled back at the ferocity of this counterattack, many tripping over the bodies of their newly fallen comrades.

Vania Bloodrummer still stood at the front of the pirates,

waving the sheriff's sword about like a madman and pointing forcefully at the militia. "Forward, fools! Death and glory, whatever! Havoc!"

"Form the line!" Da roared. "Bayonets on! Prepare to receive the pirates. God be with ye all!"

"Guide our hands to war!" several of the militia members answered as they obeyed Da's order to affix their bayonets.

Clerans stood in line with the other Entwerpi militia members, and the pirates charged forward again. He held up his tomahawk and knife, bracing himself for the collision.

"For the sheriff!" a defender cried. Everyone in the line of defenders echoed the cry as they lowered their bayonets at the advancing pirates.

"For the sheriff!"

Just then, Clerans heard a shrill cry from the back line of the defenders. "Gard out! We're flanked! Ceive cover!"

Clerans hardly had time to turn his head to see who had cried, when a fusillade of shots rang out from the shadows of the shops and houses behind the defenders. In the lights from the firing, Clerans could make out dark shapes crouched in hiding behind the militia.

So that was where the rest of the pirates had gone. They had sneaked around the lines of defense and outflanked them. Two enemy forces trapped the Entwerpi militia between them.

The pirates in front of the defenders were now almost upon them, when Da called out again over the fray.

"Follow me, lads! We cen no defend against both sides. To the upper dikes! We'll hold them off there!"

Clerans could see his Da rushing off to the north with a handful of men following, escaping from between the two opposing forces of pirates. Clerans rushed after them himself. He hadn't taken more than two steps before a hulking brute of a man leapt in his way, swinging at him with a blow of his saber.

Clerans gritted his teeth firmly together as he plowed into

the man, undeterred. Deflecting the man's sword deftly with his knife, he cut the man across the thigh with his tomahawk. Then, as the man stumbled back, Clerans continued plowing into him, striking him first in the crook of the arm to disable his sword arm, and then dealing him a decisive blow to the neck.

As the man collapsed in front of him, Clerans tried to continue after his Da, only to see another pirate closing in on him. Taking a brief glance around before engaging this next attacker, Clerans could see the pirates on either side swarming around him, as they tried to cut off the rest of the militia from following Da and escaping the envelopment. Clerans bit the inside of his cheek. He had to get through quickly, or he would be surrounded and massacred with the rest.

Just as Clerans moved forward to attack his next assailant, a gun discharged close to his ear, and the pirate before Clerans fell dead. A firm hand gripped him by the shoulder, and Clerans turned to see his brother Martyn beside him.

"Celerly now!" Martyn said as he pulled Clerans after him. "We will get through this!"

One last pirate leaped into Martyn's way, leveling a pistol at him. Martyn cast the pistol aside with the barrel of his rifle, and then beat the pirate to the ground with a single blow of his rifle butt.

Now they were free of the pirates' trap. Running forward as fast as they could, they caught up with the back line of those militia members who had escaped with Da. As they ran, Clerans heard a few musket balls whizzing past them. Behind him, there were screams and cries of agony as the pirates cut down the Entwerpi militia who had not made it out of the envelopment.

Clerans' heart pounded in his head. He tried to breathe deeply to calm himself, but it didn't seem to work. He was so out of breath that his lungs burned, no matter how deeply he breathed. Clerans scanned the small group who had escaped with his Da. There was Meriwedhr (the Pastor's son), as well as Nycolaei (the butcher), Mr. Fflemins (the tailor), and Mr. Kyliwraeth (he was a beacon tender, wasn't he?). Far out at the front, Clerans could see his Da leading the group. Clerans scanned the group again, and his heart leapt into his mouth. Where was Laendon? Laendon must have been at the dike with a complete mobilization. So where was he?

Clerans cast a furtive look back at the scene of the massacre. The pirates had torches and were setting fire to many of the shops near the square. Clerans tried to breathe deeply and calm himself, but he felt sick. Laendon couldn't be back there, could he? He must have gotten away. Surely, he had gotten away.

Just then, he heard a shout from the front of the group. Was it Da shouting? He looked up to see the upper dike wall before them. Da was already ascending the steps to the upper village, with the rest of the survivors following close behind. Just at that moment, a line of muskets fired from the dike wall above them. Martyn reacted faster than Clerans, throwing them both aside as the cobblestones all about them splintered and cracked under the hail of musket shot.

"It is another ambush!" Martyn cried, leaping back to his feet. "It is no use. Back again! Perhaps we cen hold them off at Newcourt!"

Martyn dragged Clerans after him as he ducked into a back alley that ran parallel to the upper dike. Another volley of muskets sounded in the air, cutting down many of the men who tried to follow Martyn. As Clerans looked back, he could only see five people in the alley behind them. In the dim light, he could only just make out their faces. There was Meriwedhr (Pastor Daerl's son), Mr. Fflemins the tailor, Mr. Gingrich the farrier, and the two beacon tenders, Miss Flalowen, and Mr. Chaerls. Clerans' heart sank. Da was not among them. Again, he heard screams and cries of agony behind him, and he could feel something like an oppressive hand weighing down on him. This time, there was no guesswork. He knew that Da was back there in the ambush. If he hadn't died in that first volley of muskets, then he was certainly dead now.

The seven remaining militia members rushed on, quickly coming to the Mainway. Just as Martyn was about to turn up this street and rush into Newcourt, Aarushi swooped down in front of him, letting out a shrill, warning cry and flapping her wings violently.

"What!" Martyn cried. "Another ambush, is it? Ay then, there's only one other way!"

Martyn crossed the Mainway and ducked down another back street. As Clerans and the other five followed, a volley of muskets rang out from a little way up the Mainway — though this time the shots scattered harmlessly across the cobblestones behind them. The pirates must have occupied Newcourt already. Thank God that Aarushi was there to warn them.

As Clerans continued to follow Martyn, his side ached, and his lungs burned. How had the pirates gotten into the village already? They were everywhere. Was there any place left that they had not ambushed? Clerans bit his lip as he remembered the sheriff's words about Longfinch. Yes, that pirate certainly was a mastermind of strategy. No one could have seen this coming.

"We follow the pier road," Martyn was saying. "It is the only way up into the old village. We cen only hope the pirates ha' no occupied the Upper Court yet."

So saying, Martyn turned onto the pier road. It was a little, narrow street which had once been a jetty out into the sea before the lower dikes were built and the water pumped out. The remains of the stone jetty now lay to one side of the street in a low wall as it rose to the Old Dike wall.

No sooner had Martyn turned around this low wall than he ran slap-bang into a group of pirates. This must not have been an ambush, for the pirates seemed equally surprised to see Martyn and these last six militia members. Martyn, however, hardly blinked as he bowled into them.

One pirate had the presence of mind to raise his musket at Martyn, but that was as far as he got before Martyn plowed into him, cutting him to the ground with a blow of his tomahawk. Then (snatching up the dead pirate's musket), Martyn fired it at the pirate who looked most likely to be the leader of the group. Now Clerans and the others came to Martyn's aid.

Clerans' head pounded, and he was panting. He had to keep going. He had to strike these pirates hard. A vague warning voice in the back of Clerans' head told him that he was too tense, and that he was letting his adrenaline get to his brain. What of that then? He was in the middle of a war! His father and brother had just died. He didn't have time to relax now. He had to push on and keep fighting. Singling out one pirate (a dark gnome), he made a rush for him. Suddenly, light burst through his vision, as his head throbbed with pain. Clerans collapsed to the ground, reeling. He tried to scramble back to his feet but only managed to turn over, looking up just in time to see the butt of a rifle coming towards his head.

The blow never landed. Martyn cut down the pirate who was standing over Clerans. Martyn yanked Clerans back to his feet and then shoved him aside as the dark gnome leapt at them. Expertly deflecting the gnome's sword thrust, Martyn caught him with a blow across the inside of his elbow. As the gnome recoiled in pain, Martyn struck again with a mortal blow to his torso.

That was it. They had destroyed that entire group of pirates. Clerans was wheezing, and his vision was still blurry. Martyn gripped him firmly by the shoulder and looked him in the eye.

"Ye are losing yer focus, Clerans. Breathe now; nice an' easy. There now; breathe."

Clerans breathed deeply, filling his abdomen and exhaling

slowly. Yes, his vision wasn't so blurry anymore. Looking around, he could see Meriwedhr, Miss Flalowen, Chaerls, Mr. Gingrich, and Mr. Fflemins. So they had all made it thus far. There were still the seven of them.

Martyn slapped Clerans on the shoulder. "Ye'll will get yerself killed, Clerans. Stay calm now."

At that moment, a volley of gunshots sounded behind them.

"Tar and needles!" Meriwedhr swore. "No rest fer the weary!"

"Celerly!" Martyn cried, rushing up the pier road. He slung the pirate musket, which he had taken during the fight, over his shoulder. "Follow me!"

The seven of them charged headlong up the pier road, quickly ascending to the Old Dike. Martyn seemed ready for anything as they reached the open cobblestone square at the top of Pier Road. As quick as a flash, Martyn ducked into the shadows of a shop on the edge of the square. The others followed none too soon, for at that moment, a band of about twenty pirates rushed into the square, forming a line across the top of the pier road.

"There now!" the leader of the pirates was yelling, "block 'em off, lads. They willn't get away from us now!"

Martyn smiled. "They would be jist late then. Quietly now, after me!"

And Martyn ducked down an alleyway, keeping in the shadows. As the others followed, Martyn kept a course roughly parallel to the Old Dike Road. Clerans followed close at Martyn's heels, his pulse still pounding in his chest. Where were they going? What did they plan to do, anyway? These pirates were everywhere. There seemed to be no way of escape. Surely Martyn had a plan — Martyn always had a plan.

Clerans stumbled slightly, but caught himself, suddenly realizing that he was shaking all over. Yes, he had let his adrenaline get to him. He was in no shape to continue fighting, and from the way his side was burning, he knew he was in no shape to continue running, either.

Martyn turned down another alleyway, which opened up into the Old Dike Road. Martyn paused in the shadows, looking in all directions before he entered the road. Satisfied that there were no pirates around, Martyn turned onto the road, heading west towards the High Road to Entwerp Proper. Was that Martyn's plan, then? To get out of the village?

Clerans tried to follow, but he again tripped over the cobblestones. He caught himself on his hands, skinning them badly. Without thinking, he let out a sharp cry of pain.

Martyn spun on his heels. "Ah! What wos that?"

Meriwedhr's giant hands grabbed Clerans by the shoulder and raised him to his feet.

"Martyn," Meriwedhr said in a stage whisper, "we cen no keep this up. Chaerls is wounded already, and Clerans is goin' to kill himself at this pace."

"We ha' to keep on!" Martyn urged. "There's nowhere safe here. We must get to Entwerp Proper — the rest o' the militia will be there."

The rest of the group caught up with Martyn now, ranging themselves around him. For the first time, Clerans noticed that Chaerls was clutching his side, and there seemed to be blood soaking through his overcoat.

"I cen no keep runnin', Martyn," Chaerls gasped, coughing heavily.

Martyn ground his teeth together. "Do no ye see what they are doin'? They are goadin' us like sheep. If we'll keep seekin' fer refuge in this village, they will only ambush us again an' again. There is no safe place here. We ha' to get to Entwerp Proper."

Mr. Fflemins now spoke, his voice high-pitched and strained with excitement. "But we will never make it that far. We will be killed fer certain."

"Ay," Miss Flalowen said. "An' more than likely they'll ha' ambushed the road out o' this town."

Just then, a shout sounded from further down the Old Dike Road.

Mr. Gingrich nodded grimly as he unslung his rifle, beginning to reload it. "They ha' seen us then."

Mr. Fflemins looked around in panic, like a wild rabbit cornered against a wall. "We need a refuge, where we cen lie low."

"Onward then!" Martyn urged, rushing westward again, "to Entwerp Proper — follow me!"

Chaerls took one step to follow Martyn, but he collapsed to the ground with a low groan. Flalowen rushed forward to help him.

"Martyn!" Meriwedhr cried. "We cen no cede on like this."

Martyn spun on his heels to look back. Flalowen struggled to lift Chaerls to his feet again while Chaerls coughed heavily, spitting up blood.

Just then, a fusillade of shots sounded from the road behind them, and a moment later, Clerans could hear the whine of bullets skipping across the cobblestones.

"We tain no time!" Martyn said. "We must keep runnin'."

"We cen no risk that," Meriwedhr protested, "Gard at Chaerls, then. Are we supposed to jist leave him here?"

"We're in no state to fight, either," Martyn replied. "Chaerls would certainly be killed if we stood to fight, an' by the look of Clerans an' Fflemins they'd be killed too, with their adrenaline gettin' to their heads."

Mr. Fflemins was shaking all over. "We must trive out a place to hide, a place to take cover."

"There is no sich place," Martyn said.

Another volley of muskets echoed in the air, and again Clerans heard the shots skittering across the nearby pavement.

Mr. Gingrich turned to face the swiftly approaching pirates, leveling his rifle and firing.

"Talkin' is no goin' to slow time," he muttered darkly as he methodically reloaded his gun.

Mr. Fflemins danced about wildly, terror clearly showing in his eyes. Pointing frantically at a shop door just down the street, Mr. Fflemins pulled a key from his pocket. "Ay, but that is jist there, my shop door!"

Martyn bit his lip and took a deep breath, finally nodding decisively. "Very well, then. I suppose that is our best option."

Mr. Fflemins rushed to the door of his shop, hurriedly and excitedly flinging the door open. The others followed quickly, as the pirates behind let off one more volley of shots. Flalowen practically dragged Chaerls after Mr. Fflemins into the little tailor shop, with Meriwedhr, and Mr. Gingrich close behind. Mr. Gingrich paused just before passing inside to discharge his rifle one last time into the oncoming pirates.

Clerans now reached the door and took one last look behind him before he stepped into the shop. From that shopfront, he could look right out over the Old Dike wall and see the entire lower city, the bridges passing over the mangrove swamps, the crude stands of the spice market, and the great Bay of Entwerp stretching out to the east. Clerans might have looked out on this scene on any other night to admire the calm and tranquility of that little village, but now his heart twisted up in horror. Great fires leapt up in a wide swath across the lower city, and in the stagnant air, Clerans could make out the sounds of gunshots, shouts, and screams.

Clerans shivered all over. Entwerp was taken. Sheriff Laei was dead, Laendon was dead, Da was dead — who knows who else was dead? They (the seven of them) were all that was left. How long would it be before the pirates broke into this shop, too? Would they all sell their lives dearly in a great and desperate last stand?

Martyn now rushed in the door, dragging Clerans in with him.

"Barricade the door, celerly!" Martyn cried as he slammed the door and locked it fast. "An' the windows, too. They will be here in a moment or two."

"God guide our hands to war," Meriwedhr breathed.

# 9

# CIRCUMNAVIGATION

*E*rnest dragged himself out of the freezing waters of the bay, crawling on all fours onto the shore. In the soft, mucky ground, his hands sank halfway to his elbows. His heart was pounding in his chest from the exertion of swimming so quickly for such a long distance. He just wanted to curl up in a ball somewhere and sleep until all of this nightmare was over.

Once he was well out of the water, he sat down and looked around him, sinking several inches into the reeking mud. He could see the twinkling lights of Entwerp to the north of him and the dark shape of Longfinch's man-o-war swooping down on the dike wall. Above him, Ernest could see the yawning arch of a bridge. So he must have reached the mangrove swamps at the mouth of the river — that would certainly explain all of this mud. To the south, Ernest could see nothing in the moonless night but the dark shapes of hills and mountains blotting out the light of the stars behind them. There was a damp, earthy smell in the air mixed with the stench of decomposition, and all around him, frogs and crickets chirped incessantly. If it hadn't been for the sporadic fusillades of cannon and gunfire which interrupted the stillness, Ernest would have thought it a very peaceful night.

Ernest shivered and wrapped his long arms around his knees. He really had little to complain about — other than being cold, wet, muddy, and tired. He had survived that fire-ship, and now here he was, well out of the city, and well away from any fighting that might take place. Ernest perked up at this thought. This could be just the chance he had been waiting for. He was away from the other pirates at last! For all they knew, he had died in the fire-ship's explosion. He was free now. He could climb onto one of those bridges easily enough, and he'd be off south along the coastal road before any of the other pirates knew about it. Then, he'd start a new life and be done with all this violence.

Just then, he heard a volley of cannon fire from the north. Ernest looked back towards Entwerp to see the man-o-war coming up level with the dike wall. Now and then, a barrage of cannons would light up the scene, first from the dike, and then from the ship itself.

Ernest shivered. He was certainly glad he wasn't back there. That would be sheer carnage. But wait. What was that he heard? Was it singing? Yes, he could hear it more clearly now. It was the sound of singing; a hymn, not unlike the hymns he remembered from the monastery where he grew up.

Ernest drew in his breath sharply. That nice Llaedhwythi family would be there. That nice father and his demigod sons would be defending the dike wall. Would they die there?

But then another thought came to Ernest, and it chilled him to the bone. Lexi would be in that city. That beautiful gnome maid would be in the middle of the carnage. He had been a pirate himself once, and he had raided little towns before. He knew all too well what the pirates would do to Lexi and any other woman they happened across in their destruction of that little town.

Even as this dreadful thought came to him, Ernest couldn't help but smile at himself. Had he really just thought that he had been a pirate *once*? As if that was such a long time ago! Only just the day before he would have answered to that title — the title of 'pirate' — but no more. He had taken his last order from Longfinch, and he was a free man now.

He took one last look at the bridges leading down the highroad to the south, then he fixed his eyes on Entwerp again as another volley of cannons sounded in the air. No, he would not flee like a coward. Those days were over. He would face this battle head-on, just like that young Llaedhwythi boy had done on the fire-ship. He would come to the aid of Entwerp. He would do everything he could to save the town's people. He would find Lexi and keep her safe from those ravaging pirates.

Ernest jumped to his feet and wiped what mud he could from his coat and trousers. Then he pulled out his eight-barreled pepperbox pistol. This would certainly come in handy if he were to engage in a fight. If only he had a sword, or a hatchet, or some other such hand weapon. Ah, well, it could not be helped now.

Carefully and meticulously, Ernest loaded each barrel of his pistol, and then he put it back in his breast pocket. Back to Entwerp, then!

Just then, he heard oars in the water nearby. He looked up to see six large skiffs, loaded down with pirates, moving in close to the shore. Before he had time even to think of finding a place to hide, he heard a loud voice call out to him.

"Halloo there! Is that you, Mr. Cook's mate?" It was Captain Longfinch.

All the saliva drained from Ernest's mouth, and he stood stock still. Sure enough, he could see the elfin pirate captain now, standing at the prow of the first skiff. Even as he watched, this first boat ran aground in the soft mud, and the pirates leaped out, hauling the boat high out of the water.

Longfinch walked over to Ernest with long, determined strides, a friendly smile spread across his face. "I'm glad to see that you survived the explosion."

In his mind, Ernest could see the image of Longfinch as he smiled that same friendly smile while shooting quartermaster Harold through the heart. Ernest shuddered. It didn't look friendly anymore — it was terrifying.

The other skiffs began landing now, and Ernest noted the forms of Killjelly and the albino amongst the forms of other pirates. Swords and muskets clinked, and steel flashed as the pirates piled out of the skiffs, their boots squelching in the putrid mud.

"Perhaps, Mr. Cook's mate, you'd like to join us?" Longfinch asked, still smiling.

"I, eh..." Ernest got no further before two burly pirates seized him by the shoulders. He stumbled along unwillingly when he suddenly saw his messmate Lewis amidst the throng.

"Ernest!" Lewis cried. "Blind prelates, am I glad to see you, boyo!"

The two pirates holding Ernest brought him directly up to Lewis and then released him.

"What's all this?" Ernest asked.

Lewis laughed weakly, but then leaned in close, whispering in Ernest's ear. "Just stay calm, boyo, and follow my lead. I'll get us out on this."

Longfinch barked out quick orders. "You all know your places. The village is poised to fall. Every one of you do your part, and the entire village will crumble."

The pirates snickered softly, and the greater part scampered off like a horde of rats under the shadow of the bridges. Ernest made a quick survey of the pirates who were left. There were only about twenty now, with Longfinch at the fore and Killjelly and the albino close by.

Longfinch smiled graciously. "Well then, what are we waiting for? Let's be on our way. Bring the prisoners along."

And with that, Longfinch led the way inland into the thick mangrove swamps. Several pirates moved in around Ernest and Lewis, goading them forward. Ernest smiled grimly; he must be one of the 'prisoners.' It was only then that he realized there was a third person with him and Lewis. Ernest peered at him in the dark.

"Hello, who are you?"

He was a big man, with broad shoulders and a powerful frame, yet he shuffled along like someone who has been through unspeakable misery. As Ernest spoke, the man turned his head so that Ernest could see his face in the dim starlight. Ernest caught his breath; it was Jock the Blowhoarder. So Longfinch was bringing him along, too.

"Well," Ernest exclaimed, slapping Jock on the shoulder. "Aren't you glad to be out of the dungeons, then? Though I guess we're in the same position now, me and you."

Jock cracked a wry smile. "Ay, look ye, but that does not bode well for ye then, does it?"

The small group of pirates moved quickly, following Longfinch. They slogged through the mud for nearly a quarter of a mile before turning north; climbing steeply out of the river valley and pushing through thorns and dense underbrush. Ernest struggled along as best he could, slipping and catching himself in the thick brambles repeatedly. Still, the other pirates pushed on unrelentingly, often dragging Ernest after them to keep up their pace.

They must have climbed like this for nearly a mile before the pirates stopped their ascent to walk along the edge of the steep mountains. Now and then, Ernest would look out through a break in the trees to see the lights of Entwerp glowing just below them. More shooting and screaming echoed up from the village, and lights gradually bloomed in the dark, fires burning all along the lower section of the village. Ernest's heart sank to his knees. So the destruction had already begun. Had they killed Lexi yet?

Still, the pirates continued their march, passing quickly along the winding face of the mountainside. After several more miles, the ground leveled out a little, and then the trees and underbrush disappeared completely. Looking around, Ernest realized that they had emerged on the far western side of the village and were now looking down at the main road which led inland through the mountains.

Ernest let out an inward groan. He knew where this road would lead. It would take them right to Entwerp Proper, and then to that large manor house. So that was what this small band was up to. They were going to raid that manor house again.

But then a dreadful thought came over Ernest, and the blood drained from his face. No, they were not just going to raid the manor house; they were going to open that dreadful door. Longfinch had the key now. Certainly that's what this was all about.

Lewis caught his eye and smiled encouragingly. "Courage, boyo, courage."

Without hardly pausing, Longfinch led the way westwards up the highroad. The way was much easier now that they were on a well-maintained road, and the pirates quickened their pace.

At a very brisk march then, they passed through the canyon, across the bridge, and then entered the wide dale with the twinkling lights of that great city, Entwerp Proper. Again the pirates turned off the main road, though this time they followed a small path which curved around the city in a long northwestern arch to the common grounds at the northern edge of the city.

The road was rougher and less maintained, but the pirates still kept up their quick march. They followed this winding side road for several more miles before Longfinch left this road too, trudging through the long grass of the commons. Ernest could look up and see the dark shape of the manor house before them. So they were here then. He hardly dared to think about what the rest of this night held in store. He had terrible memories of this place.

The pirates would raid the house again, and he would have to help them. Oh, how much he would rather be fighting *against* these pirates! Why did he have to be with them again? Why hadn't he fled southward when he had the chance?

But what was that in the field before them? Ernest squinted as he looked ahead. Yes, in the darkness he could just make out the shape of a lanky man, dressed like one of the Pistosians — though by his rolling stride, Ernest knew he was a sailor. The impostor strode casually up to the group of pirates and saluted Longfinch sloppily.

"How goes it then?" Longfinch asked, grinning.

The impostor laughed. "The strikers fell for it, hook, line, and sinker. They've moved on the bank now, and the whole militia's been called out on them."

"And will they attack?" Longfinch asked.

The man shrugged carelessly. "I haven't been able to talk them into actually *attacking* the bank yet."

Longfinch clicked his tongue disdainfully. "Keep trying then. The longer we can keep that diversion active, the better."

The man nodded, saluted again, and then turned on his heels, walking carelessly towards Entwerp Proper.

Before Ernest had time to think what this conversation could mean, he thought he heard the rustle of wings above him. Looking up, he saw a large hawk-like bird rushing past, heading like a speeding arrow for the manor house. Wasn't that the same bird he had seen with Lady Death the night she had spared his life? Ernest shuddered at the memory. Was it a good or bad sign that this bird was here now? Surely the bird was some ally of the Llaedhwythi people and would likely help them. That would certainly be a good thing, as Ernest wanted these Llaedhwythi men to defeat the pirates. On the other hand, as he was with the pirates now, he would likely be killed among them.

Ernest ground his teeth together. If only he could get away from these pirates!

Longfinch paused now just before the manor house. The other pirates gathered close around him.

The Archeomancer looked the house over critically. "They're still awake," he murmured darkly.

Longfinch nodded. "We'll make it quick then." Longfinch sighed contentedly and looked over his men. "On my command, rush the door and break it in. Kill everyone inside, except for the girl Ella; I would like her kept alive." The pirate captain glanced meaningfully at Jock Blowhoarder.

The pirates all nodded silently.

Just then, Ernest heard a shout from the manor house. Dark shadows rushed about at the windows. In the still air, Ernest could clearly hear bolts being drawn across the front door.

"They've been alerted, sure, baptize it," Killjelly cursed. "How'd they discover us?"

Ernest again heard the rustle of wings above him. It was that same bird. It was flying away from the house now at the same breakneck speed.

Longfinch laughed. "It's no matter. They willn't be able to resist us even if they know we're coming."

The other pirates snickered.

Longfinch turned to the albino. "Your spells are ready?"

The albino nodded darkly.

Longfinch waved his hand with a military flourish. "Take the house."

# FORSAKEN

Clerans joined the others as they hurriedly overturned desks, tables, chairs, and bookshelves, throwing them in front of the door and windows of the little tailor shop. Mr. Fflemins only watched as the others cast his books and hand-made clothes carelessly aside in their haste to bar the door. Clerans himself couldn't help but feel a twinge of regret as he trod on leather-bound books and lace dresses with his dirty boots. At the moment, there was no time to lament the damage done to Mr. Fflemins' tailor shop. For now, they need only concern themselves with their lives.

In a moment, the only piece of furniture left in the main room was a solid oak bookshelf, loaded down with reams of clothing patterns. Martyn pushed against the pile of furniture that barricaded the door to see that it was solid. Pausing for a moment, the seven defenders looked at each other. Clerans allowed himself to breathe. Were they safe here? Had the pirates seen them enter this shop?

As if in answer, discordant shouting sounded from the other side of the door. Although the door and the make-shift barricade muffled their voices, Clerans could just make out a pirate yelling, "In here! I'm certain I seed them enter here!"

Pounding fists and musket butts crashed heavily against the door, and the windows shattered, glass tinkling on the other side of the barricade.

"More than likely they'll will trive up a way to break in, now," Mr. Gingrich muttered.

Mr. Fflemins looked around his looted shop and then fixed his gaze steadily on the door, now totally blocked from view behind the pile of furniture. "You do no think that they'll will be able to break through that, now do ye?"

Meriwedhr leapt forward, seizing the remaining bookshelf. With a great heave, the huge satyr tipped the bookshelf over, spilling all of Mr. Fflemin's patterns across the already cluttered floor. Mr. Fflemins let out an involuntary groan. Carrying the solid oak bookshelf now as if it were only a bundle of kindling, Meriwedhr shoved it against the make-shift barricade.

Meriwedhr let out a great sigh. "Well then, that is the best we'll will be able to do then. We cen no help it if they'll break through that."

Suddenly, they heard gunshots from the other side of the door. Every man fell flat on the ground out of instinct. Looking up, Clerans saw no evidence that the shots had penetrated the blockade.

"Are there any other doors?" Martyn asked, turning to Mr. Fflemins. "Any other way they'll could get in?"

Mr. Fflemins nodded. "Ay, there is the back door into the alleyway."

Meriwedhr leapt to his feet. "Right then, I will make sure that is blockaded as well."

Another fusillade of musket fire sounded on the other side of the door as Meriwedhr hurried into the back room.

*Martyn and Meriwedhr in the Tailor Shop*

"What about in the attic?" Martyn said to Mr. Fflemins. "Are there any windows that gard out over the streets, or any way out onto the roof?"

"Ay," Mr. Fflemins nodded. "Both, sure."

Martyn nodded and jumped up. "Clerans, you vene with me, then — an' load yer pistol!"

Clerans scrambled to his feet, following Martyn as quickly as he could. Martyn ducked into the back room and then hurried up the steep wooden staircase (almost a ladder) which led to the attic. Clerans pulled out his pistol as he ascended the stairs behind Martyn, trying his best to reload as he climbed.

There was no light to speak of in the attic, only some dim, blue starlight which filtered in from a couple of windows on either side of the low space. The whole attic was one room, the length of the entire shop below (only about twenty feet across, but easily fifty long). From the little that Clerans could see, the attic was unfurnished, with only a few old trunks stacked up against the stone walls.

Martyn crouched in the low ceiling, hurrying over to the window which overlooked the front of the shop. Clerans followed. It was not a very large window, but it had two smaller windows placed just to either side, giving Martyn and Clerans an ample view of the street in front of the shop. Clerans pressed his face close against the window, holding his breath as he looked out so as not to fog the glass.

A group of pirates crowded around the shop, throwing themselves against the door and shooting through the shattered windows as if hoping to send a shot through the furniture behind. There were about twenty of them. Probably it was the same group that had tried to ambush them at the Upper Court. All looked like wicked sailors; most of them human, but Clerans thought he could see a few gnomes and maybe a nymph or two among the rest.

Martyn slowly pushed one of the smaller windows open, and immediately they could hear the pirates' voices distinctly.

"Harder lads, harder!"

"Baptism! It amn't no use!"

"They've blocked us out, christen 'em!"

"No, no, give it another go, whatever. I'm sure that it'll give."

"Anointment! *You* try it, then!"

"Shall we try to burn 'em out, like?"

"It's all baptized brick, you idiot."

Just then, the leader let out a loud whistle. All the pirates ceased their bustling and turned towards him.

"Order, lads!" the lead pirate said. "We'll never break in like this. Come on, then." He pointed to several of his men. "You all come with me, and we'll find out some battering ram. The rest on you all keep out a watch, for to make sure what they don't try and escape on us."

With that, the pirates split up; the greater part hurried away, while the rest loaded their muskets and stepped back from the shop front a few paces, standing like trained guards across the road.

Martyn shook his head. "They are no ordinary rabble o' sailors. They gard to be well trained."

Clerans let out his breath slowly. "That will no make it easy on us, then?"

Martyn shook his head. "Ay, no. But we are safe fer the moment, I suppose — as safe as hunted men cen be."

Martyn sat back, leaning against the cold stone walls of the attic and rubbing his forehead as if he had a headache. Clerans sighed as he looked at his older brother. He could feel a lump forming in the back of his throat.

"Is it jist us then? Are we all that is left?"

Martyn shrugged. "There *wos* firing in the Lower Village yet, which tells me that there may be some more militia left — probably jist a handful like us, holed up in shops an' houses, waitin' fer the pirates to break in."

"No," Clerans said quietly, "I meant o' our family. Are we the only ones left?"

Martyn bit his lip, but was silent.

"What about Ma, Robert, Roland, an' Laendon?" Clerans asked, suddenly feeling panicked. "An' Lexi. Was Lexi at the dike, too?"

"Calm down now," Martyn said soothingly. "Ye will get yerself excited. Jist breathe easy an' stay calm, Clerans. I need ye to be able to fight in an hour or so, an' I cen no tain ye gettin' excited on me again, an' losin' yer head, an' losin' yer life."

Clerans took a couple of deep breaths, feeling his heart rate slow. He kept a steady eye on Martyn.

Martyn sighed deeply, rubbing his forehead again. "The sheriff issued an evacuation o' the village jist after ye left. Now, whether that means all o' the non-combatants made it out, I do no know, but I 'spect that the vast majority o' them did. As fer Ma, jist before we left fer the dikes, Da gave Robert the family rifle an' told him to duce Ma, an' Roland to Entwerp Proper. I'm certain that they're safe now. Lexi, o' course, is still stayin' with Miss Elsi an' Miss Ella, at the Pickering manor, so she missed the mobilization entirely, an' will be safe there."

"An' Laendon?" Clerans asked, hardly wanting to know the answer.

Martyn paused for a moment. "He vened with us to the dikes."

Clerans swallowed and then bit his cheek. "I did no see if he'll made it out o' the first ambush."

Martyn shook his head. "I did no either." He exhaled. "I am afraid we left him behind."

"And Da?" Again, Clerans knew that he didn't want to hear what Martyn would say, but he had to ask.

Martyn rubbed his forehead again. "Ye saw as well as I did: Da was at the head o' the group which charged into that second ambush. The best I cen hope is that he wos captured an' no killed."

A lump formed in Clerans' throat again. "Neither Da nor Laendon... Do ye think that they might ha'...?"

Martyn shook his head. "I cen only hope — I cen only pray — but I do no know. What I do know is that we will no be safe here fer merri long."

Martyn looked at Clerans closely, suddenly exclaiming, "Llifsa! Clerans, ye're wounded!"

Clerans looked back at Martyn in surprise. "Am I?" And it took him several moments to remember his near keelhauling at the beginning of the evening. "Ah, yes. It's jist a few cuts from the barnacles."

"Ay, then, but let me take a gard at them an' make sure that they are cleaned an' cared fer," Martyn replied. "Vene along then, back downstairs where I cen see better."

Clerans and Martyn shuffled down the steps and entered the main room again. Here, Martyn had Clerans strip off his shirt and sit down to better inspect his wounds. While Martyn did his best to clean the wounds and bandage them appropriately, Clerans took a moment to look around the room. Someone had lighted a few oil lanterns, and they now hung from the rafters, casting a golden (almost cheery) light over the room. A strong scent of lavender filled the little shop, accompanied by a hint of thyme and ginseng — some kind of herbal concoction that Mr. Fflemins used to deter moths. The other five survivors sat in the room amidst the clutter of half-sewn clothes, scrap bits of cloth, pattern pamphlets, and spools of thread which littered the floor.

Mr. Fflemins crouched with his back slumped against the wall, viewing the catastrophic mess dismally. Standing a little way off, Meriwedhr tapped his hoof against the floor, his arms folded and his brow furrowed. Mr. Gingrich had cleared a small space on the floor, and he sat cross-legged with his rifle and two pistols laid out before him, inspecting them all closely and loading them carefully. Miss Flalowen had laid poor, wounded Chaerls in a corner in the back of the room and now leaned over him, apparently inspecting his wounds as well. Now and then, Chaerls would groan miserably.

After a few more moments, Martyn bandaged up the last of Clerans' cuts, clapping him on the shoulder heartily, and handing him his shirt back. "There, then! I expect that's the best I cen do under the circumstances. The bleedin' seems to ha' stopped, but ye'll need to tain them all re-bandaged again once we reach Entwerp Proper."

Mr. Gingrich looked up from his gun inspections. "Ye still mean to make it to Entwerp Proper, then?"

Martyn nodded. "We are safe here fer the moment, sure, but only fer the moment."

Mr. Fflemins buried his face in his hands. "Then they *will* break in?"

"These pirates," Martyn said, "ha' already shown themselves to be merri clever opponents. I expect we may tain an hour or two — maybe four at best — but then they will trive up a way to break in. They will break in, or burn us out, or blow us up, or some sich thing. If we'll stay here, we will all certainly die. We will no even last until the morning."

Mr. Fflemins sighed deeply. "Ay, an' I did no even tell my Patrisha goodbye."

"Our only hope o' living through this is if we'll cen make it to Entwerp Proper," Martyn continued. "Governor Braedhwyc will be there with the regulars an' the rest o' the militia. We'd be sure to outnumber the pirates then, an' we'll could hold them at bay." Martyn took a deep breath. "If we'll will make it out o' here, we will need a plan. First, then, we need to know what our assets are. Flalowen, how is Chaerls doin'?"

Flalowen stood slowly to her feet, turning to face Martyn with haggard eyes. "There is nothing I cen do fer him. I think he's bleedin' out from the inside, an' I cen no stop it." Flalowen slumped down against the wall and ran her fingers through her hair. Clerans looked over at the obscure form of Chaerls sprawled out on the floor. Already Chaerls' face was ashen pale, and even from the other side of the room, Clerans could hear his labored breathing.

Martyn clenched his jaw and sighed. "That is only six o' us, then. What about powder an' shot? How is everyone?"

"Still well supplied," Meriwedhr said.

All the men nodded back at Martyn.

"An' guns?" Martyn asked. "We'll want as many a piece as we cen get. I see ye all tain a rifle excepting Clerans."

Clerans nodded.

Martyn drew in a quick breath. "Ay then, Clerans ye ceive Chaerls' rifle. The rest o' ye tain pistols, too? See that they are all loaded an' attended to."

Martyn then turned to Mr. Fflemins. "An' what is there in this house?"

"Ah," Mr. Fflemins stammered, "Ah, there's scrap cloth, and the bolts I bought jist the other day..."

"No, man," Martyn cut in. "What is in this house that could be used fer a *weapon*?"

"Ah!" Mr. Fflemins said. "Well, no much, only my second rifle in the chest in the attic, an' my father's wheel-lock musket from the wars — I do no know if it'll will still fire, but it is up there."

Mr. Gingrich stood to his feet. "I will see to that, then." And he hurried up into the attic, returning a moment later with the two guns Mr. Fflemins had spoken of.

Martyn sighed, looking over the room one last time. "Well then, if that is all we tain, we will make it work. Fer now, ceive yer rests. We will all need to be ready to fight soon enough, an' I expect this might be the last bit o' rest we will tain fer quite some time."

Mr. Gingrich shook his head solemnly. "Perhaps it is the *last* bit of rest fer us."

# 11

# ROOTS

In the Pickering manor, a large fire sparkled and spat in the great stone hearth, filling the dining room with the inviting smell of cedar. It was cooler that night than it had been yet, and once they finished eating, Ella, Elsi, Lexi, and Miss Nansi moved their chairs away from the table, sitting with their backs to the fire with one fluffy, down comforter draped over all four of them. Pastor Daerl and Mr. Hydmenton were there too, posted as guards for the ladies. Both men were still sitting at the table. Miss Nansi hung a kettle over the fire, first filling it with the Pistosians' distinctive, weak beer.

"There is jist nothin' quite like ceder-smoked beer, dearie," Miss Nansi insisted. "Ye will ha' to try it."

Ella watched the kettle skeptically as it warmed. She still was not sure what to think of this Pistosian beer on its own — she could hardly imagine what it would be like warmed.

Elsi took one look at Ella and laughed.

"Ella," she said through her merriment, "You gard as if you'll are observin' some new an' strange beetle fer scientific research."

The others burst out laughing.

Ella blushed a little. "It's just wei'd to me–" Ella stopped herself, starting over and trying her hardest to say all of her 'r's properly. "It's only that I didn't expect you to warm your beer, that's all." She sighed.

Miss Nansi giggled at this. "Yer folks back at yer home never tained ceder-smoked beer?"

Ella shook her head.

Miss Nansi clicked her tongue in merriment. "Ah, what a pity."

"Ay," Mr. Hydmenton joined in, "merri true! They do no know what they are missin'."

Lexi, however, smiled knowingly at Ella. "Oh, ay. I cen relate to ye, Ella. I remember thinkin' it strange at first, too."

Ella nodded. "It's just these cultu'al–" Ella stopped herself and restarted, again trying to speak more clearly, "–cultural habits keep surprising me. You all seem so much like the people f'om my count'y, but then you do these wandom... eh, random things as if they were normal."

Pastor Daerl raised an eyebrow in amusement. "Cen ye give us an example?"

Ella laughed nervously. She was *not* about to bring up the stockings issue in public and in mixed company. She would never convert to that custom, even if no one else in this country wore stockings.

After a moment's pause, Ella said, "Well, the'e's the kissing fo'h one thing."

Elsi laughed out loud. "Oh no! Here she goes on the kissing again!"

"It's t'ue!" Ella insisted. "In my count'y, you would neve'h kiss someone unless you we'e welated–" Ella paused, "I mean unless you were *related*."

Mr. Hydmenton laughed out loud at this, turning to Lexi and waving a finger in her face. "She sounds jist like yer father now, Miss Lexi!"

Lexi laughed at this comment. "I suppose ye are right."

"Wot was it he'd say?" Pastor Daerl asked, stroking his curled beard thoughtfully.

"Oh, right! He'd say:" Mr Hydmenton furrowed up his brow as if imitating someone. "*Elderians!*" And Mr. Hydmenton burst out laughing. "As if that'll explained it all."

"Only ye could *never really* say it the way he said it," Pastor Daerl said through his merriment. "No, with the same incredulity!"

Lexi was grinning from ear to ear. "In his defense, though, he verted out to be quite a decent Elderian in the end, after he got over leavin' the Panhaplitic Church."

"Ah!" Pastor Daerl exclaimed, banging his fist down on the table. "That was what he would say! When he was really perturbed, he'd say, 'What do you take me for, eh? A *blind Rectificationist*'?"

Mr. Hydmenton laughed uproariously at this comment, but Miss Nansi made a face as of mock offense.

"Ay, then, an' now it is makin' fun at *my* kirk ye are?"

Pastor Daerl raised his hand defensively. "Well now, that wos jist what he said. Ye cen no blame the messenger."

Miss Nansi wagged her finger at the giant satyr pastor. "Ay, but I might no give ye yer ceder-smoked beer."

"Ah!" Mr. Hydmenton exclaimed. "She runs a hard bargain, then."

Pastor Daerl sighed deeply, shaking his head. "No, Lexi, yer father wos a good man, an' we miss him dearly."

The pastor sighed again, but now he looked up at Ella. "Wot o' yer family, Miss Ella?"

Ella was a bit surprised by the question. "What do you mean?"

"I do no think I'll ha' heard o' them. Tell us about yer family then. Ye're from Slyzwir, am I right?"

Ella nodded. "That's w'ight. My family is f'om a little village in the mountains, called Blisa."

"An' yer father?" Pastor Daerl asked.

"Yes, he was..." Ella stopped herself. There probably wasn't much point in telling them that her birth-father was Silas Pickering. That would take far too long to explain. She took a deep breath and started over, speaking quickly, "My fathe'h left me befo'e I was even five yea'hs old. He wanted to find his fo'tune he'e — in the Pistos Capes — but he died at sea. I don't even wemembe'h him."

Everyone sat in silence for a moment, and Mr. Hydmenton swallowed awkwardly. Ella felt ashamed. Maybe she shouldn't have spoken. She had destroyed the jovial mood everyone was in.

"I apologize," Ella mumbled.

"Oh, no, no, do no," Pastor Daerl looked at her sympathetically. "Is that, then, why ye sometimes call yerself 'Ella Pickering,' an' sometimes, 'Ella Donne?'"

Ella nodded. "Picke'ing was my fathe'h's name. Titus Donne is my stepfathe'h. He was a childhood f'iend of my fathe'h and my mothe'h, and he accompanied my fathe'h to the ship soon befo'e he died. Mr. Donne was the fo'eman fo'h a logging c'ew in the town, so he took ca'e of us when Papa died and gave us a cottage to live in — and he even paid for my schooling. A few yea'hs ago he ma'hied Mama, and now they have a little boy."

Pastor Daerl nodded. "I am glad to hear that the Lord provided fer ye. This Mr. Titus Donne sounds like a merri good man. Ye like him? He ha' been a good father to ye?"

Ella nodded, but inwardly she wanted to smirk. Of course, Mr. Donne was a good man; he was just so boring and predictable. Of course, she liked him, and of course, he was a good father to her — in the sense that he was fair and loving. Yet somehow, Ella had never been able to love him back. She couldn't find it in herself to respect him. He was a homebody and such a far cry from her daring, adventurous Papa.

"If ye'll do no mind my askin'," Pastor Daerl said softly, "how did that affect ye? Growin' up, I mean, without yer father?"

Ella played with her fingers nervously, a bit embarrassed to continue. She looked Pastor Daerl in the eye. There was no reason not to tell him. It would probably do her good to talk. Besides, Pastor Daerl was clearly a very trustworthy man who meant Ella only good. He was a pastor, after all.

"Well," Ella began hesitantly, "it was definitely difficult — especially at school, since eve'yone else had a fathe'h." Ella swallowed. "I think I was always looking fo'h Papa. He had a lot of books, and I wead them all ove'h and ove'h. And sometimes we would have men come through the village who had been at sea themselves, and I'd ask them to tell me all the sto'ies they knew about the sea, since Papa had died at sea."

"And Mr. Donne?" Pastor Daerl prompted.

Ella took a deep breath. "He was," she hesitated. She had already opened up to the pastor this much. Why not just tell him all? "I mean, he was so good to us, but I found it hard to look up to him. He wasn't nea'ly as exciting as my Papa. He was just a logging fo'eman, afte'h all."

Pastor Daerl nodded, and he licked his lips. "I lost my father, too, when I wos eight years o' age. I suppose that's somewhat different, because I remember my father, but you do no. But be that as it may, I cen see that ye already tain a better understandin' than I did at yer age."

Ella looked at Pastor Daerl closely. "How so?"

"Well then," Pastor Daerl replied. "I had a merri o' an wound from losin' my father, but I did no understand the nature o' the wound. I did no understand that it was a *relational* wound, an' it need a *relationship* to cure it. So I verted to back-sliding and wild living. Oh, ay, I was a merri intemperate youth."

"The sort that gives satyrs a bad name, eh?" Mr. Hydmenton said with a laugh.

Pastor Daerl shook his head. "Now that is no somethin' to make light at. God ha' been gracious to me, an' He ha' 'restored the years the locusts devoured.' Ay, but as fer ye, Miss Ella, ye ha' been searchin' fer that lost relationship, ha' no ye?"

Ella furrowed her brow. "I'm not su'e I follow you."

Pastor Daerl nodded. "Ye realized that the wound ye tained was a relational wound, an' ye've been searchin' fer that relationship to cure yer wound."

Ella thought on this for a moment. "I suppose that's a good way of saying it."

Pastor Daerl smiled. "So that's what I mean when I say ye are at a better understandin' o' it than I wos at yer age. It took me many years to realize that the only thing in the whole wide world that could help me and could heal me — really, the only thing in the whole wide world that would *save* me — wos the personal relationship with God the Son. Ay, an' I hope ye ha' seen that already."

Ella nodded. She had never really thought of it that way before, but what the Pastor said made sense.

Pastor Daerl now laughed apologetically. "Ah now, I'm afraid I ha' reverted to my day-job. How's the beer now, Nansi?"

Nansi nodded at the Pastor with a smile. "Jist as long as ye do no get on to yer Elderian nonsense, ye cen preach all ye like."

Mr Hydmenton burst into a fit of laughter.

"Ay," Lexi said, "ye do always edify us, Pastor Daerl."

Elsi nodded. "We appreciate it."

Just then, there was a loud tap against one of the large dining-room windows. Ella looked up, but could only see a blurred shape fluttering about in front of the window. The very next moment, the shape vanished. Before Ella had time to wonder what the shape was, one of the smaller windows above the large one shattered with no warning. Everyone started in alarm as into the room tumbled the form of Aarushi the harrier.

Aarushi landed awkwardly on the dining room table, clearly a bit stunned from breaking through the window. The harrier fluttered about for a moment before finally finding her footing on the oak table.

"Aarushi!" Lexi cried, leaping up from her chair and kneeling at the table in front of the harrier. "What is the matter?"

Aarushi paced up and down the table frantically, waving her beak about, and now and then spreading her wings wide as if trying to emphasize a point.

"Oh!" Elsi exclaimed, pale with excitement. "If only she'll could *talk* to us."

"Ay," Mr. Hydmenton agreed, peering at the harrier curiously.

Aarushi continued her odd dance on the table, and Lexi shook her head. "Martyn ha' tried many a time to teach me how to understand her, an' sometimes I *cen* understand her well enough... but when she is this excited, I cen never quite tell what she is getting at."

Aarushi whistled weakly and stood still, stomping her feet in frustration.

"It is plain enough to me," Pastor Daerl declared, standing up so abruptly that he cast his chair to the ground behind him. Everyone turned to Pastor Daerl now as his colossal form filled the room.

"It is another attack," the Pastor said calmly. "She ha' vened here to warn us that the pirates are back."

Aarushi nodded emphatically and whistled.

"Tar and needles!" Mr. Hydmenton gasped. "We must bar the door!" He dashed frantically from the room, coming back a moment later with four rifles and several pistols.

Pastor Daerl and Lexi grabbed their weapons from Mr. Hydmenton.

"Ladies," the pastor said. "I do no know where ye may best ceive refuge in this house, or if it is too late now to escape out the back door..."

"I know," Ella said, standing to her feet. She then turned to Miss Nansi and Elsi. "Follow me."

"An' no without my protection," Lexi hissed, looking her rifle over to see that it was loaded before following.

Ella dashed from the dining room into the kitchen with her three friends in tow. A thrill ran down her spine. The last time the pirates attacked this house, she had been clueless, helpless, and defenseless, yet now a new energy surged through her. She was like one of those heroines from the great stories. She had a plan, and she would see it done.

Rushing up the steep stairway from the kitchen, Ella slowed once she reached the upstairs hallway. Now, which room was it? Ah yes, this one! Ella threw open the door to the room and motioned for the others to follow her. Once inside, she slammed the door shut behind her. Bother! There didn't seem to be a lock on the inside.

"Are ye sure we will be safe in here?" Elsi asked, shaking all over as she spoke.

At that moment, there was a tremendous crash from downstairs. It sounded to Ella as if it were coming from the front door. Almost at the same instant, gunshots, shouts, and screams rang out.

Lexi knelt across from the door, leveling her rifle at it and grinning savagely. "If they'll find us, I cen take a few down, at least."

Ella's heart raced. "No, we will not be safe in this w'oom. I mean to get you out of it."

So saying, she rushed to the far side of the room and pushed aside the large dresser that sat under the window. She was now very glad that she had explored the house so well during her stay and knew of the trap door hidden here. Ella reached her hand quickly into the crack between the wall and the floor-boards, seized the hidden handle, and then flung the trap door wide open. Elsi, Lexi, and Miss Nansi looked on in astonishment.

"Why is that here?" Elsi gasped.

From the level below, Ella could hear footsteps and more shouting. Her heart sank. The pirates must be in the house already.

"Quickly," Ella urged, "climb down! It leads into the shed at the back of the house. I bet we could slip out of the'e without being seen and then run to Entwerp to get help."

Lexi shouldered her rifle and descended the trap door first. "I will make sure the way is clear."

"Ay!" Miss Nansi said, coming forward next, and nodding to Ella. "Yer a girl with a head on yer shoulders, now! I warrant we'll will all make it out o' this alright!"

As Miss Nansi disappeared down the hole, Ella motioned frantically for Elsi to follow.

Now Ella could hear yelling and cursing from nearer in the house. Was that the sound of footsteps coming up the stairs? Would she have enough time to slip down this passageway and close the trapdoor before the pirates found the room? Even if she did, suppose the pirates found the trapdoor? The only way to ensure against that was to push the dresser back in place over the top.

Elsi slid into the passage next, pausing briefly to take Ella's hand. "Ye ha' been sich a great friend to me an' my Papa. How cen we ever repay you?"

Ella looked straight into Elsi's brown eyes, and she felt a strange resolve come over her. She could not let any harm come to poor Elsi — not with what she'd been through already.

Ella smiled. "Good bye, Elsi. I'm sure you will all make it out of he'e just fine."

With that, Ella closed the trap door directly over Elsi's head.

Paying no heed to the shrieks of dismay from the other side of the trapdoor, Ella leapt to her feet and shoved the dresser back over the top. There! No one would even suspect that there was a secret passageway in this room now. Miss Nansi, Lexi, and Elsi were safe.

Ella had only enough time to take a deep breath before the door burst open behind her. Ella turned on her heels to see several pirates swarming into the room.

"That's her!" one of them shouted. "You remember the orders!"

The pirates let out a chorus of cheers and raunchy whistles. Then they seized Ella by the arms and dragged her violently from the room.

Ella could feel her throat going dry. What had she done? What had she condemned herself to?

# 12

# BAPTISM BY FIRE

Clerans and the other survivors had hardly sat for five minutes in peace before a commotion started in front of the shop. Clerans couldn't distinctly make out what was being said by the pirates outside, but he could tell they were very excited, talking loudly to one another. Then a loud crash rang out from the door.

"That would be their ram then," Martyn said matter-of-factly. "Time fer action!"

"Shall we prepare to receive them inside?" Mr. Gingrich asked darkly, standing to his feet and snatching up his rifle.

Martyn shook his head. "No, I do no think so. We must drive them back. If we'll cen foil this attempt, hopefully they will leave again, searchin' the town fer some other way to break in. They will only leave a small contingent to guard the shop an' keep us in. That is when we will strike."

Again, they heard the loud crash at the door.

"They're going to break in!" Mr. Fflemins cried, shaking all over.

Martyn smiled roguishly. "I do no think so. They ha' no even broken the door open yet, unless I miss my guess. I think I know how to drive them back. Now all o' ye, stay calm. Compose yerselves, and breathe easily — especially ye, Clerans, and ye, Fflemins. You cen no get excited again, or you will get yourselves killed."

Martyn surveyed the little band with a confident smile. Then he suddenly frowned. "Is Chaerls still with us?"

Flalowen looked up from where she slouched against the wall and shook her head. "He passed only a minute ago."

Martyn nodded and sighed. "Then we will avenge him. Ay lads, ye know what the sheriff used to pray before any engagement?"

Clerans nodded. "'Guide my hands to war.' Ay, I heard him pray that, right a'fore they killed him."

Martyn nodded. "May God guide our hands to war. May He see that we make it out o' this alive."

"Amen," Meriwedhr replied.

"Right then!" Martyn cried. "Prepare fer action. Gingrich an' Clerans, ye vene with me!"

Martyn snagged two lamps just before dashing up into the attic. Clerans and Mr. Gingrich followed close behind. Coming up to the little windows that overlooked the street, Martyn peered out, chuckling to himself.

"Ay, they will no spect *this!*"

Martyn handed the two lanterns to Clerans and then carefully pushed the window all the way open. Clerans could hear the mad cries of the pirates below. Looking out, he could see the entire group of them crowded up by the door. At the center of this crowd, four of five pirates gripped a large oak table, using it to ram against the shop door again and again. At every sound of strain or cracking from the shop door, all the pirates cheered. The leader stood a ways back, barking out orders which the pirates seemed to ignore as they bunched in tightly around the ram, as if they meant to crowd the door into breaking.

"That door will burst soon," Mr. Gingrich said.

Martyn chuckled. "Not when I am done with them." Martyn chuckled again. "Right then, Gingrich, when I give the signal, fire every gun ye tain on ye."

Martyn quickly unslung his rifle and rested the barrel on the open window, placing the pirate musket he had taken earlier just next to it. Then he pulled out his two pistols and made sure that they were both loaded. "An' Clerans," Martyn said as he worked, "when I say so, ye take those two lanterns an' throw them out the window as hard as ye cen, and right onto the ram an' the men holding it. Are ye ready?"

Clerans and Mr. Gingrich nodded back to Martyn.

"Deep breath then, everyone," Martyn said.

Clerans filled his lungs with air, and then let it out slowly. This shouldn't be too difficult; it would be no trouble at all to throw both lanterns directly onto the battering ram.

"Now!" Martyn ordered.

Immediately, Clerans leaned out the window and hurled the lanterns downward with all his might, one after the other. The lanterns shattered across the pirates' heads, spilling oil all over the battering ram and many of the pirates as well. Like the explosion of a firecracker, the oil ignited, flashing up in flames that enveloped the battering ram and the surrounding pirates.

The pirates leapt back with howls of pain, cursing, dancing about, and rolling on the ground to put out the fire that so suddenly engulfed them. Clerans watched no longer, but ducked out of the window as Martyn and Gingrich fired their guns into the confused pirates. Screams of agony added to the howls of burning rage. Martyn and Mr. Gingrich discharged all of their guns in rapid succession, then they quickly ducked back down behind the stone walls, away from the windows. They finished not a moment too soon, for the pirates quickly returned a volley of shots at the little window, shattering all the glass, and sending several shots into the attic, where they bounced off the walls and lodged in the ceiling.

Martyn crouched low to the ground, but he grinned over at Clerans. "Ah now, that outta-should slow them down."

Mr. Gingrich grinned back.

Clerans felt like grinning too. They had decisively and effectively foiled the pirates' plan. Clerans chanced a quick glance over the windowsill to smirk at the frustrated pirates. Instead, he gagged in horror. The pirates were still rushing about in all directions, some still trying to extinguish fire from their clothes and persons, while others simply yelled, shouted, and cursed. The air smelled of burning meat. These pirates deserved to be burned. Why, when he looked at them, could he only see that young striker bleeding out in his lap? Clerans swallowed. These pirates were trying to kill him. Why was he feeling sympathy for them? It was rather inconvenient.

The leader of the pirates danced about in a rage, trying to bark out orders, but Clerans couldn't make out distinctly what he was saying.

The oaken table, which they had so recently been using as a battering ram, was now a blazing fire burning just to the side of the shop's door. Several of the pirates now sported hideous and peeling burns on their faces and arms. Four or five bodies lay amidst the writhing group of pirates. Clerans couldn't quite tell if they were dead or dying. All he could see was the moonlight and starlight reflecting off the pools of blood, which now soiled the cobblestone streets.

Clerans' stomach lurched, and he ducked back away from the window. Probably his face was turning green. His heart racing, Clerans took a deep breath.

Martyn stopped smiling and nodded. "Ay, ye are right, then, Clerans; there is no reason to laugh at them. That would jist be to become like them."

Just then, they could hear the head pirate's voice finally sounding clear above the confused yells, screams, and vulgar cursing. "Stand in lines, lads, baptize it! Stop hopping about like roasting chickens, now, and get in your anointed lines. Yous there, keep a guard on that window, and shoot anyone who shows his baptized face at it. The rest of yous, get another battering ram!"

In the street below, Clerans could hear grumbling and muffled cursing, but then came the noise of feet scampering away from the shop. Martyn nodded to Clerans and Gingrich. "There we tain it now! This is our chance. We break out while they are on minimal guard."

No sooner had Martyn spoken these words than a loud crash resounded from downstairs, followed by several sharp reports from within the little shop.

"Tar and needles!" Mr. Gingrich swore, "That is the back door, or I am a dolphin."

As if in answer to Mr. Gingrich, Clerans heard a pirate's voice sounding from the back of the shop, "We're in, lads! We're in!"

Martyn, Mr. Gingrich, and Clerans rushed to the attic stairs as more shots rang out from the rooms below. As Clerans ducked down the stairs (taking three at a bound), there was a great crash. Smoke filled the room, and the pungent scent of gunpowder stung his eyes. Clerans coughed, peering closely through the smoke.

Meriwedhr stood in the center of the room, his curved horns nearly touching the ceiling as he snatched up a table from the barricade before the front door and threw it against the door to the back room, forming a second barricade against that door. Clerans could just make out the form of Mr. Fflemins leaning against the far wall and gripping his arm as if in excruciating pain. Two bodies lay on the floor, but Clerans couldn't make out their features in the smoke.

"Meriwedhr!" Martyn cried, hurriedly reloading his rifle. "Are they in?"

"Confined to the back room fer now," Meriwedhr replied,

heaving a great chair against this new barricade. "An' we, I am afraid, are only confined to *this* room."

Clerans stumbled over to the first of the bodies on the floor, checking it over quickly. It was a pirate who had apparently taken a bullet to the head. Looking up, he saw Mr. Gingrich turning over the second body.

"Llifsa!" Mr. Gingrich gasped.

"Ay," Meriwedhr nodded. "We are down another man."

Now Clerans could see the face of the second body through the clearing smoke. It was Flalowen, her eyes rolled back and frozen in a look of intense pain. A loud commotion now sounded from the other side of the door to the back room. Clerans guessed the pirates were now quickly assembling there, and at any moment they would begin breaking down the door.

Mr. Fflemins shook all over, still clutching his wounded arm. "This is it then? We are all about to die?"

"Ay," Mr. Gingrich replied, reloading his guns quickly. "An' we will sell our lives fer all they are worth!"

"Ho now!" Martyn cried.

Everyone turned to look at Martyn as he stood decisively in the middle of the room, wreathed in tendrils of gunpowder smoke. A confident smile played about the corners of his mouth. "Stay calm, an' breathe. This is our chance to get out o' here. Look to yer guns now, an' see that they are all loaded."

"Lord," Clerans muttered, as he hurriedly reloaded his pistol, "guide my hands to war!"

# 13

# WHERE THE EAGLES GATHER

With a wild yell, Longfinch and his pirates charged up the stairs to the front door of the manor house. Ernest felt a momentary thrill as he watched the pirates rush on the manor, thinking that this might now be his opportunity to escape.

To his dismay, however, three bulky and well-armed pirates stayed behind, watching the three prisoners carefully. Jock sighed, bowing his head and crossing his forehead as he muttered something religious-sounding. Lewis caught Ernest's eye and winked, mouthing the word "patience."

"Come on now," one of the pirates guarding them said, spitting on the ground. "Let's see this a little closer, eh? Why sit all the way back here? We'll miss the fun." And he prodded them up the steps to the rear of the pirate band.

The pirates flung themselves at the door of the manor house, many of them beating against it with their musket butts. Suddenly, a deep shout rang out above the commotion, and all the pirates halted. The albino strode forward, walking directly up to the door. As Ernest watched, he trembled, vomit tingling at his throat from just looking at the albino. He had seen this wizard at work, and he dreaded what might happen now.

Longfinch grinned and drew out his pistol. "Hold your guns ready!"

The Archeomancer now placed his hand on the door and muttered a few sinister-sounding words. Ernest could feel a strange pulse around him, as of many things moving through the air close by, then there was a low groan. With a tremendous crash, the great oak doors flew open.

The pirates let out a cheer, firing their guns into the open doorway. The shots filled the whole entrance with gunpowder smoke. Ernest strained his eyes. He couldn't see anyone inside defending the doorway, but then again, he could hardly see anything in the new smoke.

The pirates rushed forward with swords drawn, letting loose wild battle cries. The first had hardly set foot through the door when a fusillade erupted from inside the house. Two pirates dropped dead with strangled cries. As the rest charged into the smoky entryway, their war-whoops faltered as a tremendous bellow rumbled from out of the entrance.

Through the gunpowder smoke, Ernest could just make out a massive shape, bulling into the pirates like a force of nature. Though there was little more to see than the dark silhouette of this new-come beast, the shrieks and screams of the pirates rang all too clearly in the entryway as it wreaked havoc among them.

The pirates still outside the house with Longfinch paused, hesitant to enter this house.

"What are you standing there for?" Longfinch asked, hurriedly reloading his pistol. "Get in there and help them! It's just one of them!"

Luckily, they were saved their decision as the albino stood forward again.

"I will handle this one."

Again the Archeomancer muttered something under his breath. A sudden wind blew, seeming to emanate from the Archeomancer himself like rippling waves on a pond. The smoke in the entryway rolled back a little, revealing the massive form of a satyr.

Ernest's mouth went dry when he saw the giant with his coal-black skin and curved horns. As the smoke cleared, the giant turned. He was holding a hapless pirate in his hands, but he cast his victim aside like a rag doll. Stooping low, the satyr snatched up one of the dead pirate's cutlasses.

"Vene at me, ye heathens!"

The Archeomancer stepped forward, standing in the doorway itself, his white hair blowing back in this strange wind. He still muttered strange words as he raised his hand towards the satyr, his fingers flexed like a claw.

The satyr's eyes went wide as he looked down on the Archeomancer. "So *ye* are the little sorcerer, are ye?"

The Archeomancer only smiled, still muttering his strange words.

Ernest couldn't help but hold his breath as he watched the Archeomancer in terror. What was he about to do to this giant? Ernest trembled all over, remembering all too well what power the Archeomancer possessed. The other pirates stood still as well, eagerly awaiting the Archeomancer's next move, whether that was to make the satyr dissolve to powder or to blast him with lightning and fiery hailstones. The air thrummed with tension, like an approaching thunderhead, as the Archeomancer continued to mumble.

A look of rage spread over the satyr's face, but instead of attacking the Archeomancer as Ernest expected, the satyr stood straight, pointing his finger at the Archeomancer authoritatively.

"Ye tain no power here! By the authority o' the Almighty God, I rebuke ye!"

The pirates let out a low snicker.

"I bind ye," the satyr bellowed. "By the authority o' the Christ, I cast out all o' yer spirits. 'For all power has been given to Him, in earth and heaven.'"

The pirates were still snickering, but Ernest looked on with wide-eyed wonder. The albino shrank back as if recoiling from a deep wound, and the tension in the air fled. At the same moment, the strange wind which the albino had started came to an abrupt end. From behind the pirates, someone began laughing hysterically. Looking around, Ernest realized it was Jock the Blowhoarder. The pirates stopped their snickering and looked at Jock too, clearly perplexed.

"Ye do no know what awaits ye, Longfinch!" Jock said, then he laughed again.

With a sudden motion, Killjelly raised his pistol and fired. The satyr let out a deep bellow, collapsing to his knees.

"Where's your 'almighty god' now?" Killjelly sneered.

The pirates rushed forward with whoops and curses. Ernest watched with a growing knot in his stomach as the giant satyr fell beneath the flood of waving swords and bayonets. The pirates guarding Ernest, Lewis, and Jock now goaded them forward, and Ernest followed behind the main body of pirates sweeping into the manor house. The albino was still in the doorway, fallen on his knees and trembling all over. Ernest looked at him closely. His already-bleached face was now completely pale, and his pink eyes seemed dim and distant.

Just before Ernest passed him, Killjelly grabbed the albino by the shoulder and helped him to his feet.

"Compose yourself now, sir. Our power is strong in this house, isn't it?"

The albino said nothing but only stumbled forward.

Ernest stepped carefully around the satyr's corpse, while more shouts and gunshots rang out from further inside. His guard pushed him forward, and Ernest turned into the dining room. A fire burned cheerily in the hearth, with four chairs before it, and a down comforter draped over them. A small group of pirates leaned over a moaning form by this fireplace, stabbing it again and again with their bayonets. Streaks of blood soaked into the down comforter. Ernest felt sick.

Looking away, Ernest caught sight of a pirate on the floor, writhing and groaning while he clutched a gaping wound in his abdomen. There was blood all over the floor. Ernest's heart hammered at his chest. So much pain. So much death. And what for? Why, oh why, had he not fled to the south when he had the chance?

Lewis gripped him by the shoulder. "Courage, boyo, courage!"

Longfinch marched past now, reloading his pistol. "Search the house. I expect that girl is around here somewhere."

The pirates let out wild yells and dispersed in all directions, leaving only Longfinch, the albino, the three prisoners, and their guards. Longfinch smiled his strange, friendly smile.

"Come with me, then."

So saying, he ducked out of the dining room into the dimly lit kitchen. The guards prodded Ernest, Lewis, and Jock, and they followed. Ernest entered the kitchen just as Longfinch flung open the trapdoor. A tremor ran down Ernest's spine as he saw that door open. He had nothing but evil memories of the chamber below. In his mind, he could still hear the rabbit-lipped housekeeper's tortured screams for mercy as the albino worked on her. Ernest shuddered. Why did he have to go down there again?

Longfinch now smiled kindly at Jock. "Tell me now, did you ever see it ending this way?"

Jock spat. "I do no see, look ye, that it *has* ended, whatever."

A strange light showed in Longfinch's elfin eyes, and he licked the air. "Oh no, this isn't the end. That's certain. But really, there was no other way this would've ended."

Jock snickered. "Ay, true. God knows and plans all things to His ends."

"Did you see the bloody cadaver of that pastor in the entryway?" Longfinch asked, the slightest hint of a sneer creeping into his friendly smile. "You think god planned that? He must hate you."

Just then, Ernest heard footsteps coming down the steep stairway at the back of the kitchen. In a moment, a group of pirates appeared, hauling with them the girl Ella.

Ernest sighed. So they had her, too? Was there anything left to save from Longfinch? Perhaps Lexi was still alive. No, she was most likely lying somewhere in the ruins of Entwerp Coastal; one more corpse among hundreds. He'd seen that in his dream. But what did it matter, anyway? He could see no way that he would survive this, so why should he care if Lexi was still alive? He'd never meet her again, and even if he did, she probably still hated him.

"We have the girl," a pirate said, saluting smartly.

Longfinch smiled. "All are here then? Light your lanterns, and we will descend. You three stay up here and guard the house."

The pirates did as they were told, lighting several lanterns and following Longfinch as he descended into the passageway. Unwillingly, Ernest walked forward, stepping onto the first step, which led down, down into the chamber below. In front of him, Longfinch laughed merrily.

"This is the pay-off, lads!"

14

EXODUS

Clerans snatched up poor Miss Flalowen's rifle and loaded it while Martyn explained his plan.

"Do no ye see?" Martyn spoke clearly, but with some urgency. "Those pirates expect us to barricade the door to keep them out. What they do no expect is fer us to vene out o' this shop the very moment they're breakin' in. Listen close. They ha' only left a few guards out front while they try to break in at the back. All we ha' to do is escape through the front door, take out the few guards there, an' we will be on our way to Entwerp Proper in an instant!"

"Ay, but they will be after us jist as soon," Mr. Gingrich muttered under his breath.

"Right then," Meriwedhr said as he finished loading his huge buffalo rifle. "Let us be about it, then!"

Clerans and the others cleared away the furniture that still barred the front door, trying to be as quiet as possible as they piled it up instead against the back door. All the while, they could hear the pirates pounding against the back door, yelling and cursing.

Martyn laid his hand on the latch of the front door, looking back at his four remaining comrades. "This is it then. As soon as I'll throw the door open, we cen expect the guards to fire on us. I do no expect we will all make it out o' this."

Clerans drew in a deep breath, trying to stay calm as he gripped his new rifle. "Dear Lord, protect us all."

"Ay," Martyn said, "that is jist it. May the Lord protect us all." Martyn looked each of them in the eye steadily, first Mr. Fflemins, then Meriwedhr, then Mr. Gingrich, and finally he looked Clerans steadily in the eye. "Courage now."

"Lord," Mr. Fflemins prayed in a shaky voice, "give me strength. Look kindly upon us. Keep my Patrisha and Kati safe."

"Amen," Meriwedhr echoed.

Martyn took a deep breath, gripping the latch tightly. "Lord, guide our hands to war."

And with that, Martyn flung the door open.

All five of them charged through the doorway as quickly as they could, leveling their guns before them and firing. Meriwedhr's huge buffalo rifle sounded more like a cannon at such close quarters, and Clerans could hear several startled screams from in front of them, followed by the thunderous reports of several muskets. Mr. Gingrich (who was standing quite near Clerans) gave a muffled yell of pain and stumbled backwards.

They were in the street now, and Clerans had just a moment to look around. A semi-circle of pirates stood in the street at the front of the shop (maybe a dozen of them, no more). Already, two or three of them were doubled over, gripping at wounds and groaning. Those uninjured pirates let out a terrific yell and charged on Clerans and his comrades.

Martyn stepped out in front of the little group, casting aside the musket he had fired on exiting the shop and drawing out both of his pistols. Mr. Fflemins was desperately drawing out a saber, but his left arm hung limp at his side. Meriwedhr crouched like a lion, nimbly affixing a bayonet to the end of his huge rifle. Mr. Gingrich collapsed to his knees, fumbling at the pistol in his belt with one hand, while he clutched at his bleeding stomach with the other. Clerans drew out his own bayonet and dexterously attached it to the end of his rifle. He looked straight ahead at the line of charging pirates and let out his breath slowly.

This was it. He would fight his way through — or he would die trying. *Lord, guide my hands to war.*

Martyn's two pistols fired from Clerans' left, and two of the pirates in front of him fell dead to the ground. Then the first of the pirates was upon him. The pirate lunged at Clerans with a wicked rapier, but Clerans ducked to the side, dealing the pirate a swift blow with the butt of his rifle.

Losing his footing, the pirate stumbled headfirst to the ground. Clerans wasted no time, but stabbed him neatly between the shoulder blades with his bayonet. Turning towards his next opponent as he drew his rifle back, he saw an impish pirate leveling a pistol right at his head. Clerans bobbed to the side, but at that moment, a pistol discharged behind him. The impish pirate crumpled to the ground in a heap. Clerans chanced a look backwards to see Mr. Gingrich still kneeling on the cobblestones. Holding his appalling wound in his stomach, he could not stop the profusion of blood from seeping through his clothes onto the ground. The gloomy man dropped his still-smoking pistol and slumped down into the street, his face ashen-pale.

From before him, Clerans heard a strangled cry, and he looked up just in time to see Mr. Fflemins collapse under a pirate's sword stroke. There was another pirate rushing at him now, a short leprechaun with his teeth bared, wielding a thick cutlass. Clerans clinched his jaw as he met the leprechaun full on, deflecting the first sword-blow with his rifle barrel. The leprechaun doubled back, raising his sword to strike again. Clerans pushed in close, shoving his opponent back with the body of his rifle. He was now far too close to the pirate to use his bayonet, so he drew out his skinning knife, still holding his rifle in one hand. The leprechaun didn't see the knife as he thrust at Clerans one last time. Nimbly, Clerans parried the sword aside with his rifle and then plunged his knife into the pirate's chest. The leprechaun let out a startled scream and collapsed in a heap before Clerans.

Clerans could hear Meriwedhr letting out a great bellow. He looked around to see the giant satyr standing over Mr. Fflemins' prostrate form. With a single swing of his buffalo rifle, he cast two pirates to the ground. Martyn was fighting desperately with the pirate who seemed to be leading this small guard band, and by the look of it, that pirate leader was only about half a minute away from losing the fight. Two pirates already lay dead in Martyn's wake.

Was that it? Was that all the pirates? Had they taken them out so quickly? Just then, Clerans spotted the last pirate. He was standing just off to the side and had just finished reloading his musket. As Clerans watched, the pirate fixed his eyes on Martyn, beginning to raise the musket to his eye.

Clerans bit the inside of his lip. His pistol was all he had left. Could he make a shot that far with his pistol? He had to. Martyn's life was at stake. Clerans drew out his pistol as quickly as he could, leveled it, and fired. The pirate dropped dead. At the same instant, Martyn delivered a mortal blow to the pirate leader, letting the dead man tumble in a heap to the cobblestone street.

Clerans' heart throbbed in his head. He took several deep breaths to calm himself. Something warm and sticky trickled down his face and hands. Was that blood?

Martyn, Clerans, and Meriwedhr now regarded each other, all breathing heavily.

"That was all of them?" Meriwedhr asked.

These words were hardly out of his mouth when a loud shriek sounded just over their heads. Clerans hardly had time to look up before a huge shape fell like lightning from the sky. Clerans could only see a blur of claws, teeth, and colorful wings as the thing landed on Meriwedhr. The satyr made almost no sound as he crumpled under the impact of this flying creature.

Clerans stood stunned, hardly able to move. Now he could make out the back of this vicious creature, with its cat-like body and huge wings spread wide over Meriwedhr's corpse. It was a griffin. Hadn't Miss Ella told them that the pirates had an Eagle Griffin working for them?

The beast now turned, blood streaked across his fangs, beak, and claws. His cat-like eyes fell upon Martyn, and he froze. A hateful hiss escaped from the Eagle Griffin's beak, like the hissing of water dropped into hot oil.

"*You!*"

Martyn seemed to recognize this monster himself, and his eyes narrowed. "Ay, it is me — but this time ye ha' stepped once too far."

The Eagle Griffin hissed again. "No *one* has ever wounded *me* before and lived to tell about *it.*"

Martyn spat. "Well then, I will be sure ye do no live to tell about it." Then Martyn turned slightly to Clerans. "Clerans, reload my rifle for me."

Clerans reached out his hands to take the rifle from Martyn, but at that moment, a thought came to him. Martyn had fired his *musket* upon leaving the tailor shop, and then he had fired both of his pistols, but (if he remembered rightly) Martyn had not fired his rifle yet. It didn't really need to be reloaded then.

Martyn slung his rifle from his shoulder, as if about to hand it to Clerans, when the Eagle Griffin sprang, leaping like a tiger towards Martyn. Martyn hardly blinked as he raised his rifle and fired.

The griffin veered aside in mid-pounce, letting out a piercing shriek. Clerans could see blood flowing from the animal's left side as it struggled to its feet. Martyn drew out his tomahawk and skinning knife, jeering at the wounded Eagle Griffin. "Vene at me again, ye beast! Ye will pay dearly fer the life o' Meriwedhr!"

At that moment, there was a tremendous crash from inside the tailor shop. With horror, Clerans realized that the pirates must have broken in the back door. The first pirate leaped out of the tailor shop, looking all around at the carnage. Then he saw Martyn and Clerans.

"There they are!" the pirate called out.

Already, other pirates were piling out of the shop, leveling their muskets at Clerans and Martyn. This truly was the end, then. Clerans drew in a deep breath and let it out slowly. He might have guessed he'd die this night. First Sheriff Laei, then Laendon and Da, then Mr. Fflemins, Meriwedhr and the others... now it was his turn to die.

At that very instant, the air around his head stirred with a buzzing sound, as if many objects were flying past his ears. Was he dreaming? The line of pirates dissolved in front of him as if mowed down by a volley of rifles, yet Clerans had heard no sound of shots. Out of nowhere, the sky rumbled, and forked lightning blazed down amongst the pirates, leaving a searing pink afterglow in Clerans' vision.

Stunned, Clerans turned to look behind him just as a blood-curdling war cry filled the air. Rushing out of the shadows of the street to the east, a line of nearly three dozen Indigie warriors appeared. They were all low, square nymphs, with hideous war-paint on their nearly naked bodies. They screamed chilling battle cries, gripping slings in their webbed hands as they hurled missile after missile into the pirates' ranks. Standing in the middle of this tide of warriors was a scrawny nymph with eagle feathers tied into his hair. Raising his staff above his head, the shaman let out a savage scream, and another bolt of lightning licked over the pirates.

The pirates were clearly just as flummoxed as Clerans was at the lightning strikes, for they simply stood there as the Indigie warriors fell upon them like a tidal wave. Still screaming their war cries, the Indigies cut the pirates to the ground with their hooked knives and short spears. It was the work of only a few seconds. The Eagle Griffin had disappeared, and not a single pirate stood alive in the street.

Clerans looked on in petrified horror, gazing at the corpses of the pirates, which now lay all around in the pooling blood. A smell like burning hair filled the air. He was unsure if he should be glad this host of Indigies arrived or if he should run as fast as he could from them. Martyn held his ground, though he still gripped his tomahawk and knife tightly, and he eyed the Indigie warriors closely.

The shaman let out a demented cackle, stepping towards Martyn and touching his finger to his nose. His head was only just level with Martyn's waist, and he looked to be only skin and bones when compared with the square frame of the other nymphs, but power rolled off from him, like waves across the surface of the bay. His oily skin gleamed in the darkness like the skin of a frog.

"This is of no cause of fear," the scrawny nymph spoke in the common tongue. "We is come of to aid of you."

Martyn nodded, "Then we are merri grateful to you all." Clerans noted that Martyn had not relaxed his grip on his weapons. Clerans breathed deeply. He wasn't sure what to make of this armed (and very dangerous-looking) group of Indigies, but he knew that Martyn had traded with the tribes frequently. Hopefully, Martyn would know how to act now.

The shaman smiled shark-like. "And I is of orders to take any of the east-folk who is not *pirate* of way of Iasaqi-Woni."

Martyn nodded. "Ay then."

The shaman barked out a sharp order in his own language. Clerans knew a little Tylweni (the language of the Indigies), and he caught the imperative "take them" amidst the sentence the nymph spoke.

A group of about eight vicious-looking warriors surrounded Martyn and Clerans, motioning for the two brothers to follow them as they marched back west along the dike road.

Martyn looked over at Clerans and smiled weakly as he put his weapons back into his belt. "Well, there is no merri much we'll cen do, but do what they say."

Clerans took one last look around him before following Martyn. The little tailor shop looked so different now — had they really been shut up inside only a few minutes ago? There was the table which the pirates had used as a battering ram, still smoldering by the side of the shop door. All around the street was soaked with blood. Pirates' mangled bodies lay everywhere, Mr. Gingrich and Mr. Fflemins lying amongst them. Then there was Meriwedhr, still lying where he had fallen under the Eagle Griffin's talons. It had all happened so suddenly. Had it all really happened?

Clerans let out a deep sigh. His heart was totally numb, no longer able to register emotions. What more tragedy did this night have to offer?

# 15

# GATES OF HELL

*E*lla shuffled down the spiral staircase, slowly descending to the basement. The pirates were holding her tightly but not pulling her forcefully; they seemed almost reverent now that they were so far down. Ella's heart sank with every step she took. She had failed. The pirates had found the Gwambi Treasure after all. Now they would open the door, and all would be lost.

She reached the bottom, and the pirates directed her to a corner of the basement next to one of the moldering bookshelves. Here they let her go. Ella noticed three other captives being ushered her way. She recognized two of them as the cook and cook's mate from the pirate ship, but it was the third she was most interested in.

"Jock!" Ella cried, rushing forward and throwing her arms around the old beggar. "Oh Jock, I'm glad to see that you a'e al'ight!"

Jock took her gently by the shoulders and pushed her away. "Ella, my girl, I might wish that ye were not with me now. Av all times, look ye, this is a dreadful wan to be reunited in."

Ella couldn't help but smile a little. "Yes, it's almost poetic, isn't it? We sta'ted out this awful adventu'e togethe'h, and now he'e we a'e, back togethe'h again in time fo'h the end of it all."

Jock shook his head. "Oh no, Darlint, this is not the end by iny means. It gets more nastier here, it does."

Longfinch's voice broke in from close by. "Where's the Blowhoarder now? Where's Jock Blowhoarder?"

Ella caught her breath. So she was right! Jock was the same as Jock Blowhoarder, the famous privateer who fought for Llaedhwythi independence in the wars. That accounted for three of the four names on that note. So what of Syd Cartwright? What did he have to do with all of this? A sudden chill of excitement ran through Ella. Jock was right; this couldn't be the end. There were still so many questions to be answered, especially regarding those four names: Silas Picker-ing, Saemwel Pickering, Syd Cartwright, and Jock Blowhoarder. What did they all have to do with each other?

Longfinch pushed through the crowd of pirates and stood before Jock. He smiled a strange, friendly smile. "So, here we are at long last!"

Jock smirked. "I suppose that all depends, look ye, on what ye mean by 'here.'"

Longfinch shook his head as if he were a father reproving a rude child. "Tsk, tsk, now, Jock. Soon enough, you'll learn to hold in that tongue on yours."

"Funny," Jock replied, "For the last week, ye has been wantint nothint but for me to talk, sayint how ye were goint to loose-nate that tongue av mine. Now ye do not want me to talk? It is dreadfully confusionating."

Longfinch only continued to smile as he pulled a strange metal key from his pocket. Ella caught her breath. So the pirates had the key. They really were about to open that door!

Ella's heart pounded as she remembered Pastor Daerl confronting the door — or confronting whatever it was *behind* the door. She remembered that strange and chilling voice, her dreadful dreams, and that cryptic riddle. She shivered all over.

Longfinch waved for Jock to follow. "I thinked you might want to see this moment for yourself."

Longfinch now walked in slow — almost reverent — strides to the far side of the room, where that great, weird door stood. Jock followed dutifully behind Longfinch as the pirates made room for them. On a whim, Ella started off after Jock and Longfinch, hearing the pirate cook and cook'smate following behind her — weren't their names Lewis and Ernest?

As they reached the door, Ella looked at it again with the same sense of awe and terror. It was the same wooden door with its blackened steel supports. Ella's heart throbbed like it had the last time she was in this room. What was behind that door?

She glanced quickly around her. The pirates shuffled around them, though at a respectful distance. That wicked pirate Killjelly stood near the door, playing absentmindedly with his brass hooks, and that dreadful albino — with his white hair and pink eyes — stood just beside him, though he seemed a little disturbed. Ella shivered. Maybe this was the end after all.

Longfinch smiled at Jock. "Do you know what is behind this door?"

Jock smirked again. "I will not spoil the surprise for ye, whatever."

Longfinch laughed. "You're very considerate."

So saying, Longfinch lifted the key and put it in the lock. Everyone stood breathlessly. It was so still and silent that Ella could hear the pieces of the lock falling into place around the key. Longfinch turned the key. There was a great groan, and the dreadful door swung slowly inward, revealing the dark, yawning mouth of a passage behind.

Ella strained her eyes to see into the passage, and the pirates did the same, raising up their lanterns to shed some light inside. Ella really did not know what she expected to see, but it was certainly not this. Behind the door was only a dark tunnel with perfectly planed granite sides, sloping steadily downwards. It seemed to turn at a sharp angle about twenty feet in, so that no one could see beyond that point. Just a few feet inside the door lay a pile of something. Looking closely, Ella could see what looked to be some stone tablets and maybe some metal pots and pans in the lantern light.

The pirate behind Ella voiced her thoughts. "That's it? That's the Gwambi Treasure?"

Jock let out a loud, scornful laugh. "Did ye really believe those stories av a city of gold? If ye did iny research at all, ye would know, look ye, that the Gwambi were niver that rich av a civilization. They were warriors, not jewelers." Jock laughed again and pointed at the small pile of artifacts. "That's it, lads! I searched the whole catacombs, look ye, and that is the sum total av the Gwambi Treasure."

Ella heard many of the pirates behind her cursing loudly, but Longfinch only looked on Jock with his same friendly smile.

"Dear Jock, do you really think I comed all this way, and go'ed through so much trouble just for some gold and jewels?"

Jock looked Longfinch over carefully. Ella's body tingled with goosebumps. What was this elf captain talking about?

Longfinch stepped close to Jock, still grinning. "Do you think I would really risk the lives on so many of my men, kill an entire ship's crew on my own subordinates, and invade the fiscal capital on this ferocious nation just to make myself *rich*? Oh no, Jock, I am far more interesting than that."

Longfinch paused, still smiling his same strange smile. "I comed for *him*."

Jock's eyes went wide with horror. "Ye has no idea what ye are dealint with."

Longfinch laughed — it was a long, scornful laugh. "You

sound just like those simpletons, those religions fanatics. That's not the way I remembered you."

Jock shook his head emphatically, drawing a cross on his forehead. "He is not av the essence av this world. He was niver *meant* to be a part av it."

"On the contrary," Longfinch replied. "Don't you fanatics teach that it was God Himself who made the ghosts? Then, of course, he was *meaned* to be a part of this world. He was meaned to rule it."

"God help us all," Jock breathed.

"Do not speak like that here!" It was the albino who spoke now, vitriolic, and spewing spittle from his mouth. "You will interfere with the spells of summoning."

Longfinch smiled again. "My Order has long seeked to find one of his kind — one of these ghosts, I mean. We have searched through the ancient cities of Barberrador and even sorted through the ruins of the city of Sarnach itself. Once we were close to our aim, in Erim, at the Dunes of Ir'ahatal, but I have always known that our greatest chance of succeeding was here, in the ancient city of the Gwambi. After all, was this ghost not the most renowned of them all? Even the Hellings obeyed the orders of this ghost in the ancient times."

Jock shook his head, still looking in horror at Longfinch. "Ye has no idea what ye are enterint into. Man and ghost has niver met but with bloodshed."

Longfinch snickered. "Oh, I'm sure you're right. But that's enough talk about me and my plans — let's talk about you now, Jock."

Longfinch looked Jock up and down before continuing. "I must say, I expected you to put up a little more of a fight. You don't seem to be quite the renowned privateer that your reputation made you out to be."

"Sorry to disappoint, whatever," Jock replied, regaining some of his previous cheekiness.

Longfinch chuckled. "You have no idea how humiliating it was to be so simply defeated by you at Chiryapolis. You did it so effortlessly — it was child's play really... but I falled for it. I have spended many sleepless nights rethinking that fight, plotting how I could have winned. Ah, you were wily, and by far my most worthy opponent." Longfinch's face twitched, and he made a dismissive gesture with his hand. "There were a couple of Panhaplites who handed me my first defeat, but that was before I knew better. But you!" Longfinch smiled broadly. "You were the only one who could defeat me in my prime." Longfinch cocked his head. "I want you to imagine now how much I have plotted to get even with you."

Jock spat. "I will take that as a compliment, then."

Longfinch shook his head, still smiling. "Imagine my delight then, when I realized that in one swift move I could simultaneously take my revenge on you, and accomplish the lofty goals of my Order."

"Fine then," Jock said, throwing up his arms, "shoot me and be done with it, whatever."

"I don't want to kill you," Longfinch said, his smiled changing now for the first time into a vicious snarl. "I want to destroy you."

Jock chuckled. "Alright then, tell your wizard to cast wan av his spells on me to make me dissolvenate like butter. After all, that worked sore well on that satyr. God help ye!"

The albino let out a snarl, like that of a cornered animal.

Longfinch smiled again. "Ah yes, I'm glad you mentioned my friend here." Longfinch motioned towards the albino. "He has been of inestimable help in tracking you down. You can hardly expect that a man like you could escape the notice of others on my Order while you poked around at ancient sites, seeking to raid the sacred halls of the Gwambi and carry away what little treasure you could find as booty. No, your kind always died for their crime. Yet somehow you survived. Even after you infiltrated one of the Order's meetings and made off with our key and poor Killjelly's hand. Somehow, you still survived."

Jock chuckled to himself.

Longfinch fixed Jock with a piercing gaze. "You did what no other of your kind haved done. You *finded* the Gwambi cities, and then you *taked* from them and walked out unscathed."

Jock only smiled. "I guess I am pretty good about doint what no wan else could do, eh?"

Longfinch seemed to ignore the taunt. "Oh yes, you attracted the attention of many of my Order. My friend here, the Archeo-mancer, was seeking you too — and he nearly caught you when you were residing in Saegdhia..." Longfinch paused, looking Jock in the eye carefully, "...under the name of Syd Cartwright."

Jock was silent. He only returned Longfinch's careful stare.

Longfinch smiled now, almost benevolently. "I would not make the same mistake about you again, Jock Blowhoarder, assuming that you were a simpleton. No, I studied you. I studied you carefully, and in doing so, I discovered a very interesting man."

Jock still said nothing, though he shifted his weight nervously.

"Hold him!" Longfinch ordered.

Two large pirates rushed forward and grabbed Jock by the shoulders. Jock did not resist. He only looked at the two pirates holding him and then smirked.

"Two av them, eh? You would think ye were afraid av me, whatever."

Longfinch laughed amicably. "On the contrary, you should be *terrified* of me."

Killjelly let out a muffled chuckle.

Longfinch resumed his discourse. "Yes, Jock, I finded out just who you *really* were. You do'edn't make it very easy for me, now do'ed you? You had to use so many names so as to throw anyone off your tracks, do'edn't you?"

Jock made no reply, but he continued to meet Longfinch's gaze.

"What an interesting life story you have, Jock," Longfinch said. "I could almost write a book about you. I'm sure it would sell like hot spudnuts."

Jock's face settled into a look of cold steel. "Ye has no idea. You could niver know who I really am."

"Oh," Longfinch replied with a wide sneer. "But I do."

Suddenly, Longfinch turned to Ella. She recoiled in horror, but before she could step away, the elfin captain snatched her by the shoulder and dragged her right up next to Jock.

"You're Ella, aren't you?"

Ella nodded, terrified.

"Such a poor girl you are, living such a miserable life. Abandoned by your worthless father, who cared more about ancient jewels than he ever do'ed about his poor, lisping daughter. No, he would leave you to starvation and poverty so that he could have his own merry adventures and never come home to you. He would never take care of you and your poor mother."

Ella trembled all over, finally finding her tongue. "My fathe'h died, he was killed by pi'ates... by..."

A sudden realization came upon Ella. Hadn't Clerans said that *Longfinch* was the pirate captain who killed Silas Pickering?

"...by you?" Ella gasped in horror as she looked closely at the elfin pirate captain's benign face.

Longfinch smiled. "Silas Pickering? You think I killed him? Do you actually think that he *is* dead?" Longfinch laughed humorously. "You still don't see, do you?"

"What do you mean?" Ella gasped.

Longfinch grabbed Ella by the chin and forced her to examine Jock. "Who was your father, then, Ella? He was a sailor, right? A great and avid adventurer. He had dealings with pirates, such dealings as would make him the enemy of the dreaded pirate captain Longfinch. Is that not so?"

Longfinch glanced meaningfully between Ella and Jock. "You know this already about your father. You also know that your father was devoted to finding the Gwambi Treasure. Yet he not only seeked the treasure, but he succeeded in finding it — right here, in this very room. Don't I speak the truth of what you already know about your father?"

Ella nodded, trembling all over.

Longfinch leaned in close to Ella, and she could feel his hot breath against her cheek. "Funny, isn't it, that the man standing before you fits that description exactly?"

Ella caught her breath, peering closely at Jock. Could it really be?

Longfinch leaned in closer now, speaking in a whisper, his damp lips nearly touching Ella's ear. "Really now, why do you think Jock comed to Blisa in the first place?"

Ella's heart pounded heavily in her chest, and she looked Jock up and down. She had never seen her father, only the small picture that her mother had in her locket. It was hard to tell for certain — looking at Jock's care-worn and filthy face, marred as it was by grief and torture — but Longfinch's words made sense. She wondered how she had not seen it already. After searching for her father her whole life, had she really been blind to his presence?

Ella swallowed slowly, looking Jock full in the face. "Papa? Is that you?"

Jock set his jaw firmly, but the corners of his eyes twitched.

Longfinch let out a short laugh. "Oh yes, dear. This is your Papa. This is Silas Pickering."

Longfinch turned on Jock with vitriol. "Admit it now, Blowhoarder: that is your true name."

Jock clamped his mouth firmly shut, and the veins on his neck and forehead bulged.

"You miserable fool," Longfinch hissed. "I want you to look this poor girl in the face now and tell her. Tell her you are

Silas Pickering. Tell her why you deserted her and her mother. Do'ed you even think about them when you joined that pirate crew after leaving the ports of Slyzwir? Do'ed you do anything to provide for their well-being while you gallivanted around the oceans, playing like a privateer for the Llaedhwythi rebels? Do'ed you feel any remorse when you comed here and searched for that precious treasure of yours? Do'ed you give them any hints of your continued existence when you settled down in this city, living for years as if'n you were another bachelor who haved no cares in the world? Tell her — tell your daughter — that you abandoned her. Tell her that you do'edn't love her so much as a handful of moldering diamonds."

Jock remained silent, though Ella could see that he was shaking all over.

"Logging never was enough for you, was it?" Longfinch continued. "You haved to have an adventure. Your family and your moral rights as a father and husband were not even enough to keep you back."

Great tears now spilled from Jock's eyes, and he spoke, looking Longfinch full in the face. "You do not have the slightest idea av my life story."

"Don't I?" Longfinch taunted. "Are you not Silas Pickering, then? Come now, look this girl in the eye and tell me: are you, or are you not, Silas Pickering?"

Jock raised his eyes and stared Ella directly in the face. Ella noticed for the first time that Jock had brown eyes — deep and caring brown eyes. They seemed so large and sympathetic and yet so full of sorrow. Ella could see every furrowed line across Jock's face; each one must have been etched with suffering and pain. It seemed almost strange that in that face there did not seem to be a sign of regret — though surely her father must have some regrets if all that Longfinch said about him was true. If they were not true, wouldn't Papa seek to clear his name?

Jock's voice trembled with emotion as he spoke. "I am Silas Pickering."

The pirates all around let out a ribald cheer, and Longfinch smirked.

"I am glad you comed clean in the end," the elfin pirate captain said. "And now that your miserable daughter knows the sort of wicked and unrepentant father she has, she will die — and you, Silas, will watch her die."

Longfinch drew his pistol and turned Ella back towards himself. Ella caught her breath in surprise. As she opened her mouth, Longfinch shoved his pistol barrel into it. Ella recoiled in terror, but Longfinch held her in an iron grip. The cold steel pressed against the back of her mouth, and the taste of gunpowder stung her tongue and throat, making her gag.

She stared ahead wildly, seeing only the leering face and squinted eyes of Longfinch. She could only look on in dumb fear as Longfinch's hand flexed, his finger coming down on the trigger of his pistol.

The air split with the sound of a tremendous bellow. Out of the corner of her eye, Ella saw Jock cast aside the two pirates who were holding him as if they were only dish rags. The enormous man lunged at Longfinch.

The pistol barrel ripped violently from her mouth, and almost at the same instant, the loud report of the pistol fired from right next to her ear. Her head rang with the sound, but Longfinch released her. Stumbling back and looking towards Jock, she saw him curled up in a wadded mass on the ground. Gunpowder smoke curled all around him.

Ella fell on her knees at Jock's side, reaching out for him. "Papa!"

Jock rolled slightly, and Ella gasped. Jock had a hole in his abdomen about the size of a grapefruit. Thick, red blood already soaked through Jock's clothes and pooled on the ground.

"Papa!" Ella cried again.

Jock shook his head, his face ashen. He licked his lips and spoke softly now.

"Do not call me that, Ella, darlint, I am not..." Jock choked, reaching out with his blood-covered hand. Ella grabbed his hand quickly, looking into his deep brown eyes again. Tears spilled down his cheeks. He was struggling for breath, clearly only talking with great difficulty. "Ella, my girl, I wish I could has been your father... You deserved better... I never would have left..."

Jock groaned, leaning forward into Ella's embrace. "But he would not listen to me, Ella... He would not listen."

*Papa?*

# HEAVY LADEN

lerans and Martyn trudged after the Indigie warriors as they moved along the dike road. Martyn marched erect, brisk and alert. Clerans knew he should stay alert too, in case there were more pirates about, but at this point, what did it matter if they walked into an ambush? What were two more dead bodies added to the already mind-numbing number of dead Entwerpi militia?

They hadn't walked very far before they came to Merchani Square. Here (standing just before the kirk), a much larger group of Indigies awaited them. As they entered the square, the shaman yelled something in Tylweni to his comrades. Since he was speaking loudly and clearly, Clerans thought he could make out all the words and guess at a translation.

"The first of the having-been-rescued ones!"

Or something like that. He always had trouble with the gerunds.

The large group of Indigies looked up and let out a cheer, parting to let Martyn and Clerans pass. This seemed to be a good sign. After all, the Indigies seemed to receive them with the same friendly intentions they had claimed earlier.

Martyn and Clerans followed the path through the crowd of Indigie warriors until they came to the center of the group. There, a unit of perhaps twenty colorfully painted warriors awaited them. In the middle of these warriors stood a great Indigie who towered head and shoulders above the rest (though he still hardly came to Clerans' chest) with eagle feathers and many-colored beads tied into his hair. Clerans immediately guessed that this must be the supreme chief, the Iasaqi-Woni.

Martyn stepped forward and bowed before the Indigie chieftain, saying in Tylweni, "Good greetings do I give unto you."

"May the Great Aeparon return them unto you," the chief replied stoically.

Clerans knew enough Tylweni to translate that exchange, but as Martyn spoke again, he could not make out what Martyn was saying, other than something about gratitude overflowing and mushrooms. What was it about the Indigies and mushrooms?

The Iasaqi-Woni smiled at this, but then he frowned, saying something else in Tylweni. Again, Clerans couldn't really tell what the supreme chief said, but he thought he heard the word 'few' amidst the spew of gibberish. Clerans sighed. He really should work on his Tylweni. It would be helpful at a time like this.

As he wasn't really able to tell what Martyn and the chief were saying, Clerans took a moment to observe this crowd of Indigies. The first person he noticed, however, was not an Indigie at all, but a very tall and broad-shouldered man, standing just to the side of the elite warriors. He wore ordinary-looking clothes, though the cut and the style were certainly not that of Llaedhwyth. His face bore an expression like bewilderment. He had large hands and skin the texture of leather, no doubt from use in much physical labor. He also had a large bandage along his side and thigh. Otherwise, Clerans saw nothing noteworthy about this man. Still, there was something about this man that reminded Clerans of Miss Ella.

Just then, the Iasaqi-Woni motioned towards the big man, saying something to Martyn. Clerans strained his ears, but couldn't quite make out what the chief was saying about the big man; all he caught was a name (Titus Donne) amidst the string of Tylweni words.

Martyn now turned to this big man and touched his hat. "God bless ye, Mr. Titus Donne."

The big man looked a bit startled at this, finally saying, "Eh, thank you, eh, sir."

The chief continued to speak, and Clerans just made out the word "close alley."

Clerans looked back at the big man and started when he noticed the figure who stood beside him. Was that really Haeli Blysffi? How had he not noticed her before?

"Haeli?" Clerans gasped.

Martyn looked up in surprise. "Haeli? Haeli Blysffi? Well llifsa, it is ye!"

Haeli rushed forward, giving Martyn a hug and a kiss on the cheek. The Iasaqi-Woni looked a little perplexed, but said nothing. Haeli now quickly stepped over to Clerans, giving him a hug and a kiss as well. For the first time, Clerans realized that he was actually glad to see Haeli.

"I am merri glad to see ye," Clerans blurted out, hardly thinking. "We were no sure what happened to ye."

Haeli took a step back and looked Clerans full in the face. "Not another word, Clerans Blaeith. I tain something to say to you."

Clerans cringed. That didn't sound promising.

At that moment, a male harrier fluttered down from a nearby shop, landing at Haeli's feet and looking up curiously at her.

"Halfdan," Haeli said in surprise, "you are interrupting me."

The bird spoke in an even, emotionless voice. "Do not mind me. But I must see redemption."

"Whatever are you talking about?" Haeli asked, a hint of exasperation in her tone.

The harrier (Halfdan, as Haeli had called him) bobbed his head to the side. "That is what is about to happen, is it not?"

"Bother you," Haeli said through clenched teeth. "You are making this harder than it needed to be."

Halfdan let out a low whistle, still speaking in a dull monotone. "I sense unrighteous anger. That is a sin, you know."

With an effort, Haeli turned away from the bird, looking Clerans full in the face. There was something about her expression — perhaps the exasperation at the bird she was trying to keep down, or maybe the earnest way she was looking at him, or maybe it was just the relief of surviving this brutal night. Whatever it was, Clerans burst out laughing. He couldn't help himself.

Halfdan looked at him curiously, but Haeli sighed heavily.

"Oh, Clerans! Please do not make fun at me."

Halfdan shook his head. "That is not the laugh of scorn, but pure and holy delight. There is no sin in it."

"Will you be quiet for a *moment?*" Haeli said, grinding her teeth together.

"Again," Halfdan replied, still in an emotionless monotone, "I sense unholy anger..."

"I did not know what 'unholy anger' was until I met you," Haeli retorted.

Halfdan spread out his wings with a solemn bob of his head. "As the Apostle said, 'I would not have known sin, but for the Law.'"

Clerans couldn't stop laughing now. He really didn't want to stop laughing, anyway. It felt good, as if all the stress and carnage of the night were now washing out of him.

Haeli looked at him helplessly. "Please, Clerans, do not mock me. I mean to be serious."

"Oh no, Haeli," Clerans replied through his merriment. "I am no mockin' at ye."

"Then what is the matter?" Haeli asked.

"Matter?" Clerans said, still laughing. "Oh no, nothing is the matter, it is jist... it is jist... *ye*."

Haeli wagged a finger in his face. "But you said just now that you *were not* mocking me."

"No," Clerans said, taking a deep breath to calm his laughter. "It's jist ye are so..." Clerans trailed off, trying to think of the right word. He wanted to say 'beautiful,' but that wasn't quite what he meant (and besides, Haeli would probably take it in the wrong way). 'Funny?' No, that word still wasn't right. 'Provoking?' Certainly Haeli would misconstrue what he meant. He finally just shook his head and sighed. "I do no know."

Suddenly Clerans grinned roguishly. "Ah, but I forget myself. I was no to speak another word until ye said what ye were about to say."

Haeli sighed. "Right." She took a deep breath and then sighed again. "I want to apologize to you, Clerans, for speaking to you so harshly last time we talked. It was incredibly rude of me."

Clerans felt almost as if Haeli had stabbed him at this comment. Not at the apology, but at the sudden realization that he had been rather rude to Haeli for their whole friendship. He had avoided her, snubbed her, thought poorly of her... He should be the one apologizing to her.

Haeli sighed again. "I know you were being a good friend to me at the time, and you were trying to help me — probably more so than anyone else was. So I guess I wanted to thank you for that, and apologize too."

Clerans shook his head, smiling nervously. "Ah no, Haeli, do no worry about it."

"Of course I worry about it," Haeli replied. "It was awfully animal of me, and totally unacceptable."

Clerans sighed. "Well, I forgive ye, Haeli, o' course I forgive ye." He sighed again, the words felt foreign and awkward on his tongue. "I jist cen no help but feel that I outta-should be the one apologizin' to ye."

"Whatever for?" Haeli asked.

"Well," Clerans paused. How was he to say it? "I ha' no been the friend I should ha' been to you all this time. I hope ye cen forgive me fer that."

"Clerans Blaeith," Haeli replied, placing her hands on her hips. "What a silly thing to say! Was not it you who killed those two pirates before they... What do you mean you have not been the friend you should have been?"

Just then, Martyn walked over to them, looking between Clerans and Haeli with clear amusement. "An' what is goin' on here?"

"Clerans is being ridiculous," Haeli replied, a grin spreading across her face.

Martyn shrugged. "Ay, but what else is new?"

Haeli giggled. Clerans couldn't help but think again (as he had thought before) that Haeli had such a musical laugh.

Martyn now turned to Clerans. "Well, Clerans, it will probably relieve ye to know that these Indigies are indeed fightin' on our side o' this war. They mean to kill all o' the pirates as repayment for a blood feud with them."

Clerans nodded. "Well, that is providential fer us, then."

"Ay," Martyn replied, "an' I'd say they arrived in the nick o' time. However," Martyn motioned to the big man, "I am given to understand that this man tained a merri to do with the Indigies showin' up when they did."

The big man stepped towards them now, raising his eyebrows inquiringly. "What, eh, what was that?"

Martyn nodded graciously. "We are merri indebted to ye, sir.

If ye an' yer allies ha' no arrived, I and my brother would be dead."

The big man wrinkled up his brow. "Eh... er... You are... eh... You are welcome, then."

"Oh yes," Haeli said suddenly, regaining her composure, though her eyes still sparkled with merriment. "This is Titus Donne — Ella's step-father."

Martyn stood bolt upright in alarm. "Llifsa! Miss Ella! I ha' been sich a fool!"

Clerans looked at Martyn closely. "What do ye mean?"

Martyn rubbed his forehead anxiously. "Ay, these pirates would certainly be after her. Do ye think any o' them might ha' gotten through to the Pickering manor by now?"

As if in answer to this question, Clerans heard the frantic fluttering of wings above him. Before he could look up, Aarushi descended to the ground in front of Martyn. She seemed to be in a state of total agitation, hopping about and whistling, hardly standing still for an instant. Halfdan took one look at Aarushi and stepped backwards in dumb astonishment.

"It is the Pickering manor, is it no?" Martyn asked her.

Aarushi nodded forcefully and whistled.

Martyn hurriedly unslung his rifle from his shoulder, checking it to see that it was reloaded. "Right then, Clerans, we must cede back into action."

Titus looked at Martyn closely, his face beginning to turn pale. "It's not Ella, is it? Is she in danger?"

Martyn slung his rifle back over his shoulder. Putting one hand on the butt of his pistol, he looked Titus in the face. "No if we'll cen do anything about it, sir."

# 17

# IMPRECATORY

Ernest watched as the body of Jock Blowhoarder crumpled to the ground before Longfinch's pistol. Somehow, it didn't seem right that such a renowned privateer captain should die so ignominiously. But what was Ernest supposed to do about it?

Ernest had never felt any camaraderie towards Jock, yet now, as he saw Ella leaning over his bleeding body, Ernest couldn't help but feel sympathy for the old privateer. Jock was the only person who had beaten Longfinch in a fair fight. He didn't deserve to die like this. But if Jock was dead, who was going to stop Longfinch now?

Longfinch smiled kindly, looking back at his men. "Will someone give me another pistol for the girl?"

"Certainly not!"

Ernest jumped in alarm. That was Lewis speaking. The faerie cook stepped towards Longfinch with a pistol leveled at the elfin captain's head. Vitriol consumed Lewis' eyes; rage and grief wrinkled his fatty forehead. Ernest backed away unconsciously. He had never seen Lewis with so much hatred spread across his wide face.

"Certainly not!" Lewis said again. "I willn't let you kill one more helpless soul."

The pirates all reached for their guns, but halted as Lewis said, "Don't you dare! The moment any on yous makes a move, I'll shoot the captain dead."

Lewis strode up to Longfinch, keeping the pistol aimed steadily at the captain. "You're a heathen, and you deserve to have the fires of hell lick your miserable carcass clean."

Longfinch smiled disarmingly. "And I understand you mean to send me there?"

"Too long," Lewis replied, "too long I've helped you, and I've done your bidding, and I've done your dirty work, but no more! This is where it ends. Right here. Blind prelates!"

Longfinch nodded. "Alright then, you have me. What will you do with me, then?"

Lewis eyed Longfinch testily. "You and your men are walking out on here and leaving this city. That's what."

Longfinch let out a great sigh. "Ah, I see."

"Don't mock me, sir," Lewis warned. "Blind prelates! I could kill you right here."

"That does you no good, see," Longfinch said, beaming. "The moment you kill me, you lose all of your bargaining power. My men will shoot you in an instant."

Lewis showed his teeth. "Ay, then justice would be done to both of us. Too long have you offended God with your presence on this earth. I'd have half a mind to kill you here and do Him a service."

"Ah, yes," Longfinch said, "but unless I miss my guess, you're just as guilty."

"I can only hope that God is mercy," Lewis replied. "That's what I've readed, anyhow."

Lewis looked Longfinch over closely. "Now stop your babbling and give the order. Tell your men to march out on here at once."

Longfinch only smiled. "You know, Lewis, I liked you."

Lewis' eyes narrowed dangerously.

"You were so..." Longfinch searched for the right word. "Well, I never could tell what was going on in that head of yours — behind all on those smiles. You reminded me of myself in that way. Well done. I mean that as a sincere compliment. You've done here what almost no one else on earth haves ever managed: you surprised me. I'm not used to running into an obstacle which I do'edn't foresee and plan for."

Lewis brandished his pistol menacingly. "Don't test my patience."

"Because I like you," Longfinch said, "I will teach you something — one of those cardinal rules on warfare that you're violating." Longfinch shrugged, giving the room a theatrical smile. "See, the only time that you should ever *show* your opponent your weapon is when you're using it. To show your weapons for a threat defeats the purpose of the weapon."

"I'm warning you," Lewis hissed.

"Tell me, cook," Longfinch replied. "Have you ever killed a man before?"

Lewis squinted his eyes fiercely. "I'm about to, Helen Maria! Now give the order. Tell your men to walk out on here. It's your last chance before I give you to the demons in hell as a play-toy."

Longfinch sighed, turning back to his men. "Alright then, you heared the faerie."

At that instant, Ernest noticed that Longfinch was fingering something behind his back. Before he had any time to cry out in warning, Longfinch turned back to Lewis and struck. Longfinch's hand shot out like a viper, a small knife clamped in his fist.

Neatly, Longfinch sliced Lewis across the wrist. Lewis cried out in pain, dropping his pistol. Longfinch's other hand lashed out like a whip, catching the pistol in mid-air. With the dexterity of a wildcat, Longfinch spun the barrel on Lewis and fired. Lewis made no sound as he collapsed in a heap to the ground.

"Was that a good enough lesson for you?" Longfinch asked, beaming.

The pirates let out a ribald chorus of laughter.

Ernest screamed in disbelief, leaping to Lewis' side. This couldn't be happening. What was all of this blood here for? No. Ernest refused to believe this. He could see plainly enough the truth that Longfinch had shot Lewis straight through the heart. Lewis was already dead. Ernest seized his messmate in horror, cradling him in his arms and ignoring the blood which now soaked his friend's clothes. This couldn't have happened. Lewis couldn't be dead. How could Lewis be dead?

"Have mercy on his soul," Ernest prayed, hardly even knowing why he was saying it. "Have mercy on his soul, Lord!"

Ernest again looked at Lewis, staring him in the eye. How could those eyes, which once twinkled with merriment, be lifeless? This had to be a bad dream. Lewis couldn't actually be dead.

Above him, Ernest could hear Longfinch speaking again. "Baptize it. Will someone give me a pistol for the girl? I'd rather not use my knife."

Just then, a loud crash rang out from the entrance to the basement. Were those muffled gunshots? A moment later, a pirate rushed down the stairs.

"Captain Longfinch!" the pirate cried. "It's the regulars, sir. They're moving in on the house. They're breaking in!"

"Anointment," Longfinch cursed. "I was hoping they'd be a little later. Ah, well, it is what it is. You know the contingency. Cweel will just have to find us on the other end."

"Come on, lads!" Killjelly yelled. "Form in your line! Make ready to receive them!"

The pirates quickly ranged themselves before the bottom of the staircase, fixing bayonets to the ends of their muskets before leveling them at the stairs. Ernest's heart pounded as he watched. How many regulars were there? Might they be in enough strength to overpower Longfinch? Ernest wasn't sure if he should be relieved or terrified at the prospect.

Technically, he was still a pirate, so the regulars could shoot him on sight. Then again, they might be his only chance of escaping from Longfinch and his crew. Still, Ernest had a dreadful feeling that this attack was no surprise to Longfinch. No, the elfin pirate already seemed to have a plan ready to execute.

Ernest felt hopeless. Here he was, a captive of his old captain, and he could do nothing except watch and worry. Captain Holgard, Quartermaster Harold, Jock Blowhoarder, the nice Llaedhwythi family, Lexi... everyone he knew and cared about was dead. Even Lewis — dear Lewis — was dead. What was there left for Ernest? Perhaps it would be a mercy to die today.

Ernest took one more look around the room, and a sudden realization came over him. Everyone had forgotten about him. All the pirates were getting ready to fight the regulars when they came down the stairway. Longfinch and Killjelly were standing behind the lines, barking out orders. The albino was standing just to the side, looking on knowingly. Then there was Ella leaning over Jock, weeping. Ernest turned and stared into the dark opening of the Gwambi passageway behind him. A chill ran down his spine as he remembered that he still had his pepper-box pistol on him, and it was loaded.

Ernest looked again at Ella, then back at the passageway. Was it worth risking? Now he looked down at Lewis, staring deeply into his messmate's lifeless face. A growing resolve filled Ernest's heart, even as a deep-seated anger flooded his veins. Longfinch and his pirates had killed Captain Holgard and his crew. Longfinch had killed all of those people in Lexi's village, and now he had killed Lewis.

Longfinch would never kill again.

Ernest set Lewis gently on the ground, then he straightened up to his full height, staring resolutely at Longfinch and the pirates at the far side of the room. They all had their backs turned to him, too busy to notice the scrawny little gnome and his pepper-box pistol.

At that moment, more shouts came from the stairway, followed by more gunshots. They were close, and the loud reports echoed harshly in the confines of the basement. Several of the pirates discharged their muskets up the spiral stairway. More gunshots from further up the stairs answered a return volley, and a pirate doubled over in pain. So the regulars were almost here.

Ernest took one step towards Ella and touched her shoulder gently. She looked up at him, tears streaming down her cheeks, and a look of hopelessness etched on her face. Ernest motioned for her to be silent.

"On your feet, Ella, and softly, now," Ernest whispered.

As Ella stood, Ernest turned back towards the other pirates. Slowly and deliberately, Ernest drew out his pepper-box pistol and cocked it. He looked carefully at all of those pirates with their backs towards him. Most of all, Ernest looked steadily at Longfinch. He allowed his anger to wash over him. It throbbed in every part of his body, tingling in his fingertips. He set his jaw, his face as sharp as flint.

Enough was enough. He was a pirate no more. It was good that he had not fled to the south when he had the chance. He was glad that he was right here, right now. Finally, he would do what he had been too much of a coward to do before. Longfinch would get what he deserved.

Ernest spoke loudly, slowly, and clearly, "May God damn you all."

The pirates paused, and Longfinch turned his head, that same disgusting smile on his face.

"What was that?"

Without a moment's hesitation, Ernest pulled the trigger. He felt the familiar recoil against his arm, like being pounded on by a sledgehammer. All eight barrels fired simultaneously, vomiting flames and smoke behind the charges. Several strangled cries rang out in front of him, but Ernest could see nothing in the sudden smoke that filled the room.

Turning quickly, Ernest seized Ella by the hand and dashed for the Gwambi door. In a moment, he was through, stumbling over the pile of artifacts, and then running at breakneck speed down the passageway. The sounds of shouting, cursing, and wails of pain followed behind him. Then a fusillade of gunshots echoed in the narrow passageway. Ernest cringed as several musket balls ricocheted off the walls.

Then he reached the turn in the passage. Dashing around it, he found himself presented with a wall of darkness. He could not slow down. He had no other option. This was his only way to escape from the pirates.

Ernest plunged forward, feeling in front of him with one hand while dragging Ella along behind him with his other. He could see nothing. In a moment, he crashed into a wall. Groping desperately in the darkness, he felt an opening in the wall to his right.

He rushed forward again, but suddenly felt nothing beneath his feet. Catching his breath, he pitched forward and landed face-first on what felt like a staircase. He continued forward now, tumbling head over heels, still dragging Ella behind him. Together they toppled down, down, down…

# 18

# FROM WHERE DOES MY HELP COME?

Clerans, Martyn, and Haeli rushed through the common lands north of Entwerp Proper, heading directly for the Pickering Manor. Close behind them, Titus Donne ran with just over a dozen Indigie warriors at his heels. The leader of these Indigies was a young woman nymph. Clerans had pieced together that she was a shaman's apprentice of some kind and that her name was Tiya. Above the group flew the two harriers, Aarushi and Halfdan.

As they came within sight of the great house, Clerans noticed several groups of men in gray uniforms loitering outside.

"It is the regulars!" Clerans cried.

"Praise be to God," Martyn replied. "We are no alone."

They all rushed forward and soon came right up to the steps of the large house. At the top of the steps stood Governor Braedhwyc, flanked by his regulars. The lanky governor held a long horse-pistol in one hand and a saber in the other, his left eye twitching spasmodically as ever.

As Clerans, Martyn, and the others arrived, the governor turned towards them. He started, looking with some alarm at the Indigies in their war-paint, but he seemed to recover on the sight of Martyn and Clerans.

Martyn saluted smartly. "Militia, sir, fresh from the dikes."

Governor Braedhwyc wiped pus from his eye and looked at Martyn and Clerans closely. "You are the Blaeith boys, are no you?"

Clerans saluted as well. "Ay, sir."

"We ha' vened," Martyn said, "to aid our friends, the Pickerings."

The governor nodded. "Ay, well you are jist in time then." He turned back to the regulars, who were standing by. "Get on with it then. Clear the house!"

The regulars needed no further bidding. They immediately plunged into the house, each one holding his rifle ready. Governor Braedhwyc motioned for Martyn and Clerans to join him up on the porch.

"The strikers tipped us off to this." The governor shook his head and chuckled bitterly. "O' all people, it wos the strikers!"

"Are they under control?" Clerans asked, remembering what the sheriff had told him about the strikers besieging the bank.

Governor Braedhwyc snorted. "Of course no. They jist wanted to distract me from their attack on the bank." And the Governor shook his head. "But they'll be in fer it themselves when the lord protector finally lets his dragoons loose on them."

Clerans' jaw dropped wide open. "Caedmon Wilkins? And his dragoons? He is here now? In this town?"

Governor Braedhwyc waved his hand dismissively. "Oh, enough o' that. Ye will see him in good time, I'm sure. Fer now, we tain a house to clear."

"How many pirates are inside?" Martyn asked, unslinging his rifle.

"The report is about twenty," Governor Braedhwyc replied. "But we ha' only seen three or four o' them so far. No doubt they are hiding somewhere inside. No fear though, we'll will root them out."

"And hostages?" It was Haeli who spoke now as she climbed up to the porch. "Is there anyone else inside?"

Governor Braedhwyc nodded. "Ay, the word is that Miss Nansi, Elsi Pickering, and Lexi Blaeith are all safe with Doctor Heyl."

Haeli sighed heavily. "Then Ella is still inside."

"What's that now?" Titus asked, trudging up to the porch himself.

"Ay," Martyn said, ignoring Titus' question. "An' Pastor Daerl and Mr. Hydmenton were both on guard duty tonight." Martyn turned to the governor. "Wos there any news o' them?"

Governor Braedhwyc made a disgusted face and motioned towards the open doors of the manor. "Ay. We did."

Martyn and Clerans followed the governor as he ducked through the open door. Clerans glanced at the door and noted that there were only small dents on the door (as of pummel marks from a dozen rifle butts), but that could hardly account for enough force to break in such solid oak doors.

Martyn had only just stepped inside when he caught his breath. Clerans looked around to see what had arrested Martyn's attention and stopped dead in his tracks. There, lying in a mangled heap on the ground, was the body of Pastor Daerl. It looked to Clerans as if the pirates had bayoneted the amicable satyr to death — and long after death, at that. His stomach lurched at the sight. Taking a deep breath, he exhaled slowly.

"Haeli," Martyn warned, "Ye will no want to vene in here."

"I do not care," Haeli replied forcefully. "I am following you."

Before Martyn could stop her, Haeli stepped inside the door, gasping in horror herself as she saw Pastor Daerl's body. Titus and the Indigie warriors were next to enter. The Indigies showed no emotion on their stoic faces; only the leader, Tiya, furrowed her brow sympathetically. Titus, however, leapt back like a man who has set his foot on live coals.

"Heaven preserve us!"

Halfdan fluttered to the ground at Titus' feet, saying in his dull, emotionless voice, "Blasphemy is a grave sin, Titus."

"Blasphemy?" Titus retorted, his voice rising to a high pitch in his excitement. "That was a sincere prayer!"

Halfdan whistled, apparently unconvinced.

Martyn put his arm around Haeli's shoulder. "Steady now. Steel yer nerves. I am afraid this may only be the harbinger o' what else we'll may trive in this house."

At that moment, Clerans heard a gunshot from the kitchen. This was followed by a second, and then a shout from a regular.

"By the saint's beard! Here they are!"

Governor Braedhwyc hurried towards the cry, and the others followed right behind him. As they passed through the dining room, Clerans noticed Mr. Hydmenton's body lying face-first before the fireplace with bayonet wounds in his back. Clerans ground his teeth together in anger and frustration. How could the pirates do this? Would this carnage never end?

Miss Ella then was the only one to be found. Though with a twinge in his stomach, Clerans wondered if he really wanted to find Ella. He dreaded what state she might be in now. No, the pirates wouldn't have killed her. They wanted her alive, didn't they?

As Clerans entered the kitchen, he saw the trapdoor to the basement lying wide open. Two dead pirates lay before it, and all the regulars stood in formation around the passageway with their muskets pointed down the open shaft. Clerans could just make out the sounds of shouting and cursing wafting up the stairway.

Clerans swallowed. So the pirates were back at the door again. Had they opened it, or were they simply making their stand down there, prepared to fight vice and vail until the last man fell?

"Alright then," Governor Braedhwyc said. "No a moment to lose. We ha' lost two good men already in this house. Down we scend. Pair off in twos, and hold your guns at the ready. I doubt but that they tain a reception party fer us below."

The regulars obeyed smartly, stepping down the stairs in pairs, one after the other. Martyn put his hand on Haeli's shoulder.

"Take up the rear now, Haeli. I will no tain ye getting hurt." With that, he turned to Clerans. "Shall we?"

Clerans flashed a weak smile. "Ay, then."

With that, the two brothers descended after the regulars. Clerans unslung his rifle (it was poor Miss Flalowen's rifle, really), double-checking to see that it was loaded. Then he touched his pistol, his tomahawk, and his skinning knife to reassure himself. Yes, he was ready. But oh, how much he wished he didn't have to fight again!

The regulars came quickly to the bottom of the first flight of stairs, pausing on the wide landing before descending the spiral staircase. Clerans smiled grimly as he looked at that narrow spiral staircase. Yes, that would lead them straight to the basement, but no doubt there would be a line of pirate muskets waiting at the bottom of that stairway. It would be near suicide to descend it.

"Onward, lads," Governor Braedhwyc urged, wiping puss from his eye. "By God's aid, we will ceive them."

The regulars nodded and continued forward, still in pairs of two, slowly descending the spiral staircase. If Clerans stood on his tiptoes, he could just see over the heads of the regulars to the two at the front. They stepped forward carefully and cautiously, their rifles pointed in front of them at every turn. Now Clerans and Martyn descended the spiral stairway, Clerans standing on the side of each step closest to the center of the spiral, while Martyn took the outside.

The regulars in front paused, and one of them took off his tricorn hat, tossing it ahead of him down the stairs. In a moment, two loud gunshots broke the silence, sounding louder than thunder in the close confines of that stairwell. Clerans cringed involuntarily.

"Ay then," the regular whispered, "There's nothing fer it."

He nodded at his companion. The two regulars suddenly leaned around the corner of the spiral staircase and fired their rifles, ducking quickly back around the corner. A barrage of gunfire answered the regulars' shots. Clerans ducked down as low as he could as the charges ricocheted off the granite walls around them.

The regular and his comrade at the front crouched low, taking cover behind the corner of the stairway as they reloaded their rifles.

"Steady now!" Governor Braedhwyc cried.

"Ay sir!" the regular called back. "I am believin' that we will ha' to make a dash o' it, sir."

Governor Braedhwyc nodded. "Ay then, rifles ready! Put on your bayonets, sirs!"

The regulars obeyed with smart precision. Clerans, too, affixed his bayonet to the end of his rifle. He tried to breathe deeply and calm his racing heart. It would be a bloodbath down there.

At that moment, Clerans heard a voice which sounded clearly from the basement below. Clerans perked up at the sound of it. That sounded like that pirate Ernest, the one who had helped him aboard the fire-ship.

"May God damn you all!"

Suddenly, the whole passageway shook with the sound of an enormous gun discharging — something between a buffalo rifle and a cannon. Harsh shrieks, screams, and curses echoed through the stairwell from the pirates below, followed by several more gunshots.

"Now is it!" Governor Braedhwyc called. "For God, Llaedhwyth, and Entwerp!"

The regulars rushed forward with a great yell, charging down the spiral staircase like an avalanche. Clerans and Martyn followed behind the last pair of regulars. Ahead of him, Clerans could hear metal ringing against metal, screams, moaning, and an occasional gunshot. As Clerans reached the bottom of the stairs, however, he could see nothing in the thick gunpowder smoke that filled the little room. Realizing that his rifle would be useless with such limited vision and space, Clerans snatched up his knife and tomahawk, wading into the smoke with his eyes keen and alert, looking for any pirates to engage.

# 19

# REVELATIONS

All around Clerans were shapes blurred in the smoke, but were they friend or foe? Suddenly, the shape of a man loomed towards him. Clerans raised his weapons, standing poised to strike. Yet as the smoke broke from around the figure, Clerans could plainly see that it was a regular.

"Haloo!" the regular shouted. "Ye are no a pirate."

Clerans lowered his knife and tomahawk. "Ay, then, where are they?"

Suddenly, there was a gunshot from close by, followed by the sound of an enormous door slamming shut.

"After them!" a voice called out through the smoke (it sounded like the regular who had led the charge).

The rest of the regulars shouted all at once.

"After what?"

"Ay, and where?"

"Well, are there any pirates here?"

"Here is one! I tain him pinned!"

"Do no ye shoot, Alfyn! I am no a pirate."

"Is that ye, Michel? I cen no make out a thing in this smoke."

Clerans coughed heavily. The smoke was smarting his eyes now.

"Where ha' they vened to, then?" That was Governor Braedhwyc's voice.

Clerans tried to peer through the smoke, but still could see nothing more than shadows. This was no use. They wouldn't have any order until this smoke cleared. Clerans backed up until he touched a wall. He stood there, waiting for the smoke to settle somewhat.

The regulars continued to shout at each other for several more minutes. Finally, Clerans noticed openings of clean air swirling about in the smoke. Slowly but surely, the thick, gray smoke dissipated, clearing enough for Clerans to see the entire room.

Governor Braedhwyc stood nearly in the center of the room, scowling and wiping pus from his eye while the regulars scurried about around him. As the smoke cleared, they settled down a bit, regaining most of their previous composure. Scanning the room quickly, Clerans noted that the only pirates in the room were perhaps half a dozen corpses on the ground. Two regulars also lay on the ground wounded, being helped by their comrades who had wounded them in the confusion. But where were the rest of the pirates? Surely there had been more in this room. Then Clerans noticed the officer and Martyn standing right before the Gwambi door on the far side of the room, prying at it with their knives.

"Wos that it?" Governor Braedhwyc asked.

"They got away," the officer said through clenched teeth.

"Ay," Martyn added, "I saw perhaps ten o' them disappear behind the door before they closed it."

Clerans now noticed Haeli, Titus, and the Indigies stepping down the stairway into the chaos. The Indigie warriors looked at the chaos disdainfully.

"What happened?" Haeli asked, waving the gunpowder smoke away from her face.

Titus scanned the room anxiously. "Where's my daughter? Where's Ella?"

As if in answer, a halting voice spoke. "Titus?"

Everyone seemed to pause at the sound of that voice. Clerans peered at where he thought he had heard the voice, but saw only several bodies lying on the ground. As he watched, one of the bodies moved slightly. Turning on his side, the speaker showed his face. He looked to be a large man, though he was now crumpled up and gripping his stomach tightly. Clearly he was wounded, as blood pooled all around him. Clerans couldn't help but wonder why this man hadn't bled out yet, except that an extraordinary will kept him grasping tenaciously to life.

"Titus Donne? Is that ye?"

Titus glanced at the dying man hesitantly, but took a step towards him. "Yes, that's me. Do I... er... do I know you?"

"No," the man replied weakly. "Ye have niver seen me before in yer life."

"How do you know my name, then?" Titus asked, pausing.

The man coughed heavily. "Ye got my message. Is that why ye are here?"

"What?" Titus asked, clearly perplexed.

"In the bread... The affidavit," the man choked and then broke off coughing again.

A light seemed to spread across Titus' face. "That was you? You are the man?"

The man winced, as if in excruciating pain. "Not much time... now... Titus, come here."

Titus walked forward quickly and knelt beside the dying man. Clerans looked closely at this scene, trying his best to make sense of it all.

The dying man reached out with his bloody hand, taking Titus by the shoulder. The man winced again. "I meant to... in

Blisa. I... was... stopped, before I..." The man coughed again, breathing deeply, yet he seemed to choke on his own breath.

Titus looked with great perplexity into the dying man's face.

The man shook his head, clearly struggling to breathe. He placed his bloody finger on Titus's chest and tapped it a few times. Suddenly, as if calling upon his last remains of strength, the man sat up and looked Titus full in the face.

"Ye have," the man said with an effort, "been good to Ella. I has given you what I could. Take care av her now."

And with that, the man collapsed, his breath catching in his throat and sounding no more. Clerans furrowed his brow. How strange! It was almost as if that man had held on to his life just long enough to talk to Titus.

"Tar and needles!" Martyn suddenly exclaimed. "It is Mr. Silas!"

Clerans looked closely at the now-dead man. Martyn was right! That *was* Mr. Silas, only just recognizable through the blood and bruises on his face. What was he doing here?

"Silas?" Titus started. He looked closely at the dead man and then shook his head. "Oh, no, that's... Ah, of course, I see. It's like he said, then."

Clerans nodded. "Ay, ye are right. It *is* Mr. Silas Pickering."

"Silas Pickering?" Titus looked the dead man in the eye, scrutinizing him. He shook his head and sighed. "Extraordinary. What, eh, a... they *do* look very similar."

"What's that, now?" Martyn asked.

Titus only shook his head. "I knew, eh, that is, one of my closest friends was named Silas Pickering, but eh, eh, this is not him. It's... ah... a coincidence."

Clerans was unsure what to make of this scene. What did this mean? How had Sir Silas gotten here? Hadn't Miss Ella said that Sir Silas was her father?

Clerans' thoughts were interrupted as he noticed Haeli out of the corner of his eye. She was standing directly in front of the

Gwambi door. What was she doing there? Clerans didn't have to ponder this long, for Haeli suddenly reached into the folds of her dress and pulled out a strange metal key. Clerans caught his breath. Haeli had a key? Perhaps the pirates hadn't taken it from her after all! No, they must have, for they clearly had opened the door already. There must be two keys then.

Haeli slipped the key into the lock, yet the key wouldn't turn. Haeli gripped it in both of her hands, clearly twisting the key with all of her might, yet it still did not turn. Letting out a groan, Haeli pulled the key out of the lock and slumped to the ground dejectedly.

"I should have known it would not fit the lock," she murmured.

Martyn looked at Haeli curiously. "Llifsa! Ye are full o' surprise, Haeli."

"Right then!" Governor Braedhwyc ordered. "Clear out o' the way, we'll will break the door down."

Haeli stood up quickly and moved to the side, standing near Clerans as the regulars swarmed around the door, beating at it with their rifle butts.

The Indigie leader (Tiya) now walked over to Haeli and shook her head. "It is of no use," she said in the common tongue. "The door has many enchantments on it. They will never break it down."

"But where is Ella?" Titus suddenly asked, standing up and looking over at Haeli and Tiya as if they could answer him.

Martyn put his hand comfortingly on Titus' shoulder. "I am afraid that she is behind that door with the rest o' the pirates."

"What?" Titus gasped, trembling all over. "My Ella? What will they do to her? We have to get her out. Can't we get the door open somehow?"

Tiya shook her head again. "As I said, it is of no use."

"But is there another way?" Titus asked desperately. "I came for her. I can't leave my Ella to die."

Haeli suddenly stood bolt upright, seizing Tiya by the shoulders. The little nymph looked rather surprised by this, but she stared at Haeli steadily.

"The tower!" Haeli exclaimed.

Tiya said nothing, but only looked darkly back at Haeli.

"You have climbed it?" Haeli asked.

Tiya nodded slowly.

What was this they were talking about? The tower? Surely Haeli wasn't talking about the Gwambi Tower. No one had survived climbing that thing.

"Do not you see? That's our only other way," Haeli said. "You know how to climb it. You must show us."

Tiya let out a deep sigh. "One can not simply..."

"Oh, do be reasonable!" Haeli cried. "Ella is in the Gwambi city now. She is going to die if we can not get some help to her. Surely you can help us."

Tiya took a deep breath. "She follows the one true God?"

"Absolutely," Haeli replied.

Tiya nodded, though Clerans could see a look of dread in her eyes. "Then for His sake, I will climb the tower."

Haeli nodded, releasing Tiya. "Thank you. Then, Titus, you will come with us. And Martyn, you too."

Martyn raised a perplexed eyebrow. "What are ye talkin' o', Haeli? I tain the defense o' the city to worry about. There are still pirates out there..."

Haeli looked Martyn in the eye with intense determination, pointing her finger in his face. "Martyn, I am going to climb the Gwambi Tower, and I am going to enter their city in search of Ella."

"Oh!" Titus exclaimed. "That's eh... that's wonderful. Good for you."

"You know," Haeli continued, still lecturing Martyn as if she were a teacher and he were a naughty six-year-old child, "that I would much rather you come with me and help me, but if you are obstinate, I will go without you. But tell me, what would you do if anything should happen to me?"

Martyn shook his head and sighed. "Alright then, I suppose I must."

"Ay," Haeli replied, "You must."

Just then, boots scuffed down the spiral stairs. Clerans looked up just in time to see a strangely uniformed man descend to the basement. He wore russet brown from his thigh-high leather boots, to his felt trousers, leather riding chaps, woolen undercoat, many-pocketed greatcoat, which hung from his shoulders and fell all the way to his knees. The hat on the man's head was not tricorn like those of the Pistosians, but it was short (almost like a helmet) with a narrow rim all around it. Clerans noticed a curved saber hanging from the man's hip next to a long horse-pistol. In his left hand, the man carried a very long rifle.

Clerans' pulse quickened. It was a Federal Dragoon. In the flesh!

"And is the Governor here, look ye?"

The governor looked up, wiping pus from his eye. "Ay? What is it?"

The dragoon touched the brim of his hat. "Captain Smydhac says he is ready to charge."

The governor waved a hand dismissively. "Merri well. And I do no care if you'll will kill them all."

"Very good." And with that, the dragoon was rushing up the stairs again.

The regulars paused in their assault on the door.

"Should we help them?"

"Are the strikers at the bank, then?"

Governor Braedhwyc massaged his temples. "We've got enough with the pirates, then. Let the dragoons ride the strikers down. It's what they deserve, anyway."

Clerans swallowed, once again thinking back to the young

striker who had died in his arms. He could envision the dragoons in their russet coats, galloping in like heroes from a book, cutting down all the strikers for what they saw as a righteous cause.

His guts roiled. How many men would die in the attack on the strikers? And how many strikers would die, too? And all the while, the pirates were looting and tearing Entwerp Coastal apart. It was madness. All the bloodshed with the strikers was so pointless, and distracting them from the real threat the pirates posed.

Like a flash, Clerans remembered the letter Haeli had given him, and he knew what he had to do. He knew the streets of Entwerp better than anyone else. He could get to the bank long before the dragoons.

Just like that, he was off, shooting up the stairway like a cannonball.

"Clerans!" Martyn called out after him.

"Got a delivery!" he replied, not bothering to look back. "See ye when this is over!"

20

# YEA, THOUGH I WALK

Slowly and shakily, Ella picked herself up. She hurt all over from her fall, and her head throbbed — she must have hit it on a stair when she fell. But where was Ernest? She could see nothing — it made no difference whether she had her eyes open or closed. Stagnant air surrounded her, with only the feeling of cool granite beneath her feet.

Bending down, Ella felt the ground around her. Her fingertips touched cold stone so smooth and well-planed that there hardly even seemed to be dust on it. Ella continued to grope forward, and then her hand touched something soft and warm. She recoiled out of instinct, but then she felt the warm thing more closely. Yes, it was clothing and a body. It must be Ernest. But he was so still and didn't even flinch as Ella touched him. Ella's heart jumped. Was he dead? Was she stuck in this eternal blackness with only a dead body to keep her company?

Slowly, she felt up to his head. He was lying on his face, though, so Ella couldn't feel very well if he was breathing or not. Finally, she got her fingers against his neck. To her relief, she felt a steady pulse.

Ella let out her breath in a great sigh. So he was still alive, but he must have been knocked out cold. She slumped to the ground next to Ernest and groaned. Really, he might as well be dead. She might as well be dead, too. Whatever were they to do? She couldn't see a thing. She couldn't hear a thing. It was just totally dark and heart-numbingly lonely.

Ella buried her head in her hands and wept. Why had this all happened to her? What had she done to deserve this — this darkness, this misery, this loneliness? Hadn't she had enough hardships?

What was she even supposed to be thinking just now? She felt like her whole world had collapsed into itself. How many long years had she yearned for her father, wishing she could have met him, trying to learn about him? Now, she had finally found her father — alive, after all of those years. Yet he wasn't at all the person she had imagined him to be. What was it all to mean? Was he really the father she deserved? Was God punishing her?

No, even as she thought this, she knew it was a ridiculous thought. God didn't vindictively punish people for their bad actions — that would be legalism. No, perhaps this wasn't punishment from God, but perhaps it was simply the natural outcome of her decisions. After all, she had left her family's house on that fated night in Blisa to bring Jock that loaf of bread. Was all of this, then, just an outcome of her mistake? Otherwise, if all these trials were not a result of something *she* had done, then they must result from something God had done. That would mean that He had planned for all of this to happen to her. But why?

Ella wiped the tears from her cheeks, but she was still sobbing. "God," she whispered. "Can You hea'h me?"

It was at that very moment that she remembered what Pastor Daerl had said earlier, about a relational wound needing a relationship to heal it — a personal relationship with God — hadn't he used that phrase?

Ella sighed deeply. "I just wanted to find my fathe'h. I just wanted to know who he was. Is it w'ong of me to want to know who my fathe'h was?" It was an honest question, and she sat there in the total blackness with her ears strained and her heart open to an answer. She almost expected to hear a still, small voice answer her out of the darkness.

She heard no voice, but suddenly a verse from the scriptures came to her mind. "We were given a spirit of adoption, by which we cry out, 'Papa, father!'" Ella stopped crying now, wiping tears from her eyes again. Of course, God was her father. That's always the way they referred to Him at church: God the Father, God the Son, and God the Spirit. Was that supposed to be an answer? If God was her father, then she wasn't supposed to be looking for her birth-father?

But that was a silly thought, after all. Was she really supposed to say, "God is my father," and forget all about her real father as if she did not need a real father? Certainly, that sounded very spiritual and holy, but it was also completely unsatisfying. She had never known her father. He had left her — abandoned her, if Longfinch was to be believed. Surely it was no sin for her to seek her very own birth-father.

And yet, she had found him now, though she might as well still be without him. Before, she had felt only a dull aching in the background of all her life, and now her heart throbbed and burned. Her father was certainly dead now, and by the look of it, he had been a very careless and selfish man, anyway. Perhaps she would have been better off forgetting all about her father from the beginning.

But that was no good, and Ella knew it. Pastor Daerl had been right. She had a relational wound — a papa-sized hole in her heart, and she couldn't simply ignore it. Of course, she *had* to look for him. She *had* to know who her father was. Now that she had found him and met him — though she still hurt, and she still had a hole in her heart — she at least *knew* who her father was. Perhaps the hole would heal in time.

Ella shook her head. Surely knowledge was not that much of a cure. But what was that Pastor Daerl had said about needing a relationship to heal? Certainly that made sense. She didn't really want to know who her father was; she wanted to know her father. She wanted to sit beside him and hear him tell stories while they curled up under a blanket in front of the fire on a long winter night. She wanted to hear her father laugh when she made a witty remark. She wanted to feel her father's warm arms holding her when she was hurting. That's the cure she needed. That's what would make that hole in her heart heal. Knowledge was not enough. She needed a relationship.

Even at the thought of it, Ella started sobbing again. The darkness and loneliness closed in around her, taunting her. The stark stillness was almost palpable, as if that cold air was freezing claws, extended and flexed, ready to torment her. She had no father — no good father, anyway. She had no father that she could ever know, or leastways, no father whoever wanted to know her.

That must be it then. God was her father, of course — in the sense that He wanted to know her and love her — but He could never be what her real father might have been. God could never really hold her when she was hurting, for instance.

Ella paused at this thought. Certainly, the idea of God physically holding her in His arms seemed absurd, but was it? If God was really all-powerful (which she believed) and if He was really her eternal Father — a *good* Father, as He claimed — then wouldn't it be part of his role to physically comfort her? In the same way that all of this thick blackness seemed palpable to her, couldn't God's love and comfort be just as, if not more, palpable? If God was really a *person* with feelings, and if He really wanted to know her *personally,* then it only made sense that He would interact with her *personally.*

A personal relationship with God. Hadn't that been something Pastor Daerl had said? If that didn't mean God palpably, physically comforting her, then what did it mean?

Ella took a deep breath and wiped the tears from her eyes again. "God," she prayed. "I guess I don't weally know You very well — on a pe'sonal level I mean. I may know a lot *about* You, but I don't know *You*. Somehow, it seems like that's the answe'h to all of this."

Ella paused. She could still see nothing, and her voice seemed insignificant, as if it were sticking in the stagnant air. Or perhaps the obscene darkness was gobbling up her words.

"I don't know," she continued. "I'm not su'e how this wo'ks. I only know that I want You. I've been looking fo'h something my whole life, and w'ight now, You a'e the only one who can give it."

This sounded silly. Ella sighed. "I guess I don't know what I'm saying. I don't know what I'm weally p'aying fo'h."

No sooner were the words out of her mouth than she felt the answer. It wasn't like a voice or anything she could hear, and it wasn't like a thought from her own brain. She simply felt it, as if it were words in a book she was reading.

"Do you really need to pray *for* something in order to pray?"

Ella could feel a lump in her throat, and she wept again. "I don't know," she cried. "I don't know anything anymo'e! Do I have a father? Did he abandon me? Does it even matte'h? I don't know, I just don't know. All I know is that I hu't, and I want it to stop. I hu't weally badly, and I've been hu'ting fo'h so long now that I don't even know if it *can* stop."

Her voice caught in her throat, which was just as well, as she could think of nothing else to say. She simply sat there with her arms wrapped around her knees, rocking back and forth as she wept. Somehow this wasn't the same hopeless, lonely weeping of a moment ago. This felt different. She was weeping, yes, but she didn't feel alone anymore. Someone was there in the room with her, listening to her — someone who truly understood and knew her.

As this thought came to her, she felt a very pleasant, warm sensation all around her. Whether it was actually physical warmth or just an emotionally warm feeling, she couldn't say, but the distinction didn't matter anymore. What was the big difference, after all, between physical warmth and spiritual warmth?

Ella smiled — she couldn't help it — even as the tears streamed down her cheeks. So that was what a hug from God felt like.

# 21

# STRONG TOWER

Haeli pushed through the forest underbrush doggedly, determination in every step. Sure, she was tired. It had been a long day already, marching with the Twengoli through all their forest trails to get to Entwerp in time. But what did that matter? She had to keep going. Exhaustion was not a horse she would ride right now. Anger. Fury. Shame. Those would do for now. Those were the horses that could actually give her the energy she needed at the moment. She had let the pirates get that key, so now she had to fix the problem. Her Da had given her those keys, and he had said... but no, Haeli would not let her mind go there. She was not to think about her Da right now.

Responsibility. There, that was something she *could* think about. She had caused this problem, so she would take responsibility for it. Ella was in trouble, and it was all her fault. If she had simply not been so careless, the pirates would never have captured her and taken her key. She was lucky to be alive and even more lucky to have the second key. But she couldn't fail this time. She had to get into the Gwambi city somehow and save Ella. That was her responsibility.

Behind her, she could hear the others trudging through the underbrush. Just behind, Martyn was moving aside a branch to walk through. To her right, Tiya-Aenji padded on webbed feet, dampening the sound of her footsteps. Then there was Titus Donne, forcing his way through the trees and stepping on every stick there was to step on, sounding like an elephant announcing his approach to the entire world. Above her, the soft beating of wings announced Aarushi and Halfdan as they floated through the night.

"Haeli," it was Martyn speaking, probably objecting to this enterprise — again. At least he sounded like he was losing steam. "Haeli, this is sheer madness. What do ye mean trekkin' through the woods like this in the dead o' night?"

Haeli shook her head, not even turning around. "No, Martyn, I have already told you, and I will not change my mind. This is the only way to rescue Ella."

Her father's voice sounded in her mind. "Once you make a plan, you can not hesitate in seeing it done."

"Well, if it's the only way," Titus said, crashing through a spruce tree. "Then, eh, it's, I suppose, eh, the only way."

"Right," Haeli said, "and we cannot waste a moment. Who knows what those pirates are doing to her? Get a lantern if you must, but we can not dally."

"It is no the dark I am concerned about," Martyn said, "it is the exhaustion. Ye may be right that we must needs to hurry, but what help will we be to Ella after hiking all day an' night?"

Haeli said nothing, but she clamped her jaw tightly. In her mind, she could hear her brother's voice, coaching her just like when he was teaching her to climb a tree.

"That's it. Steady on. You've got this. Eyes forward. Never look down. Do not overthink it."

She just had to keep going. True, she had never been to the Gwambi Tower before, but she was certain she could reach it easily enough. After all, it was just at the top of this ridge — surely no more than four miles away.

So she plodded on. The thick underbrush of the lower forests soon gave way to wide groves of aspen and birch. The night was black with no moon to light their way. Haeli had to grope in front of her in places to see that she was not walking into anything. Even so, she stumbled over several logs and bumped into a couple of trees in the darkness. Looking up, she could just see the stars twinkling at her through the canopy above, as if they were playing hide and seek between the leaves. The stars were so bright that night, as if they were trying to light up the night in the moon's absence. The two black shapes of Aarushi and Halfdan passed overhead. Haeli shook her head and faced forward again.

Forward, yes, that was the way. She would not look back. She couldn't let herself overthink this.

Now they came into a little meadow, and Haeli could see the ridge high above them. Yes, there was the Gwambi Tower too, standing out stark and bold against the star-points of the night sky. She had to get there. That was her last chance of fixing all the problems she had caused.

Olyfia had said that she had seen Sir Saemwel on the tower after going through the door in the basement, so the two must connect. She only had to climb to the top of the tower, enter it, and find the connection point.

Haeli was panting now, and her throat hurt. Why did her throat hurt? Surely that wasn't from exertion. No, it hurt as if she were about to cry. But that was absurd. Why should she cry? She had nothing to cry about. Even as she thought this, her heart began to throb. This was ridiculous. She was *not* going to cry. She had nothing to cry about. Rage was the horse she was choosing, and she would ride that emotion until she had Ella back.

Haeli felt a dull, foreboding voice in the back of her mind, saying that this was not at all about Ella, but she pushed it aside. Again, that was a ridiculous thought. Of course, this was all about Ella, or at least mostly about Ella. Hadn't she agreed to help Ella in any way that she could? Then, of course, when Ella was in trouble, she would do all that she could to help Ella — especially if *she* had caused the trouble in the first place.

It really was just that simple. Ella was in trouble, and Haeli was going to stop it. That was all there was to it.

Almost at that instant, Haeli pushed between two aspen saplings and found herself right up against a cliff face. Groping to her left, she found that the ground sloped up slightly in that direction, so she walked along to the left, skirting the face of the cliff, always straining to see if there was a way up or around the cliff.

She went on like this for nearly a mile before the cliff broke up into steady, rising ground, and they could again climb up the mountain as before. However, this detour took Haeli well away from her intended course, and she had to backtrack considerably before she could see the tower in front of her again.

Haeli continued her confident trek towards the tower, but before she made another half mile, another cliff blocked her way. This cliff, though, was considerably smaller, and she found a way around it quickly.

Still, her legs ached, and her heart beat heavily as she breathed deeply and steadily from the labor — and her throat still hurt. Haeli ground her teeth together. She could do this. She had the strength. She just had to keep pushing herself. She could do this.

*Tower in Darkness*

And so she plodded on for several more miles, skirting around a few more cliffs and continually forcing her way through the trees and underbrush. Finally, Haeli noticed that the gnarled specimens of pine trees all around her were much smaller than the massive spruce trees nearer the valley. Then, like bursting out of the sea, Haeli pushed through the last branches of the trees, finding herself at the treeline, with only patches of tough grass and loose rocks before her. Only a few hundred feet above her, standing out starkly against the brilliant stars of the night sky, lay the ridge of the mountain, with the Gwambi Tower rearing up high and proud above it.

She caught her breath just at the sight of it. She had never been so close to the tower before, though she had seen it often enough from the valley. Even now, she wasn't very close to it, but she felt a great sense of doom all around her.

The others scrambled up just behind her, so Haeli pushed herself onward. She kept her eyes on the ground, concentrating on each step as she plodded onward. It only seemed a moment later that she looked up, finding herself on the top of the ridge. She could look out from here and see the twinkling lights of Entwerp Proper in the dale behind her. Looking out to the east, Haeli could see the dark mass of Entwerp Bay, like undulating ink in the night, and beyond that she could see the even darker surface of the ocean, blending almost seamlessly with the sky far out on the horizon. There was another mountain ridge before her to the east — with the Entwerp river running between these two steep ridges — and this blocked much of her view of Entwerp Coastal. Even so, she could see a red glow from that village and billows of smoke rising to obscure the starlight. Haeli shivered all over. What was left of Entwerp Coastal after the raid? She hardly wanted to know.

Haeli swallowed, and with a great act of willpower, she turned towards the Gwambi Tower. She was now standing at its very base, and it rose above her, tall and foreboding, like a fell monster, blocking out all the stars behind it. It seemed to be nearly fifty feet high and made of rough and natural granite, as if the tower itself was no more than an extension of the craggy mountain. Even its ramparts bore that same strange look — rough and irregular, like stones upon a rocky pinnacle — where they sat so high above her.

Haeli shivered all over, that strange dread coming over her again as she looked at the tower. Her heart throbbed in her chest like the deep beating of the Twengoli's tribal drums. Suddenly, she realized she could no longer feel rage. She had worn that horse out. All she wanted to do was collapse where she stood and rest.

So this was it. This was the Gwambi Tower.

Martyn, Titus, and Tiya-Aenji stumbled up the ridge behind her. Haeli turned to face them, swallowing back her dread and forcing a smile. "Alright then, Tiya-Aenji, show us how to climb the tower."

"Hold on a moment," Martyn interjected, shaking his head at Haeli. "This ha' ceded on too long as it is. I cen no let ye keep on."

Haeli took a deep breath. She had to keep feeling rage. That was the only way she could keep going. "Martyn, I have told you already; we *have* to do this. There is no other way."

"This is madness," Martyn replied, speaking in a low, calm voice. "People die on this tower every year. Ye cen no simply climb it, now."

Haeli ground her teeth together. "Stop wasting time. We will climb the tower, because we *have* to climb the tower."

"Haeli," Martyn said soothingly. "Do we even know what we are walkin' into?"

Haeli wrinkled her brow. "What do you mean?"

Martyn now turned to Tiya-Aenji. "Ye indeed ha' scended the Gwambi Tower a'fore?"

Tiya-Aenji nodded slowly.

"An' ye ha' been inside the underground city o' the Gwambi?" Martyn asked.

Tiya-Aenji shifted her position nervously, but she nodded again.

Martyn looked at the little nymph closely. "What is it like?"

Tiya-Aenji took in her breath sharply and then exhaled. Putting her webbed hands over her eyes, she shivered all over. "It is darkness."

Titus trembled a bit. "Eh, you said, eh... darkness?"

Tiya-Aenji nodded, her face turning grim. "It is tunnels upon tunnels, and mazes upon mazes. I have only entered once, but I am told that it is sixteen levels down — straight down to the roots of the mountains. It is terror, and it is horror. If the darkness will not destroy your wits, then *he* will devour you."

Titus's eyebrows shot up in alarm. "What was that? Who is 'he'?"

Tiya-Aenji turned to look Titus in the eye, speaking in a low, even voice, as if she were forcing herself to remain calm. "The god of the Gwambi, he whose name is a secret of the shamans of my people. He who sends his lightnings from the shaman. It was he who ruled the Gwambi with an iron hand and an orb of lead."

Haeli could feel the hair on her scalp rising at this speech. It was preposterous, though; it couldn't *really* be true. These were just the superstitious stories that the shaman told to his acolytes. Tiya-Aenji may follow God now, but she clearly held on to many of the animistic beliefs of the Twengoli. Still, standing there in the shadow of that strange and menacing tower made all that Tiya-Aenji said seem plausible, if not absolutely true.

Titus' eyes were wide in terror. He was opening and closing his mouth, but nothing came out. Martyn alone seemed unfazed by this description of the nebulous 'he.' He simply looked at Tiya-Aenji carefully and soberly. He didn't seem incredulous at all. Surely Martyn didn't believe what Tiya-Aenji had just said? Ah, but Martyn *was* an Elderian, so he still might believe in these spooks and magical trumpery.

"Then what is he?" Martyn asked. "Is he a demon? Or some monster o' the ancient times? An orcling, or a bloodless?"

Tiya-Aenji shook her head darkly. "He is of a different substance altogether."

Martyn straightened up in alarm. "Ye do no mean to say that he is a Helling, surely? I thought that the scriptures were clear that all o' the Hellings were destroyed."

Tiya-Aenji again shook her head. "No, he is not of the Hellings, though in their time he was a close ally with them. No, he is one of those demons who joined with the Devil in the great orgy at Sarnach, when all the kings of the earth joined together and slaughtered Aydon, the prophet of the Almighty God, sacrificing him on the high altar of Sarnach to the Devil himself. Yes, he is one of those demons who was cursed by God to inhabit a physical body, so that though he be a spirit in life and eternality, yet he would feel the pangs, needs, and cravings of every fleshly beast."

Martyn nodded. "Ye mean that he is a ghost?"

Tiya-Aenji nodded.

Titus shook all over. "Lord preserve us!"

At that moment, Halfdan and Aarushi fluttered down from the sky, landing near Martyn's feet. Halfdan looked up at Titus and shook his head. "That had better be a sincere prayer, because otherwise, that was blasphemy, which is a grievous sin."

Haeli shook her head in disgust. "How could you ever believe this nonsense, Martyn?"

Martyn furrowed his brow. "How could I no? It is written out clearly in the scriptures."

"It is not nonsense," Tiya-Aenji insisted. "I have met him before." Even as she spoke, all the color drained from her face. "I shudder to remember that meeting; I have no words to describe its terror." Tiya-Aenji took a deep breath. "But that was before I was a follower of the one God."

Halfdan nodded, still speaking in his dull monotone. "Yes, yes, you have no need to fear now. After all, do you really think that an ancient, powerful, desperately evil, supernatural, villainous demon could hurt you?" And Halfdan let out a hollow laugh.

Titus looked at Halfdan with some confusion. "Was, eh, that is, eh... are you trying to be encouraging?"

Tiya-Aenji nodded, clearly attempting to regain her composure. "The harrier speaks the truth, for we need fear no power of the Devil. The Spirit of the Almighty God lives within all of us. By His power are all the powers of darkness bound and defeated."

Haeli looked at Tiya-Aenji closely, then at Martyn, Titus, Halfdan, and Aarushi. Why was she the only one who seemed to have trouble believing all of this rubbish? Of course, demons didn't walk the earth anymore. That age had ceased.

In her mind, she heard her father's voice, as he had spoken many times to the Elderians about the supernatural. "The physical is all there is. God, the earth, you, your emotions — it is all physical. You can not appeal to anything else."

Martyn took a deep breath. "Tell me then, Tiya, how long are we likely to be down in those tunnels?"

Tiya-Aenji shook her head. "Who can say? Perhaps a few hours, perhaps a few days."

"Do ye know the way?" Martyn asked. "That is, could ye trive yer way through those tunnels back to the Gwambi door?"

Tiya-Aenji again shook her head. "As I said, I have only entered those dark halls once before, and I have only a vague memory of them. I think that I might be able to guide you to the great Lower Hall and the Pillars of Sacrifice, but that is all."

Martyn nodded and then turned back to Haeli. "There we are. We certainly cen no try to climb the Gwambi Tower tonight, then. If we'll are likely to be down there fer many days, then we will need our rest now. Also, we will need provisions and lanterns."

Haeli rubbed at her temples. "But we do not have a moment to lose." Her rage was flagging. She had very little energy left, and she was having trouble saddling up any emotions powerful enough to carry her on. "We can't waste time." It sounded lame even to her ears. And she really wanted to believe it.

Martyn nodded. "Ay, we cen no *waste* time, so we must use it wisely." He now turned to everyone else present. "Aarushi an' I will cede back to Entwerp an' collect some provisions. The rest o' ye stay here an' get some rest. One o' ye should probably stay up an' watch until I return. At dawn we will tain breakfast, an' then we'll will climb the tower and resume our attempts to rescue Ella."

Haeli crumbled to the ground. Rest. Yes, she needed rest. But only to keep going on. She would not look back. She had to press on. She had to save Ella.

2 2

<br>

# CALLED

Clerans gasped in air as he pounded across the cobblestone streets of Entwerp Propper. His pulse pounded in his head, and his side ached from his exertion. But he had to ignore that. He had to get to the bank before the Federal Dragoons.

Thankfully, the streets were brightly lit, and few people were out at this time of night, so Clerans had nothing in his way. And he knew these streets like he knew the ties on his boots. He was off down one main road, then ducking down the alley, then cutting across an allotment, vaulting a fence, scampering over the roof of a shed, and then dropping back to the street. Southward, ever southward, by the straightest road, just like he was delivering an urgent Company letter to the bank. If Clerans had the breath for it, he would have laughed at the irony. He was delivering a message alright, though it wasn't for the Company. But if that one-armed striker took a bullet for him, the least Clerans could do for the strikers was deliver Haeli's message to them.

Once or twice, he heard something behind him, almost like footfalls. Was Martyn following him? But Clerans didn't waste the energy to look behind him. It didn't change what he had to do.

Finally he came up to the park outside the bank, hurtling down the road. All at once, he realized that the black shape in front of him was a wagon thrown over on its side. He saw the rifle barrel glint just in time to come to a screeching halt.

"Ho there! Halt where ye are!"

Clerans threw up his hands. "Dike militia!"

"Clerans?" The person before him lowered her rifle and stepped out of the shadow of the overturned cart.

"Lexi?"

Lexi snorted and slung her rifle over her shoulder. "Ye ha' *got* to keep out o' the way o' these strikers. One o' these days I'll am goin' to shoot ye, and then wot would yer mother say to me?"

Clerans leaned over, hands on his knees, gasping for breath. "I ha' to… I ha' to get to the bank. 'Afore the dragoons."

Lexi straightened up. "The dragoons? Are they finally goin' to clean this up?"

Clerans looked about him, suddenly realizing that nearly a dozen town militia and gray-clad regulars crouched in the wagon's shadow. Just to the side, a couple of men lay on stretchers, while a dark form leaned over them. Was that Olafr, Dr. Heyl's faerie apprentice?

"It's about time they get rid o' those strikers," someone muttered.

"No." Clerans gasped, still trying to catch his breath. "I must talk with them. The strikers, I mean."

Olafr looked up at Clerans, squinting at him in the darkness.

"By the saint's beard, is that ye Clerans Blaeith?"

"The same," Clerans replied, sucking in several long gulps of air. He had to stop his racing heart.

"Llifsa, Clerans!" Olafr exclaimed suddenly. "Ye are wounded."

"Me?" Clerans shook his head. "Oh, no, that wos only the barnacles..."

Lexi cleared her throat. "An' wot o' yer escort?"

Clerans blinked. "Escort?"

Lexi motioned behind him. To his surprise, Clerans found two Indigie nymphs standing just behind him (a boy and a girl), and neither full-grown. Though the girl carried a *kukri* strapped to her hip, and the boy had a sling and bag of stones hanging from his shoulder, neither appeared to be a warrior. As Clerans looked back at them, they stood still, simply staring at him. Clerans licked his lips. What did they want from him?

The girl pointed at him with her webbed hand, speaking in the common tongue. "We is for to come with you. As declares Tiya-Aenji Li."

Clerans nodded. Was Tiya-Aenji the shaman's apprentice? Clerans shrugged. "As ye wish, then, an' I'm sure I won't stop you."

Clerans looked at the two Indigies, and they looked back at him mutely. With another deep breath, Clerans turned back to Lexi.

"Will ye let me through, then?"

Lexi sighed deeply and then waved him on. "But do no get yerself shot."

Clerans moved forward, peering around the upturned wagon. In front of him was just the open square before the bank, though ranged along the front steps of the bank lay make-shift barricades of desks and cobblestones. That must be the strikers' positions. But would they fire on him if he approached? The best he could do was walk forward slowly, with his hands visible, so that they knew he meant them no harm.

Clerans moved out from behind the wagon's cover, stepping forward slowly. Much to his surprise, the two Indigies kept pace just behind him.

"What are you doin'?" he whispered.

The girl simply blinked. "We is for to come with you."

Clerans shook his head. "Your shaman's apprentice, Tiya-Aenji, ay? Why would she want ye here?"

The girl only shrugged. "We must be obeying only."

Clerans sighed, walking forward again, keeping his steps slow and deliberate. As he crossed the open space, the nymphs followed at his heels, their webbed feet slapping noisily on the cobblestones.

"Well then," Clerans whispered, hardly daring to take his eyes off the strikers' barricades. "I s'pose I'll outta-should introduce myself. I am Clerans Blaeith."

"We is of knowing," the girl Indigie replied. "The Li said unto us your name."

Clerans nodded. Had the strikers seen him yet? How would he know? Dear God, let them not shoot first. "Ay then, an' what might your names be?"

The girl pointed to herself, "Sydni-Efylyn," then she pointed to the boy, "and is my brother Nōlistrw-kagwyr."

"Nōli!" the boy protested loudly, thumping himself on the chest with evident pride.

The girl rolled her eyes, but Clerans cringed at the noise. Still, he forced himself to remain calm, and continue slowly forward.

"I like that. It is a merri o' easier to say." He swallowed nervously, risking a glance back towards his two nymph escorts. "How about I call you two 'Sydni' and 'Nōli'?"

Nōli nodded with satisfaction, and his sister shrugged dispassionately.

Clerans had just turned back to the bank when a loud report rang out, and an instant later, the cobblestones by his feet sparked and chipped, a bullet skittering and ricocheting past.

Clerans froze, his mouth suddenly dry.

For several moments, he stood there in perfect silence. Was

that meant to hit him, or had the strikers missed him on purpose?

"Halloo?" Clerans said in a hoarse voice.

Another gunshot rang out, the charge whining off to Clerans' left.

At last, a rough voice called out from the darkness at the front of the bank. "An' no another step!"

Clerans held up his hands. Hopefully, there was enough light that the strikers could see he meant no harm. Though perhaps they had only missed him because they couldn't see him properly.

"I'm jist here to talk."

There was a moment of silence, and then the rough voice spoke again. "Time fer talk is over!"

"Ay!" another voice added. "The bank is ours!"

"Jist as soon as we'll break in the vault."

At that moment, a regular called out from behind Clerans. "Wait until the dragoons come! You cen no stand up to the lord protector himself!"

"Anoint the lord protector!" the striker replied. "An' anoint every baptized one o' the dragoons!"

Clerans took a deep breath. "Cen all o' you shut up?"

Silence followed for several moments, and Clerans faced back towards the strikers' barricades. He thought he could just make out the dark silhouettes of men amidst the shadows.

"Now, I came here…"

Another gunshot cut him off, and Clerans winced as it shattered the cobblestones by Nōli's feet. The young nymph squeaked with surprise and shuffled closer to his sister.

"We don't want to hear it!" the striker yelled.

Clerans grit his teeth, a sudden rage filling him.

"Now you look here!"

Another gunshot, and the bullet whined quite close to his head, but Clerans refused to be intimidated.

"I ha' been shot at enough tonight, an' watched the sheriff murdered by pirates, an' hacked enough pirates to death myself, an' watched my friends bleeding to death, an' I ha' been through all that, an' I'm still here, an' I'm goin' to talk to ye, an' I'm no goin' to be frightened off by ye yellin' an' shootin' at me, a'cause ye are too thick to listen to reason!"

"Reason?" the striker yelled back. "An' we ha' never heard 'reason' from you lot."

"Did ye say the sheriff is dead?" the second striker asked.

"Enough o' that," the first hissed.

"Listen to me!" Clerans roared.

The first striker snorted. "Ay, an' ye tain one thing to say, an' *one* only."

"Look!" the second striker broke in, "and is no that Indigies he ha' got with him?"

There was a moment's pause.

"Oh, ay, he tains two o' them."

"He's that younker from the meeting!" the second voice broke in.

"When we burnt down the cottage?"

The second voice coughed. "He wos the one suggesting suing under Indigie Law, an' trial by moa fer the Company."

The first striker snorted and then yelled out something in Tylweni.

Clerans blinked. "I am sorry, I am no merri fluent."

"No ye!" the striker hissed, and then yelled out some more in Tylweni.

Clerans frowned, not sure how to respond to this, but at that moment, Sydni spoke up behind him. She was speaking rapidly, but Clerans caught the words "Iasaqi-Woni," "Company," and something about the verb, "to right" — but no, maybe that was the gerund of the verb, so that would be something about "the making-right one," or something. Clerans took a deep breath and let it out slowly. He should really learn Tylweni better.

There was a brief silence as Sydni finished speaking, and the first striker let out a low whistle.

"See?" the second striker said. "He's the genuine deal."

The first sighed. "Ay, but ye are making it a merri o' hard to intimidate him."

Clerans took a tentative step forward. "No need fer intimidating here."

Another gunshot rang out, and Clerans froze.

"I was no talking to ye!" the first striker snarled. "Now I said ye could only say one more thing, an' that wos it!"

Clerans blinked. "That wos never it! How cen ye count *that* as my only thing to say?"

"There it is!" the first striker called out. "He ha' said one more thing. Now off ye go. It's seizing the bank we're tryin' to do here, an' ye are distracting us."

"Give him a chance, now," the second striker broke in.

"Intimidating?" the first cut in with a stage whisper. "Ye are supposed to be intimidating?"

The second groaned quietly, and Clerans was certain he was rolling his eyes. "Look, younker, we cen only let ye say one more thing, an' then ye do ha' to leave."

The first clicked his tongue. "What wos that? That wos almost *polite*."

Clerans licked his lips. Come to think of it, what exactly had he come here to say? He had a vague thought about showing them the letter and talking about suing the Company under Indigie Law, but it sounded like they already knew about his proposal. So why was he here? How was he supposed to get these strikers to leave the bank before the dragoons started slaughtering them? He briefly considered mentioning the dragoons again, but no, surely they knew all about the dragoons. The threat of violence would not intimidate these strikers. Most of them were beacon tenders who lived in a constant threat of violence or bodily harm for their vocation.

Clerans cleared his throat. "Ye will let me say one thing more?"

"Ay," the first striker said, "that's a waste o' yer sentence. Now off you scend."

The second striker cleared his throat, and the first sighed.

"Fine then. What ha' ye got to say?"

"That spokesman o' yours," Clerans waved his hand in the air vaguely. "The man who… he's the one who speaks all the time, and gets all passionate about siegin' the bank an' all?"

"Ay," the first striker said slowly. "We know who ye mean."

Clerans nodded. "Where's he from?"

Silence met this question.

"What beacon did he tend?" Clerans went on.

"An' how should I know?"

Clerans threw his hands up. "Ye cen ask him. Jist ask him, an' see what he says."

There was a long moment of silence.

"Is that all?"

Clerans sighed. "Jist listen to what he says, an' see if he'll will give ye a straight answer." A sudden idea came to him. "An' see *how* he says what he says."

"What do ye mean?"

"Like," Clerans licked his lips again. "Listen to see if he'll say 'amn't' instead of 'am no', or if he'll say, 'what' instead o' 'that', or 'comed' instead o' 'came'."

The second striker broke in with a stage whisper. "He does talk like that, though."

"Ay," the first yelled back at Clerans. "An' what would any o' that prove?"

Clerans sighed. "Ha' ye ever talked with a sailor? That's how they talk."

A long silence followed this statement.

"Come along, man!" Clerans yelled. "I ha' been fightin' pirates all night. I cen tell ye, I know what pirates talk like."

"Pirates?" the first voice called back. "Ye callin' him a pirate?"

Clerans threw his hands in the air. "Ye tell me!"

After a moment's silence, the second voice spoke again.

"Does no hurt to ask him, now does it?"

"Ay," the first voice said slowly. "Does no hurt to ask him, but we'll ha' to be cunning about it."

"We cen be cunning!" the second striker replied. "We're always cunning, ye an' I."

Clerans backed up slowly. "I am leavin' now?"

A gunshot rang out.

"Ay! An' ye better be leavin'!" The second striker yelled. Then, in a stage whisper, he added. "How was that? Intimidatin' enough?"

A sudden exhaustion came over Clerans as he shuffled back to the militia's barricade, the two Indigies following. Hopefully, he had done enough. He had been through enough tonight, and now he simply wanted to lie down and forget about the village, the bank, the pirates, and all of it, and just sleep.

Tonight, he would settle for a bed on the cobblestones.

2 3

# SHEOL

Ella didn't know how long she sat beside Ernest's unconscious body. Even surrounded by that thick, oppressive darkness, she felt somehow safe and warm. The darkness was no longer a fell beast with claws penetrating her very soul. Now it was near and safe, like a wing that sheltered her from prying eyes. Ella could hear Ernest's gentle breathing. She yawned heavily.

Now that her heart had stopped racing, she realized just how tired she was. After all, she would usually be well asleep by this time of night. But was it still the night? How long had she been down in this darkness? After a few moments, Ella settled down, laying her head on Ernest. He really was the only pillow around, and so long as he was asleep, he wouldn't mind, would he?

Ella sighed deeply and contentedly. It was strange to feel so safe and comfortable down in this dark pit. She knew that this was more than just a feeling. She *was* safe. That was a fact. God had come to her, and He was with her now. She could hardly be safer back home in her bed in faraway Blisa.

She had her eyes closed, yet Ella was never sure if she slept or not. Suddenly, she heard a loud shout echoing through the darkness. Ella sat bolt upright, and the hair on her head stood on end. What was that? Was there someone in the tunnel with her?

All at once, she saw a bright light. More than likely, all she saw was the fitful rays from a lantern, yet in that utter darkness, it seemed to her as if it were the rising sun. All at once she could see the staircase which she had tumbled down, and at the very top of this stairway she could see the light gleaming off the walls of the strange granite passageway.

Ella crouched wearily over Ernest's still-sleeping form. What was this light? She felt exposed without the cover of her darkness.

Then the figure of a pirate loomed up in the doorway at the top of the stairs. He held a lantern before him and moved hurriedly, looking back over his shoulder warily. Ella froze. The top of the stairs was so far up from where she sat that Ella could not make out many of the pirate's features, yet she saw the glint of the lantern light reflecting from the twin brass hooks at the pirate's left side. It was Killjelly. Ella sat petrified, without the presence of mind to find cover from Killjelly's prying light. But where would she hide, anyway?

Killjelly cast a brief glance down the staircase. Ella sat in breathless silence. Could he see her? Surely he had to be able to see her. Ella hoped that the darkness was thick enough that Killjelly could not see to the bottom of the stairs. Ella muttered a quick prayer.

"Lord, don't let him see!"

After a moment Killjelly turned away, holding his lantern before him as if he were gazing down another passageway.

"Ay then! This way, sure. After me, lads."

Killjelly disappeared, seeming to pass into another tunnel. Yet his was not the only light. As Ella sat there watching, several more pirates passed by the doorway at the top of the stairs, many holding lanterns of their own. Ella couldn't make out many of their features, but she was pretty sure that she identified the albino as he walked by. What of Longfinch? Ella couldn't tell if he was among the group or not. There were probably only a dozen pirates shuffling past the doorway, and if Longfinch was not among them, then where was he? Had Ernest killed him with that gun he fired?

As quickly as they came, the lights disappeared again, and Ella sat in total darkness once more. Straining her ears, Ella could just make out the sound of the pirates' boots shuffling through the passageway above her, their low voices dying away into silence.

Ella took a deep breath. So, she was not alone in these tunnels after all. She was no longer safe just sitting here. Suppose the pirates came back? Really, she had sat at the bottom of this stair for too long already. It was time for her to act. It was time for her to do something.

But what was she to do? Obviously, she must find her way out of this darkness, but how? Her only fear in retracing the passageway back to the Pickering manor was running into the pirates again, yet they seemed to be moving deeper into this maze of passages. In that case, finding her way back to the basement would be the safest thing, as that would be the direction the pirates were not heading. The only question that remained was could she retrace her steps to the Pickering basement in sheer darkness? And even if she could, had the pirates closed the door behind them? How would she get the door open?

But then there was the matter of Ernest. Surely she would have to take him with her — it was the least she could do for the poor gnome after he saved her from the pirates. Yet what *was* she supposed to do with him? He seemed so completely unconscious that Ella wasn't sure if she could wake him or not. Still, it was worth a try.

Ella reached out with her hands, feeling for Ernest. She quickly found his shoulders and then shook him forcefully.

"Ernest!" she whispered. "Ernest, can you hear me?"

She continued shaking him for some time, yet Ernest made no signs of waking up. What if he were in a coma? She had read about people sleeping for days in a coma — or worse, never waking up at all. Ella felt her former panic coming over her again. No, she couldn't go there. She couldn't let herself lose her head.

"Oh God, please help me now," she breathed.

Just saying that helped to calm her panic a good deal. After all, if God had so clearly come to her and comforted her just a moment ago, would He really desert her now?

It was no good just sitting here. She may as well do something. Ernest would wake up eventually. Standing slowly to her feet, Ella stretched her hands out in both directions. She hoped she might feel a wall — or something — in the darkness, to give her an idea of her surroundings. However, all she could feel around her was that same cool, stagnant air.

In front of her, Ella knew there was a stairway. So what was behind her? She walked slowly backwards, her arms still spread wide, reaching, hoping, aching, to feel something — anything — in that total darkness. With each step, she still felt nothing. She could almost believe that there was nothing in this darkness, that she was standing in an eternal void with only the stone floor beneath her feet. Ella shuddered at this thought. Of course, that couldn't be true. Of course, there were walls to this place... somewhere. She tried to remember what her surroundings had looked like in the light from Killjelly's lantern, yet the stairway was all that she remembered.

Still, Ella continued to edge backwards. She could imagine a great chasm in the floor behind her and wondered what she would do if she took a step and her foot landed on empty air. She forced this thought out of her mind. There was nothing she could do about it, and no way to know if there was a chasm behind her, so she had best not worry about it.

Now a more rational thought came to her. She was backing up directly away from the stairway. Suppose then that she was in a very straight passageway and she was simply walking down it? If that were the case, she might walk for a long time before she reached a turn in the passageway and thus bumped into a wall.

Really, all she needed to do was to find a wall. If she was indeed in a passageway, then she would only need to take a few steps to her left or right in order to find a wall. Then again, she might be in a room, and the walls to either side of her might be just as far away from her as the wall behind her.

If she was in a room, how large must it be? Ella couldn't think exactly how she should know. If only she had counted her steps! As it was, she had only a vague feeling of how far she had walked away from Ernest, but she also suspected that her idea of how far she had walked was probably too large, being skewed by her worry, hesitation, and the darkness.

The genuine danger would be if she was in a sizeable room and began walking too far to either her left or right and then lost track of where Ernest was lying in the darkness. As long as she backed straight up, even if she didn't know how far, she need only walk straight forward again and she would find Ernest and the stairway. If she was in a passageway after all, then she had no fear of losing her way to the left or right, as the passageway would easily lead her right back to Ernest.

But how could she know if she was in a passageway or a large room? Perhaps she should take ten more steps, and if she had not reached a wall yet, she would walk straight to her right. She would count her steps carefully so that she could find her way back to where she was now, and that way she could still find her way back to Ernest.

Deciding that this was the best thing for her to do, Ella continued to walk backwards. One... two... three steps...

She had hardly taken six more steps before her back touched something cold and smooth. Feeling a bit relieved and excited, she turned around and felt the wall with both of her hands. Sure enough, it felt like the same smoothed granite as everything else in this catacomb. There! Now she had reached a wall. Did that mean she was in a room?

Ella, with her left hand touching the wall and her right hand stretched out in front of her, began walking steadily to her right, counting her steps carefully. She placed her feet one after another, touching the heel to the toe of the next with each step. That way, she could be sure that all of her steps were the same size, as each of her steps would be the length of her foot.

At her seventeenth step, she reached another wall. This was clearly the corner of a room. Now Ella walked along this wall — thirty-two steps — until she reached the next corner, crossing over a doorway of some sort at step eleven. Pretty certain now that she was on the side of the room that the stairway was on, Ella walked along this wall. Sure enough, at step eighteen the wall fell away, and, reaching down, Ella could feel the first steps of the stairway to her left and the warm body of Ernest to her right. Good! She had not lost her way.

After a moment's consideration, Ella continued to walk along the wall, past the stairway. After fourteen steps, she reached another wall. Following this, and passing across another doorway, Ella reached the far wall again in thirty-two steps. Clearly then, she was in a moderately large, roughly square room — thirty-two steps one way, and thirty-two the other.

Ella walked back along the walls until she reached Ernest again. At least she knew what her surroundings were like. But what was she to do with Ernest now?

At that moment, Ella could feel her heart pound heavily in

her chest, and she trembled all over. Sweat formed on the palms of her hands, and her throat went dry. What was going on? Ella strained her ears in the darkness, but could hear nothing.

Dread was coming over her. She felt as if some sinister essence had just entered the room. Ella looked around, but she could see nothing. The darkness was closing in on her again, like jaws closing around her feeble body. This was exactly how she had felt when Pastor Daerl confronted that *thing* behind the door! Ella's heart sank to her toes. She *was* behind the door now. Whatever that *thing* was, it was in this maze of tunnels with her.

Just then, Ella heard the sounds of labored breathing from the far side of the room, right about where she had felt that first doorway. The sound was like the gasping of a man about to die, or else the choked and gurgling breaths of a rabid animal. Ella shuddered all over. That was not Ernest's breathing. It was that *thing!* It was in the room with her.

The sound of this breathing was clear in the silence, and a rush of cold air blew over Ella. She trembled, petrified in terror. Her heart pounded in her ears like beats on a great drum. But what was that now? Could she hear chanting far, far away, or was that still the sound of breathing?

That breathing grew louder, as if that *thing* was coming closer. What had it said to her earlier? That there was nothing she could do to escape it? Was it going to kill her? Her tongue clung to the roof of her mouth. She could not cry out or scream. She could only shake in fear.

"Ella Pickering."

The voice that spoke was dry and husky, sounding more like the voice of a beast than a man. Ella clasped her clammy hands together, sweat trickling down her back. How did this *thing* know her name?

The voice chuckled in the darkness, and Ella smelt a whiff of sulfur in the stale air.

"You are not the first Pickering to cross my path." Again, the thing chuckled.

Now Ella heard a dreadful scraping noise, like the sound of fingernails scraping against stone. Her knees buckled, as if she were about to pass out.

"Did you get my note?" the voice asked.

Again, Ella smelled the scent of sulfur, though this time she could feel a breath of hot air on her cheeks. Was the *thing* so close to her then that she could feel its breath? Ella tried to take a step backwards, but something cold closed over her wrist. It felt like a claw, at the same time both rotting, yet full of virile strength.

"Poor Ella," the thing hissed, its hot breath on her ear. "You never knew your father, did you? But I knew your father well! Wouldn't you love to know what I know? But I forget myself — I already wrote to you about it."

Ella shook all over, sweat now pouring down the back of her neck. Bile rose in her throat at the touch of this dreadful thing. Her knees were buckling. A deep sense of dread washed over her. She was totally at the mercy of this dreadful *thing*. There was nothing she could do.

"O God–!"

That was the only thing Ella could make her mouth say, yet even as she spoke it, the thing released its hold on her wrist. A wild snarl sounded in the darkness, and again Ella could smell sulfur in the air.

"He will not save you. He can not hear you now!"

Ella trembled all over, and her heart pounded in her chest. That thing was still near her, but why had it let go of her? Was the name of God so distasteful to it? Suddenly, she remembered the hymn that the Blaeith family had taught her on the first night she had spent in their house. The words came unbidden to her lips, as her tongue suddenly came free. She sang now in a low, halting voice:

*"The love of God expels the da'kest places,*
*All shadows fall befo'e His many g'aces.*
*And in His p'esence eve'y fea'h is banished,*
*Within His comfo'ts, sorrows swiftly vanish."*

As she sang, she felt a great freedom washing over her. She could still hear the breathing of that *thing* in the room with her, and she could smell the sulfur of its breath, but her heart no longer pounded in her chest, for now there was another Presence in this room. There was a bright Presence which made the labored breathing halt and hesitate. Ella couldn't help but smile. She could feel that same pleasant, warm feeling that she had felt earlier. It was the presence of God, yet now it seemed to be inside her — emanating from her. Her fear completely dissolved, and she turned to face the sound of the labored breathing. She was singing now at the top of her lungs.

*"Then what to Him are all the wo'ldly wiles?*
*For He will keep me th'u' my eve'y t'ial.*
*No sin, o'h so'ow, man, o'h devil's scheming,*
*Can w'est me from my Fathe'h's loving keeping.*

*"Oh, Lo'd, I look to You! Be my defende'h,*
*A'ay You'hself in You'h victo'ious splendo'h.*
*And then foreve'h I will sing You'h p'aises,*
*When You'h g'eat love consumes the da'kest places."*

At this last word, a sudden, unearthly wail filled the room, something between the scream of a wounded horse and the howl of a starving lion. Ella could feel a chill run down her spine at the noise, but at the same instant she felt a flush of triumph. She could hear the labored breathing let out an injured hiss, and then there was the sound of scraping — claws against the granite floor — as the *thing* scurried away down the passageway whence it came.

"You will never be rid of me! You belong to me — just as your father belongs to me!"

Ella let out a great laugh, not in merriment, but in triumph. God was with her! What was she afraid of?

At that moment, Ernest let out a cry and gasped for breath.

So *now* he was awake.

# OUR DAILY BREAD

*H*aeli was falling, falling, falling. All she could feel around her was the rushing of wind. She was surrounded by utter, eternal blackness. But where was she falling to? What had she fallen from? Was she falling at all? Perhaps she was merely floating, suspended in an everlasting void. But how had she gotten there?

Now she could hear something above the sound of the rushing wind. What was it? It sounded almost like the sound of a great canvas flapping in the wind. Or perhaps it was the sound of wings, very large wings. Was it that Eagle Griffin again? Had he come back?

Suddenly, there was a flash of light in the darkness, a small ray cutting across her face like the slash of a sword. As she blinked stupidly in the sudden light, Haeli saw a great reptilian creature floating just above her. It was a pteranodon, though she had never seen it from so close, with its membranous wings, its scaly body, and its strange, beak-like head. It looked at her with wild eyes.

Haeli let out a startled cry. The reptile opened its mouth, revealing two lines of razor-sharp teeth. It was going to eat her.

As the pteranodon leaned close to her with its open mouth, instead of sinking its teeth into her, it breathed out a stream of fire. Haeli shrieked and turned away, but she found the fire rushing up to meet her from the other direction as well. Yet this was not just fire. She could hear, amidst the crackling and spitting of normal fire, screams, and howls of agony. This was the mouth of hell, yawning up at her.

She writhed and clawed at the air, trying to get out of the way, trying to move. But the wind continued to rush past her. She was still falling, falling, falling, and hell was waiting for her.

She covered her face with her hands. Perhaps if she did not look, this nightmare would end. Yet as soon as she could not see anymore, the sensation of the rushing of wind stopped. She could feel something else under her now. It was solid, flat, and cold.

Slowly and carefully, Haeli took her hands from her eyes. Before her, she could see the dim light of the moon shining through a window. All around her, there were shelves and barrels. She was sitting on the ground in the storage room of her father's fort.

No! How had she ended up here? Why was she here? Just in front of her, Haeli saw an obscure bundle stretched out on the floor. At first glance, she knew exactly what it was.

She wanted to turn her eyes away; she wanted to run. She wanted to wake up — but she could not. Her eyes were riveted to the scene before her, as if something were holding them in place. Haeli's body moved without her bidding. Slowly, she crept towards the obscure bundle.

No! Haeli, stop! Don't go any further! You know what it is. You do not have to see it. You do not want to see it.

But still her body continued to creep forward until she was kneeling right next to the obscure bundle. It was a body, a human body. Of course it was! She knew that already. Why had she come to look at it? She knew who it was. Why couldn't she

look away? Why couldn't she run? Why couldn't she turn her mind to something else?

But her eyes slowly looked over the body until they came to rest on the face. It was her Da — her own dear Da!

But who else would it be? Of course, it was her Da. She could hardly have a dream now without him. But why could she not look away? Why did her eyes force her to linger on her Da's dead face? In her waking hours, she could control her body, she could control her mind. Why couldn't she in her dreams?

Then she heard a low and sinister snickering. Her eyes turned slowly towards the sound of the snickering, and Haeli saw a black form — a shadow almost — obscuring the moonlight before the window. It was narrow, dark, and baleful, but Haeli could not see its face. It was cloaked with darkness. The stench of sulfur filled Haeli's nostrils, and she coughed.

"What then?" the shadow said. "Did you really think I did not exist?"

---

HAELI WOKE WITH A START, a chill sweat covering her body. It was still very black outside, but she thought she could see the slightest hint of red light around her. Haeli groaned. She did not want to wake up. She felt more tired and achy now than she had before she fell asleep. Then again, what was the use of trying to doze off again? She would only have another of those terrible nightmares about her father and that... that... shadow-thing.

Haeli slowly opened her eyes all the way. The first thing that met her eyes was the foreboding shape of the Gwambi Tower. She closed her eyes again and groaned. Why had she ever thought it was a good idea to come to the Gwambi Tower? Why had she ever set out on this stupid trek?

Ella... responsibility... the keys... it all sounded silly to her now. But what else was she to do? She couldn't just forget about all of this and go home. There was no home waiting for her.

No, she had decided to climb the Gwambi Tower, so she would do just that. She would not second-guess herself now. She was not about to dredge up all of her reasons from last night and tell them over to herself. No, that would come too close to remembering. But that was not the right word. 'Reliving' was closer to it. She was not about to relive yesterday. Today was today, and that was enough for her.

Haeli rolled over and opened her eyes again. She was lying on a soft patch of grass — soft compared to the rest of the mountain ridge. She tried to remember exactly what had happened the previous evening. Martyn, Aarushi, and Halfdan had left, going back to Entwerp for provisions, but Haeli couldn't remember them returning. Nor, for that matter, could she remember falling asleep. She had probably dozed off while she waited. Then who had wrapped this blanket around her? Certainly, she didn't have it with her when she climbed the mountain. A light breeze brushed past her cheeks, and she shivered, pulling the blanket around her more tightly. Anyway, she was glad to have it now.

Tiya-Aenji was sleeping next to her, wrapped up in a similar blanket. Not too far away, Haeli could see the shapes of Martyn and Titus sleeping on the ground themselves. Titus was snoring rather loudly. In the midst of all four of them, lay two small packs — these must be the supplies which Martyn brought back with him from Entwerp.

Looking to the horizon, Haeli could see a hint of rose-gold forming far away to the east. The only other lights in the sky were the thousands of stars which looked down, winking at her. This, however, was not enough light to make out anything distinctly. The mountains, the surrounding ridges, the trees, and the bay below were just dark shapes of varying shades of blackness.

If she looked closely towards the bay, though, she could just make out a dim glow from behind the ridge which obscured her view of Entwerp Coastal. Was the village still burning? Looking back to the west, Haeli could see a few lights in the dale below, most likely coming from the few houses in Entwerp Proper which were awake at this early hour.

Another breeze passed over the ridge — this one stronger than the last — and Haeli shivered. It was freezing this morning, so high in the mountains. Had it frosted? She couldn't tell in the dim light.

Haeli slowly stood to her feet. If she was going to be awake, she might as well move around and try to stay warm. Haeli walked slowly up to the packs which Martyn had brought back with him. She was curious about what provisions he had stuffed in them, but to open them and look inside would mean bringing her hands out from under her warm blanket. No, she had best simply walk along the ridge for a bit, stretching her legs and getting her blood to circulate.

Someone stirred behind her, and Haeli looked over to see Martyn rubbing sleep from his eyes. He let out a tremendous yawn and then stood to his feet, looking suddenly very alert. He smiled at Haeli as he folded up his blanket and put his tricorn hat on.

"Ye could no sleep?"

Haeli shook her head.

Martyn nodded sympathetically. "Ye gard as if ye'll are freezin', Haeli. Vene along then. We ha' best get a fire started."

So saying, Martyn walked over to a little fire ring which sat by the tower on the lee side of the wind. Haeli could now see a small pile of logs and kindling. How had that gotten there? Martyn must have made it ready last night before going to sleep himself.

As Martyn set the fire, Haeli slumped down at the base of the tower, feeling ashamed of her actions the night before. She had been a beast, not listening to anyone else or taking any time to see what they thought or felt. Yet all the time, Martyn had been looking out for her. He had even made sure that she — and all the others, too — would have a warm fire to wake up to.

She had acted like she was the only one doing something selfless by trying to help Ella, but every single person on the ridge with her right now was just as, if not more, selfless than her. After all, why was Titus here? He had tracked his step-daughter from the other side of the world, and even now, he didn't complain about sleeping on the hard ground. Tiya-Aenji was only there because Haeli had bullied her into coming. And Martyn — well, Martyn only ever acted in someone else's self-interest. Why did Martyn even put up with her?

Martyn now sat next to her with a contented sigh, watching the first few flames of the fire lick at the wood. He had no time to enjoy the fire, for at that moment Aarushi and Halfdan fluttered up, carrying a rabbit in each of their talons.

"I see we are in time for the breakfast," Halfdan said in his dull monotone.

Martyn nodded thankfully. "Ay that ye are."

Aarushi whistled and dropped the rabbits into Martyn's outstretched hand.

Pulling out his skinning knife, Martyn dexterously skinned and eviscerated three of the rabbits, leaving the last one whole for the two harriers to pick at. Spitting the three skinned rabbits on the ramrod for his rifle, Martyn hung them over the fire.

Haeli watched these preparations without a word.

After a few minutes, Halfdan cleared his throat. "You are all determined to enter the Gwambi tunnels?"

Martyn looked back at Haeli inquisitively, but she said nothing. Martyn nodded as he turned back to Halfdan. "I ha' no heard that the plan ha' changed at all."

Halfdan bobbed his head. "That is as I expected." He looked

at Aarushi for a moment before continuing, "We have seen the village — Entwerp Coastal."

Martyn sighed. "Is it bad then?"

"Yes," Halfdan replied. "I am afraid it is rather bad. I mentioned it because we harriers must consider where we may be of most use. It is our vocation, after all, to be at all times where we are most needed. That is why God separated us from the dumb beasts and endowed us with sapience."

Aarushi whistled in affirmation.

"You will no be venin' with us, then?" Martyn asked.

Halfdan shook his head. "The tunnels are no place for a bird. I must look to the village and see what help I may give."

"I understand," Martyn said. "If that's yer plan then, ye cen trive out my brother Clerans. I'm sure he would appreciate yer help."

Halfdan straightened up and spread out his wings. "Very good. I must leave at once, then. The lady Aarushi will stay with you until you enter the tunnels."

Aarushi whistled and nodded her head.

"Very well," Martyn said. "Thank ye fer yer help thus far, Halfdan. May ye be o' good service fer the defense o' the village."

Halfdan beat his wings with a flurry of feathers, and in a moment he was soaring high above the mountain ridge. He circled once around the tower and then floated down towards Entwerp Coastal, disappearing from sight behind the ridge.

Martyn leaned back against the Gwambi Tower contentedly, propping his feet up by the fire. Haeli could only stare into the fire. She really wished she could just sleep — sleep for a long time with no dreams.

"Ah, now," Martyn sighed, "is there any smell so grand as the smell o' roasted rabbits in a crisp morning's air on the mountain?"

Haeli smiled. She wanted to laugh. She wanted to come back with some witty reply that would make Martyn laugh. But the thought of Martyn laughing made her hear Tomas' laugh in her memory. A lump formed in her throat, and she couldn't swallow it down. That's all she had left of most of her family now — a memory of a laugh.

Haeli cut her thoughts short and looked away. She had to think of something — anything — to keep her mind from drifting back to the past. Looking towards the eastern horizon, she fixed her attention on the first few rays of the sun leaping up from behind the sea. All around her, the ground suddenly twinkled silver as the sunlight revealed the hoarfrost, which had grown overnight like lichen.

Why did the morning have to look so beautiful? It was as if the entire world were happy, as if the world *enjoyed* turning and the sun *enjoyed* rising. Couldn't they see that everyone down here was suffering? Couldn't the sun, the stars, and the earth — just for once — be a little more depressed?

Martyn gave a wide smile, closing his eyes and breathing deeply.

"What a morning, ay?"

Suddenly Martyn's face contorted, and he flinched. "That's smoke I smell, is no it?"

Haeli blinked. "Smoke?"

Martyn stood suddenly, his eyes going wild. "Wood smoke. Wood smoke. It's—" Here he suddenly cut off, falling to his knees, and vomiting onto the ground.

Haeli was too stunned to respond. What was happening?

After a moment, Martyn stumbled back to her, slumping on the far side of the fire.

"Sorry," he mumbled, wiping his mouth. "It wos jist the smell o' the fire... It set me off... reminded me..." And he cast a look towards Entwerp Coastal. Smoke tendrils rose from below, standing out starkly in the pure light of dawn. So the village really was still burning.

Haeli took a deep breath. "How many people do you think died last night — good people, I mean, not the pirates?"

Martyn hunched over, repressing a shudder. "A merri too many."

Haeli looked at him closely for a moment before looking away. "Do you need a hug?"

Martyn snorted. "A hot meal an' a bath, more like."

Haeli suddenly thought back to that warm bath that Mrs. Blaeith gave her after the pirates assaulted her in the alley, and she gave an involuntary shudder. "I know what you mean."

Martyn wiped his hands over his face. "I'm sorry, Haeli. I should no be like this. I should be happy." He blew out his lips, then took a deep breath. "God is good, an' He is in control o' this."

Haeli wanted to spit. "That's literally the definition of spiritual bypassing, Martyn."

Martyn did his best to force a smile, but it wasn't convincing. "But God *is*, is no He?"

Haeli snorted. "You have every right to vomit right now, Martyn. No one expects you to be happy."

Martyn prodded at the fire with his boot. "An' this is where ye give me yer mother's lecture about yer emotions being like horses, and you outta-should ride them and no' pen them away?"

Haeli gave a mirthless chuckle, staring into the fire herself. "Very wise woman, my mother."

Martyn suddenly frowned. He regarded Haeli closely for a moment and then looked away.

"What?"

Martyn shrugged. "Nothing. It is no really my place."

Haeli arched an eyebrow, simply staring at Martyn.

Martyn didn't meet her gaze for a moment, and at last he held up his hands. "It's jist — are ye followin' her advice, yerself?"

Haeli's stomach suddenly twisted into a knot. "What do you mean?"

Martyn waved a hand dismissively. "Look Haeli, I jist want to be sure ye are doing alright."

Haeli swallowed hard and stared into the fire.

Martyn took a deep breath. "God really is in control. Ye know that."

Something snapped inside Haeli. "God doesn't care."

Martyn blinked. "O' course God cares."

"God?" Haeli asked, her cheeks flushing with a sudden rage. "No. He doesn't care a hand's-breadth. If He cared, He would have answered me."

Martyn licked his lips slowly. "What did ye ask Him?"

Haeli glared at him for a long moment, tears suddenly obscuring her vision.

"'Why,'" she finally said. "I asked Him 'why,' and He still has not answered me."

To Martyn's credit, he waited several moments before speaking again. "Ye must be strong, tain courage, an' wait..."

"Do not say it!" Haeli snapped angrily.

Martyn took a deep breath, as if he were plunging into a lake. "Haeli, I think ye either need to ride these emotions till they are all spent, like yer Ma says, or salve them up with some spiritual by-passing." He gave a hollow chuckle. "Like me." The smile he gave was forced. "Ye can no do neither."

Haeli looked away, focusing her attention on the steadily rising sun, and blinking the tears out of her eyes. "You know what Da would say about all this?"

Martyn swallowed. "I do no know."

Haeli cast him a bitter look, her voice sticking in her throat. "Well, that makes two of us."

# 25

# CHURCH COUNCIL

Clerans woke suddenly to the feeling of someone shaking him by the shoulder. Looking up and squinting against the sudden light, his mind struggled to explain what he was seeing. A man in a russet brown coat and a wide-brimmed hat was leaning over him. His coat parted briefly, giving Clerans a glimpse of pistol-butts, and the hilt of a saber. Suddenly, Clerans sat bolt upright, wide awake. It was a dragoon — one of the Lord Protector's own Federal Dragoons.

How long had he slept? The sun looked as if it had risen a few hours ago. What had happened while he was asleep? Had the dragoons attacked the strikers in the bank? Surely any fighting would have woken him. Clerans glanced about him, seeing Lexi still at her post behind the upturned wagon. Olyfr lay in a bundle of coats nearby, fast asleep next to the wounded men he had been tending to the night before.

"There, now," the dragoon said with a smile. "I trust that ye restit well, whatever?"

Clerans nodded, hurriedly standing up and straightening his clothing. What he wouldn't give for some kind of uniform right now. But he was militia through and through. He could only hope he didn't look too shabby to this dragoon. "Ay, sir, an' what are my orders, sir?"

He tried to smile and look confident.

"No orders, no orders," the dragoon assured him, "that was not what I was wakint ye for. But there is a council av war, look ye, and Caedmon Wilkins wants a representative av the dike militia for the discussionation."

Clerans blinked. "Lord Protector Wilkins?" For a moment, he couldn't think of anything more to say. "But...the dike militia...I'm..."

"The only one left," Lexi cut in.

Clerans' stomach lurched. "The only one left." He suddenly felt exhausted all over again, slumping over as the memories of Sheriff Laei, and Meriwedhr, and Mr. Gingrich, and all the others washed over him.

"Yo ho!" the dragoon exclaimed, catching Clerans by the shoulders to steady him. "None av that now! Look ye, I'll be sure to see you rested wanst ye give yer report to the lord protector."

"Caedmon Wilkins?" Clerans said, swallowing heavily. "He is here, then?"

"Ay," the dragoon replied, "he and Captain Smydhac, and the governor, look ye, and 'heir waitint on ye for to begin."

Clerans took one deep breath, quickly strapped his weapons back on. The dragoon waved him to follow, and turning a corner in the street, Clerans found five other dragoons, all mounted on stocky horses. Taking the reins of his horse from one of his companions, the dragoon mounted, and offered a hand back to Clerans.

"Ye will have to ride behind me, look ye."

Clerans nodded, but just as he took the dragoon's hand to haul himself up behind the man's saddle, a loud cough sounded behind him.

Turning quickly, Clerans found Sydni and Nōli standing there, arms crossed, and glaring.

"We is of coming together with you," Sydni said, eyes narrowed.

The dragoon furrowed his brow, looking back at Clerans. "Are they part av yer militia, too?"

Clerans sighed. "It's complicated."

Sydni eyed him closely, raising an eyebrow.

"Ye'd best bring them along, too." Clerans hauled himself onto the horse behind the dragoon. "If there is room?"

The ride back to Entwerp Coastal did not take long. The dragoons set their chargers at a quick trot, and before long, Clerans was crossing through the canyon and emerging on the other side of the mountains.

As the crags on either side of the canyon fell away, Clerans craned his head around the dragoon to better observe the scene which spread out before him. The road stretched out before them, winding down into the mass of houses and shops below, where it diverged into the village's many streets, alleyways, and terraces. The village itself seemed to sit poised on the steep slopes of the mountains' feet, its dikes and terraces looking as if any moment they might slide into the black mouth of the bay.

Great billows of smoke rose from the Lower Village, and even from this distance, Clerans could smell the acrid hint of burning wood in the air. He bit the inside of his cheek in disgust. The Lower Village was where all the new wooden houses were. A fire would nearly decimate that section of the village. It was hard to tell if any fire still burned, however.

Smoke rose from the Upper Village too, but the fires there were clearly less extensive. The houses and shops in that section of the village were mostly stone, after all, so the fire could only burn so much. With some satisfaction, Clerans noted that there was no smoke in the Old Village, or Coastal Village sections of Entwerp. Did that mean that the pirates had not made it that far? Or did it simply mean that the pirates could not get fires started amongst the low stone buildings of those areas?

The entire scene was eerily quiet. There was no bustle or murmur of voices as would usually fill the village at this time of the morning, but why should there be after such a night? More surprising to Clerans was that there was no sound of fighting. Where were the gunshots, the cannon fire? Were there still pirates in the village, or had the Indigies fought them off?

Clerans shook his head. He just had to get down there. That was the only way he would know what was going on in the village and what he could do about it.

At last the dragoons reined in their mounts in Merchani Square, in front of the Company offices. Clerans dismounted and the dragoon leader waved across the square towards the kirk.

"There ye are. 'Hey will be waitint for ye in there."

After taking a moment to see that his clothing was as presentable as he could manage, Clerans strode quickly across the square to the kirk. His heart was beating heavily in his chest. Was he really about to join in a war council with the lord protector himself?

Cautiously (almost reverently), Clerans climbed the steps on the outside of the kirk. Yet just as he reached out with his hand to push the door open, he heard webbed feet padding up the steps behind him. Clerans turned quickly to see Nōli and Sydni still dutifully following him.

"No here," Clerans said.

The two Indigies paused and looked up at him.

"You cen no follow me in here," Clerans said. "It is to be a war council. We cen no tain jist anyone cedin' in."

Sydni, evidently the mouthpiece of the duo, wrinkled up her brow in confusion. "But we is for to follow you. As declares of the Li."

Clerans shook his head. "I do no mind ye followin' me (even

if I'll do no know why this 'Li' told ye to), but ye may no follow me into the council."

Sydni nodded dutifully. "It is as you say. We will be for awaiting you without." And with that, she and Nōli backed away, seating themselves like miniature sentries on the bottom step.

Clerans turned back to the door and shook his head. What had he done to deserve these two Indigies' company? It was not a bad thing (Clerans supposed it might come in handy to have two little Indigie assistants with him at all times), yet it was awkward, all the same.

Clerans now pushed open the big oaken doors of the kirk and slipped inside. The light from the many stained-glass windows poured down upon a large table which stood at the front of the kirk just before the pulpit. Several men leaned over the table, while others sat in the pews of the kirk nearest to the front. As Clerans entered, walking down the center aisle towards the table, all the men present looked up at him.

Clerans recognized a few of those assembled, though most of them were unfamiliar to him. Governor Braedhwyc — standing by the table with two other men — was, of course, the foremost of those present whom Clerans knew. Then, too, Clerans noticed the Twengoli Chief (wasn't he called the Iasaqi-Woni?) sitting with great dignity on one of the pews with the shaman and a few of his brilliantly painted bodyguards. Clerans also noticed the harrier, Halfdan, who had accompanied Haeli and the Twengoli, standing on the table with a look of great sobriety.

With some surprise, Clerans recognized Mrs. Blysffi sitting in the pew beside the Iasaqi-Woni, Yohni (her Indigie ward) sitting close beside her. What were they doing here? And why were they with the other Indigies?

Of the other dozen or so men present, about half of them were in the gray uniforms of the Entwerpi regulars, while the other half wore the russet cloaks and greatcoats of the Federal Dragoons. Clerans, however, did not look too closely at these men, sitting as they were scattered across the front pews. His attention was focused on the two other men who stood with Governor Braedhwyc at the table. One of them was a very stocky man in the uniform of a dragoon, yet with a large red feather sticking out from his wide-brimmed hat. The other man was tall, broad at the shoulders, dark featured, and clean-shaven. He wore the same russet riding-cloak that the dragoons wore, though the rest of his uniform was gray like the regulars'. As Clerans entered, this man looked over at him with keen blue eyes.

Clerans' heart leaped to his throat – his pulse beating in his head. This man must be Caedmon Wilkins, the lord protector himself! Clerans hardly dared to take a step forward. What was he supposed to do in the presence of such a great man?

The man looked Clerans up and down closely. Clerans saluted as smartly as he could. What would he say if the lord protector asked him something?

The lord protector turned to Governor Braedhwyc. "The representative of the dike militia, I presume?"

Governor Braedhwyc nodded, wiping pus from his eye. "Ay, sir, Clerans Blaeith is his name, sir."

At his name, Mrs. Blysffi and Yohni turned around sharply, concern in their eyes as they looked him over.

The lord protector turned back to Clerans and looked him up and down again. His face betrayed no emotion. Clerans looked briefly down at his boots and noticed with some horror how disheveled and dirty his clothing was (smeared as it was with blood and other filth). He could feel his cheeks growing hot from embarrassment. How could he come in front of his Lord Protector looking like this? He felt starkly out of place next to all the regulars and dragoons in their clean, snappy uniforms.

The lord protector now spoke again, his accent clear — though now and then, Clerans detected a hint of the southerling brogue.

"We are glad that you could join us in the council, young Clerans. I confess, look you, I do not know how the dike militia has fared of late. You are the first I have met thus far. Tell me, look you, where have you all been?"

"I'm afraid, sir," Clerans replied, swallowing nervously, "I'm afraid, sir, that I am all that is left, sir."

The Lord Protector's eyes widened in a look of both astonishment and distress. "Ay-eigh! The entire dike militia slaughtered then?"

Clerans nodded. "All but my brother an' I, sir."

Mrs. Blysffi's eyes flashed, and she inhaled sharply.

Shaking his head ruefully, the lord protector said, "I see. I was not aware, look you, that when I asked for a representative of the dike militia, I was asking for the *only* member of the dike militia alive. Still, young Clerans, we are thankful to the Almighty God that He has preserved you to this day. And so we welcome you into this council — even if you are the youngest member present. Your very appearance speaks that you have done your duty in defending your home, and for that, you have earned a seat among the oldest of us."

Clerans nodded gratefully. He felt a little shaky.

Caedmon Wilkins motioned at the map that lay out on the table. "Young Clerans," he said, "please tell me exactly what happened at the beginning of last night. In particular, look you, I would like to hear every detail you can remember of the enemy's attack."

Clerans hurried forward. He could feel his knees shaking a little. What was he to say? He had never delivered an official military report before, especially not to the lord protector of the entire nation!

Taking a deep breath, Clerans looked over the map carefully.

It was a map of Entwerp Proper, Entwerp Coastal, the bay, and the surrounding roads. After taking one more breath to brace himself, he pointed to the battery (or where the battery had once stood) on the map.

"The pirates sent a fire-ship, sir, straight towards the battery. Sheriff Laei sent me to board the ship while he manned the battery. He told me, sir, that if I'll could no vert the ship aside from its course, I wos to give him the signal, an' he would open fire on the ship in hopes o' detonatin' the ammunition before it reached the battery."

"Very good," Caedmon Wilkins nodded, "A very sensible plan. I would have done the same."

This reaction from the lord protector encouraged Clerans. He breathed deeply and continued a little less stiffly. "Ay then, sir. Well, after boardin' the ship, I..." Clerans licked his lips. How much should he say about that pirate Ernest?

"Well, sir," Clerans said, "I got in a fight with the pirate who wos steerin' the ship, an' he threw me overboard a'fore I could vert the ship aside or give the signal to Sheriff Laei. Consequently, the fire-ship landed at the docks, here," Clerans motioned to the docks at the far northern end of the city below the battery. "When the fire-ship exploded, sir, it destroyed the foundations o' the battery, sir, and... well, ye cen see the remains o' that battery now, sir."

Caedmon Wilkins nodded gravely. "It was with some great astonishment myself that I heard that the renowned Entwerp Battery was destroyed. Look you, it was very hard to believe."

"Ay, sir," Clerans said, glancing up from the map for the first time to look the lord protector in the face. "I ha' served as barrel monkey a merri o' an times in that battery, an' never did I think that a pirate could bring it down so celerly."

*Clerans Gives His Report*

"Still," Caedmon Wilkins replied, "we might have guessed that Captain Longfinch would be capable of such a bold and seemingly impossible feat. This is not the first time for him to accomplish the impossible. Look you, he is a master of strategy."

Halfdan cocked his head to one side. "God, and God alone, can accomplish the truly impossible. Man may only do what is *seemingly* impossible."

"Were ye at the dike defenses, younker?" Captain Smydhac asked, clearly ignoring Halfdan's remark. "What happened there?"

"Ay," Governor Braedhwyc agreed, wiping pus from his bad eye, "I am merri interested myself as to how the defenses crumbled."

Clerans swallowed. All the horror and bloodshed of the previous night suddenly washed down upon him. He bit the inside of his cheek, taking a moment to compose himself. After taking a deep breath and looking back down at the map to avoid the eyes of his three commanders, Clerans resumed his report.

"The pirate man-o-war was hovin' in towards the Fisher's Docks, here," he pointed to the place on the map. "We took our stand along the dike wall."

Clerans paused and swallowed. In the ears of his memory, he could still hear the deafening pounding of the cannonade mingled with the pitiable groans and shrieks of wounded men. Clerans shuddered. He had to keep talking. Caedmon Wilkins needed to know what had happened. It was his duty to give the detailed report. He must not let himself shrink back from that horrendous memory.

"The fighting wos fierce and bloody, sir," Clerans' voice choked, but he forced himself to continue. He did not dare look up at the Governor, the dragoon captain, or the lord protector. He was certain that if he looked away from the map, he would lose all of his nerve.

"Sir, I wos in the back o' the line, so I did no see the whole engagement merri clearly, but I know the pirates were usin' some kind o' grenade made o' dynamite, I think. Yet then their captain called them to halt, an' issued a challenge to Sheriff Laei to engage in single-handed combat."

"Captain Longfinch did this?" Caedmon Wilkins broke in.

Clerans still did not look up, but he shook his head. "No, sir, he called himself Vania... Vania Blood-something."

"Vania Bloodrummer," the lord protector said with a sigh. "Ay, that would be Longfinch's chief officer. Yet, look you, do you mean to say that Captain Longfinch was not the officer in charge of the attack on the dike wall?"

Clerans nodded again. "Ay, sir. It wos that Vania Blood-rummer who wos the only pirate officer at the dike, sir."

Caedmon Wilkins clicked his tongue contemplatively. "So the villainous captain had already split off from his crew *before* the attack."

Governor Braedhwyc nodded vigorously. "Ay sir, that must ha' been when he began his raid on the Pickering manor, where I trived him up."

"Yo-ho!" exclaimed the lord protector. "I am most interested to hear what transpired there, as I believe it may reveal Longfinch's true aim in all of this. But, look you, let us first hear the rest of the account at the dikes." So saying, Caedmon Wilkins turned back to Clerans.

Clerans still kept his eyes focused downward on the map. Taking a deep breath, he continued. "I think that Vania Blood-rummer cheated, or anyway, he must ha', fer he beat the Sheriff in the duel, even though he outta-should ha' lost. Once the Sheriff wos dead, the pirates charged us again. We formed our lines an' returned fire, but then another group o' the pirates attacked us from behind. Somehow they must ha' outflanked us while the Sheriff and Vania were fightin'."

Clerans took another deep breath. He really didn't want to continue, but he knew he had to. "We were trapped, sir, or about to be, an' my father tained the foresight to get out o' the envelopment. He gave the orders to follow him so that we could resume our stand where we could better defend ourselves."

"Where then did you retreat to?" Caedmon Wilkins asked.

Clerans pointed to the Dike Plaza, where the dikes of the Lower and Upper Villages joined. "Here, sir. We thought we could hold them off on the upper dikes. Yet when we were almost there, they ambushed us again. Me, my brother, and five others escaped the ambush an' made fer Newcourt, here," again Clerans pointed to the spot on the map.

"The pirates laid an ambush fer us there, too, sir," Clerans continued, "but we saw it in time an' retreated to the Upper Court — here — jist a'fore the pirates got there themselves. After that, sir, I do no know what happened to the rest o' the dike militia, if there wos anyone else. We ceived cover in the tailor shop — here — an' defended it desperately until my brother an' I were the last men standing. We would ha' been killed ourselves ha' no the Twengoli arrived jist then and rescued us."

"Ay!" Governor Braedhwyc added, motioning to the Iasaqi-Woni, who was sitting somberly on one of the front pews. "We owe our current position entirely to our friend and ally here: the Iasaqi-Woni of the Twengoli tribe. Without his counterattack on the pirates, we would ha' lost the entire village."

Caedmon Wilkins nodded to the nymph chieftain courteously. "I thank you, sir, for your timely assistance in this campaign. We owe you a deep debt of gratitude."

The Governor translated this into Tylweni for the Iasaqi-Woni, and the great chief nodded back to Caedmon Wilkins politely.

"*Efybsaeiwsas eyl peyswsey faelei swt meba swmaechthw 'ne*" the Indigie war-lord said and then pronounced an unending string of Tylweni words. Clerans tried his best to follow, but could only pick up a pronoun here and there. The great chief was certainly using courtly vocabulary which Clerans was not familiar with.

Thankfully, Governor Braedhwyc translated. "The Iasaqi-Woni says that he is delighted and humbled to at last meet the great Supreme Chief o' the east folk. He wishes ye a long life, fair health, an'... well, sir — to translate the phrase literally — he wishes ye the mushroom. He says also that he is happy to aid us in our fight, and he considers us as blood-brothers in our feud against the pirates."

The Iasaqi-Woni nodded regally, seeming to understand that the governor had finished translating his speech, for now he spoke again. This time, Clerans caught the word 'pirate' (in the common tongue) amidst the Tylweni words.

Governor Braedhwyc wiped pus from his bad eye as he translated again. "The Iasaqi-Woni has offered to cooperate with our warriors for the pirates' destruction."

Caedmon Wilkins nodded. "Please tell him again that we are honored to have him as our ally in this fight. We accept his offer. And please tell him in the most respectful way you know. I would have him understand how much we respect his aid, look you."

The governor translated what Caedmon Wilkins said, and again the Iasaqi-Woni nodded somberly.

As the governor finished, Caedmon Wilkins addressed him again, "With that, Governor, tell me what our position is in the village now."

The Governor cleared his throat to answer, yet just before he spoke, the great oak doors at the front of the kirk burst open loudly. Turning suddenly, Clerans saw two men dressed in the gray uniform of the regulars, marching briskly and hurriedly into the sanctuary. One of the two men held a roll of paper in his hand. They advanced quickly to the front of the room. Clerans slowly backed away from the table and took his seat on the nearest pew.

The two regulars saluted Captain Smydhac, Caedmon Wilkins, and Governor Braedhwyc smartly. The one with the roll of paper handed it to the governor.

"The tally, sir!" he announced.

Then, just as briskly and suddenly as they had entered, the two regulars marched back out of the kirk, the *tramp, tramp, tramp,* of their boots echoing in the high vaults of the ceiling.

# 26

# YOU ARE NOT ALONE

*E*rnest sat bolt upright, sweat pouring down his face. What had he been dreaming about? It must have been a nightmare. His heart pounded loudly in his chest, and he was gasping for breath. He looked around wildly, trying to regain his bearings, but it was just as dark as if his eyes were closed. He waved his arms and touched something nearby. It felt warm — like a living thing. Almost as soon as Ernest touched it, he jumped back.

"Who's there?" he screamed. "What do you want?"

"Sh! E'nest!" a voice replied in an urgent whisper. "Not so loud!"

That was Ella's voice! But of course it was. After all, he had dragged her down here. It would only make sense if she were with him when he woke.

But why was he so shaken? What had set him on edge?

"Sorry," Ernest said, in a much lower voice now. "I don't know why I'm so riled up. I'm shaking all over. It's like I haved a nightmare or something of the sort."

"No," Ella replied quietly. "It wasn't a nightma'e, it was... it was a..." She trailed off.

Ernest groped around some more, finally standing slowly to his feet. "It was a what, now?"

Ella seemed to hesitate. Ernest peered into the darkness where he could hear Ella's voice, but he couldn't see her.

"I think it was a ghost," Ella finally said.

Ernest jumped. "A ghost? You don't mean there's a ghost down here with us?"

"Well," Ella replied, "that's the best I can make of it."

Ernest continued to stare in Ella's general direction. It was strange how this young woman talked. She seemed calm, and even confident. If there really was a ghost in this darkness, they were all as good as dead. How could she be so calm about it?

Ernest cleared his throat. "Now you are certain that there is a ghost?"

"Oh, yes," Ella replied. "If not a ghost, then some other demonic powe'h."

Ernest paused for a moment. That didn't sound any better. "Does that concern you?"

"I don't know," Ella replied. "He a'eady came fo'h us, but I sang a hymn and he left us."

Ernest raised an eyebrow. "You singed to him?"

"Yes," Ella replied. "God was with me. I mean, He w'eally was w'ight he'e with me. And I guess He chased the ghost away."

Ernest looked at her critically, though he knew that Ella couldn't see the expression of incredulity on his face. This didn't seem likely. Perhaps Ella had knocked her head when they tumbled down the steps and she had just dreamed this all up. After all, why would a hymn scare off a creature as supernaturally terrifying as a ghost?

Even as he thought it, Ernest remembered how the albino had collapsed to his knees when that satyr spoke to him. What was it that satyr had said? Something about rebuking by the authority of the Almighty God? The albino could break through solid oak doors, fell trees, dim the stars, and even enter the minds of people — Ernest had watched him do all of these things. So why would a few words from a satyr make the albino hesitate, unless there was some real — and mighty — power in them?

Yet hadn't Lewis told him that the followers of the true God had defeated demons by simply invoking His name? If that was true, there *must* be some great power in Him. If Ella was right, and God was *with* her, then perhaps she hadn't dreamed it after all. Maybe she had frightened a ghost away in the same way that the satyr had frightened the albino. But what did Ella mean that God had been *with* her? How could God be *with* anyone? Wasn't He in heaven?

There! His eyes must be adjusting now. Ernest could now make out the outline of Ella standing before him.

"Ah," Ernest sighed. "Now I can see you. I think I'm getting used to this darkness."

Ella recoiled. "Oh no, it's not you — the'e's a light!"

These words were hardly out of her mouth when another voice sounded in the darkness.

"Eh? What was that? Do'ed you hear something?"

The voice spoke from a little way off, and Ernest turned to face it. He could just make out a doorway in the face of the granite wall before him. There seemed to be the smallest hint of a light emanating from this doorway.

"What now?" It was a second voice speaking. "I do'edn't hear anything."

"Shush now!" the first voice replied. "Listen!"

There was silence for a few moments, but Ernest could tell that the light was becoming brighter now.

"Here now!" a third voice hissed. "We have to get back to Longfinch. There's no point in getting so far away."

"No, no, no," the first voice said. "I *hear'ed* something. We're going to find out what it was."

Just at that moment, Ernest saw a lantern appear on the

other side of the doorway. Three figures — clearly pirates, two of them hulking leprechauns, and one a man — stood behind the lantern, stepping in front of the doorway. Ernest gazed at them with wide eyes, for a moment petrified by their sudden appearance.

One of the leprechauns pointed a long finger at Ernest and Ella. "There now! What do'ed I say? It's that cook's mate and the girl."

Ernest quickly snatched Ella by the hand again and turned to run. But where would he run? By the lantern light, Ernest saw another stairway in the middle of the room, leading down into a black void below. Darkness. Yes, that's what they needed to escape from these pirates.

Ernest rushed forward, dragging Ella after him as he plunged down these stairs. Behind him, metal rang as one of the pirates drew his sword.

"After them!"

Ernest rushed forward, careening down the steps. He could hardly see anything now and suddenly realized that he might miss his step again and knock himself out. But he didn't dare to slow his pace; he couldn't let those pirates catch him. They'd kill Ella — or worse — and they'd probably kill him, too, after they had tortured him. He was defenseless as he was, without his pepper-box pistol loaded. All there was for him to do was to run. If he could evade these pirates and hide — even for a few minutes — he could get his pistol loaded. Then he might stand a chance.

Suddenly, he stepped forward but found that there was not a step in front of him; he was on level ground — a landing of some kind. Staggering a little in surprise, he rushed forward again, only to catch himself again as the passage before him fell steeply in another staircase. Ernest only just regained his balance before plunging down this second stairway.

Behind him, he could hear the sounds of the pirates rushing

down the steps. He dared not look back, lest he trip. Really, though, he couldn't see what was ahead of him, anyway. Just then, he heard a gunshot in the passageway, followed by the sound of a musket ball skittering and ricocheting down the stairs.

Now he stumbled out onto another landing. He tried to slow himself, in case there might be yet a third stairway in front of him, but there was no need, for at that moment, he crashed into a wall. Ernest groped desperately to his right, hoping that the passageway might continue in that direction. There wouldn't be a dead end right at the bottom of a stairway, would there?

Ah yes, the passageway continued to Ernest's right. He shuffled forward, moving as quickly as he dared. Another gunshot echoed in the darkness, and the ball struck the granite wall behind him.

There! His caution was rewarded: there was another stairway ahead of him. Ernest dragged Ella down this third stairway. When would this descent end? He really needed to find a place where he could hide for a moment and reload his pepper-box pistol. If only there were a side tunnel he could duck into. That would be perfect.

He felt with his right hand for the wall, still holding Ella's hand in his left. His fingers touched the wall to his right, and he could feel the smooth granite rushing along his fingers as he continued to rush down the steps. Then, suddenly, the wall to his right ended. It was not a passageway, but simply the end of the wall. Was there a chasm off the stairs to his right? If only he could see in this darkness!

After descending only a few more steps, he came to another landing. This time he caught his balance quickly, though Ella pitched forward. He pulled back on her hand just before she crashed to the ground on her face. Ernest could feel open, cool air in front of him and guessed that the passageway continued straight ahead. But what was off to his right? Why had the wall ended?

Ernest shuffled over to his right, reaching out with his hand and taking small enough steps that he could catch himself should the ground beneath him suddenly end. But no, there was the wall again. There must be a passageway going in the opposite direction from the main passage, though off to the side of the stairs.

He could hear the pirates behind him still, but he could not see their light yet. Perhaps they were not as mad as he, to go rushing pell-mell into the darkness.

Ernest quickly doubled back in the opposite direction, keeping to the far side of the passage from the stairway. He felt out with his right hand as he walked, and he could feel the stairs going up one step at a time. This would be perfect. The pirates would likely continue forward down the main passage. They wouldn't think to double back down this passage. Yet, even as he thought this, he felt the stone underneath the stairs suddenly give way to an entrance of some kind. This was even better! There was a small passageway leading underneath the stairway! This would be the perfect place to hide while he reloaded his pistol.

Pulling Ella after him, Ernest ducked inside this small passage beneath the stairs. The pounding of his pursuer's boots reached the top of the third stairway. They would be down in a moment.

# 27

# HEART OF STONE

aeli didn't meet Martyn's gaze again. She did her best to swallow back the lump in her throat, and vigorously scrubbed any tears that spilled over her face. But it was only a few moments before Titus and Tiya-Aenji edged up to the little campfire. Tiya-Aenji was staring closely at Haeli, while Titus cleared his throat awkwardly, and refused to look at either Haeli or Martyn. Neither of them seemed at all weary after spending the night in the open air. Haeli couldn't help but think how they looked too happy this morning, as well.

Titus coughed and glanced at the three roasting rabbits self-consciously. "Is that rabbit?" he asked.

Martyn nodded. "Ay, it is: rabbit roasted over cedar logs."

Titus let out a thrilled-sounding sigh. "Oh, there's nothing quite like it. It's so... eh... so good."

Martyn grinned and prodded the rabbit with his long knife. How could he go from nearly vomiting in grief to grinning so quickly? "An' ye are in luck then, as I think it is done."

And in no time at all, Titus and Tiya-Aenji were sitting before the fire themselves, cutting off pieces of the roasted rabbits and talking. Why did they have to be talking so much?

Really, it was Titus who was doing most of the talking. He had his feet propped up before the fire just like Martyn, and he was jabbering away like a drunken parrot. Martyn smiled and nodded the whole time while he, too, stuffed the roasted rabbit down his face.

"Roasted rabbit," Titus was saying glibly. "Yes, now that reminds me of the time four winters ago when I was out trapping in the mountains near Blisa. You see, eh... well, I was caught in a snowstorm while crossing the pass..."

Haeli watched them all in disgust. How could they be sitting there looking so cheery, like school children on a summer solstice? By looking at them, anyone might have guessed that they were just camping out on the mountain ridge for the fun of it.

They were about to embark on a dangerous journey to save Ella, for goodness' sake! Couldn't they all be a little more somber? Didn't any of them care about Ella, or was Haeli the only one?

"Well, I know now," Titus was still jabbering, "that it was a day and a night. Of course I, eh... I couldn't tell up there in the clouds, with the snow all around. I think they call it... call it... what was it now? Whiteout?"

Martyn nodded. "Ay, a whiteout? I ha' been in one o' them a'fore."

Titus nodded, stuffing more rabbit in his mouth. "Ah! Then you know exactly what a predicament I was in. But you see, after, eh... well, after all of that, I suddenly sniffed the air, and what do you think I smelled, but roasted rabbits!"

Martyn cut off one of the rabbit legs and offered it to Haeli. Haeli only stared back at him. She was not about to *eat*. That was the last thing she wanted to do right now.

"And it was Eunice's cottage I was smelling," Titus went on. "Eunice — eh, now, that is, eh... Ella's mother, you see... ah... and this was before we were married. You see, eh... well, she was cooking rabbit over her fire, and that was what I was smelling. And I do believe that saved my life. You see, eh, I couldn't see the cottage, but I could smell! So I followed that smell, eh... the smell of roasted rabbits, I mean..."

"Haeli," Martyn spoke softly, "you need to eat."

Haeli shrugged, not at all sorry that she was interrupting Titus' annoying story. "I really do not feel like eating."

Martyn nodded slowly. "Haeli, jist take the food and eat."

"I am sorry if I do not feel like stuffing my face while I listen to your silly conversation," Haeli murmured. She hadn't meant to say it so bluntly, but the words came out loud enough for all to hear.

Martyn, Titus, Aarushi, and Tiya-Aenji sat for a moment in stunned silence.

After a moment's pause, Martyn said, "Haeli, what is all o' this about?"

"What do you mean?" Haeli snapped, clenching her fists.

"This vening up to the tower, this insistence to enter the tunnel... what is all o' it about?"

"To save Ella, of course," Haeli replied.

Martyn shook his head. He was still holding out that roasted rabbit leg. "But what else?"

"What are you accusing me of?" Haeli asked defensively. "This has always been about saving Ella, and that is *all* it is about!"

Martyn only looked at her closely and pursed his lips.

Haeli shook her head angrily. "Why are we still sitting here, wasting time? Am I the only one who cares about Ella anymore? Why are the rest of you still dawdling? Come now: put out the fire! Let's get climbing that tower."

"Haeli!" Martyn said sternly, raising his voice just a little. Haeli drew back in alarm. Martyn had never raised his voice at her before. All of her resentment seemed to melt away in an instant. Was Martyn yelling at her?

Martyn held out the roasted rabbit's leg forcefully this time. He spoke in a level yet authoritative tone, "Haeli, ye are goin' to sit down an' eat this."

"But Martyn..." she began to object, but Martyn cut her off with a dismissive wave.

"I do no want to hear another objection from ye. Ye are exhausted, physically, mentally, an' emotionally. Ye are in *no* state to climb that tower. Ye need to eat."

Haeli looked at the roasted rabbit's leg disdainfully. Perhaps she should apologize for her harsh words, but she couldn't quite bring herself to it. She couldn't even bring herself to take the rabbit's leg from Martyn.

Martyn sighed. "Haeli, if ye'll will no eat, then I will ceive ye back to Entwerp right now. I cen tell ye are pale already from hunger an' exhaustion, an' if ye'll will no eat this now, then it is no safe fer ye to continue."

Slowly and bitterly, Haeli reached out and took the rabbit's leg from Martyn. As she chewed it slowly, she hardly dared to look him in the eye. The rabbit meat felt rubbery and tasteless in her mouth, and she could hardly choke it down. She could sense the gaze of Titus and Tiya-Aenji on the side of her head, and her face felt hot and flushed with shame. What a fool she had made of herself. Why had she even come on this stupid trek?

No, Ella was down there still. Ella needed their help. Haeli couldn't let her own damaged pride stop her from giving aid to Ella. She knew how to save Ella, and she had to do it — and if she had to eat some humble pie in the process, so be it. She'd probably come out better for it.

Martyn leaned forward now and put his hand on her shoulder. "Haeli, ye know I love ye like my own sister. I want to help ye, do no ye see that? I do realize that right now the help ye need an' the help ye want may be two merri different things."

Haeli choked down a piece of the bland rabbit meat, not daring to look up at Martyn.

"I am sorry," she whispered.

Haeli spoke in such a low voice that she was not at all certain that anyone heard her. Yet that was the best she could do. She couldn't bring herself to say it again.

"There's no easy way through this." Martyn squeezed her shoulder. "Maybe we cen both cry together when this is over." And he gave a hollow chuckle.

Haeli swallowed the rabbit meat. She had already lost control of her emotions once this morning, and look at what it had done: insulting Titus and Tiya-Aenji. No, she would not give her emotions rein again. Whatever her mother said, Haeli knew she could not let herself ride the horses of her emotions. That would only lead to her hurting people. From now on, she needed to be unfeeling, and strong. She needed to be stone.

2 8

# MEDIATOR

The governor slowly and somberly unrolled the piece of paper that the two regulars had given him. His face twitched as if in suspense, and he gave a great sigh.

"Well, sir," he said to the lord protector, "as ye asked what our position in the village is, this tally will help to tell ye."

Governor Braedhwyc shook his head and rolled the paper back up, turning to Caedmon Wilkins.

"After the Twengoli drove the pirates out o' the Old Village, the pirates put up their stand in Newcourt and Lower Court." The governor tapped on the map at the two plazas several times. As he continued his report, he pointed out each location as he named it. "With the help o' yer dragoons, sir, we forced the pirates away from the Fisher's docks — here — during the night."

"Are the Fisher's Docks the only place where the pirates might land their man-o-war for retreat or reinforcements?" Lord Protector Wilkins asked pointedly.

The governor shook his head. "No, sir, in a high tide ye cen make planks to a ship most anywhere along the dike. That is why my regulars an' I — with the help o' this harrier here —

conducted another counter-attack before sunrise this morning, sir, shortly, a'fore ye ceded to the village."

Halfdan nodded his head solemnly.

Clerans blinked. So the dragoons had been busy in the village all night, then. What of the strikers? Had the dragoons indeed made no more move on the bank?

Governor Braedhwyc now directed the Lord Protector's attention to the map again. "We ceded down from the north — here — right at the docks, an' we pushed down hard an' desperately along the dike wall, through the Dike Plaza. We tained cannons to support us, an' we drove the pirates back. We could no ceive back any o' the streets further into the Upper Village, but at least we now hold the entire dike wall between my regulars, yer dragoons, an' the Twengoli."

Caedmon Wilkins stared at the map closely, as if he were carefully considering every location the governor pointed out. "Then the pirates are cut off from their ship?"

The governor nodded, wiping pus from his bad eye. "Ay sir, that wos my intention. I wished to isolate them a'fore they tained time to settle into their position. We tain them surrounded now."

"Yo-ho! Well done, governor," Caedmon Wilkins said, rapping his knuckles on the table. "Our position is certainly less desperate than I was afraid."

"Then again, look ye," Captain Smydhac said with a wry smile. "Ye do always fear the worstest, sir."

The dragoons all chuckled.

Caedmon Wilkins only smiled. "Optimistic-pessimism is what my father would have called it. It's a good military habit, look you, captain."

Then the lord protector turned back to the governor. "And what of the pirates then? How do they stand?"

The governor shook his head. "Well sir, they ha' tained all

night to dig in an' barricade their position. I am merri afraid that it will prove almost impossible to dislodge them now."

"Not impossible," Halfdan said in his dull monotone, "if God is against them."

"Very true," Caedmon Wilkins replied, a hint of a smile playing about the side of his mouth as he nodded at the harrier.

"And what was the tally ye just received?" Captain Smydhac asked.

The governor sighed deeply. "Ay then, sir, when we reclaimed the dike, we trived up the remnants o' the dike militia. I ha' no yet heard the full tally from the Fishers' Docks, but the initial tally o' the dead is about a hundred to a hundred and twenty militia members. My regulars are still tryin' to identify them."

Clerans felt his heart sink at this statement. A hundred men dead at the Fishers' Docks? That must be all the men and women who could not get out of the pirates' first ambush. He could feel a lump forming in his throat. Had they found Laendon among the dead?

The governor sighed again as he looked over the roll of paper. "This tally is o' the dead near the Dike Plaza, jist where the dike o' the Lower Village joins the dike from the Upper Village — my regulars ha' jist finished identifying them all."

Clerans felt his heart skip a beat. That was where they were ambushed the second time — with Da leading the retreat. It was Da who had charged first into the ambush. Surely Da's body would be among the others at that place. Clerans could not think of any way that his Da could have escaped the carnage. Yet was his Da's name on the list? Had they found his body?

The governor wiped pus away from his eye. "Here are the names o' those fallen near the Dike Plaza."

The governor read the list slowly and with tremendous gravity, his bad eye twitching at each name. Clerans' heart sank to his toes as the governor proceeded, waiting with dread to hear the name of his father — "Henri Blaeith" — among the rest.

> "Jim Middlynness — tradesman,
> Nycolaei Burdan — tradesman,
> Persyfl Guthro — carpenter's apprentice,
> Ffraenc Kyliwraeth — beacon tender,
> Jon Haelred — tradesman,
> Aelyster Coman — baker's apprentice,
> Jon Luukamys — tradesman,
> Henri Chaefenoch — dock-hand,
> Jock Selsymer — tradesman,
> Sigfryd Myleynli — tradesman,
> Luranc Invertn — beacon tender,
> Sebaestian Aebernathi — tradesman."

The room sat in a somber silence for several moments. Clerans waited breathlessly, certain that the governor would continue. That could not be the end of the list. He had not heard his Da's name yet. Clerans was certain that his Da was among the dead. There was no way he could have escaped.

The governor continued to look at the roll of paper, and he heaved a great sigh. "In all, the number o' the dead at the dike near the Dike Plaza is nine men, an' three boys."

Clerans sat bolt upright. What was this? His father's name was not on the list? Could this really be true? No, his Da could not have survived the headlong charge into the ambush. He *had* to be among the dead. Perhaps his body had been misidentified by the regulars for someone else?

The lord protector heaved a deep sigh. "I pray that their souls were all right with God. But tell me, look you, how many men were there in the dike militia?"

The governor furrowed his brow, but then shook his head,

looking over at Clerans. "I am uncertain. How many men were there, Clerans?"

Clerans bit the inside of his cheek, trying to remember, while his mind still reeled with the possibility that his father might not be dead after all. "Ah, sir, I do no remember precisely. But I do no think we tained more than two hundred defendin' the dikes. Perhaps we tained a hundred-eighty?"

Caedmon Wilkins nodded slowly. "Let us say there were only a hundred and sixty then. But look here, governor, you say there were a hundred and twenty men found dead at the Fishers' Docks, plus the twelve found near the Dike Plaza, and the five comrades of young Clerans who died defending the tailor's shop. Look you, that means there are still perhaps twenty men unaccounted for."

Clerans caught his breath. Could that really be true? Had twenty more of the dike militia escaped the massacre? Where were they, then? Was his Da possibly among this group of survivors? What about Laendon? Could he have survived, too? Clerans' heart beat heavily at the thought. Suddenly, he remembered the night before, when he and Martyn had sat in the attic of the tailor shop together. They *had* heard gunshots in the Lower Village. There *must* be more survivors.

The governor stroked his chin thoughtfully, yet before he could make a reply, the oak doors of the kirk burst open again. As Clerans looked to see what this new interruption might be, he saw two of the federal dragoons accompanying three swarthy, unshaven men. Clerans guessed in a moment that these three men must be strikers. Clerans' stomach tightened. Was it too much to hope his conversation with the two strikers in front of the bank had done any good?

Two of the strikers were very large, heavy-set men who looked as if they had spent far too many nights tending beacons in the open air of the coastal mountains. These two beacon tenders carried between them a third man (bound and gagged with thick ropes), holding him tightly by the shoulders. Clerans caught his breath. It was the spokesman, the same man who had murdered all those strikers in Miss Nansi's house.

"The envoy from the strikers, sir," one of the dragoons said as they advanced towards the table at the front of the sanctuary.

Reaching the table, the two beacon tenders threw the spokesman to his knees in front of the lord protector.

"Here ye are, sir," the older of the two beacon tenders said. Clerans blinked. Perhaps he was wrong, but it certainly sounded like the voice of one of the strikers he had spoken to the night before. "We cede here now to reply to yer terms. In short, we are drawin' back from the bank, an' will confine ourselves to Nychweni Square fer the present."

Caedmon Wilkins nodded, looking closely at the man who now knelt before him, bound and gagged. "And what of this man?"

The two strikers curled their lips disdainfully.

"Well, sir," the younger of the two replied, jabbing the bound man in the rib with the toe of his boot, "*that* man is the reason that we moved against the bank in the first place, an' our bindin' him an' gaggin' him is the reason fer us leavin' the bank in the second place."

Clerans prickled with anticipation. It was indeed the same voice. These two were the same men who had tried to intimidate him in front of the bank.

"Ay, sir," the older agreed, pulling the younger striker back from the spokesman. "Ye see, this here villain ha' been quite vocal throughout this whole strike, an' he ha' been the one who started the idea o' besiegin' the factories, an' burnin' those cottages on the north o' town, and it wos he who talked the greater part o' us into attackin' the bank last night."

"Despite the advice o' us elders," the younger one added quickly, jabbing the bound man with his boot again.

"Ay," the older striker said, pulling the younger man back

again, and nudging his shoulder reproachfully. "That's true, certain."

"So we started to thinkin'," the younger of the two added, moving back towards the spokesman despite another nudge from the older striker. "An' we realized that none o' us knew where this man ceded from, what beacon he tended, or how he wos let go by the Company. We simply believed that he wos a striker jist like us who once wos a beacon tender." The younger striker drew back his foot, clearly gearing up to kick the spokesman. "But then–"

"–Ay then," the older one cut in, pushing the younger aside before he could kick the spokesman. "That is when I said, 'He does gard a bit more like a sailor than a beacon tender.'"

"Ay," the younger of the two affirmed, stepping closer to the spokesman, again jabbing him in the ribs with his boot before the older striker could stop him. "An' he does talk like one, too, does no he?"

Clerans cleared his throat. He couldn't help himself. "An' you two figured that all out on yer own, did you?"

The older striker turned on Clerans, looking him over slowly. At last, recognition dawned in his eyes, and his lips cracked into a smile. "We might ha' tained *some* help."

The spokesman made a muffled noise through his gag, as if in protest. The two strikers clicked their tongues disapprovingly, and the younger kicked him in the ribs.

"Here now," the older striker growled as he grabbed the younger striker by the shoulder and pulled him back. "Do no do that in front o' the lord protector, will ye?"

The younger striker shook his shoulders from his comrade's grip. "Ay? An' why no?"

The older man just shook his head and turned back towards Caedmon Wilkins. "Well now, an' the short o' it is, that this man here is a pirate. Pure an' simple. Never wos a striker to begin with. Jist pretended to be to humbug us all."

"Are you saying then," Caedmon Wilkins asked levelly, "that this man, look you, was a liaison for Captain Longfinch?"

"Do no call him a liaison, sir!" the younger of the two strikers protested. "That makes it sound too official. Call him what he is: a treacherous, sneakin' spy, who wos usin' us to help the wicked pirate captain." And with that, the younger of the two strikers spat on the bound man.

The bound man simply slumped his shoulders sullenly and glared up at the lord protector.

"Un-gag him," Caedmon Wilkins ordered.

Captain Smydhac reached out and pulled the gag from the man's mouth. The bound man stared up at the lord protector defiantly.

"Do you deny this?" Caedmon Wilkins asked. "Are you indeed working for Captain Longfinch?"

The man sneered. "Sorry, cap'n, ye're too late to stop us now. Ye've already lost. Longfinch ha' already taken what he comed fer, an' it will be the death o' ye soon enough!"

"I will take that as an admission of guilt then," Caedmon Wilkins replied. "Captain Smydhac, clap this man in irons, look you, to await a more thorough sentencing after we retake the village."

"Ay, sir," Captain Smydhac motioned to the two dragoons who had accompanied the strikers into the sanctuary. Stepping forward, the dragoons lifted the bound man to his feet and dragged him out of the kirk.

The younger of the two strikers stamped his foot indignantly. "Are no ye goin' to shoot him? Does no Llaedhwythi law give ye permission to shoot any pirate on sight? Ay, an' he jist admitted to bein' a pirate!"

Caedmon Wilkins shook his head. "The law says that any officer of the law *can* shoot a pirate on sight, not that he *must*, look you. If I were you, I would be careful about pressing the justice of the law too firmly, as you and the other strikers are also in just danger for violation of the law."

The younger of the two licked his lips nervously, but the older one spoke. "Ay sir, an' that is why we ha' ceded here with our proposal."

"Proposal?" Governor Braedhwyc asked, clearly suspicious as he wiped pus from his bad eye.

"I am listening," the lord protector said.

The older striker turned on Clerans. "Do ye tain it, then, younker?"

Clerans blinked, taking a moment to guess what the striker was saying. "Ah! Ay."

Rifling through his coat pockets, Clerans came up with a packet of papers Haeli had given him — the papers formally calling the Company to a lawsuit under Indigie Law.

Mrs. Blysffi noticed the package and went suddenly stiff, looking at Clerans with keen interest.

"There now!" the older striker said, taking the packet and handing it to Caedmon Wilkins. The lord protector frowned, looking from Clerans to the strikers, and then opening the packet.

"We are formally suing the Company," the striker said.

Governor Braedhwyc snorted. "An' what good do ye think that will do you? How could the courts look favorably on you after the mess you ha' caused?"

The striker held up a finger. "Ay, but I never said *which* court, now did I?"

The lord protector raised an eyebrow. "What do you mean, look you?"

The striker only winked and then turned to the Iasaqi-Woni. This man was good. Clerans could not help but admire his dramatic flair. Maybe he should have done more to talk with the strikers from the beginning. Here was a man after his own heart.

The strikers said something in Tylweni, and the Iasaqi-Woni cocked his head to listen. Governor Braedhwyc went stiff in alarm, his mouth falling open.

"What is he saying?" Caedmon Wilkins asked.

The Iasaqi-Woni held up a hand and turned to Mrs. Blysffi, speaking in hushed tones. For a moment, the two of them exchanged whispered words in Tylweni, Mrs. Blysffi bowing her head respectfully, and the Iasaqi-Woni nodding slowly. The shaman chuckled to himself, adding a few words himself. Llifsa, Clerans wished he could speak Tylweni himself.

At last, the Iasaqi-Woni turned to the older striker, giving a quick sentence. The striker bowed respectfully and turned back to the lord protector.

"Ye see, sir, the Company ha' done us many wrongs, but they all occurred in Indigie land…"

Caedmon Wilkins glanced over the papers in Haeli's packet quickly. "And per our agreement with the tribes, crimes in indigenous land must be prosecuted under indigenous law…"

"What is this?" Governor Braedhwyc wiped pus from his eye and scowled.

Caedmon Wilkins searched the striker's face. "You are serious? You mean to drag the Company officials up for a trial by moa?"

The older striker only shrugged.

"No!" the governor said, and he turned to the Iasaqi-Woni, speaking a few words in Tylweni. The shaman replied instead, speaking several harsh words. The Governor paled.

"Oh, ay, they are serious."

Mrs. Blysffi now cleared her throat. "The Company must be brought to account for their crimes. The Twengoli and all the tribes of the cape are ready to demand their laws be upheld in this matter."

"My Lord Protector," the governor said, turning to Caedmon Wilkins in alarm. "Ye cen no take this request seriously."

Caedmon Wilkins simply raised a hand. "By the Almighty God, we must." And he suddenly chuckled. "Taking the Company to trial by moa?" He chuckled again. "No, but it is just in a way."

"But my Lord Protector," the governor cut in.

"This is justice," Caedmon Wilkins cut him off. "We all know that the Company is corrupt, but we can do nothing about it. Per our compromise with the Indigies, however, *they* can. We must uphold their decision."

At that moment, a fusillade of gunshots sounded from outside the Kirk. Everyone froze.

Caedmon Wilkins quickly scanned the room of soldiers. "I was not imagining that sound then, look you, you all heard it?"

"Ay, sir," Captain Smydhac replied grimly.

At that moment, Clerans heard several shouts outside the kirk. Was that an alarm of some kind?

Caedmon Wilkins slapped the table forcefully with his open palm. "There we have it, sirs. Deliberation is over. Call up your men. We move now to prepare for action."

And with that, the entire group of soldiers leapt from their seats, rushing towards the door. Clerans followed in the mad rush. Each man was hurriedly checking his weapons to see that they were ready for action.

"Captain Smydhac," the lord protector was saying, "send a message to the dragoons still stationed at the bank at once. Tell them that their service is required here post-haste."

As Clerans rushed out the door, squinting in the sudden sunlight, he shook his head. What fresh trouble awaited him now?

# THE SHADOW

Ernest pressed himself flat against the wall and held his breath. He was just inside the entrance to the little passageway, and he could hear the pirates pounding down the steps over his head.

The dull light of a lantern dawned in the main passageway, the heavy footsteps of the pirates stopping at the bottom of the stairs. The light bounced about for a moment, and then Ernest heard the pirates rushing forward again, the sounds of their footsteps dying away into echoes down the passageway. Slowly, the light faded, leaving Ernest in total blackness once more.

Ernest let himself snicker. That was almost too easy.

"Well done," Ella whispered in his ear.

Ernest snickered again. "Oh no, it isn't done yet!"

And with that, he pulled out his pistol. He could still see nothing in the darkness, so he worked slowly, reloading the pistol by feel alone. Just as he rammed tight the first of his nine barrels, he felt a strange chill run over him. Was that a breeze? No, it couldn't be. His heart pounded in his chest, sounding like drums in his ears. What was going on? All at once he felt like a hunted rabbit, with a wolf on his scent.

Something stirred on the stairs above him. A noise at once grating and terrifying, like the scratching of claws across granite, or the sound of an axe blade against a whetting stone. Ernest stood stock-still with his ears perked forward and listening. He could hardly think to finish loading his pepper-box pistol.

But there was that sound again! It descended the stairway. But what was it? It couldn't be footsteps, could it? If it was, whoever — or whatever — it was certainly taking its time coming down each stair. Yet now Ernest heard another sound, and it made every hair on his head stand on end. It was *breathing*; a slow, grating, wheezing, as of a man — or a creature — who does not have many breaths left to take. Yet, even as Ernest listened, he trembled. Somehow, he could sense that the *thing* that was breathing was near to death, not in the sense that it was near to dying, but that it was juxtaposed to death — a near neighbor.

It was at that moment that Ernest remembered what Ella had said about a ghost. Was this it, then? Was there a ghost descending the stairs above him? Ernest shivered in terror. He could only hope that he might escape the notice of this ghost as easily as he escaped the notice of those three pirates.

Ernest stood completely still, holding his breath. The thing — the ghost, or whatever it was — seemed to reach the bottom of the stairs, for Ernest could hear it pausing for a moment, still wheezing. Then suddenly, the breathing stopped. Ernest strained his ears to listen, but he could not make out any sound. He trembled all over. What had happened? Had he just imagined all of that, or was there really a ghost in the darkness out there? Ernest's mouth was now completely dry. If the ghost found them, what would it do to him?

Ernest tried to remain still, but he was shaking. He could hardly keep his hands steady, and he dared not try to reload his pistol now. Besides, what use would his gun be against a supernatural foe? At any moment, Ernest expected to feel clammy, ghostly hands seizing him by the throat.

But just then, he heard a sound in the darkness. It was footsteps, but not those of the ghost. Now he could hear the pirates' voices again.

"Come on! There's got to be another passage around here. How else'd he give us the slip?"

"There wasn't a point in turning around! He was ahead of us, like I sayed! We should of keeped going!"

"No, no, no, we would of seed him, if'n he was ahead of us."

"What's Longfinch going to say, eh?"

The dim light returned to the main passageway. They were coming back for him then. They'd find his hiding spot soon enough. Ernest could now just see his pistol in the darkness. Hurriedly, he rammed the rest of the barrels and cocked the flint back. There, now he was ready! Just let them *try* to find him now. They wouldn't live to regret it.

Suddenly, an injured scream rent the air. Every hair on Ernest's body bristled at the sound. What was happening?

"Get it off on me!" one of the pirates screamed.

More screams, howls, and moans echoed off the walls of the passageways, mixed with curses and an intermittent gunshot.

"Kill it! Kill the baptized–" the cry cut short in a horrendous, blood-curdling scream of pain.

The light wavered slightly, and then suddenly, all was silent again. Ernest trembled all over. What had happened? Dare he step out of hiding to find out? The lantern still filled the passageway with dim light, enough that Ernest could now clearly see.

"What just happened?" Ella whispered, her voice shaky and strained.

"I'm sure I don't know," Ernest said. "Daren't we look?"

"What else would we do?" Ella replied. "We can't just stay he'e."

Ernest nodded, swallowing hard. He told his legs to move, but they didn't obey him right away. After an intense mental battle, Ernest's feet finally took their first step, sluggishly. Ernest held his pepper-box pistol in front of him while he stepped out into the main passageway. Ella followed just behind.

There, perhaps twenty yards down the passageway, the lantern was sitting gently on the ground. Something lay near the lantern, but Ernest couldn't quite make out what it was from this distance. Looking all around, Ernest could see nothing else in that dreary passageway, no sign of the pirates or the ghost.

Ernest's timidity turned into panic. Where were the other pirates? What had happened to them? Ernest rushed forward now, glancing suspiciously all around the tunnel. Had they ducked down some side passage? No, there was nothing here, only the smooth, granite walls. Ernest quickly reached the lantern, with Ella right on his heels.

How very curious! The lantern looked as if it had been set softly on the ground. It simply sat there, filling the wide passage with its amber light. Then, with a recoil of horror, Ernest noticed what surrounded the lantern. It was bones. Three piles of bones lay scattered around the circle of light, carelessly tossed to the ground. Several of these bones were whole and stood out sharply in the light, yet most of the bones were broken. But there were also bits of clothing — torn to pieces and scattered all around with the bones — as well as a pistol and a few cutlasses, which were twisted out of any useful shape.

*Ella in the Catacombs*

Ernest slowly bent down, trembling all over. Reaching out, he picked up a bone and looked at it carefully. His stomach quivered inside him. It looked like the bone of a man's fore-arm, but there were teeth marks all over it, as if something had gnawed it clean of any flesh. Ernest dropped the bone in horror, still trembling uncontrollably. Was this all that was left of those three pirates? Had they been devoured in such little time? But what could have done this? Was it that ghost Ella was talking about?

Surely not. This couldn't be all that was left of those pirates. If those pirates were just killed, he would see blood; lots of blood. But there was no blood, only bones. Surely these must be *old* bones that were just placed here to frighten him. Nothing could have killed these pirates, devoured them, gnawed the bones clean, and licked up all the blood so quickly.

Just then, Ernest heard a low chuckle behind him. He jumped and turned around, yet he could see nothing but the wide passage illuminated by the light of the lantern. Yet even as he looked, he heard that breathing again, close and near.

"So they all will pass. So quickly does the grave devour his victims."

Ernest recoiled in terror at the voice. "Who's there! What do you want!"

The voice only chuckled again.

"Be gone!" Ella shouted, speaking with more confidence than Ernest could muster at that moment. "We do not fea'h you!"

Ella could speak for herself. Ernest more than feared that thing. And that was understating the matter.

"You should," the voice replied.

Ella pointed her finger towards the voice, singing loudly and confidently.

> *"The love of God expels the da'kest places,*
> *All shadows fall befo'e His many g'aces.*

*And in His p'esence eve'y fea'h is banished,*
*Within His comfo'ts, sorrows swiftly vanish."*

A loud hissing filled the passageway, and Ernest shook all over. What was Ella doing? This ghost was about to devour them and lick their bones clean! How could she be singing at a time like this?

"Do you really think you can evade me forever?" the voice wheezed with a vicious growl. "Know that I will always be there, waiting in the darkness around you, ready to destroy you."

Ella only continued to sing,

*"Oh, Lo'd, I look to You! Be my defende'h,*
*A'ay You'hself in You'h victo'ious splendo'h.*
*And then foreve'h I will sing You'h p'aises,*
*When You'h g'eat love consumes the da'kest places."*

Now Ernest heard a low snarl, like the snarl of a wild dog that has just been kicked.

"Never again!!"

The cry rose in a piercing wail through the tunnel. Then Ernest heard what might be the sound of claws scratching against the floor. Suddenly, he saw something in the dim light. It was strange, wild, and obscure, little more than a shadow, rushing away from them, flitting up the stairway, and then vanishing into the darkness.

Ernest trembled all over. It was a ghost then, and it was going to kill them.

# ASCENSION

As Haeli finished chewing the last pieces of meat off the bone, Martyn took out his bayonet and scattered the fire with it. He stomped out any live coals and was about to throw aside what was left of the rabbit carcasses when Aarushi whistled. The harrier was looking at Martyn closely, almost pleadingly.

Martyn shrugged. "Ay then, if ye'll think there's good eatin' on them yet, then they are yers."

Martyn tossed the carcasses in front of Aarushi, and she whistled joyfully.

"Alrighty then!" Martyn exclaimed, picking up the two packs of provisions. "Shall we set about it, then?"

Martyn put on one of the packs himself and tossed the other one to Titus. Then Martyn looked closely at Tiya-Aenji.

"Ye say ye ha' scended the tower a'fore?"

Tiya-Aenji stood to her feet slowly — almost fearfully, Haeli thought — and she nodded. "Ay, I have climbed the tower."

Martyn pursed his lips. "Well, I may as well say that though I am a decent climber — if I'll may speak fer myself — I am no too keen on startin' to scend this tower. I ha' heard o' far too merri men diein' in the attempt." Martyn paused and looked at Tiya-Aenji keenly. "So then, I assume there is some trick to it?"

Tiya-Aenji hesitated. "Ay, there is a 'trick' — if you can call it that. There is only one way up the tower. I know it, and I can show it to you. But..." and she trailed off, as if afraid to continue.

Martyn raised an eyebrow. "But?"

"The reason," Tiya-Aenji continued cautiously, "the reason that so many of your people die climbing the tower is because it is under a spell."

"A spell?" Titus exclaimed.

Haeli looked at Tiya-Aenji closely. Haeli really did not want to be a jerk all over again, but she felt like rolling her eyes. She had liked Tiya-Aenji at first, but these superstitions were testing her patience. But no, she would not let her emotions get control of her again. She had a heart of stone.

Tiya-Aenji nodded gravely. "To my people — to the Twengoli — this tower is a haunted place, and the people will not come near it. However, once a year the Shaman may enter to give sacrifice to the spirit of the Gwambi. And on that day he may bring his apprentice — the Li — to initiate into the secret rites of Shamanship."

Martyn nodded. "An' that is how ye scended it a'fore? As the Shaman's apprentice, I mean?"

Tiya-Aenji nodded. "As I said already, it was before I knew the true faith."

"We cen thank God then," Martyn said with a smile, "that ye still remember the way up the tower."

Tiya-Aenji held out her finger. "Ay, I remember the way, but I also remember the many ceremonies and sacrifices that the Shaman performed before he even dared to lay his finger upon the tower. For whoever tries to climb this tower without appeasing the ghost who dwells within... that man will face the wrath of the ghost while he ascends it. The tower is deceitful, and the very stones will turn themselves against you for your destruction. Do you not see? That is why so many men die trying to climb it. The ghost has cursed this tower."

Titus shivered all over. "Heaven preserve us!"

Martyn nodded, but he winked roguishly at Titus. "Ay, an' be thankful that Halfdan wos no around to hear ye, or he would be pesterin' ye about swearin'."

Titus laughed nervously.

Martyn turned back to Tiya-Aenji. "Tiya, I do no fear any curse, either from a shaman, or a ghost, or a pagan god, fer that matter. There is nothin' that any o' them cen do that will 'separate me from the love o' God which is in the Christ.' Ay, now that's straight from scripture, that is."

Tiya-Aenji nodded. "You speak the truth. The power of God which is in us will overcome all the powers of darkness."

Haeli couldn't help but think that Tiya-Aenji looked rather timid for the confidence with which she attempted to speak.

"Then may the Almighty God be with us!" Martyn cried. "Now, show us how to begin."

Tiya-Aenji took a deep breath, and then she padded softly over to the tower on her bare, webbed feet. Touching its rough sides with her webbed hands, she felt all around the base of the tower twice before she finally paused over a little depression in the ground. Here, she knelt down, pulling out her *kukri* knife and using it to dig into the ground. To Haeli's surprise, the earth in that depression seemed loose, and in no time at all, Tiya-Aenji had dug nearly a foot into the ground.

As Haeli looked over Tiya-Aenji's shoulder into the hole, she could see a small stone slab at the bottom. Tiya-Aenji wedged her *kukri* along the side of the slab and then carefully pried it up. Below the slab was a small compartment with four oblong objects concealed inside.

Snatching up the contents of this compartment, Tiya-Aenji stood to her feet. Haeli looked closely at the four objects in Tiya-Aenji's hands. They were tools of some kind. At first glance, Haeli thought they were long knives, about three hand-breadths in length, but now she saw that what she had mistaken for blades were actually rather thick and not sharpened at all. The entire tool was made of one solid piece of iron, the one end being round, as if meant to fit in your hand, while the opposite end was flat, coming to a keen point.

"These are the *alwmli*, the mystic climbing tools," Tiya-Aenji said. "None but the Shamans and the ghost even know that they exist. See, I am already breaking the rules by showing them to you." Tiya-Aenji took a deep breath. "But the Spirit of the Almighty will protect me."

Martyn took one of the tools from Tiya-Aenji and balanced it in his hand. "Tar and needles, this feels like it would hold the weight o' an elephant!"

Tiya-Aenji smiled ruefully. "Only if the *tower* would hold that weight. See here," she held up one of the *alwmli* next to the granite surface of the tower. "You may force the blade into the cracks between the stones, and thus use these *alwmli* to climb up the tower. However, there is only one path up the tower where the cracks are spaced evenly so that you can climb from crack to crack."

Martyn nodded. "Seems simple enough."

Tiya-Aenji shook her head. "Except that there are only enough *alwmli* for two climbers. Only two shamans ever climb the tower at one time."

Martyn nodded. "Ay, I ha' noticed that. We will ha' to scend it in turns then. Here, Tiya, ye and Haeli should cede first."

Martyn pulled a long rope from his pack and handed it to Haeli. "You two, tie yourselves together. That way, if either o' ye'll slip while you climb, then the other cen catch you."

Haeli nodded. Yet, as she tied the rope about her waist, Martyn stopped her.

"No like that, Haeli. It will slip right off o' ye. No, ye need a harness, see — it ha' to wrap around yer thighs as well."

And with Martyn's direction, Haeli tied her end of the rope into a proper harness. She couldn't help but think that it was a rather awkward thing, and she had a bit of trouble getting into it, even in her loose, square-hemmed skirts. She had to hike her skirts up well above her knees to get the seat of the harness between her legs.

She thought little of this at first while Martyn was helping her, but then she noticed Titus watching, eyes downcast, his entire face as bright as a tomato. He wasn't from Llaedhwyth after all, and Haeli did not know what the Slyzwirians considered proper and modest. Certainly, Haeli had never seen Ella bare her knees, and she was pretty sure that Ella wore stockings all the time. Perhaps it was indecent in Slyzwir for a girl to bare her knees. But what could she do about it now?

Haeli simply shook her head and turned her attention to the tower, trying to block out any thought of Titus and Slyzwirian customs. There was no point worrying about it. Titus probably already thought poorly of her.

By this time, Tiya-Aenji had tied her harness at the other end of the rope and fastened it around herself with skill and poise. There was about ten feet of rope between the two of them.

The little nymph handed Haeli two of the *alwmli* solemnly. "O Lord Almighty," Tiya-Aenji breathed, "guide and protect your children! Foil the curses of the evil one! Save us from death and its many fears. We commit our cause to you. We pray that you will deliver us by Your name."

"Amen!" Martyn and Titus echoed.

Tiya-Aenji took a deep breath and walked up to the base of the tower. Haeli couldn't help but notice that she shook as if terrified. And now, for the first time, a twinge of fear crept into Haeli's heart. She really did not know what she was getting into. Tiya-Aenji knew better than anyone else what awaited them at the top of the tower, so if she was terrified, perhaps every one of them should be terrified as well. But no. She would not ride that horse. She would feel no fear. She had a heart of stone.

Tiya-Aenji wedged the blade of one of her *alwmli* into a crack between the enormous granite blocks that made up the tower. Then, drawing herself up on this *alwmli,* she wedged her other *alwmli* into the next crack higher up.

Haeli noticed that Tiya-Aenji's lips were moving. What was she saying? Haeli strained her ears to listen, and she thought she could make out what Tiya-Aenji was saying:

"O Lord Almighty, guide and protect your children! Foil the curses of the evil one! Save us from death and its many fears. We commit our cause to You. We pray that You will deliver us by Your name. O Lord Almighty, guide and protect your children..."

She was praying the same prayer, repeatedly. Haeli felt her heart sink as she realized that the prayer which Tiya-Aenji had just given was not just a prayer that one might give as a courtesy before starting on an adventure; it was a sincere, desperate cry for help.

"You must put the *alwmli* exactly where I do," Tiya-Aenji called down to Haeli as she hauled herself up to the next crack, pausing her prayer for just a moment. "There is only one way up the tower, and you must follow it exactly — or risk falling."

Haeli tried to calm her nerves as she, too, stepped to the bottom of the tower. This was ridiculous. She had no reason to be terrified. She had climbed before. What about that time, only a few days ago, when she had climbed up that cliff after the white-haired man chased her over the edge? She had made it up that cliff just fine, and she hadn't even had any climbing tools or protective equipment with her then. No, she had nothing to fear now. She had a heart of stone.

Haeli thrust her first *alwmli* into the first crack between the blocks of the tower. She took a deep breath.

The only reason that Tiya-Aenji was so afraid was because

of that ghost she kept talking about. But Haeli knew better than to be afraid of such a superstitious story. There were no ghosts. Haeli breathed again, reassuring herself. This was the modern era; the era of magic had passed. There were no goblins anymore, or curses, or spells of black magic... No, there was nothing to be afraid of.

As Haeli climbed the Gwambi Tower, her heart pounded in her throat. This was absurd! She was acting like she was afraid, but she wasn't afraid. She had no reason to be afraid. Tiya-Aenji might be afraid, but she wasn't.

Haeli forced her *alwmli* into a crack between the vast granite blocks of the tower and then drew herself up on it. No, she was not afraid. She had just allowed Tiya-Aenji's superstitions to rub off on her, that was all.

She forced herself to look up. She knew better than to look down. Focusing her attention on Tiya-Aenji above her, Haeli continued to climb, drawing herself up steadily and thrusting her *alwmli* into the next crack as she came to it.

Really, it wasn't that difficult going. After all, the *alwmli* fit nicely in each crack, and once she wedged them in firmly, they easily held her weight. As for her feet, the tower was uneven enough that she easily found a toehold, so that at no point did she feel in the least unsteady.

Still, Tiya-Aenji muttered to herself, "O Lord Almighty, guide and protect your children..."

Haeli shook her head. Why was Tiya-Aenji so terrified?

Just then, Haeli heard something above her head. It sounded almost like a flag snapping against itself in the wind. She looked up with some apprehension, but at that moment, she felt the *alwmli* that was holding her weight slip free from its crack. Haeli let out a startled cry, but she quickly caught herself with her feet, hanging tightly onto her other *alwmli.*

"Haeli!" she heard Martyn call from below her. "Are ye alright?"

Haeli's arms trembled. She had been too careless. How could she let herself get careless?

"I am alright!" Haeli replied, looking back over her shoulder and trying to smile at Martyn. With some surprise now, she saw how high up she was. Martyn and Titus both looked small from where they stood at the bottom of the tower. She must be halfway up already.

But then, Haeli felt dizzy, and she felt as if she might tip backwards off the tower. Haeli immediately turned her head and looked hard at the unmoving granite block in front of her nose. She took a few deep breaths to calm the dizziness in her head. Why had she been so careless? She had to concentrate.

Haeli turned back to her work, looking up at the tower she had yet to climb. Tiya-Aenji had paused her ascent and was looking back at Haeli. She did not seem to be affected by the height.

"Are you ready to continue?" Tiya-Aenji asked kindly.

Haeli nodded. Reaching forward, she wedged her *alwmli* into the crack from which it had slipped — this time she was certain to drive it in as far as the *alwmli* would go. This time, it held her weight, and she began ascending the tower again with minor difficulty.

From then on, Haeli took great care to thrust her *alwmli* as deeply as possible into the cracks between the stones. She watched Tiya-Aenji carefully and thrust her *alwmli* into the exact same cracks that Tiya-Aenji did — though really, there wasn't much need to watch as closely as she did, for the way was pretty self-explanatory now. Still, Haeli had learned her lesson. She would not be careless again.

Tiya-Aenji kept muttering her prayer, "O Lord Almighty, guide and protect your children..."

Haeli grunted as she hauled herself up and thrust her *alwmli* into the next crack. Again she heard that sound, as of a flag in the wind. What was that noise? Looking up, she could see nothing but the odd parapet at the top of the tower. Perhaps there was a flag or an old piece of cloth up there, blowing in the wind?

Yet now, Tiya-Aenji hauled herself up carefully, and Haeli could see that if the little nymph reached out her hands, she could grab onto the battlements at the top of the tower. That was it, then! They were almost there.

Haeli couldn't help but wonder about this tower. She had heard so many stories of the many people who died trying to climb it. Yet how was that possible when she had climbed it so simply? Perhaps having the *alwmli* made all the difference. Or perhaps knowing where each of the cracks were was the only reason she had found this task so simple.

True, it wasn't exactly simple. Haeli was sweating, and she could feel the strain of the long climb now. She would be happy to get to the top and rest a bit.

Tiya-Aenji reached up, grabbed hold of the top of the battlement, and hauled herself up. Yet she had hardly gotten her head above the parapet when a deafening scream rent the air. Two huge, black wings loomed above her from over the edge of the tower, snapping in the wind as they unfurled.

Tiya-Aenji started back in surprise and lost her grip on the battlements. Haeli caught her breath. Tiya-Aenji snatched at her *alwmli,* which still protruded from the last crack between the blocks of the tower. For a moment, Haeli thought that the little nymph had caught herself, but then Tiya-Aenji's small webbed hand slipped from the handle of the *alwmli,* and down, down she tumbled.

# A REMNANT

Clerans and the rest of the war council rushed out the doors of the kirk, following the lord protector. As he pushed through the doors, Clerans looked over the square in front of the kirk to see if he could determine what had caused the shouts of alarm. The fresh smell of smoke mixed with the acrid odor of gunpowder wafted over him. Unless he was imagining it. Glancing about him, however, Clerans could see nothing out of the ordinary except a knot of six regulars standing in the square's eastern corner, talking with each other and fidgeting about like excited, gray pigeons. The regulars had their backs turned to the kirk and clearly had not noticed the sudden appearance of the war council.

Lord Protector Wilkins descended the steps of the kirk with the poise of a mountain lion.

"What is the alarm, sirs?"

The regulars turned quickly, clearly startled and overawed at the sudden appearance of the lord protector himself. The regulars saluted hurriedly.

"Lord Protector, sir!" they hailed almost in one voice.

Caedmon Wilkins waved his hand, a hint of amusement playing about his mouth. "Ay, gentlemen, and what, look you, is the cause of this commotion?"

The regulars looked from one to another, clearly uncertain who should speak. Clerans noticed now that there was not an officer among them to serve as a spokesman for the group. Governor Braedhwyc now stepped forward, saving the regulars any further embarrassment by pointing to one.

"Ye there, give yer report, sir!"

The chosen regular stood straight with an immaculate salute. "Sir!" he cried, then he waved in the general direction of the Lower Village. "There is a disturbance in the Lower Village, sir! Gunfire an' the like, sir."

"Among our ranks, or the ranks o' the Twengoli?" Governor Braedhwyc asked.

"Are the pirates trying to break free, look you," Caedmon Wilkins added, "and get back to their ship?"

The regular shook his head vigorously. "No, sir, the disturbance is comin' from *within* the area held by the pirates, sir."

Governor Braedhwyc's face twitched as he furrowed his brow in thought. "The pirates are no fightin' amongst themselves, are they?"

The regular shrugged. "There were gunshots, sir, an' they fer certain are no attackin' at our line along the dikes."

Caedmon Wilkins clapped his hands together with a wide smile. "Yo-ho! It would be worth a wager that this might be the rest of the dike militia, look you."

At that moment, a dragoon galloped into the square from along the Old Dike Road. Reining to such an abrupt halt that his horse's hooves skidded on the cobblestone, he saluted Captain Smydhac, the lord protector, and the governor.

"Sirs, all," the dragoon said. "It is takint a look you best should be."

"Lead on!" Caedmon Wilkins ordered.

The dragoon rushed down the Old Dike Road a few blocks, with the entire council following quickly behind.

Clerans rushed after, coming up just behind the governor. His mind rushed with questions. What kind of disturbance was this in the middle of the pirates' position? Clerans still remembered the gunfire he had heard in the Lower Village shortly after the Twengoli had rescued Martyn and himself. Martyn had said that he thought there might be more groups of dike militia holed up in shops to defend themselves from the pirates' invasion. Could this disturbance be one such group? Had more survived the pirates' envelopment?

But now a greater question came to Clerans. If his Da's body was not found among the dead near the Dike Plaza, was it possible that Da could be among this group of survivors?

The dragoon leading the way now reined in his horse, stopping at a spot along the Old Dike Road which commanded a clear view across the whole Lower Village. Clerans looked out and caught his breath. How familiar this view had once been to him! The Lower Village had been such a tidy sight, laid out with its neat rows of low houses and shops all along the winding streets. It had been one of the prettiest sights in the village, for it was all picturesque timber construction. But what a desolate and ruined placed it looked now! Large swaths of the wooden houses lay in ashes, like great festering scars across the village, smoke still rising from their burned-out shells. Even some of the stone structures lay in ruins, shale roofs caved in, or walls crumbled after contact with the scorching flames.

The dragoon pointed towards a small square where the houses and shops were a little more intact. Clerans recognized the square at once as the Lower Court. Looking at it closely, he noticed several rapid puffs of smoke rising from the windows of a shop on the square's eastern end. A few moments later, the sounds of gunshots echoed up to them.

Suddenly, Clerans saw shapes of men swarming into the

square from the streets around. It was hard to tell at this distance, but he was pretty certain that they were pirates. More puffs of smoke flashed from the windows of the shop, and again the sounds of gunshots reverberated over the village, this time mingled with shouts and screams.

"It is the survivors av the dike militia, it is," the dragoon said, "sure as heaven!"

Caedmon Wilkins pursed his lips. "Does anyone, look you, have a telescope, or a glass of any kind?"

Captain Smydhac immediately pulled out a pair of field binoculars and handed them to the lord protector.

Caedmon Wilkins peered through the binoculars for a long moment, his jaw set tight, his face as emotionless as flint. Clerans watched in breathless suspense, looking at the lord protector and then the Lower Court.

This was clearly a fight of some kind, and if the men in the shop were not survivors of the dike militia, then Clerans could not imagine who they would be. What was going on? Now and then the wind blew straight into Clerans' face from across the Lower Village, bringing with it the steady sound of gunshots along with the acrid sting of smoke.

Finally, the lord protector lowered the binoculars from his eyes and shook his head. "Ay-eigh, I can not distinctly tell, look you. But surely that must be the dike militia in that shop. Who else would they be? It is certainly the pirates who are attacking it."

"May I'll see?" the governor asked.

Caedmon Wilkins handed the binoculars to Governor Braedhwyc, who now looked through them himself onto the action in the Lower Court.

Clerans groaned internally. If only he could see what was going on!

Suddenly, from down in the square, there was a bright flash

of light, and a pillar of smoke rose from the middle of the Lower Court. A loud report followed a second or two later; even at this distance, it sounded loud and close.

Governor Braedhwyc jumped back, taking the binoculars from his eyes and wiping pus from them before peering through the binoculars again.

"Tar an' needles!" he exclaimed, "I think they'll are tryin' to break out!"

"Who is?" Caedmon Wilkins asked.

"The militia — assumin' it *is* the dike militia." Governor Wilkins pursed his lips into a frown. "It is a merri difficult to see it, with all o' the smoke now, but I think that they ha' ranged themselves in front o' the shop there, an' they are fighting desperately."

Another fusillade of shots reverberated up to them, mixed distinctly with yelling, screaming, and groaning. That was certainly the sound of desperate fighting — Clerans knew that too well.

"How many are there?" the lord protector pressed.

"I cen no tell distinctly through that smoke," the governor replied. "Oh, wait now! Well, it is clearin' some. If only a wind would blow it all back so I'll could see." The governor let out a deep sigh. "Well now, I cen make out ten or twelve men distinctly, an' they are in Pistosian clothing. Perhaps there's more inside, hidden from my view?"

Halfdan suddenly settled on the parapet of the dike wall just before Caedmon Wilkins and the governor. He nodded his head courteously, but spoke in a dull, monotone voice. "If you would like, Lord Protector Wilkins, I can fly down there, count the numbers, and see if I can contact the militia."

"Ay, do," Caedmon Wilkins said with a nod, "and at once, my noble harrier."

With a flurry of wings, Halfdan fluttered up from the wall

and then glided through the air towards the Lower Court. Clerans could see the harrier growing smaller and smaller until he looked like little more than a floating piece of cloth in the sky as he circled around the square where all the action was occurring.

Oh, if only Clerans could see what was going on! Was his Da down there among the survivors?

"Are we certain?" Caedmon Wilkins said, turning back to the governor who was still peering intently through the binoculars, "Are we certain, look you, that we are actually watching the dike militia?"

The governor pursed his lips. "Ay then, but I do no know who else it might be. I cen no recognize anyone distinctly..."

The lord protector suddenly turned around and looked over the group of people behind him.

"Young Clerans," the lord protector exclaimed.

Clerans jumped in surprise, saluting quickly and smartly. How did the lord protector still remember his name?

"Come here then, look you," Caedmon Wilkins ordered, motioning to the governor for the binoculars. "See if you can make anything out of this."

Clerans accepted the binoculars from the governor mutely, and then he peered through them towards the Lower Court. At last, he could see!

The smoke from whatever charge it was that had exploded a moment ago was now much abated, and Clerans could make out the scene pretty clearly. As the governor had said, somewhere around ten men stood before the door of the little shop, engaged in fierce combat with the pirates. A smoking crater now filled the center of the square, and pirates' smoking bodies lay strewn all over the cobblestones. The militia must have set off that explosion then, in an attempt to break out.

Yet the attempt seemed to be failing. The few men who stood before the shop, though fighting for all they were worth, were not making any headway; worse, they seemed to be falling back before the ruthless rush of the pirates. But wait! One of the militia was down! The pirates swarmed into the gap formed in the militia's thin line. The brave men quickly closed the line tighter, backing slowly closer to the door of the shop. Just then, Clerans saw more puffs of smoke coming from the windows of the shop, and many of the pirates fell back, clearly struck dead by the rifle fire.

"Ay then," Clerans said, finally speaking. "The governor is right. There are eight men (ay, I count eight now) standin' before the shop, tryin' to fight their way out, and there are more inside (I cen no tell how many). But the pirates are drivin' them steadily back. I cen no tell fer certain, but there must be nearly forty pirates, an' more are arrivin' every minute."

Clerans shook his head and heaved a great sigh. "Ah, sir, they will no make it. We must do something, or they will never survive!"

"Do you recognize any of them? Is it indeed the survivors of the dike militia?" the lord protector asked patiently.

Clerans peered hard through the binoculars. He could only just see the faces of the men, but could hardly be sure enough of their features to identify them clearly. Clerans could feel the blood rushing hot in his veins as he watched the action. He had been in just the same place last night. Could his Da be down there now? He looked closely at each of the men before the little shop, trying to identify them as best he could by the clothing they were wearing and their manner of moving — ah, but it was hard to see much at all, with the pirates pressing hard against the men, and the men themselves dancing about like maniacs trying to defend themselves.

Clerans let out his breath slowly and licked his lips. "It is certainly the dike militia, sir." He paused, still looking closely at the men fighting. "I think, sir... no, I'm pretty certain that I cen see Seth Morrys — he is the miller on Busyway Street, sir. And then... yes, sir, that's pretty clearly Culym Alculi, sir, the dwarf blacksmith from Broadway."

Suddenly, a loud cry wafted across the distance from the Lower Court. Clerans saw the men before the shop deliver one last volley at their assailants before rushing all at once back into the shop. At the same moment, every window in the shop blazed with smoke and fire. The pirates who rushed at the retreating militiamen fell back, some falling dead, while others toppled over the corpses, writhing on the ground with shrieks of agony.

Yet as the last man entered the shop and turned to slam the door behind him, he presented the profile of his face to Clerans' view for just an instant; but an instant was all that Clerans needed to recognize him.

"It is my brother, sir!" Clerans cried desperately. "It is my brother Laendon, sir! Oh, we must do something! We ha' to save them!"

"What ha' happened, then?" Governor Wilkins asked breathlessly. "What wos that cry fer?"

"They ha' fallen back," Clerans replied, his heart pounding in his chest. "The militia, I mean, they ha' retreated into the shop. The pirates are rushin' forward now, an' tryin' to beat in the door. No, wait... what is this? They tain torches, sir. Ay, an' they are layin' bundles against the shop. They are goin' to burn them out, sir. We must do *something!*"

Clerans looked up at the lord protector desperately. His pulse throbbed in his head.

"Oh, sir!" Clerans pleaded, "I know what it is like to be pinned up inside some shop, waitin' fer the pirates to kill you one by one. Please, sir, ye *must* do something right now, or every man in that shop will die! That is my brother in there!"

At that moment, there was a clatter of hooves on the cobblestones of Merchani Square. Clerans looked back to see over two dozen dragoons (probably newly come from Entwerp Proper), reining in their horses and dismounting.

Caedmon Wilkins turned suddenly on Captain Smydhac. "Sound the order to assemble for war, Captain. We advance on Newcourt. With God's help, we will draw the enemy's strength away from the shop where they threaten our countrymen."

# PRINCE OF THE POWER OF THE AIR

*H*aeli gripped her *alwmli* firmly and braced her feet against the tower just in time. As Tiya-Aenji fell, she landed right across Haeli's back before continuing to tumble downwards. The blow took the wind out of Haeli, but she still held on tightly. In a moment, the rope snapped tight, and Tiya-Aenji dangled from the end. One of Haeli's feet slipped at the sudden jolt to her harness, but she kept her grip. Thank God, Tiya-Aenji was so light.

Yet Haeli had no more time to think about this, for at that moment, she felt a shadow falling on her from above. She looked up just in time to see the black, lizard-like shape of an enormous beast launching itself from the top of the tower. Though Haeli did not get a good look at it before it vanished from her view, she knew what it was. The pteranodon. So *this* was its lair.

The dragon screamed again. It was close by, but so shrill that Haeli could hardly tell where it came from, whether from the other side of the tower, or else from directly behind her. All Haeli knew was that the great flying reptile was not above her. She dared not turn her head and look for the pteranodon lest she lose her grip and both she and Tiya-Aenji fall to their deaths.

"What is it?" She could hear Titus shrieking excitedly from the ground.

A gun fired from down on the ridge. Another ear-piercing scream cut through the thin mountain air.

"Haeli!" Tiya-Aenji screamed in warning.

But what was she supposed to do? She was stuck there, totally exposed to the flying reptile's attack.

At that moment, Haeli felt a rush of air all around her, and a shadow fell over her. The pteranodon screamed again, this time as if the beast was right at her ear. Haeli clung tightly to her two *alwmli* and bowed her head close against the tower for protection. She dared not look now.

The great membranous wings beat the air just behind her, then, like the flick of a whip, they lashed her across the back. The blow startled her more than it hurt, since surely the beast would not risk injuring its own wings, but Haeli cringed away just the same, her palms sweating as she clung desperately to the *alwmli*. In a moment, that creature would snap at her with its toothed beak.

"Don't shoot!" Titus was shrieking from the base of the tower. "Don't shoot! You'll hit Haeli!"

Just then, Tiya-Aenji let out a wild scream, like the scream of an injured puma. The rope that held her and Tiya-Aenji together jerked suddenly. Was Tiya-Aenji climbing up it?

The pteranodon seemed to hesitate, and the beating of the wings stopped for a moment. Then Haeli felt Tiya-Aenji's webbed hand grab the harness where it wrapped around her waist. The rasping sound that came a moment later was the only way Haeli knew the little nymph had drawn her *kukri*. Tiya-Aenji was still screaming, dangling from Haeli, holding on to the harness with one hand and thrashing about like a wild thing.

The pteranodon let out another scream, and then the shadow fell back a little. Another gunshot rang through the air, and Titus let out a triumphant cheer. Out of the corner of her eye, Haeli could see the wings of the pteranodon disappearing behind the other side of the tower. Was it over then? Had Martyn shot it?

Haeli now felt Tiya-Aenji's hands on her shoulder, and the little nymph scrambled up until she was standing on Haeli's two *alwmli*. Haeli looked up. Tiya-Aenji was staring down at her. Haeli trembled all over, and her pulse pounded in her head.

"Well done," Tiya-Aenji said. She was panting, her already-oily skin gleaming even more with perspiration.

"Well done yourself," Haeli replied with a nervous laugh. "Did they — Martyn I mean — did he..."

Tiya-Aenji shook her head. "I do not think so. It is still in the air, at least."

Haeli sighed. "Are we still in danger, then?"

"You will still need to hold on, in case I fall again," Tiya-Aenji replied. "I will have to free-climb back up to my *alwmli*."

Haeli nodded, planting her feet firmly against the tower. She gripped the handles of her *alwmli* tightly, then looked back up at Tiya-Aenji.

Beginning her muttered prayer again, the little nymph slowly ascended the tower. Haeli imagined that it must be a hard climb for Tiya-Aenji without her climbing tools. After all, though the surface of the tower was rather rough and uneven, providing ample bumps for footholds, very few of those bumps protruded far enough to grab hold of. Tiya-Aenji only needed to climb about eight feet up to reach her *alwmli*, but Haeli hardly knew how she would do it. Was it even possible to free-climb that distance? Haeli gripped her *alwmli* more tightly now, bracing herself in case Tiya-Aenji should fall again.

The little nymph woman took her time, slowly climbing up the tower. She trembled from the exertion. With a prick of apprehension, Haeli realized that she, too, was trembling. If Tiya-Aenji fell, would she even have enough strength to catch her again? Or perhaps she was still trembling from the excitement and adrenaline rush of the pteranodon's attack.

Tiya-Aenji now reached out with her webbed hand and grabbed the handle of her *alwmli*. Haeli let out a great sigh of relief. So that was done. Tiya-Aenji was safe for the present.

Just then, Haeli heard the pteranodon scream again, though this time the scream was not so near.

"There it is!" she heard Titus shouting excitedly.

Again, she heard Martyn firing his rifle, the sharp report echoing loudly in the thin air. What was going on down there? Had Martyn shot the pteranodon this time? Where was the pteranodon?

"Do not look down, now, Haeli!" Tiya-Aenji was saying. "I need you to keep holding on, in case..."

Tiya-Aenji hauled herself upward, now grabbing onto the edge of the battlement. Haeli braced herself as firmly as she could against the tower. Might there be a second pteranodon on that tower?

With a great heave, Tiya-Aenji drew her chest over the parapet and then slithered over onto the other side. Haeli looked up anxiously as she saw Tiya-Aenji's webbed feet disappear over the edge of the tower. She was at the top then! She had made it. Below her, Titus let out a triumphant cheer.

Now, Tiya-Aenji's round head popped over the edge of the tower. "It is up to you now!" she called down to Haeli as she reached down and pulled her *alwmli* free from the last crack.

Haeli took a deep breath, then she drew out one of her *alwmli,* hauled herself up as high as she could, and thrust it into the next crack. She was climbing again. Haeli took her time, taking care to thrust each *alwmli* into the cracks as far as it would go. She breathed steadily as she continued her ascent.

Even with the care Haeli took, she still climbed this last

section of the tower much more quickly than Tiya-Aenji had. Finally, she thrust her *alwmli* into the last crack, then, drawing herself up once more, she grabbed hold of the battlement. The stone was rough and slick with dew.

Haeli clamped her teeth together and then hauled herself up and over the edge. In an instant, she was toppling over the other side of the battlement. Quickly, Haeli got to her feet, and she looked around. Tiya-Aenji was standing not far away, leaning up against the inside of the battlement. The little nymph's head barely came past the height of the lowest part of the crenels. Tiya-Aenji's mouth was wide open. She was panting and gripping the front of her shirt, waving it to create a wind up it. Haeli smiled. Tiya-Aenji surely wasn't that hot — the air was quite cool up so high — more than likely she was just trying to breathe better as nymphs breathed through their bellies as much as through their lungs.

Haeli now turned to observe the top of the tower. The whole parapet couldn't have been over twelve feet from one end to the other. The stones on the inside here were just as smooth and well-planed as the outside of the tower had been rough and uneven. Hunched up against the far wall of the parapet lay a strange pile of dried marsh-grass, twigs, mud, bits of cloth, and other trash. As she looked at it closely, Haeli noticed that this pile was hollowed out at the top to form a sort of bowl.

A chill ran down Haeli's spine. Was this the pteranodon's nest? No wonder it had attacked them so viciously. And if Martyn had not shot the pteranodon yet, then they could all be sure that the dreaded flying lizard would be back. Surely it would not abandon its nest.

Haeli pointed to the nest and turned to Tiya-Aenji. "Was that there when you were up here last?"

Tiya-Aenji shook her head, still panting.

Then Martyn's voice called down from below. "How is it up there? Are you safe?"

Haeli leaned over the battlements and waved down at Martyn. "We are alright, but the pteranodon's nest is up here! You did not kill it yet, did you?"

"No," Martyn hollered back. "Do ye see it from up there?"

Haeli looked all around her, for the first time taking in the scenic view. She was so high up! She was at a near-level with many of the mountain peaks along the ridge, and she could see for miles in every direction. The air was thin and cold, yet it tasted sweet in Haeli's mouth. For a moment, the view took her breath away, but then Haeli regained her focus; the pteranodon — she was looking for the pteranodon.

Scanning the sky above her for a moment, the only thing Haeli could see in that open, blue expanse was the sun, still hanging low in the eastern sky above the sea. Then where had that monster gone? She looked across the mountain ridges and peered — as best she could — into the valleys and ravines, hoping to see the pteranodon flitting about close to the ground. Still, she could see no sign of that winged reptile. But it might be there for all she knew; the beast would be hard to see against the wooded slopes of the mountains.

Haeli leaned back over the battlements. "I can not see it."

Martyn shook his head. "We ha' best be quick then! Send down the *alwmli.*"

As he spoke, Aarushi fluttered up to the top of the tower. Haeli handed Aarushi one of her *alwmli*, and then the harrier flew back to Martyn, depositing the sacred climbing tool in his hand. Aarushi repeated her flight until she brought all four of the *alwmli* down to Martyn. Meanwhile, Martyn and Titus hurriedly tied themselves together in harnesses.

Haeli looked on anxiously from the top of the tower. Surely the pteranodon would come back. Martyn had better hurry! What would he and Titus do if the pteranodon attacked them mid-climb? And what would she do from up here? If only she had a rifle herself! She was a good enough shot to be a threat to that flying reptile — if she had a gun.

She could see Martyn and Titus discussing something briefly, and then, as if coming to a consensus, Martyn approached the tower and began to climb. Haeli could tell, even from this height, that Martyn was starting at the same place that Tiya-Aenji had started. Martyn was clearly moving cautiously, thrusting each of his *alwmli* deep into the cracks between the stones before he trusted his weight to them. Still, Martyn was climbing rapidly. He moved with such confidence and poise, as if he had done this sort of work his whole life. Haeli shook her head. Martyn was always like that, confident and capable at whatever he lay his hand to, as if God had given him an extra measure of talent. Why did everything go so easily for him? Really, it wasn't fair.

Martyn hardly climbed six feet of the tower when Titus began his climb. He thrust his *alwmli* into the tower slowly and, with difficultly, furrowing his brow in great concentration, like a toddler first learning to read. Couldn't he hurry? Who knew when the pteranodon would return?

Haeli ground her teeth together in frustration. Yes, Titus was certainly slowing Martyn down. Martyn would stop now and then to let the big Slyzwirian man catch up. Though perhaps Titus wasn't so slow and clumsy as he appeared; nearly anyone would look clumsy compared to Martyn.

Yet Haeli's thoughts were interrupted as she heard Tiya-Aenji catch her breath. Before Haeli had time to turn around and look at the little nymph, Tiya-Aenji's webbed hands grabbed her by the waist, pulling her back from the edge of the battlements. At that same instant, Haeli heard those great wings snapping open as the loud scream of the pteranodon sounded in her ear.

For a moment, Haeli was tumbling about on the stone parapet, tangled together with Tiya-Aenji. Then somehow she found her feet again. In front of her, the gigantic frame of the pteranodon blocked out the sun as it perched on the edge of the battlements. It was quite a stunning sight; Haeli had never observed the dreaded creature so closely.

Its huge, gray wings were spread wide, hanging over the tower on both sides, yet its body was comparatively small, not much larger than a vulture's. It had no feathers on its wiry frame, only dull scales and small hairs which bristled like spikes. The lizard's shiny, black beak and crest gleamed with the sun behind them, and its claws curled tightly around the stones that formed the battlement. The pteranodon stared down at Haeli with squinted, snake-like eyes.

Haeli took in all of this in a moment — for a moment was all she had before the beast sprang at her. The pteranodon screamed again, then threw back its wings, launching itself at Haeli. Haeli could see the creature's beak streaking through the air towards her, and she threw herself to the side.

One of the great wings slammed her in the face, and she toppled forward onto her hands and knees. Before she had time to scramble to her feet again, she felt the pteranodon's scaly claws seize her by the ankle, sinking easily into her flesh. Haeli cried out in pain. The dreadful reptile stood poised above her, ready to strike at her again with its wicked beak.

"Haeli!" It was Martyn's voice, floating up from below. "What's happenin'? Are ye alright?"

Haeli lashed out with both of her fists, letting out a cry of rage. She had nothing to fight with, but she had to fight back. A mute beast would not best her. With considerable force, Haeli struck the pteranodon several times in the body, and it drew back with another scream. But the creature did not release its hold on Haeli's ankle. It flapped its wings furiously to keep its balance against Haeli's onslaught. The wings struck Haeli across the face, stinging like the blows of a whip.

*Haeli and the Pteronodon*

Suddenly, Tiya-Aenji appeared between Haeli and the pteranodon, her *kukri* drawn. Bellowing out her same unearthly warcry, the little nymph struck at the pteranodon, delivering several powerful blows with her knife, one to the claw that held Haeli, and two more at the pteranodon's small body.

Haeli hurriedly scrambled to her feet, backing away from the winged reptile as it recoiled under Tiya-Aenji's assault. Why could she still feel the creature's claw around her ankle?

Haeli looked around desperately for a weapon, or a large stone, or something she could use to fight off this reptile. She had to help Tiya-Aenji, but how? Tripping on her injured foot, Haeli tumbled into the nest on the far end of the tower. At that moment, Haeli saw a strange, oblong object in the tumbled mess of dried grass and mud. Could it be an egg?

As Tiya-Aenji now struck out at the pteranodon's head, the ghastly reptile batted her hand aside with the edge of its beak. Then, as the creature seemed to regain its composure, it swatted Tiya-Aenji to the side with a single blow of its wings. Tiya-Aenji toppled over, landing heavily against the inside walls of the battlements.

Haeli snatched up the egg in both hands, standing to her feet and turning back defiantly to face the pteranodon. She could see Tiya-Aenji with her back against the battlements, brandishing her *kukri* desperately as the pteranodon hunched over her like some dark and hideous vulture.

"The devil have you!" Haeli screamed, holding the egg over her head for the creature to see.

The pteranodon turned away from Tiya-Aenji for a moment and let out another ear-piercing scream. Haeli could tell that it was gathering itself to pounce on her again. Taking a deep breath, Haeli hurled the egg over the edge of the tower.

The pteranodon screamed again, launching into the air and flapping hurriedly after the falling egg. One of its wings just brushed Haeli as it flew by, and then it was gone.

# 33

# FOEMEN AT THE GATE

As the shrill sound of the dragoons' bugles pierced the air, Clerans rushed along the Old Dike Road, following just behind the stately figure of the lord protector. The dragoons and regulars who had been in the council all hurried down the road as well, while the reinforcements from Entwerp Proper brought up the rear.

Clerans paused for a moment in his forward rush to look at the Lower Court through the binoculars one last time. Yes, sure enough, the pirates had paused in their preparations to burn down the shop where Laendon and his comrades were taking cover, and they were now all looking with concern at this impromptu regiment of Llaedhwythi soldiers.

Having fallen behind while taking this look, Clerans pushed himself to hurry ahead again, elbowing his way through the mass of moving men until he was back at the front. He was certain that they were about to engage the enemy, and he wanted to be among the first to fire on the pirates. They would pay dearly for what they had done to his home and family!

In no time at all, Caedmon Wilkins and his followers entered the Upper Court. Here, a group of about ten regulars and twenty Indigie warriors already stood guard. A look of relief seemed to spread over their faces when they saw the lord protector and his reinforcements arrive.

On the eastern end of the Upper Court, about thirty yards past the opening in the old dike where the road ran downhill to connect the Upper Court to Newcourt, a barricade blocked the whole road. The barricade had clearly been compiled of plunder from the nearby houses in great haste last night. Stray timbers and pieces of furniture protruded from it at odd angles, but the barricade looked quite sturdy. All across the top of the barricade crouched the swarthy forms of pirates, humans, leprechauns, and gnomes, mostly, with their muskets trained forward as they huddled behind tables, bookshelves, and couches. Behind the barricade, Clerans could see the tall schoolhouse (one of the very few two-story buildings in the entire village) rising like a great sentinel, its large, red brick chimney seeming to look down on the pirates disdainfully. The guards in the Upper Court seemed unwilling to get too close to the barricade, hardly daring to approach as close as the old dike wall.

Caedmon Wilkins marched forward until he was in the opening of the dike wall, just before the road sloped down towards the barricade. The regulars quickly drew up their line along the road to Caedmon Wilkins' right, joining with the line of dragoons who formed a line of their own on the lord protector's left. Captain Smydhac stood in front of his dragoons, and Governor Braedhwyc stood just to Lord Protector Wilkins' right by his regulars.

Clerans took his place in the front line of the regulars, quickly making sure that his rifle was loaded and ready. He could see the pirates leveling their muskets at the line of Llaedhwythi men, but no one fired. Clerans guessed there were only about twenty pirates on the barricade, yet more pirates were swarming up to the top of this make-shift barrier, holding their guns at the ready.

"Do we fire, sir?" Captain Smydhac asked. "We should strike now, look ye, before 'hey all finish assemblint!"

"No," Caedmon Wilkins replied, "I do not mean to risk open combat with them just yet, look you. We have already accomplished our objective. They are leaving those souls from the dike militia alone."

Captain Smydhac shook his head in consternation. "Ay-eigh! It is shot 'hey should all be; ivery mother's son av 'hem!"

Just then, a tall, swarthy figure climbed up to the top of the barricade. Clerans recognized him at once; it was that villain Vania Bloodrummer. Clerans clenched his teeth in anger. He could feel his blood boiling inside him. If he didn't have good discipline over himself, he would have raised his gun right then and there and shot that cocky swordsman dead.

Clerans could hear Sheriff Laei's voice from those many training sessions.

"Breathe, Clerans. Relax. Ye cen no let yerself get excited. *Ye* must be the master o' yer self, no yer emotions. If yer emotions rule ye, then... well, that's a quick way to get yerself killed."

Clerans breathed deeply, trying to calm himself. Yes, he was letting his emotions take too much control of him. He had to relax. He had to remain calm. If they were about to come to a fight, he had to be calm. Martyn was not here to protect him if he lost his head again.

Vania Bloodrummer did not crouch for cover like the other pirates at the top of the barricade, but he stood up tall and tauntingly for all to see.

"Which is!" the pirate swordsman said, tossing his raven hair in the wind. "Who do you think haves comed to see us, lads? Is that the lord protector hisself?" And he flashed a roguish smile.

Caedmon Wilkins simply looked at the pirate steadily. "And if I should venture a guess, look you, I should say that you are Vania Bloodrummer, chief officer under Captain Longfinch, and former spezhetary captain under the doSeqtir Kafals?"

Vania bowed low in a taunting manner. "You confuse me with Captain Pennywraith. I wasn't ever a spezhetary. Couldn't abide their hats, whatever."

The lord protector smiled disdainfully. "I have come, look you, to deliver my terms for your surrender."

"Which is very good," Vania replied with an impudent smile. "I was only just now wanting to give you *our* terms."

"I will not hear your terms," Caedmon Wilkins replied authoritatively. "You will accept mine, look you, or suffer the consequences."

"What consequences?" Vania Bloodrummer asked, toying with the handle of his saber.

"I will reduce you to a powder," Caedmon Wilkins replied. "I will show you the same mercy that you showed to my dike militia. Not a single one of you will survive my harrowing."

Vania chuckled. "That's a bold threat, your excellency. Do you really think you can carry it out against the crew of Captain Longfinch?"

The pirates let out a cheer.

"And where is your captain, then?" Caedmon Wilkins asked loudly.

Vania Bloodrummer paused, but he did not reply.

"I will tell ye where," Governor Braedhwyc broke in, "we tain him blocked up in a hole in the ground, with my men to guard him an' shoot him should he stir himself."

"Baptism!" Vania replied, spitting in the governor's direction. "That's just what you think, now isn't it? Well then, you don't know Captain Longfinch very well if'n you think what he hasn't already planned his way out, whatever!"

The pirates cheered again.

"I will give you my terms," Caedmon Wilkins said, "and they will apply to your captain too, look you, should he ever show his head."

A couple of the pirates spat in Caedmon Wilkins' direction

at this last comment, but the lord protector paid them no heed as he continued. "My terms are as follows:

"First, you all will immediately release the men you now hold captive in the shop in the Lower Court. Any harm which you do to a single one of them, I and my men will do to every one of you."

Some of the pirates snickered at this, and someone jeered back, "And I'd like to see you try, anoint you!"

"Second," Caedmon Wilkins continued, "you will lay down your weapons on that barricade and then assemble — unarmed, I repeat — in this Upper Court. Whereupon my men will bind you and bring you to Triumvria. There, we will give you each to a different merchant ship to serve as a compulsory deckhand for no less than three years' time."

"Here now!" a pirate jeered back. "You really think what we'll go along with that?"

The other pirates laughed.

Caedmon Wilkins still stood unmoved. "Those are my terms, and they are the only way, look you, that you will escape the full extent of the Llaedhwythi law."

Vania Bloodrummer only grinned. Clerans couldn't help but think that the pirate swordsman looked an awful lot like a shark. "Which is, perhaps you had better hear my terms then."

"As I told you before," Caedmon Wilkins replied. "I will not hear your terms. The only terms that I will accept, look you, are my own."

"Which is!" Vania exclaimed with some contempt. "Look at this high and mighty pride what these baptized people have, whatever."

So saying, Bloodrummer motioned to the other side of the barricade. After a moment's pause, two more pirates climbed to the top of the barricade, carrying a hostage each. Clerans could tell at a glance that the two hostages were Mr. Dawdi, the cartwright, and his young son; they had been among the dike militia the night before. Both Mr. Dawdi and his son were bound but not gagged, with bruises on every visible part of their bodies. Clerans bit the inside of his cheek in anger.

"My lads haved a bit of fun with these two last night," Vania Bloodrummer said, drumming his fingers on the hilt of his saber. "But we haved the mercy to leave them alive, with nothing cut off, whatever."

The pirates let out a chorus of bawdy laughter.

Caedmon Wilkins only looked at Vania. His eyes narrowed, sharp as daggers, but the lord protector said nothing.

Vania now pulled out two pistols from his belt, holding them dramatically in his hands. "Which is, I'd be more than happy to change the situation."

The pirates laughed again.

Mr. Dawdi pulled himself forward, clearly trying to wrestle himself free from the pirate who held him. "Mr. Wilkins, sir!" he cried, his voice cracked and hoarse. "Mr. Wilkins, sir, do no mind me, sir. I do no care fer myself; only think o' my son, sir. He is jist a boy. If there is anything ye'll cen do–"

But before he could get out another word, a pirate stepped up and rammed his musket stock into Mr. Dawdi's stomach. Mr. Dawdi doubled back at the blow, gasping for air.

Vania turned back on the lord protector with a sneer. "You heared the man then; think of the boy. You wouldn't want any harm to come to him now, would you?"

"Present arms!" Captain Smydhac bellowed.

The dragoons responded with poise and precision, shouldering their rifles as one and presenting a line of glittering bayonets in the morning sun.

The regulars looked at the governor inquiringly. Looking back at the dragoons first, Governor Braedhwyc wiped pus from his bad eye and then repeated Captain Smydhac's order.

"Present arms!"

The regulars obeyed quickly and deftly, though Clerans

thought they lacked the finesse with which the dragoons had acted. Clerans too shouldered his rifle, aiming directly for Vania Bloodrummer's heart. As soon as Governor Braedhwyc gave the order to fire, that pirate would be dead. Clerans would not miss at this close range.

Caedmon Wilkins remained perfectly still and perfectly silent.

Vania Bloodrummer pointed his pistols nonchalantly at Mr. Dawdi and his son. "Which is, here are my terms: you will withdraw your men from the dikes at once and allow us to board our ship unharmed."

"Or what?" Governor Braedhwyc replied, his face twitching in anger. "Ye kill those two innocent men, I suppose?"

"Oh no," Vania Bloodrummer replied with a smirk. "*You* will be the one who kills these two 'innocent men.'"

Caedmon Wilkins now spoke again. "I do not make bargains with pirates, look you. You will accept my terms or suffer the full punishment of the law."

Vania shrugged. "Well then, you've just contemned these two men to their deaths. *You* are responsible for what follows."

And he leveled his pistol at Mr. Dawdi's head.

"Please, sir!" Mr. Dawdi whimpered. "My son... he's only a boy..."

Caedmon Wilkins' jaw clenched, and the veins stood out on his throat. "You would attempt to impute your crime on me?"

Vania Bloodrummer fired his pistol, and Mr. Dawdi collapsed in a heap at the top of the barricade. The pirates let out a cheer mixed with laughter. With a smirk of pleasure, the pirate who had held Mr. Dawdi now kicked his body savagely. The corpse rolled forward slightly and then toppled down the near side of the barricade, lying there for all of the Llaedhwythi men to see. Clerans bit the inside of his cheek harder. Above the noise of the pirates' ribald laughter, he heard the young Dawdi boy sobbing.

Vania sneered, casting aside his first pistol and leveling his second at the young Dawdi boy's head. "You could have saved them, but you didn't."

"You have an abysmal view of morality," Caedmon Wilkins replied, his blue eyes flashing with anger. "Abysmal. I mean that, look you, in every sense. Do you really think that I will be held culpable for your sins? No, sir. I will not fall prey to your guilt-manipulations. You, and you alone, will bear the guilt for that man's death, and the death of his son, should you choose to pull that trigger now. Any harm you do to him will be held against you in my court, but more importantly, it will be held against you in the court of the Almighty God in the Last Day."

"Baptize you!" a pirate yelled out in reply. "Christen the lot of you!"

"If you will not take caution for your life," Caedmon Wilkins bellowed in response, "take caution for your soul!"

"Shall we fire?" Governor Braedhwyc asked, looking to the lord protector.

Caedmon Wilkins clenched his teeth, giving a slight shake of his head.

Vania only flashed another roguish smile before he lowered his pistol a little and fired. The charge struck the young Dawdi boy in the right knee. Letting out an ear-piercing scream of pain, the young boy writhed in agony in his captor's grip, his right leg now dangling from him like a wet washcloth. Even Governor Braedhwyc flinched at the sight. Clerans could feel his knees shaking in anger. He was still looking down the barrel of his gun at Vania Bloodrummer. If Governor Wilkins would just give the order, he would kill that villain!

Vania Bloodrummer cast aside his second pistol and now turned to face Caedmon Wilkins, a smile of delight spreading over his twisted face as he put his hands on his hips. "It's your last chance, your excellency. Do you want to save the boy's life? Will you accept my terms?"

Caedmon Wilkins took a deep breath and then let it out slowly. "You have my answer already, you dog."

Vania Bloodrummer callously drew out his saber. "Have it your way, then. You were the one who ignored that father's pleas, whatever."

So saying, the lanky pirate took a step towards the Dawdi boy and delivered a single stroke across the young boy's neck. A smile played about the Bloodrummer's face.

"Fire!" Caedmon Wilkins hissed, his voice tight with emotion.

With a sound like thunder, Clerans and the others discharged their guns.

Bloodrummer had just enough time to pitch the Dawdi boy's corpse after his father, before he ducked below the barricade. Not a single pirate fell, as they took cover in time, the bullets peppering their defenses harmlessly.

Again, the pirates cheered, but Vania's voice rose above the others. "Which is, your excellency, you'd better hope I don't get my hands on any of those other men in that shop by the Lower Court. If I do, whatever, I'd really enjoy making you watch what I'd do to them."

"Baptism," Governor Braedhwyc cursed. "Shall we charge them?"

The lord protector turned to face his men, letting out a long breath and clenching his fists. Clerans could see his eyes flashing like blue flame under his military cap.

"Gentlemen," he finally said. "That is all the business we have here for now. We will reconvene our council at the kirk. In the meantime, resume your guard of the pirates' position. If you see any pirate attempting to escape from the area we have confined them to, look you, show him no mercy."

34

## THE ETCHINGS

$\mathcal{E}$lla was shaking all over. Ernest stood mutely beside her. It was over, yes, but she was still shaking. She should feel happy and exhilarated; after all, she had just chased that ghost off a second time. God had helped her again! Shouldn't she be excited?

Yet somehow it had felt different this time, as if there was no power in the hymn, or else that God wasn't standing beside her this time. But that couldn't be true. God wouldn't desert her now, would He? Ella trembled all over. But what would happen next time? That ghost said he would come again. Would the hymn even scare it next time?

"O God, help us," Ella breathed.

As if Ella's words gave him permission to speak, Ernest let out a loud gasp — was he just now breathing?

"What the baptism was that?"

"I assume it was the ghost," Ella replied, trying to sound confident.

"Oh, yes, I'm certain of that," Ernest said, "but I meant what was *that*? What just happened?"

Ella swallowed. "Well, I guess I sang a hymn."

"I heared that," Ernest turned to look at Ella closely. "Obviously, you singed a hymn, but what does that have to do with anything?"

Ella shrugged and licked her lips. "Maybe it doesn't like hymns?"

Ernest turned back to look up the dark staircase, and he trembled all over. "Or maybe he just let us go... for now."

The hair on the back of Ella's neck stood up at this suggestion. That was not a thought she wanted to entertain. But what if it were true? What if the ghost had really left them alone just because it wanted to and not because the hymn had any power over it? Maybe the ghost was satisfied after eating those three pirates, and it would come after her and Ernest later, once it was hungry again. She tried to still her hands from trembling, but she couldn't.

"We must get out of he'e," Ella said.

Ernest shrugged. "That's true, but how are we supposed to do that, eh?"

Ella pointed back up the stairs. "We have to go back up. I think we could find our way back to the Gwambi doo'h — the one we ente'ed by."

"Are you mad?" Ernest cried. "You want us to go right back up those steps? You want us to follow that... that... *thing*?"

"That's the only way we know to get out," Ella replied.

Ernest shook his head emphatically. "No, never, and not even in a hundred years!"

Ella ground her teeth together in frustration. "How else a'e we supposed to get out of these tunnels?"

"We will find another way." Ernest crossed his arms in front of his chest and looked at Ella determinedly.

Ella shook her head. "Don't be an idiot. How would we eve'h find anothe'h way? Just look at this maze of passageways. How do we even know that the'e *is* anothe'h way out of he'e?"

"We'll have to find another way," Ernest said. "If'n we go up those stairs right after that ghost, it's certain to eat us alive — both of us."

Ella shook her head in frustration. "That's a w'isk we have to take. What's the alternative then? We wande'h a'ound in these tunnels until we sta've to death?"

Ernest shrugged. "I imagine that's a more pleasant way to die than being eaten alive by some supernatural monster-thing."

Suddenly, Ella heard a loud clanging sound coming from the stairway. Both she and Ernest froze. It sounded as if it had come from a good way up the stairway, probably a few levels above them. Ella strained her ears in the darkness. It was so still and silent in those passageways that she probably could have heard a feather falling to the ground two stories above her.

Yes, there was definitely some kind of noise coming from up those stairs. It was really only an indistinct shuffling, but now and then Ella thought she could hear something metallic. Then, all at once, Ella could distinguish the sounds of voices amidst the muffled rustling.

Ernest caught his breath. "It's Longfinch!" he whispered.

Ella's heart sank to her toes.

"See what I mean?" Ernest continued in a very low voice. "We *can't* go back up those stairs. If'n the ghost doesn't eat us, then Longfinch will kill us."

Ella ground her teeth together in frustration. Ernest was right. They couldn't go back now. She took a deep breath and let it out slowly. What were they to do now? How were they going to get out of these God-forsaken tunnels? Was there any other way out?

Suddenly, the image of the Gwambi Tower flashed through Ella's brain. Of course! Sir Saemwel and her father had made it to the tower through this maze. Now she had to do the same! A sense of resolution filled Ella's heart again, and she straightened up. There was still another way out of these passages. She had come into these tunnels following her father's footsteps, and now she would follow his footsteps going out.

Ernest picked up the lantern. "At least we have a light now."

Ella nodded. "Yes, and I know whe'e to go."

Ernest looked at her hopefully. "You know how to get out on here?"

Ella shook her head. "Not the way to it, but I know that the'e *is* a way."

Ernest nodded, still speaking in a low voice. "Then we'd best get moving before Longfinch catches up on us." He looked down both ways of the large passageway. "What do you say, Ella, forward or backward?"

Ella glanced down the long straight passageway before them and then down the narrower passage which curved around the stair. "Fo'wa'd — and quickly!"

And so they hurried forward, guided by the light of the pirates' lantern. Soon the stairway behind them disappeared into the darkness — and so too did the grisly remains of the three pirates. The passageway before them stretched out straight and even for as far as the lantern could cast its light. Walking forward as briskly as she could, Ella glanced around at the walls, as if to assure herself that nothing was stalking them.

Soon she noticed that the passageway was larger now. The roof was considerably higher than it had been at the stairway, and the walls were farther apart. After walking for about another hundred yards, Ella guessed that the walls had now widened to about twenty or thirty feet apart. It seemed much less like a passageway now and more like a grand hall.

Yet as they walked on, Ella suddenly noticed something on the right side wall of the passageway ahead of them. Was it writing of some kind? Intuitively, Ella rushed forward for a closer look.

"Ella!" Ernest hissed in a low voice, but then he followed her, the lantern bouncing up and down with every step, making the light leap and dance in the great hall.

Ella quickly came up to the marking on the wall. It was not writing at all, but an image — or perhaps a very complex hieroglyph — etched into the granite surface of the wall. The image was of a ship with ragged sails, but it was a strange and small ship, the like of which Ella had never seen before. On board the ship, Ella could just see the faces of a few dozen men — all gaunt, with hollow eyes — as they peered over the sides of the ship. The etching was so peculiar, so compelling, Ella almost felt as if she could feel these sailors' pains and longing for land as she gazed upon this strange picture. And the etchings were so strange — so smooth — almost as if no one etched them, but they had simply grown out of the granite like lichen.

But what was this picture, and what did it mean? Ella peered closely at it and caught her breath. It seemed so ancient and distant, and yet at the same time, imminent and very present. She was quite certain that this picture had really *happened.* Those men on that ship were really men with real faces. It was like gazing into the past — though how far into the past, Ella could not say. Did this image have anything to do with this network of tunnels?

Then Ella noticed another picture a little way down the tunnel. Ella walked quickly over to this next picture and looked at it with the same spell-bound awe. It was the same ship from the first etching, only now it was cast upon a great reef, floundering like some injured sea-monster as the cruel waves beat upon it. The gaunt-faced men, however, were on shore, making some kind of burnt offering upon a beach before high mountains.

But now what was this? There was another picture, much closer now: little carved faces — strange and wild — peering out of the thick forests at the gaunt-faced men. What were they? Savages of the forest? Little nymphs like the one who had brought Ella to Entwerp? Yet the picture continued, and as Ella looked down the great hall, she could see these strange carvings all along the wall for as far as the little lantern cast its light.

She glanced at the next etching. There were the gaunt-faced men again, building tiny houses and fires, and they were hunting with crude spears and skinning gigantic animals. For the first time now, Ella noticed women among the gaunt-faced men, with a few weak children. They were all dressed in furs, huddling before fires. Now, Ella saw rows and rows of dead men on the ground, away from the fires. They seemed to be the gaunt-faced men, and they were emaciated and almost skeletal. Thick drifts of snow swallowed up the pile of the dead. It must be the wintertime then, a time of starvation, sickness, and death for these gaunt-faced people.

Ah! but in the next picture, Ella caught her breath in horror. There were the little savage men whom she had seen earlier, only now they looked even more wild and savage. Some were small and scrawny, and others were very square-looking, with great, unkempt beards. They bore spears, knives, and other weapons that were hooked like claws or cruel beaks.

The wild men were attacking the village of the gaunt-faced men, killing, dismembering, and devouring them. Those few that survived were fleeing into the forest or huddling together in caves.

In the next etching, the gaunt-faced people were together again, and they stood around a great blazing fire. They held their gaunt faces towards the sky as if petitioning some deity for help. Ella's heart stirred within her as she looked at this etching. How could she not feel for these poor people who were wrecked on a foreign shore, starving, and hunted down like animals? It was only natural that they should look to God for help. Yet as Ella looked closer at the picture, a sudden chill ran down her spine. Those were not logs in the fire, but bones. The body of a child was even now being consumed in its blaze.

The next etching was larger than all the previous pictures, and its details were unmistakable. There was an extensive structure made of stone, with a large chimney and smoke billowing out of it. Was it a great kiln, or perhaps a forge? The mountains rose high above this structure, and the sun — etched in glorious detail — looked over all, carved into the wall almost where it touched the ceiling.

The gaunt-faced men entered one side of this structure, hauling in strangely shaped rocks. Out the other side of the structure they emerged again, carrying swords, spears, shields, and helmets — the women carried shovels, sickles, hoes, and devices which looked not unlike wheelbarrows.

And now the women and their scrawny children bent double with their hoes over cultivated ground. The gaunt-faced men looked on, laying stones together to form grand houses and the walls of fortresses. Yet in the forest behind, Ella could again see the leering faces of that savage people who had so nearly wiped out the gaunt-faced men during the winter.

And now the gaunt-faced men had lined themselves up in array as for battle — swords, spears, axes, and pennons flying in the wind — and the savages were fleeing before them. It must have been a great battle, or perhaps this was an entire war depicted in one picture. And what a picture it was! It stretched from floor to ceiling, continuing for nearly ten feet down the passage. Ella could see the mountains, the forests, and the burning sun above all. Behind every rock and tree hid figures of the savage people, with the gaunt-faced men running after them. The dead savages littered the ground as the gaunt-faced men chased them up the mountains and down the river valleys.

But then, the gaunt-faced men emerged from the forest again, driving the savages before them like cattle. Now they did not look like gaunt-faced men anymore. They stood upright — proud and cruel — many bore whips in their hands instead of swords. The wild men crouched before them, stripped naked, covering their faces in shame. Many bore yokes on their shoulders.

And the etching that came next was just as large and impressive, yet Ella's stomach turned within her as she looked at it. It was another blazing fire — like the one before — only this one was much larger and more hideous. At the center of the fire lay dozens of the bodies of the savages, burned to skeletons in the blaze. All around the fire, the gaunt-faced men stood about proudly in their mighty armor. The other savages knelt before them. More savages now tilled the cultivated lands, while the women sat by, eating grand feasts and growing fat.

What a dark and dreadful history this was! Ella now looked to the next etching and gasped in awe. It was the figure of a man, tall and imposing, larger-than-life over Ella. Even in this stone etching, Ella thought he looked very handsome — yet somehow dark and cruel. The picture showed him in full armor, with a sword and a spear at his side, and a helmet in his hands. The sun shone brightly above his head, and beside him — though much smaller than him — stood seven other mighty men, all similarly dressed in full armor.

Etched in great detail beneath the feet of this great warrior were women, cattle, sheep, and servants, row upon row. Yet now, running along the bottom of the wall, Ella could see strange figures — still hieroglyphs of some kind, though more like writing than the rest of the pictures. This etching blended into the next, where Ella saw another great chieftain, standing in a similar posture, with his lords and warriors about him, and his wives, servants, and subjects beneath his feet.

Yet now there were cities too — great stone cities — and strange towers and shrines. And the pictures spread larger now, with etchings running out onto the floor and up onto the roof.

And there was another great image of a man, followed by another, and another, all standing in their armor, with their nobles around them. Their faces were all clearly drawn, so that

Ella could make out their features perfectly — the proud look in their eyes, the gaunt, almost hungry look to their jaws. Their subjects and dominions spread all around — across the floor, across the ceiling, and filling the opposite walls. The pictures here changed from simple etchings into something greater, with painted colors and a vibrancy and realism that Ella had never seen before.

It was an impressive network of scenes and pictures — fortresses, temples, ziggurats, and magnificent palaces built with high pillars. There were great bridges too, spanning rivers and canyons, and mighty ships sailing along the coast. Slaves bent low beneath the whips of their masters, and workers drew ore from deep mines. There were great armies too, marshaling to the sound of trumpets, and joining battle in tumult and bloodshed. Scattered through these scenes of prosperity and violence, Ella could see great fires consuming sacrifices of cattle, slaves, and children. All of this, Ella could see as it took place beneath the eye of each great ruler.

And there were more markings, too, running along the bottom of the wall. First they looked hieroglyphic, like the markings Ella had noticed at first, but with each successive ruler, Ella could see the markings changing slightly and subtly until she was certain that it was a writing system of some kind. Now it was a strange curving — almost serpentine — script, scrawled out in three lines along the bottom of the wall.

But then — of a sudden — came a great etching with no ruler, and no nobles, and here even the writing stopped abruptly. This etching was less clear, and for the first time, Ella could see the marks of chisels upon the stone. And what a dreadful picture this was; a vast network of violence and destruction! There were cities ablaze with fire; towers crumbling to the ground. Armies chased other armies, leaving behind piles of dead bodies. There were fires at the top of the ziggurats now, and piles of skulls at their base. Even in the temples and the palaces, Ella could see the warriors chasing and killing each other.

Then Ella paused. On the wall before her was the image of another man, towering up great and tall like the rulers before, only this man was taller, leaner, and more cruel-looking than any before him. His eyes were hollow and devious-looking, and his fingers seemed to clutch like claws at the end of his bony arms. Was he even a man at all? He, too, stood in full armor with a sword at his hip, but about his neck hung a strange and dreadful-looking dagger. There were no nobles around this figure, but only storm clouds and lightning.

Beneath this figure's feet, in a long line, stood about a dozen men, each clothed in strange robes, as of a priest. Beneath these priests, the people were hiding their faces, bent over double and digging. There were no palaces or fortresses now, only temples. In each temple, Ella could see many pillars standing by themselves in the middle of the temple, the bodies of human sacrifices piled up in their midst. All around these temples, everyone was digging, burrowing underground like rabbits in a great terror.

Ella could hardly bear to look at these dreadful images anymore, but she was spellbound, hardly able to take her eyes off the etchings. Yet as she looked for the next picture, she saw to her great astonishment that there was no other picture. Yet the pictures had not simply ended, the entire wall had ended.

Ella looked around and saw, to her surprise, that just in front of her, the hallway ended. It seemed to open up into some great room — so great that the light of their little lantern could not illuminate it. Before her, Ella could only see several large stairs leading downwards into a great blackness.

Yet right at the end of the passageway, almost directly before Ella's feet, she could see writing again. The lantern lit up the words clearly, and Ella gasped as she looked at them. It was not the same script that she had seen on the walls before — this was the Pistosian script.

*Dhω hw mnc mi dw vot vid mi*
*Dhω hw baei mi dw vot wovt mi,*
*Dhω hw yws mi dw vot vω mi.*

"What is it?" Ernest spoke in a low, raspy voice. "What does it mean?"

Ella swallowed. She knew those words all too well. She guessed what they said even before she sounded them out. "It's a widdle," she finally whispered, her throat suddenly feeling dry and hoarse. "'Those who make me do not need me, those who buy me do not want me, those who use me do not know me.' I've hea'd it befo'e..."

Ella suddenly noticed that the light was trembling. For the first time, she looked back at Ernest, to see that he was shaking all over. The scrawny little gnome shook his head, pointing with accusation at all the weird etchings in the hall they had just passed through.

"I don't like it, not one bit! There's something evil at work here."

With sudden horror, Ella noticed something behind Ernest. Why had she not thought to look back before? Ah, but these etchings had drawn her in and slowed her down. There, off in the darkness of the passageway behind, Ella could see a glimmering light, as of another lantern.

35

# STRATAGEMS

Halfdan perched on the table at the front of the sanctuary as Caedmon Wilkins, Governor Braedhwyc, Captain Smydhac, and the rest of the council waited silently. Clerans sat on the edge of his seat, waiting to hear what the harrier would say.

"They are in a desperate plight," Halfdan said in his dull monotone, "as I am sure you all have guessed. They have no food, no water, and very little powder left. The member of the militia who I spoke to confided in me that there is only just enough powder left between them for three shots to a man."

Caedmon Wilkins shook his head. "And their numbers, look you? How many defend that shop?"

"Seventeen men," Halfdan replied emotionlessly. "Seventeen men in the shop, and I counted two-hundred thirty-one pirates in total."

Caedmon Wilkins shook his head again, but said nothing. Clerans could sit still no longer. He knew Laendon was among those desperately defending the shop in the Lower Court. But what about Da? Might Da have survived the slaughter near the Dike Plaza? Was he with Laendon and the other survivors?

Clerans stood to his feet, looking directly at Halfdan. "Did you get their names?"

Halfdan looked at Clerans blankly. "Of all two-hundred thirty-one pirates?"

"No," Clerans replied desperately, "of the militia. Did you get the names of the survivors?"

Halfdan shook his head. "I did not take the time."

Clerans slumped back into the pew dejectedly. In some ways, it would be better simply to know for certain that his Da was dead. This uncertainty was unbearable.

Caedmon Wilkins took off his hat and dropped it on the table, running his fingers through his short, black hair. "Ay-eigh! This certainly complicates our position, gentlemen."

"May I suggest," Governor Braedhwyc said, wiping pus from his eye, "that we make an immediate offensive on the pirates' position in the Lower Village? We'll outta-should strike hard, and we would be sure to drive them back. If they'll only tain two-hundred some men, then—"

"Two-hundred thirty-one," Halfdan corrected.

Governor Braedhwyc waved his hand dismissively. "So, some two-hundred."

"There is no reason to round the number," Halfdan replied. "We know that the exact number of pirates is two-hundred and thirty-one."

Captain Smydhac shrugged. "Ay, but ye might has missed a few when ye counted."

Halfdan looked at the dragoon captain blankly. "No, I counted all of them. There are two-hundred and..."

"Regardless," Caedmon Wilkins broke in, "a full frontal offensive would be ill-advised. They could hold off an army ten times their size, look you, from their position in this village." Caedmon Wilkins sighed. "And if this Vania Bloodrummer is a decent strategist, then he could hold off a force over twenty times his strength. Take it from me, look you, I've done it before myself."

The dragoons nodded soberly.

Governor Braedhwyc furrowed his brow pensively, his bad eye twitching steadily. "But there must be a way..."

"If we make any attack on the pirates' position," Caedmon Wilkins said, "if we wish to rescue those men, look you, we must do it in a way that risks fewer lives than we are trying to save. We are guaranteed to lose over seventeen men, look you, in an open attack."

Governor Braedhwyc drummed his fingers on the table in contemplation.

Caedmon Wilkins sighed deeply. "As it is, time is on *our* side. I have already sent word to Admiral Maeli of the Megalytian Cape fleet. He, I estimate, should arrive here at Entwerp in a week's time. He will bring with him three third-rate frigates, and that should make quick work of the pirate's partially manned man-o-war in the bay. With their ship taken, look you, the pirates will have no other option but to capitulate, or starve to death under siege."

Caedmon Wilkins paused for a moment before continuing. "If they wish to escape, then their only opportunity will be in this next week. We can defeat these pirates, look you, if we can but contain them until Admiral Maeli arrives."

"That will do *us* well," Captain Smydhac replied, "but what av those men trapped down in the Lower Court, look ye? If 'hey have no food and water, then 'hey will ivery wan av 'hem be dead in a week, whether or no the pirates cen drive 'hem out."

"Very true," the lord protector said. "That still must be thought on."

Governor Braedhwyc banged his fist suddenly on the table. "What if we'll gave the pirates a counteroffer?"

Caedmon Wilkins looked at him closely. "What do you mean?"

"S'pose we told the pirates that we would let them go back to the ship if they'll released our men from the Lower Court unharmed?"

Caedmon Wilkins sighed heavily. "I do no wish to sound callous, but, look you, this is the infamous pirate Longfinch we are dealing with. Surely you know of all the coasts and towns he has ravaged in his career. Shall we really just let him go now?"

Caedmon Wilkins looked around the room, but no one answered. "We may save the lives of our seventeen men, for sure — assuming the pirates do not double-cross us, which is a distinct possibility, look you. But suppose we save the lives of our seventeen men; think of the hundreds more men, women, and children, that Longfinch and his men will kill because we did not stop them here!"

Caedmon Wilkins struck the table with his fist. "Yo-ho! No, gentlemen! I mean to stop that dreadful pirate here and now. We must not cave to his guilt-mongering tactics, look you. We must stand firm and see him surrender, or — as I think the more likely — we must destroy him."

"Yo-ho!" several of the dragoons shouted out in affirmation.

Halfdan nodded somberly. "The curse of the Almighty God is upon Longfinch and all of his men. As the scriptures say, 'The wicked man's calamity will fall upon him swiftly.'"

At that moment, the doors to the kirk opened. Clerans wondered who in the world could interrupt the council now, yet, as he turned around to look, he saw to his horror his little brother Robert wandering in. Robert looked with wide eyes at all the soldiers assembled at the front of the kirk, but he walked down the center aisle steadily. What on earth was Robert doing here? He should know better than to interrupt an important council of war.

"Robert!" Clerans hissed. "What are you doing here?"

As if in answer to Clerans, a dark shape darted out from underneath one of the pews, tackling Robert like a puma.

Clerans leapt up with some alarm, rushing forward to help his brother. Robert was on the floor, wrestling with the phantom assailant, and he cried out sharply. Yet, as Clerans reached Robert's side, but before he drew out his own knife, he recognized Robert's attacker.

"Nōli!" Clerans cried in annoyance. "What is this fer?"

Nōli looked up, and Clerans saw that the little nymph held a knife to Robert's throat. Clerans threw himself forward, snatching up Nōli's wrist and then swiping the knife deftly from the nymph's webbed hand.

Nōli let out a long string of gibberish in protest, but Clerans paid it no heed as he pried the Indigie off of his brother. Then, holding the slippery Indigie in his two hands, Clerans heaved him as far from him as he could.

Nōli landed in a heap on the ground a few feet away, but he leapt back to his feet in an instant, still spewing out gibberish. Sydni now appeared from the shadows to stand beside her brother. She was looking up at Clerans reprovingly.

"My brother says he does of your bidding. That is of why he is attacking of the intruder."

"He was no doin' my biddin'!" Clerans replied sharply, more than a little annoyed. "I did no tell him to attack my brother."

Robert got to his feet shakily, his eyes wide with astonishment as he looked at the two young Indigies.

Sydni shook her head. "But it was clear that you did not want of him here."

"Ay," Clerans reported, "an' fer that matter, I did no want *you* two here either."

Sydni shook her head. "We is of *orders* of the Li. The Li declared that we remain with you."

"But we already established," Clerans replied in great frustration, "That those *orders* do no include you two followin' me into this council!"

Before Sydni could make a reply, the voice of the Iasaqi-

Woni rose loud and harsh from the front of the kirk. Clerans could not make out any of the words that the great chief said, but both Nōli and Sydni wilted under them. Without another word, the two little Indigies turned and slipped quietly out of the kirk.

Clerans turned now to see Caedmon Wilkins, Governor Braedhwyc, Captain Smydhac, and everyone else in that room staring at him. Had they been watching this entire scene? Clerans felt his face flush. He wanted to disappear. Why did this have to happen to him? He had done nothing disruptive; it had been his brother and that pesky Nōli person! Why did he have to be the one to receive all the embarrassment from it?

"Lord Protector Wilkins, sir," Clerans stammered. "I am merri sorry, sir, I did no mean to disrupt the council, sir..." Clerans could think of nothing more to say.

Caedmon Wilkins stared at Clerans steadily and then burst into a fit of laughter. He tried to speak twice, but could not get any words out through his merriment. Clerans simply stood there awkwardly. Now what was he supposed to do?

Finally, Caedmon Wilkins regained control of his tongue. "Do not worry, young Clerans, there is no harm done. In fact, it might do us all some good to have a good laugh after the recent events."

Clerans nodded dutifully, uncertain what to say to this.

Caedmon Wilkins now addressed himself to Robert. "Do you, young man, come with business for the council?"

Robert answered softly, clearly intimidated by the lord protector's presence. "No, sir." Robert hesitated for a moment. "I was cedin' fer my brother, sir."

"Very well," Caedmon Wilkins said. "Perhaps the two of you should confer outside, then?"

Clerans nodded. "Ay, sir, that will be fine."

With that, he took Robert by the shoulder and dragged him from the kirk.

Robert had better have a very good reason for this, Clerans thought.

# 36

# ANATHEMA

"**B**ut what does it mean?" Ernest asked, still very perplexed by this whole situation. What were all of those pictures on the wall about, and what in the world did that riddle have to do with anything?

Ella, however, seemed to pay no attention to him. She simply stared at him dumbly — or was she staring past him? Ernest growled in frustration.

"But what *does* it mean?" he asked again.

Ella simply kept staring into the distance, as if unable to speak for a moment. But was she really just staring away vacantly, or was she actually looking *at* something? Ernest turned and followed Ella's gaze. There was a light, far down the tunnel.

"Blind prelates!" Ernest cried. "It's Longfinch! We shouldn't have stopped."

Ella jumped, looking at Ernest in horror. "Blind whats?"

"Hurry then!" Ernest urged, ignoring the question. How was he supposed to explain righteous cussing to her at a time like this? "We must get away! No doubt he's already seed us by now!"

So saying, Ernest rushed forward, gripping the lantern

firmly as he plunged into the darkness ahead. Yet no sooner had he crossed the scrawled writing on the floor than he hit something. He couldn't say that he hit a solid wall, for whatever he encountered was not solid — at least not in the traditional sense — but what had he run into? For a moment, he felt as if he were plunging into a thick liquid of some kind, but then he could go no further.

He stepped back in alarm and then plunged forward again. Once more, he felt the same heavy feeling around him, and then he could go no further. Ernest strained with all of his might to push himself forward, but his feet simply slid on the ground as if he were pushing against a wall. But there was nothing in front of him! The light from the lantern still continued before him, revealing the same smooth granite floor and the stairs leading down into the darkness of the great room beyond. At that moment, Ella rushed forward herself. She, too, came to a stop with a startled cry just where Ernest had been stopped.

"What is it?" She gasped.

Ernest looked back over his shoulder. The light in the passageway was brighter now, and Ernest could see that it came from at least six different smaller lights — probably the many lanterns that Longfinch and his pirates bore with them. In that moment of silence, Ernest could make out the steady footsteps of the approaching pirates.

"Baptize it!" Ernest hissed, looking all about him like a cornered rat. "What's the matter? We must get away!"

Again, he hurled himself at the blackness at the end of the passageway, but again, he hit the same *something* that blocked the entrance to the great room beyond.

"It's black magic!" Ella said in horror. "It must be black magic!"

Ernest looked in desperation from the invisible *something* blocking their way to Ella and then to the steadily advancing lights. They were trapped. There was no way out of this.

Suddenly, Ernest heard a voice calling to them from down the passageway. It was Longfinch.

"Glad to see you here, cook'smate! And thank you kindly for waiting for us."

The echoing of laughter trickled down the passageway towards him.

Ernest snatched up his pepper-box pistol and pointed it down the passageway at the advancing lights. "Stay where you are! Not one more step, or I'll blow your brains out!"

Yet the words were hardly out of Ernest's mouth when his pistol suddenly seemed to ignite in his hands. With a cry of pain, Ernest dropped his gun. It landed heavily on the ground, smoking and hissing like water poured into boiling oil.

Ernest looked up in alarm, his pulse beating at a mile a minute. What had just happened? He could now make out the faces of the pirates in their lantern light. There was Longfinch at the head, with the albino and Killjelly off to either side of him, and the rest of the pirates — six or eight of them — following in a close cluster behind.

For a moment, as Ernest looked on Longfinch, his panic subsided, and he felt a bit of satisfaction — Longfinch was limping badly, and he had a make-shift bandage tied about his waist, which bore very clear bloodstains on it. So then, Ernest's pepper-box pistol had done its work earlier.

But then the panic came back over Ernest. What would Longfinch do to him now? Ernest swallowed hard. He had a dreadful feeling that there would not be a quick death in store for him at the pirate captain's hands.

"What's the matter, cook's mate?" Longfinch asked with the hint of a taunt in his voice. "Why don't you run? You aren't cornered, are you?"

Ernest's heart beat hard and fast, and his mouth was now totally dry. There was nothing he could do. They would capture him and Ella again, and God only knew what would happen to him then. He had heard stories of Longfinch taking prisoners and skinning them alive, or boiling them alive in pitch and tallow. He hadn't believed those stories at first, but now he wondered if they might be true. Would that be his fate, then? Or could Longfinch have a darker and more terrible death in store for him?

Ernest, you are a dead man.

The thought came loud and clear in his head. At first, he shrank from this thought in terror, but suddenly he felt a strange, calm resolve come over him, not unlike the feeling he had experienced just before firing on Longfinch in the basement.

He was a dead man — or as good as dead, at any rate. What did he have to fear then? He was already bound to die in the worst and most horrendous way possible. Nothing he said or did now could add to his pain. He was free, totally free, to do or say whatever he liked. At best, he might irritate Longfinch so much that the captain might kill him quickly. Now there was something to hope for!

Ernest looked at the approaching lanterns with an extraordinary thrill. This was the chance of a lifetime! How often had he wanted to snub Holgard with some insolent statement! Well, now he need not hold back; he could tell Longfinch just what he thought of him.

Ernest smiled, a little surprised at himself. "Welcome, welcome, your honor. We couldn't have all the adventure without you now, could we?"

Longfinch and the other pirates were very close now, and the elfin pirate captain stopped a few feet away from Ernest, regarding him closely.

"You seem rather plucky for not having a gun."

The albino chuckled at this comment.

*Longfinch and the Etchings*

"Oh, yes," Ernest said, motioning to the red-hot pepper-box pistol on the ground. "I was leaving it there for you. Would you like to touch it? It's quite cool."

Longfinch stared at him. "You're rather cheeky of late."

Ernest grinned wickedly. "And you're rather *limping* of late."

He could tell that this touched a sore spot, as for once the elf did not smile.

"Oh, I'm sorry," Ernest replied, surprising himself with his own impunity. "Did I do that to you? Well then, perhaps you should have your momma kiss it; that'd make you feel all better, for sure."

Ernest had seen nothing but strange, deceptive friendliness in Longfinch's eyes, yet now he saw them suddenly glow in a seething rage. This was enough to unsettle Ernest, and he quickly closed his mouth, stepping back a few paces.

Longfinch said nothing for a moment, but then he stared past Ernest and smiled again. "I have often wondered if it is the loss of blood and body parts that kills a man, or if it is possible to kill a man simply by inflicting enough pain on him. Or would he live on, undying — though he wished to die — in a state of perpetual torment? How much pain can man endure before life leaves him?" Longfinch now looked long and hard at Ernest. "You may have to be my experiment."

Ernest swallowed, all of his cockiness leaving him. Yet he still did not feel any fear. He seemed overcome with a great and deep-seated anger. "You killed my messmate," Ernest said, in a low voice, "and you killed all of those people in that town. You can do with me whatever you will then, but I am certain that there is no earthly torment you can contrive which will match the eternal agony you will feel on the Day of Judgment!"

Longfinch laughed derisively. "And what do you know of the afterlife, pirate?"

"I am not a pirate," Ernest snapped. "I amn't like you."

"That is very true," Longfinch nodded knowingly. "Tell me, cook'smate, have you ever spoken with a god?"

Ernest was a bit taken aback by this question, unsure how to respond.

Longfinch clearly saw Ernest's uncertainty, and he laughed. The albino laughed as well. "Prepare yourself then. Perhaps you willn't speak of the Day of Judgment so quickly again."

Longfinch turned away from Ernest now, walking over to the strange, etched mural on the wall. He laid his hand on the image of the great and hideous man at the end of the mural. "And what is this Day of Judgment to you? Some myth that you have seen acted out on a monastic stage?"

Longfinch looked at Ernest keenly, but did not wait for a reply. "But see, I believe in a god who is real. See here?" Longfinch pointed to the peculiar curved dagger that hung about the image's neck, then he motioned to the albino. The albino smiled darkly and pulled out a dagger from underneath his cloak. Ernest started in horror. It was the same dagger — curved and wicked-looking with jewels on its hilt, which glinted in the lantern light.

"And these!" Longfinch motioned to the strange grouping of pillars in the temples around the hideous image. "You see these? Ah! But I get ahead of myself. First, we must enter the hall."

Ernest motioned towards the invisible wall dramatically. "Please, then, enter."

Longfinch smirked. "You couldn't get in, could you? You stupid fellow, didn't you read the riddle? Don't you see? You can't enter until you answer the riddle."

Longfinch motioned dramatically to Killjelly, who now read the riddle, his dark face gleaming in the lantern light. Ernest couldn't help but shudder. There was something distinctly sinister in that leprechaun's eyes, almost more sinister and more dreadful than Longfinch.

"Those who make me do not need me; those who buy me do not want me; those who use me do not know me."

Killjelly paused soberly, almost reverently, still staring at the scrawled letters of the riddle.

Longfinch smiled at Ernest. "Luckily for you, it's an easy riddle. Haven't you guessed it yet?"

Ernest only stared back dumbly. He wanted desperately to say something witty, but he couldn't think of anything to say.

"You are standing in it," the albino said, a queer look in his eyes.

Ernest looked all around at the strangely etched walls, then he looked back at Longfinch inquiringly. "A tunnel? Is that the answer to the riddle?"

Longfinch only smiled his same friendly-yet-wicked smile. "A tomb."

37

## THE WAY

Haeli's heart pounded heavily inside her. The pteranodon was gone for the moment. But would it be back? Hurriedly, Haeli rushed to Tiya-Aenji's side, helping the little nymph back to her feet. Tiya-Aenji was shaking all over, and she had a nasty-looking gash on her forehead.

"Are you alright?" Haeli blurted out.

Tiya-Aenji didn't answer, but only pointed to Haeli's ankle. Looking down, Haeli could see the pteranodon's claw still clamped tightly around it, and blood was now running down and soaking her shoes. Tiya-Aenji reached out and quickly pried the claw from Haeli's leg.

"Here," the little nymph said, "let me wrap it."

Yet before Tiya-Aenji could do anything more, a loud cry rang out from below them.

"Heaven preserve us!"

It was Titus.

Haeli rushed to the edge of the battlements and peered over them anxiously. There were Martyn and Titus, now just over halfway up the tower, and the pteranodon was swooping up at them from below. Titus' face was white in terror, and he gripped tightly to his *alwmli* as if that might save him.

"We'll die for certain!" Titus wailed, his voice rising to a high pitch in his excitement.

Haeli ground her teeth together. Would they never get rid of this monster? If only there was something she could do! If she only had a gun, she was certain she could shoot the pteranodon.

In a moment, the winged lizard was upon Titus, flogging him with its wings and pecking at him with its beak. Haeli noted with some satisfaction that it didn't claw at Titus, but held back its one good claw to hold the bloody stump that was left of its other claw. Martyn now gripped only one of his *alwmli*, snatching up his long horse-pistol in his other hand and leaning out from the tower dangerously.

"Don't shoot!" Titus was shrieking as he buried his head against the tower to protect it from the pteranodon's attack. "Don't shoot! You'll kill me!"

"Jist one clear shot," Martyn cried. "That is all I need!"

Yet as Martyn spoke, the pteranodon looked up, backing away from Titus for just a moment. Martyn wasted no time firing his pistol at the ghastly reptile. The pteranodon let out a vicious scream, beating its wings furiously. Martyn must have hit it then or grazed it, at least.

Yet the monster was not done. It wheeled away from the tower for a moment, circling back with its eyes fixed on Martyn. Haeli caught her breath. Could she really do nothing but watch?

With his brow set like flint, Martyn snatched up the limp rope of his harness and wrapped it tightly around one of his *alwmli* until it was quite taut. Then he let go of his hold, dangling now in mid-air with both of his arms free.

The pteranodon swooped down upon him, its beak extended and its eyes wild with fury, a deafening scream issuing from its mouth. Yet as it bore down, Martyn unslung his rifle, and, with a calm but sure motion, he raised the sights to his eye and fired.

The pteranodon's scream was cut suddenly short, and its wings went limp. Like some overgrown bat, the reptile fell from the sky, its membranous wings flapping against the rising wind. Then its lifeless body struck the mountain ridge, crumpling into a shapeless mass.

Haeli slumped down, leaning her back against the inside of the battlements. Her heart still pounded in her head, and she still gasped for breath, but she felt a great surge of relief washing over her. It was over. They had done it. They had killed the pteranodon.

But what if Martyn had missed? What if the pteranodon had attacked Martyn — or worse, what if the pteranodon had *killed* Martyn? What would Haeli have done then? After all, she was the one who had dragged Martyn along on this crazy expedition. What would she do if she were responsible for Martyn's death?

Tiya-Aenji now squatted in front of Haeli, tearing off a piece of cloth from her shirt and then pulling out a small package of skins from some hidden pocket in her dress. "Let me see that ankle."

Haeli lifted her leg off the ground slightly and let the nymph do her work. Tiya-Aenji first unwrapped the skins from around her package. Inside, Haeli could see what must be some sort of ointment, though it was the color and consistency of a soft cheese. Haeli immediately smelled a very pungent odor as Tiya-Aenji lathered this ointment onto the strip of cloth.

Haeli winced as Tiya-Aenji wrapped this makeshift bandage around her wounded ankle. The ointment stung, though the stinging felt soothing after the piercing pain of torn flesh.

Haeli leaned her head against the stone walls of the battlements and closed her eyes, taking several deep breaths. Oh, how exhausted she was! That shouldn't come as such a surprise.

After all, she had hardly slept last night. Why had she kept pushing herself on and on? Why had she convinced herself to go on this fool's errand, anyway? She was too weak to keep going. She had let her emotions overcome her just now when the pteranodon attacked Martyn. She had just felt so helpless. But that was no good. She had to do better. She had to keep herself calm. She had to make her heart a heart of stone.

Haeli took another deep breath and then moaned. She had determined that she was going to save Ella. She had gotten this far, and now she had to keep going. Yet Haeli suddenly felt that familiar pain in her throat. Was she about to cry? Why was she about to cry? This was absurd. She had nothing to cry about.

Stone. Her heart was stone. She couldn't afford to mount up on some horse of emotion right now.

Behind her, on the other side of the battlements, she could hear sounds of grunting. Haeli shifted over and pulled herself to her feet, looking over in time to see Martyn appear over the edge of the battlement. Quickly and nimbly, the Blaeith boy vaulted onto the top of the tower. His face was flushed with a look of victory and adventure.

"I tain half a mind to climb back down and gard over that dragon merri well," Martyn was saying. "I would no be surprised if a specimen like that were o' great value fer a student o' natural history. No doubt we'll could make a fortune sellin' that carcass to a museum, maugre leavin' it as waste to rot up here."

Then Martyn noticed Haeli's bandaged leg, and he looked down at her sympathetically. "Ye are no hurt badly, I hope?"

Haeli swallowed back the pain in her chest. Her eyes were suddenly stinging, as if they meant to tear up. No. She was not about to let this happen. Taking a deep breath, she forced the pain away, giving Martyn a confident nod. "I'm fine."

Martyn gripped her shoulder encouragingly. "It is alright, Haeli, ye'll do jist fine now. I know God will see ye through."

Haeli flinched. "Just like he saw my Da through?"

Martyn looked down, but before he could make a reply, Titus' head appeared over the edge of the battlements. With some grunting, he tumbled over onto the parapet of the tower. Scrambling to his feet, Titus breathed heavily and looked around with wide eyes. Looking at Haeli closely, he pointed to her bandage.

"Ah, I see that she's gotten you, too. That ointment really stings, doesn't it?"

It took Haeli a moment before she remembered how Tiya-Aenji had bandaged up Titus after his fight with the mother moa. Was he trying to commiserate with her? Haeli certainly didn't appreciate having her pain compared with his.

"Right then," Martyn said suddenly, "where from here? Is there a way into the tower?"

Haeli quickly looked around the parapet again, realizing for the first time that she had seen no opening into the tower from up here. Had their climb been for nothing? Was there no entrance here, after all?

Tiya-Aenji pointed to the pteranodon's now-deserted nest. "It has built on top of the door."

Martyn strode forward quickly, grabbing a great armful of the dried grass, mud, and debris that made up the nest, and heaving it over the side of the tower. With a second armful, he threw over the rest of the nest, revealing in its place a strange, iron-reinforced trap door with a keyhole directly in the middle of it.

Martyn shook his head and clicked his tongue. "I should ha' known that there would be another door."

Tiya-Aenji nodded soberly. "There are three doors, one on each of the entrances to the catacombs, each thickly enchanted with many spells."

"Catacombs?" Titus asked in alarm. "Now you use that word. That's, eh, that's not very reassuring."

"There are more entrances, then?" Martyn asked.

Tiya-Aenji shrugged. "So the shamans say. This is the only one I have entered."

"But it's locked," Titus said. "How do, eh, do we open it?"

Tiya-Aenji turned to Haeli. "You have the key, do you not?"

Haeli swallowed, suddenly feeling apprehensive. "Well, I have *a* key at any rate."

What if her key was the wrong key? What if it wouldn't unlock this trap door, just as it wouldn't unlock the door in the Pickering's basement? No, but it had to. Sir Saemwel had been out on this tower, so one of his keys had to undo the lock. Perhaps that was the whole reason he had two keys in the first place; one for the door in the basement, and one for this door at the top of the tower.

Haeli quickly walked over to the trapdoor. Pulling out her key, she fit it into the lock. She hardly dared to breathe as she now turned the key. It worked! The key turned smoothly, and the bolt drew aside. Haeli let out a deep sigh of relief. So their climb had not been in vain!

Martyn now lifted the trapdoor open. As he did so, a strange, musty breeze blew out from the entrance. Haeli caught her breath and shivered all over, not from a physical or bone-chilling cold, but from a sinister and soul-chilling cold. The darkness below the trap-door was thick and almost palpable. Haeli could just see the beginnings of a spiral staircase in the entrance; a deep blackness shrouded everything else.

Martyn let down his pack and quickly pulled out a lantern. "We begin our descent then?"

Tiya-Aenji trembled all over, her face now completely pale. "O Lord, be near your children! Guide and protect us..."

Martyn pulled out his horse-pistol, using the flint and steel to light his lantern. "Titus," he was saying, "you should have a lantern in your pack as well."

Titus nodded, unstrapping his lantern from the side of his pack.

Once Martyn had both lanterns lit, he straightened up and looked Tiya-Aenji squarely in the eye. "Do ye want to duce the way?"

Tiya-Aenji shook her head vigorously. "Not for all the gold of Arimanes!"

Titus looked at her nervously. "What, eh, what is, er, that is to say, why not?"

Martyn looked at Tiya-Aenji closely. "Ay, what are we about to encounter? What should we expect?"

Tiya-Aenji trembled all over. "We enter *his* domains, do you not see? We are not simply descending into the tower, but we are descending into hell; a realm that serves a false god and does not care for the Almighty God."

"Ay," Martyn nodded, and gave a shrug. "So ye ha' said a'fore, but what do we need to fear a false god? He is *false,* after all."

Tiya-Aenji only looked at him with terror in her eyes. "His power is great. I shudder even to remember it."

Martyn flashed an encouraging smile. "Come now. There is no power — no height, no depth, no principalities o' men or angels — that can overcome the power o' the Almighty God which indwells us through his Spirit."

Tiya-Aenji took a deep breath, nodding slowly. "Even so, you speak the truth."

Martyn held out his lantern dramatically into the darkness of the entrance. "Then let the truth lead on, an' let it illuminate all darkness!"

So saying, he plunged down the staircase into the darkness.

# 38

# HERE AM I, LORD

As soon as Clerans closed the big oak doors of the kirk behind him, he turned on his brother sharply.

"What wos that fer, Robert?"

Robert lowered his eyes and sighed pitifully. "I wos tryin' to trive ye up."

Clerans held up his hands in exasperation. "An' so ye waltzed into the *council*? What were ye thinking, Robert?"

Robert sighed again. "Clerans," he whispered. "We did no even know if ye'll were alive. We heard..."

But here Robert broke off, sobbing.

Something caught in Clerans' throat, and he let his breath out slowly. "I am sorry, Robert. I outta-should no ha' spoken so harshly to ye..."

Robert was still sobbing, but he tried to finish his sentence. "We heard that the militia wos destroyed. Ma sent me to trive ye, an' Martyn, an' Laendon, an'..."

"Robert, I'm sorry," Clerans said again, cutting his brother off before he could mention Da.

Robert took a deep breath, trying to compose himself. "I

promised myself I would no cry if I'll trived ye still alive," Robert smiled halfheartedly.

Clerans sighed, then he threw his arms around his little brother. "Oh, Robert! I am still alive, praise God!"

For a moment, Clerans thought he might cry too, but he swallowed it back.

Robert sighed deeply and pushed himself from Clerans' embrace. "I promised Ma that I would tell her how you all were." Robert swallowed. "I see ye are alright — if a little battered an' bruised."

Clerans smiled weakly. "Ay, a *little*." He looked down at his many bandages, his ripped clothing, and the minor cuts and bruises that were not treated. Wasn't he supposed to see Olafr to get his bandages replaced?

Robert looked at Clerans hesitantly. He licked his lips several times, then finally he said, "An'... an' the others?"

"Oh!" Clerans replied enthusiastically, "Martyn an' Laendon are alright. Ye cen tell Ma that they will be safe fer now. Martyn is climbin' the Gwambi Tower with Haeli Blysffi an' Miss Ella's stepfather (it is a long story), an' Laendon is with the rest o' the militia in the Lower Court, surrounded..."

"The Gwambi Tower?" Robert asked with wide eyes.

Clerans shrugged dejectedly. "Alright, so I s'pose neither o' them is merri safe then."

Robert sighed deeply. "Then..."

Clerans looked at his brother inquiringly. "Then, what?"

Robert hesitated, "Then, Da... is he..."

Clerans bit the inside of his cheek. "We ha' no trived him yet."

Robert looked as if he were about to cry again. "I knew as much, I knew ye would no all be alive..."

"That's no what I said." It came out more harshly than Clerans intended. "I did no say that Da wos dead, I only said that we ha' no trived him yet. He wasn't with the other dead.

He..." Clerans swallowed. "He *must* still be alive, Robert. I jist ha' to trive him."

Robert nodded gloomily. "Well then," and he sighed again. "That wos all I ceded fer. I hope ye enjoy yer council."

And with that, Robert turned and walked back down the steps, his shoulders slumped and his head bowed.

Clerans heaved a great sigh himself as he watched his little brother leave. Poor Robert! Clerans half-wished that he could leave this cursed fighting and rejoin his family. But no, he had to keep doing his duty. He had to keep defending that village until he had defeated the pirates. Slowly, Clerans turned to the doors of the kirk and slipped back inside.

As Clerans entered the sanctuary, the men of the council looked up. Yet when they saw that it was only him, they continued speaking.

"Longfinch is a master of strategy," Caedmon Wilkins was saying, "and that is why he has never been caught. He has three or four prearranged contingency plans for every possible scenario. His crew knows precisely what to do and when to do it. He becomes drunk on planning and ecstatic on success. It is what he lives for. Look you, what makes Longfinch such a formidable opponent is not that he makes perfect plans, but that he plans perfectly."

To this, Halfdan let out a low whistle from where he perched on a pew in the front row. "Only God's plans are infallible. The plans of man are never perfect."

Governor Braedhwyc wiped pus from his bad eye as he looked at Caedmon Wilkins. "Then explain this to me: Longfinch goes through the trouble o' blowin' up the Entwerp battery, an' then he jist invades this small manor house on the north o' town, leaving the bank an' all the real pillage fer the strikers? That does no make any sense."

Clerans hurriedly resumed his seat next to Yohni, listening closely to the discussion.

Caedmon Wilkins sighed. "Simply because we do not have an explanation, does not mean there is none, look you. The pirates' effectiveness speaks to the cunning strategy. Besides the unheard-of feat of destroying the Entwerp Battery and demolishing the famed dike militia, Longfinch arranged for the strikers to serve as a decoy so that you would keep most of your forces at the bank instead of stopping him at the dikes. It was clearly a well-thought-through plan."

"Then why the manor house?" Governor Braedhwyc insisted, slapping the map on the table. "Why was that his target, an' why — if he'll planned this so well — did no he tain an escape plan to get out o' the manor house when me an' my men attacked him there?"

Caedmon Wilkins shook his head. "Perhaps he *meant* to retreat behind the door. Perhaps that was his strategy all along. Look you, I do not pretend to know why."

"I know why," Clerans said hesitantly, standing back to his feet.

Caedmon Wilkins looked at him closely. "You do?"

"Ay, sir," Clerans replied. "It is a bit o' an long story, but I tained a friend who was captured by the pirates, an' she heard *that* much o' their plans."

The entire council sat in silence, looking at Clerans intently. Clerans took a deep breath. "It is the Gwambi Treasure, sir. It is behind that door at the Pickering's manor. That is what Longfinch is after."

Caedmon Wilkins ran his hand through his hair as if in deep thought. "Gwambi Treasure? Yo-ho, this is all about the Gwambi Treasure?" Caedmon Wilkins shook his head. "That treasure has caused me enough trouble as it is."

"Sir?" Governor Braedhwyc asked inquiringly.

Caedmon Wilkins sighed. "It is once or twice a year that some fool adventurer presents a petition to the parliament and me for permission to seek the Gwambi Treasure — or worse, to buy it from us in advance!"

Governor Braedhwyc looked at the lord protector closely. "An' what is the trouble with that, sir?"

Captain Smydhac chuckled.

Caedmon Wilkins sighed again. "Ay-eigh! The trouble is that a good many of the MPs are in favor of selling the treasure — or selling treasure-seeking license — to whoever wants it. It would certainly be a steady way of repaying some of our war debts. But then there's the other MPs — and myself among them— who believe that since the government does not *own* the Gwambi Treasure, we can not morally, or with a clean conscience before God, sell it as if we owned it. Of course, that line of argument will never wash for the other side, look you, until we can find someone who *does* own the treasure."

"Very well put," Halfdan said in his emotionless voice. "Your stand for moral perfection is most laudable."

Caedmon Wilkins shook his head. "As I said, I have had enough troubles with that treasure... but now we have a pirate captain — Longfinch no less — tearing apart the fiscal center of our nation in his attempt to find it himself."

The lord protector now turned back to Clerans. "However, young Clerans, this certainly explains Longfinch's motives pretty well. It makes sense of everything."

Captain Smydhac shook his head. "It does not explain why he had no plan av evacuating the manor house."

"True," Caedmon Wilkins agreed.

"Unless," Governor Braedhwyc offered, wiping pus from his bad eye, "is it possible he *tained* no plan, and we caught him at the one weak point in his strategy?"

Caedmon Wilkins shook his head. "It would seem uncharacteristically sloppy of Longfinch. Do you know, is there another way out of the tunnel he retreated into? Might he be able to come out somewhere else and then rendezvous with his crew?"

Governor Braedhwyc shrugged. "No one ha' been down there a'fore."

Caedmon Wilkins sighed. "Then I suppose there is nothing more we can determine there. The best we can do is continue to guard that door and wait for news of Longfinch appearing somewhere else. In the meantime, if we can defeat his crew here in Entwerp, or even capture his man-o-war, I reckon we will begin to unhinge his plan."

"That's all sore well, sir," Captain Smydhac said, "But we still has not come to ony better conclusion as to what to do about those seventeen men in the Lower Court."

Caedmon Wilkins nodded. "That is true. I have not given it any further thought. You do not happen to have a plan, do you?"

Captain Smydhac flashed a roguish smile. "Well, as the fact av the matter is, I *would* happen to have a plan."

Caedmon Wilkins sat down on the table. "Alright then, let us hear it."

Captain Smydhac folded his hands together pensively. "Well, sir, as ye said yerself, it would be foolish to make an open attack on the pirates' position. It would risk too mony lives, it would. But if we wait ourselves, then the men in the Lower Court will starvinate, or thirstinate, or run out av powder when the pirates next attack."

Captain Smydhac tapped on the table with his pointer finger. "So then, what we need is simple, and it solves our conundrum. We need to get provisions to the men in the Lower Court."

Caedmon Wilkins nodded. "Ay, that is simple enough, but—"

"But the execution av the thing!" Captain Smydhac replied, tapping his finger on the table more forcefully. "The execution av the thing is the fiddly-bit. Yet we awnly need a volunteer who can slip through the pirates' position with provisions. Send a volunteer every few days, and if we can get those men a week's worth av provision, then we are set until Admiral Maeli arrives."

"An' how do ye propose we get a man through the pirates' lines?" Governor Wilkins asked.

Captain Smydhac nodded. "Ay, sir, that is the trick, that is! But that, too, maun have a simple answer. We cause a *diversiona-tion*." Captain Smydhac nodded knowingly. Then he began pointing to points all across the map. "We order our men all along the dikes to fire on the pirates' position, to make 'hem think we are about to attack 'hem all along the line. Perhaps we could even use some av the cannons and fire on their barricade in the north av their position. Yo-ho! That would distractinate 'hem in a jiffy!" And Captain Smydhac chuckled to himself.

Caedmon Wilkins nodded. "And while we are distracting the pirates, a volunteer laden with provisions sneaks through to our men in the Lower Court?"

Captain Smydhac nodded. "Ay sir, that is just the gist av it."

"And how does the volunteer get back?" Caedmon Wilkins asked.

Captain Smydhac shook his head. "He does not. He maun volunteer to bring the provisions to the Lower Court and then stay there with the dike militia."

Caedmon Wilkins took a deep breath, studying the map. "And we repeat this as many times as necessary until Admiral Maeli arrives?"

"Ay, sir," Captain Smydhac rapped his knuckles on the table.

Caedmon Wilkins nodded his head. "I like it. It is a good plan — at least it is as good as any plan we are like to come up with, look you."

Governor Braedhwyc nodded too. "I agree. I like the simplicity o' it."

"All we need now is a volunteer," Caedmon Wilkins said, looking around the room.

Clerans hardly had to think. He stood to his feet. "Send me."

It only made sense, Clerans thought. His brother Laendon was there in the Lower Court, and so it was his duty as a brother to see that Laendon got the provisions. Besides, if he delivered those provisions, then he could finally see if his father was alive and among the survivors.

"Send me," Clerans repeated.

Caedmon Wilkins looked him up and down and nodded, turning to Governor Braedhwyc. "What do you say, Governor?"

The governor nodded too. "Ay, sir, he's one o' the most capable youths in the village. He would see it done if anyone could."

"It is decided then," the lord protector proclaimed. "Now Clerans, look you, how much do you think you can carry?"

Yet, just as he said it, Yohni stood up beside Clerans. The little nymph first looked at Clerans with his dark eyes and then looked at the lord protector, saying simply, "Two are better than one."

Caedmon Wilkins looked over at Captain Smydhac. "What do you say, captain? I would agree. The two of them could carry more provisions, and besides, the younker and the nymph would both be well-suited to sneak through the pirates' lines."

Captain Smydhac smiled, "Ay, sir, but to complete the proverb, it is a *third* volunteer we would be needint."

In response to this, Halfdan fluttered up onto the table. "I will go with them," the harrier said in his dull monotone. "They would do well with a winged guide."

"There we have it," Caedmon Wilkins said, slapping his hand on the table. "That settled, we can but look to God Almighty for success in this endeavor. May He bless us and frustrate the attempts of Longfinch and his crew."

"Amen!" the entire council echoed.

39

# SACRIFICE

$\mathcal{E}$lla was trembling all over, hardly able to think in her terror of the pirates. So, they had captured her again? She looked at Captain Longfinch and shivered all over. She was afraid of Longfinch, yes, but not with that wild, other-worldly dread with which she feared the white-haired beggar. And then there was Killjelly, standing there with that dreadful look in his eyes, his brass hooks glittering in the lantern light — she feared *him* most of all!

As Killjelly read the riddle, her whole body tingled in horror, every hair standing on end — as if the very words which that hooked leprechaun spoke were torture. But what was this strange feeling which had come over her? She felt dull and heavy, and her heart beat against her chest as if it were the throbbing of a great drum. She had felt this way ever since she had run into the invisible wall. Her thoughts seemed to ooze about in her brain like chilled sorghum. All that she could distinctly make of her thoughts was the question 'what?' and the dreadful answer, 'black magic.'

Yet as Longfinch now said, "A tomb," the heavy feeling seemed to fall off of Ella, almost as if she were bursting out of a

353

wide pool of water into the fresh air again. Her heart still throbbed heavily inside her, and she could hear her pulse in her ears.

"Take them," Longfinch ordered, smiling his strange smile.

A pirate stepped forward and grabbed Ella by the wrist. His hand was sweaty and trembled a bit. Was he terrified, too? So then, Ella thought, this strange passageway unsettled even her adversaries. She did nothing to resist the pirate who grabbed her, but only looked at Ernest. He scowled and looked inclined to put up a struggle as two more pirates moved to seize him, but he remained still as they took hold of him.

Longfinch snickered softly. "Where's your fight now then, oh brave warrior?"

Ernest spat, but then he flashed a cheeky smile. "It wouldn't be fair to fight back now. After all, there's only ten of you. I'll have to wait until there'd be enough to have an actual fight with."

"And you think we are alone?" Longfinch asked with a peculiar look in his eyes.

Without waiting for an answer, Longfinch walked forward, crossing directly over the scrawled writing of the riddle on the ground. Ella waited breathlessly for the pirate captain himself to halt as he ran into the invisible wall, but nothing happened. Longfinch continued forward with no impediment, stepping briskly down the few steps into the darkness beyond the passage. Killjelly and the white-haired man followed close behind the captain, and then the pirates dragged Ella and Ernest after them.

As they left the passageway, the pirates' lanterns lit up the darkness just enough that Ella could make out that they were in an enormous room, so large that the light did not even reach the walls or ceiling. All Ella could see was that same smooth, granite floor stretching out into the darkness on all sides. Now and then she would see a massive granite column rising upward until it vanished into the darkness of the vault above. These must be supporting the ceiling, she thought, but why could she not see the ceiling?

"At last," Longfinch was saying, "we are in the Great Temple itself! Who would have thinked it possible, eh?" Longfinch chuckled to himself.

Both Killjelly and the white-haired man mumbled something affirmative-sounding.

"It is so rewarding, isn't it?" Longfinch continued, now speaking in a louder voice, as if addressing the whole of his crew. "All of that planning, all of that scheming — and it paid off so well! Holgard mutinied just as we guessed, and we taked his ship to destroy the famed Entwerp Battery. Now we've infiltrated the fiscal center of this warlike country right under the nose of their most prestigious leader. Ha! Now tell me, is there anyone else on earth who could have pulled off this raid?"

Killjelly chuckled. "No, sir. Longfinch, and Longfinch alone could do this."

"That is, after all, why we chose you," the white-haired man said in a low tone.

Ella felt a chill run down her spine. There was something in the tone of that man's voice — something in the lilt of Killjelly's chuckle — that seemed dreadful and sinister.

Longfinch turned around and faced them all with his wide smile. "Come then. Let us make our Order proud."

"Please, sir." It was one of the pirates in the back of the group who spoke now. Ella turned to look at him, and she could tell that he was trembling in fear. "Please, sir," the pirate said again.

"What is it?" Longfinch asked, his voice dripping with compassion.

"Please, sir," the pirate said again, "but you keep talking as if'n we've won, or conquered something or other. Yet I can't help but think... how are we going to get back to our ship?"

Longfinch only grinned. "Tell me, what need would we have of a ship, if'n we owned the entire world?"

The pirate looked perplexed, but said nothing.

Longfinch only winked. "Trust your captain. We are about to have the aid of a god. Look! See!"

Longfinch pointed ahead into the darkness.

Ella strained her eyes, and the pirates held up their lanterns. Though she could not make out more than a few obscure shapes amidst the blackness and shadow, Ella could feel a great dread filling her soul. A black feeling came over her, as if she were about to enter a very evil place. In these tunnels, darkness seemed almost a physical thing, but now she believed she was about to come to a place where evil was just as palpable.

In that moment, Ella knew that she did not have the strength to continue. Whatever lay before her in the darkness was too much for her. It would overcome her. There was nothing she could do. She needed a savior; but all she had was Ernest.

Longfinch continued forward, and the other pirates followed — though their steps became slower and more hesitant. As they advanced, the lights illuminated the obscure shapes before them. They were pillars, standing all by themselves, each about ten feet high. They stood straight, unadorned, and they supported nothing. As the light shone on them more clearly, Ella could make out that there were seven such pillars standing in a rough circle. The whole ground within this group of pillars rose to a dais of sorts made of impeccably planed granite. All along the edges of this dais, Ella could see small slats in the floor, like drains for a sewer.

She looked over the entire scene closely and shuddered. This was a very eerie place. The riddle had said that this was a tomb. Could it be? In what way was this a tomb?

Longfinch stepped onto the dais and looked all around at the seven pillars, a light of triumph in his eyes. Killjelly and the white-haired man followed him onto the dais, but the other pirates stopped, standing in the shadow of the pillars before the dais.

"Who has walked where a god once walked?" Longfinch asked. "Who has spoken face to face with a god before?" and he smiled. "We *will* make our Order proud."

The albino simply stood to one side of Longfinch, looking at him closely. Killjelly stood on the other side of Longfinch with that same blank look on his face. Ella couldn't help but think that they looked like actors — or perhaps demons — standing on a stage together; Longfinch in the middle with his wild-eyed triumph; the white-haired man on one side like a cloaked wolf; Killjelly was on the other side, his sharp nose looking just as hooked and dangerous as the hooks on his left hand.

Longfinch motioned to the white-haired man. "Let us begin then. Call up your incantations."

The albino pulled out the wicked jeweled dagger again, and he drew it from its sheath. The blade flashed like starlight in the lanterns' dim glow. Ella drew back. There was something terrible about that dagger; its blade was too brilliant, as if it might not actually be a part of this world. Ella trembled in terror. She could hear that pounding in her head again; was it really her heart, or was she hearing great drums beating far, far away in the darkness?

"I will begin the summoning," the white-haired man said, "but to fulfill all things, we must have the blood of a sacrifice. We must have the blood of man."

Longfinch chuckled. "Luckily for us, then, we have two prisoners." Longfinch motioned with his hands towards Ernest and Ella. "Which one then? Would the scrawny gnome, or the weakling human, be more to his tastes? Does the god prefer the blood of a man, or the blood of a woman?" And Longfinch smiled broadly. He looked more closely at Ella. "Personally, I think there would be something poetic about cutting the throat of Silas Pickering's daughter as a sacrifice, after he so blatantly violated our sacred Order."

Though Longfinch had been speaking to the white-haired man, it was Killjelly who answered him, "It is not a sacrifice if it costs you nothing."

Longfinch turned to face Killjelly now, smirking. "Do you mean that I should sacrifice one of my men?"

Killjelly only looked back at Longfinch intently, his eyes narrow and gleaming in the lantern light. Ella shuddered at the sight of him. "What the god likes best is the blood of one of his own followers. That is a *true* sacrifice."

Longfinch looked at Killjelly closely for a moment. His eyes narrowed, and he seemed as if he were about to open his mouth and speak, when the white-haired man struck at Longfinch's back like a cobra. Ella saw the blade of the terrible dagger flash for a moment in the lantern light, and then it vanished into Longfinch's back.

Longfinch let out a startled cry, and he dropped to the ground like a rock, writhing in agony on the dais. Ella looked on in speechless horror. She could hear the drums louder than ever in her ears. Deep down, she knew that there was something darker and more evil going on beyond the simple betrayal. Yet none of this seemed real. How could any of this really be happening? It seemed like a play. The white-haired man, Longfinch, and Killjelly were just actors on a stage.

Yet now Longfinch was struggling to his feet, something wet soaking through his clothing. Certainly, this was no play! Longfinch got to his knees, but seemed unable to rise any further.

"So that is it, then!" Longfinch spoke through clenched teeth, looking accusingly at Killjelly. The white-haired man simply stood to the side, still holding his dreadful, dripping dagger.

"All of this time," Longfinch hissed, "all of this time I was worried about Holgard mutinying. But now I see that it was you

I should have been watching. If'n only there was some strength left in me, I'd kill you! Then at least we'd die together." Longfinch motioned to the pirates who stood before the dais. "Why are you standing there? Aren't you going to defend your captain?"

The pirates all took a step back, mute horror filling their faces. Were they all — like Ella — then paralyzed with the gravity and dread of this awful place?

Longfinch turned back to Killjelly and shook his head bitterly. "I thinked you were loyal. I suppose I shouldn't have maked that assumption. Of course, you would turn against me in the end. What pirate willn't kill his captain at the last?"

Killjelly shook his head, speaking gravely and seriously as he helped Longfinch to his feet. "You are my captain on the ship, and I would never turn against my captain. Don't you see that this is a great honor that I give to you? What greater thing can a man do than to die for his god? No. I am making the decision that you couldn't have maked for yourself. Now you will be immortal."

Longfinch laughed, coughing up blood. "If'n that's what you think, sacrifice yourself, then."

Killjelly shook his head. "Someone must be left to take control. You forget, you are my captain on the ship, but in the Order, I am your senior. This was a duty you owed me. Besides, I have to clean up after myself."

Longfinch only coughed again, clearly about to collapse, but Killjelly held him on his feet. "Don't you see, Captain? This is all for the best. You will receive the fame of a legend, and the albino and the rest of our Order will receive their religious satisfaction."

"And you?" Longfinch gasped.

Killjelly smiled. "Power. But come, let us make an end of this."

Killjelly seized Longfinch by the hair, tilting his head back and exposing his neck to the white-haired man. Ella could hardly bear to look on, but she seemed to have no power at all over her body. She was rooted to that spot, and her eyes were drawn irresistibly to this sickening drama.

The white-haired man stepped forward slowly, briefly blocking Ella's view of the scene as he made one last sweeping stroke with his dagger. Longfinch collapsed to the ground without another sound. Ella could see very little of the elfin captain, with the albino standing in front of him, only the pool of blood that spread steadily on the dais. So that was what those drains were for; this was not a dais — it was an altar.

The white-haired man now turned to face the pillar on the far side of the dais, holding the bleeding sacrificial dagger above his head in his right hand. He spread his arms over his head, as if he were receiving a benediction. His hideous white hair fell about his shoulders, and he stood motionless for a moment. Killjelly stepped back and knelt on the edge of the dais just behind the white-haired man.

The albino man muttered strange words now, swaying back and forth as he spoke. Then suddenly he stopped and stood still for a moment. Ella noticed that he was drenched in sweat. Every muscle in his body seemed tense and poised.

"I address you now!" the white-haired man finally said. "Do you answer me? What shall I call you, but that what you are? You are Grave, you are Tomb — you are Death itself. Or shall I call on you in your own language, after the tongue of the Gwambi? *Throcmordyn.*"

The name rolled off the white-haired man's tongue. Ella could almost hear it reverberating and echoing in the darkness. But was her mind simply tricking her? The drums were louder now. Was she really hearing them in her head, or were they actually sounding far away in the darkness? She could feel a great heaviness all around her, as if she were trying to breathe in water and not air.

*"Throcmordyn,"* the white-haired man repeated. "I summon you from your haunts and wake you from your hiding. I invoke your name so that you will answer me! Were not the whole Gwambi peoples yours? Did you not govern them with power, majesty, and dread? Did you not once rule these halls as the god of an entire people? Come, we ask you: do so again!"

Again, he paused. There should have been a deathly silence in that dreadful hall, but Ella's whole body throbbed with the beat of those drums. She stared in horror at the pillar on the far side of the dais.

But what was that? There was a sound, as of claws scratching — or else chains dragging — along the ground. Ella could hardly breathe. Were her eyes playing tricks on her? No, surely that was a dark *something* just at the base of the pillar. But what was it?

The white-haired man suddenly threw the sacrificial dagger on the ground with such force that it broke in two. "Do you answer me?"

Out of the darkness beyond the pillars there came a dreadful sound, as of someone clearing his throat. Ella stood completely still, totally paralyzed in fear. Even Killjelly looked up in alarm. The white-haired man only stood still, every sinew and ligament in his body taut, sweat pouring down his head and drenching his clothing.

Then a horrendous voice spoke out of the blackness, "Who is it that calls upon me?"

40

---

## A CHORD OF THREE STRANDS

A cold, miserable drizzle filled the air as Clerans and Yohni shuffled slowly down the Shore Road along the edge of the Lower Village. The sun had set about an hour ago, and in its absence, the clouds rolled in over the top of the bay. Already, a thin fog filled the village, and Clerans was pretty certain that it was thickening as time went on. The rain settled in pools in Clerans' tricorn hat, and if he tilted his head down at all, the rain would pour off his hat in a small cataract in front of his face.

Clerans carried two heavy packs crammed with as much dried food as he could carry, while Yohni carried two small kegs of gunpowder, one under each arm. They simply needed to descend into the Lower Village and find a way through the pirates' defensive lines to reach the Lower Court. Clerans felt certain that they would manage just fine.

Captain Smydhac had briefed them just before they had headed out, and Clerans reviewed the whole briefing in his head. They were to approach the edge of the Lower Village, but not descend into it until they heard the cannon-fire from the northern end of the village. After a few minutes (letting

Caedmon Wilkins conduct a thorough bombardment of the pirates' lines in the north), Clerans and Yohni were to move in to the Lower Village.

But what were they to meet with in the Lower Village? Captain Smydhac had only mentioned vaguely that the pirates had a line of barricades "a smidgeon into the Lower Village." Did that mean that Clerans and Yohni would need to climb over a barricade in order to get the supplies to Laendon and the rest of the remnant? That would certainly be a delicate business. Clerans doubted the pirates would completely abandon their defensive line in the Lower Village, no matter how great of a bombardment Caedmon Wilkins performed on their northern lines.

Clerans adjusted the pack on his back. Yes, this might be a difficult mission (a "fiddly bit" as Captain Smydhac said), but they could do it. They would get these supplies to the survivors of the dike militia. Clerans sighed. But was his Da among those survivors?

Just then, Clerans heard the sound of wings beating against the drizzly air. Looking up, he saw Halfdan descending out of the light fog, beating the rain back with his wings as he alighted on the windowsill of a shop just at hand. The harrier ruffled up his feathers and shook the rain off himself.

"I would wait here," Halfdan said in his emotionless voice. "Once the bombardment begins, you can turn right down the next street, and that will take you directly into the pirates' line."

Clerans nodded and set down the pack in his arms. "Ay then, that sounds reasonable enough."

Just then, Clerans heard the distant boom of a cannon. Several more deep, resounding reports followed this, lingering in the heavy air like thunder. Clerans let out his breath slowly. So the bombardment had begun. The fusillade of the cannons was an all-too-familiar sound to Clerans from manning the battery for so many years. He guessed that there were perhaps twenty cannons, each firing in rapid succession. Even at this great distance, Clerans was pretty sure he knew the caliber of the cannons firing. Most of the guns certainly were fifteen-pounders (probably re-purposed dike cannons), though from the low rumbling reports of a few of the cannons, Clerans guessed that Caedmon Wilkins had salvaged a couple of thirty-four-pounders from the ruins of the battery. Yes, that bombardment would certainly clear away any make-shift barricade the pirates might crouch behind!

The second volley of cannon-fire now sounded, and as Clerans strained his ears to listen, he thought he could hear screams of agony and the sharp reports of muskets.

Clerans bit the inside of his cheek, turning slightly to Yohni. "Shall we let them fire off another two volleys, then? An' then we will try to get through?"

Yohni nodded somberly.

Yet suddenly, Clerans heard a strange noise in the growing fog behind them. It almost sounded like the pitter-patter of small feet against the wet cobblestones. Clerans drew out his pistol and pointed it in the general direction of the noise.

"Stand an' report yerself!" he cried.

As if reluctantly, two forms stepped out of the shadows and padded down the street towards Clerans. Clerans lowered his gun, shaking his head in annoyance.

"Sydni? Nōli? Are you still followin' me, then?"

Sydni nodded gravely. "The Li declared unto us..."

"Bother the Li!" Clerans replied. "Do no I tain a say in this matter? If you'll are to follow me around everywhere, the least you cen do is get my permission."

Sydni looked at Clerans closely with a blank look on her face. Was she simply unable to conceive of this idea, or had Clerans used some vocabulary that she did not know?

"Gard here," Clerans said after a long sigh. "I am about to

enter the pirates' lines, an' I cen no tain the two o' you followin' me. It will be too dangerous."

Sydni nodded. "All the more reason of for our aid of you."

"This is absurd," Clerans replied, glancing over at Yohni for support.

Yohni only shook his head, muttering, "Thus are all the Gwambi. If only *my* tribe, the Skratsi, had come for our allies..."

"Ay then, Yohni," Clerans said. "Cen ye tell these two? Maybe if they'll cen hear it in their own language..."

Yohni shook his head, scowling darkly. "I do not speak their tongue. Who would want to speak Twengoli?"

Clerans looked back at the two little nymphs, fixing them with a very severe gaze. "No, this ha' ceded far enough. You two may no follow me any farther. An' I do no care what the Li declares!"

Sydni looked as if she were about to reply when Nōli tugged at her arm, whispering some string of unintelligible gibberish into her ear. Sydni made some equally unintelligible (though impassioned) reply. Nōli shrugged, whispering something else into his sister's ear. Sydni heaved a brief sigh and then turned back to Clerans.

"It is of compromise, then, which is for why I speak."

Clerans raised an eyebrow, skeptically. "Compromise?"

Sydni nodded solemnly. "If you is for objecting, but the Li has thus declared, then it is of compromise that we must admit to of."

Clerans bit the inside of his cheek, trying to make out this little nymph's meaning through her garbled grammar.

Sydni pointed to herself and then to her little brother. "You is of wishing that we do not follow you? Then let be this as our compromise: one shall stop in the following of, and instead return unto the Iasaqi-Woni."

Clerans looked at Sydni closely. "So one o' you will keep following me, and the other one will leave?"

Sydni nodded, pointed at herself again and then pointing at her little brother. "You is of to choose between."

Halfdan whistled softly. "No good will come of letting a *heathen* join this mission."

Clerans looked over at Yohni, but Yohni only shrugged without a word.

Clerans let out his breath slowly. In the silence, he could hear another fusillade of cannon fire. "Ay, Halfdan, but I do no see as I tain a choice."

Sydni nodded her head emphatically, and Nōli giggled.

Suddenly, Yohni pointed to Nōli. "Make that one carry your second pack. That will be of use."

Clerans shrugged. "Very well then."

Nōli let out a little squeal of glee, rushing forward and struggling to lift Clerans' second pack of provisions onto his back. The pack looked to be about the same weight as Nōli himself. For a moment, the little nymph tottered under the heavy load, but then he regained his balance, looking up at Clerans expectantly.

Clerans couldn't help but smile down at the little nymph. "Merri well then."

Glancing back at Sydni, Clerans just saw her little shadow disappearing into the fog up the street. Clerans let out a heavy sigh.

"Alright then, on we cede!"

Halfdan fluttered into the air, and in a few moments, he disappeared into the drizzle above them. Clerans hiked up the pack on his back and then started forward himself, turning down the street to his left, while Yohni and Nōli followed close behind.

The rain drizzled down from Clerans' hat, and his heart pounded in his chest. He was heading into enemy territory then. What would he meet with on the next street?

Another round of cannon-fire rumbled in the air. Clerans

breathed deeply and steadily. He would not lose his head like he had when the pirates first attacked. He would stay calm, and he *would* get the provisions to Laendon. Above him, Halfdan's wings flapped softly in the drizzle, and behind him, Yohni and Nōli's webbed feet slapped against the cobblestones. Still, Clerans fixed his eyes ahead. He could make out very little in the dark and gathering fog.

They passed a long row of shops on their right, while side streets converging with the road occasionally interrupted the shops on their left. After passing this second side street, the shops suddenly ended on either side of them. Clerans was pretty sure from his memory of this part of the city that they should cross a more major street here, yet he could make out no shops or houses on the other side of the street. Surely the fog was not so thick that he could not see the other side of the street, was it?

Clerans paused for a moment and looked ahead. At a distance through the fog, he could just make out a few sputtering lights, like will-o'-the-wisps dancing in the gloom. Yet the lights looked to be in a line. Clerans could also see tiny pinpoints of glowing red which looked almost as if they were on the ground in front of him. It took Clerans several moments before he could make sense of what he was looking at. He smelled the pungent odor of burnt wood and heard the hiss of rain on live embers.

The next two blocks of houses and shops, then, were now only piles of ashes and burnt-out hulls. Clerans must then be looking across a desolate expanse of cinders. The line of sputtering lights must be lights along the pirates' barricade at the far end of the expanse.

Clerans bit the inside of his lip. So then, the pirates had not simply been burning the Lower Village for the fun of destruction. They had purposefully cleared an open area in front of their defenses. It was a no-man's-land of sorts. The lord protector was right. These pirates had planned perfectly. Clerans sighed. It would be rather hard to approach the line of the barricade unseen then — though the thickening fog would help.

Halfdan alighted on the ground before Clerans. "The remnants of a building are just ahead and to your left," the harrier said. "You can find cover there."

Clerans nodded. "What about the barricade? How heavily is it guarded? Do ye think we'll cen make it through?"

"I will investigate," Halfdan replied, and he fluttered into the air again.

Clerans now peered intently into the fog. Yes, just to the left, he thought he could see the shadowed outlines of some kind of building. Crouching forward slightly, Clerans crept ahead. He could still hear the soft footsteps of Yohni and Nōli behind him. Hopefully, any pirates guarding the barricade were too far away to hear those footsteps themselves.

Clerans breathed deeply, trying not to cough at the smoke in the air. So it began! He was leaving safety behind him now.

"God, protect us," Clerans whispered.

41

## DAMNED

*E*rnest could feel a heavy throbbing all around him, and he looked in horror at the pillar on the far side of the dais. Was he dreaming, or had he really heard that voice?

Beside him, Ella shrank back, clutching at his side for support.

The albino stood on the dais, his hands still raised, the sweat seeping through his cloak. He was trembling all over, but whether from exertion or excitement, Ernest couldn't tell. Killjelly fidgeted a little where he was kneeling on the hard granite dais, but he, too, peered ahead at the pillar on the far side.

Then Ernest noticed a dark something at the base of the pillar. It looked very much like a shadow, only there was nothing there to cast a shadow. As Ernest looked at it closely, he couldn't help but think that it looked as if all the darkness in the room was drawing itself together — almost of its own will — and making for itself a shadow that no light could dispel.

Yet as Ernest looked, he could see that the thing was growing, as if it were rising out of the granite floor and seeping out from the pillar. It was more than a shadow now, for it had depth. A tremble ran down Ernest's spine. Could that be the same shadow that he had seen in the passageway? Could that be the ghost?

The thing reached about six or seven feet in height, and then it stopped growing. The albino looked on with a look of sheer ecstasy on his face. Ernest didn't dare to move as he looked at that shadow. He hardly even dared to breathe.

But what was it? Was it really the ghost, or was it only a shadow, after all? It seemed so still, so motionless, that for a moment Ernest believed that he had only imagined the thing growing. Surely this was all just a trick of the lantern light. There was nothing there at all. It was just spooks in the darkness. His mind was in a state to believe anything!

Yet then the thing moved, and at once Ernest could see its outline: a head, arms, and legs like a man. As the thing moved, Ernest could hear that scratching noise which he had heard in the passageway. He no longer had any doubts; this was the ghost!

Ella whimpered and gripped him more tightly. But what good would that do her? He was just as likely to end up in that thing's belly as she was.

The shadow stepped slowly onto the dais at the far end from the albino. As the lantern light shone clearly on the shape, its dark shroud of shadow seemed to fall off of it like a cloak. For the first time, Ernest could see the ghost in hideous detail. Its face was the first thing that Ernest noticed, how the skin was so thin and drawn so tightly across the skull, that at first Ernest thought the ghost had nothing but a skull for a head. But he could see the creature's eyes sunken back in his head. They were slitted like a dwarf's eyes, bright yellow and unblinking.

Its cheeks were tight and hollow, revealing the jaw underneath them. Its lips, too, were thin and colorless. Upon its head the ghost wore a strange turban, yet from the folds of moth-eaten cloth, Ernest could see spikes protruding, as if it wore a crown underneath.

Now the ghost took one more step forward, and Ernest looked over the rest of his dreadful frame. The creature's whole body was emaciated, wizened, and skeletal, like the body of a prisoner who has not eaten for several fortnights. Despite this, Ernest could not but marvel at the power and strength with which the creature carried itself. Its fingers were so narrow, long, and bony, that they looked more like the claws of a bird of prey than fingers.

The ghost wore armor exactly as the kings had worn in their etchings on the wall of the passageway. He wore a strange breastplate which looked as if it were made of many bands of iron, all woven together into a solid piece. His legs were covered as if with a sort of tunic, with only his thighs shielded with that same peculiar armor. His arms, however, were bare, and his skin looked moldered in the lantern light. At the ghost's waist hung a short sword, which was curved but very thick. Ernest guessed it must weigh nearly thirty pounds, and he wondered how on earth this sickly-looking creature could heft it.

The ghost took one more step forward and then stopped, as if purposefully displaying itself in the lantern light. Suddenly, a great stench wafted over Ernest, and he nearly gagged. It smelled like rotting sewage, or decaying meat, or the foul odor of a festering wound — or perhaps all three at once. Was that dreadful stench coming from the ghost? After the creature had stood motionless and silent for nearly a minute, it spoke, its voice sounding cracked and strained with age, and yet somehow dreadfully potent.

"Why do you summon me?"

The albino slowly lowered his hands, looking at the ghost in great wonder, as if unable to speak for the moment. The ghost returned his gaze, staring blankly and expressionlessly at all the pirates with his golden eyes.

"I am Throcmordyn, whose name you have invoked. Why do you summon me?"

"We wish for you to retake your former station," the albino finally replied. "Have I not spoken of you what is true? Did you not rule the Gwambi civilization as a god?"

The ghost laughed, a stale and rasping laugh. "For five hundred years, I walked among the mortals. And for two thousand more, I have haunted these halls of death. I have eaten no meat for three hundred years — until today. Why should I again rise from the darkness? Why should I now quit my haunts?"

The albino reached out his hands towards the ghost, as if in a petition. "We are in a generation of people who doubt that there were once gods who ruled upon the earth. They draw power from ignorance and skepticism, and they teach others to do likewise. Even now, your enemies rule the ground above you and preach of only one benevolent god whom no man can see."

The albino paused for a moment and then continued. "You must rouse yourself and arm yourself in fury. We will be your servants, priests, and captains. With your aid, we will conquer this whole earth — for what could stand against your great power? Even the mighty empires of Hrufang and Kelmar would fall before you. We will rebuild your temples and erect a thousand altars. Yearly will the people of the earth come before you to worship. They will slaughter sacrifices on your altars and give you the honor you deserve in the blood of their sons and daughters."

The ghost drew out his sword in one swift motion and held it so that the lantern light twinkled off its gleaming blade. Ernest could not help but marvel at how easily the ghost held that massive weapon.

"You speak with much learning, oh man, for all of these things I did when I ruled the Gwambi. I was worshiped as a god, and only I know the exact number of the thousands and thousands of men, women, and children that my priests sacrificed on this very altar."

The ghost stepped forward again, pricking the lifeless body

of Longfinch with his wicked blade. There was a strange and sinister gleam in his eye. "Nothing pleases me so much as the death of man."

The albino spread his arms wide again. "Come then! Bind yourself to me. Let me be as your arms, your legs, and your mouth. I will be your representative, and your high-priest, and the mediator between you and all the world."

The ghost stepped forward again. He was very close to the albino, and the stench was worse than ever. Ernest could hardly stand to breathe. His heart rose in his chest, and he felt as if the whole air was pounding against him, as if he were at the center of a great drum which some giant continued to beat upon.

"And the rest of these?" the ghost motioned to Killjelly and the other pirates.

"They shall be your servants, as I am. You shall make of them as you choose, whether slaves, or priests, or captains. And there are more of us who wait on the ground above. For they are in a desperate struggle with your enemies."

The ghost let out a low growl. "I know of the people of Entwerp, and of their country, Llaedhwyth. And I know of Caedmon Wilkins, their leader, who proclaims his one invisible god, and how he blasphemes me. For though I linger in this darkness, I know of all that happens in the light."

The albino nodded. "Certainly. Then you must rouse yourself for battle. Let us first destroy the people of Entwerp and ravage all the nation of Llaedhwyth. We shall capture Caedmon Wilkins and sacrifice him on this altar. He shall pay for his blasphemies with his life."

The ghost laughed again, that same rasping laugh — almost more of a cough than a laugh. "So! And it would please me well."

The albino raised his hands higher, and he bowed his head. "Come then! Bind yourself to me. Arise in your fury and work again those works which you did of old, when you were a god on this earth. Let this whole earth be yours once more!"

The ghost took in a deep breath of air, and it sounded like the great gulping of a geyser as it sucks in air after erupting. Reaching out his claw-like hand, the ghost gripped the albino's hair tightly. Ernest watched with a twinge of horror. Somehow, he had not been willing to admit to himself that this ghost was a physical thing; it was too dreadful to be admitted. In his mind, the ghost was only a spirit, or a shadow, something purely spiritual in nature. Yet now, as he watched those long, bony fingers mingling with and grasping the albino's long, white hair, Ernest realized with a mind-numbing terror, that this ghost was indeed just as much a physical being as it was a spiritual being.

"Even so," the ghost said, gripping the albino by the hair so tightly that Ernest thought it a wonder that it did not pull out all the albino's hair.

There was a moment's pause, and Ernest drew in the scene's horror. The ghost and the albino seemed at that moment joined, as if in some great link between this world and the world of demons — for surely this ghost must be a demon himself, even if he were in a physical form. The albino stood poised and tense, sweat streaming down his body. The ghost seemed relaxed, but as if collecting his strength for a great pounce, holding the albino tightly by the hair with his left hand and his thick sword in his right.

Yet looking on the ghost and the albino, the two seemed to blend, so that Ernest could not say if the ghost looked as if he belonged to this world, or whether the albino looked as if he belonged to the world of demons. Killjelly still knelt on the edge of the altar, as if he were kneeling on the edge of a great cliff with only darkness before him. Ernest trembled all over, and he could feel all the pirates around him drawing back. Ella buried herself deeper against Ernest's side. There was something dark, dreadful, and very evil in this place. It seemed to throb in the air, like some sinister sprite that wafted past him in the stench, brushing against his clothing and touching his face with cold, clammy hands.

"I pay my homage to you, Throcmordyn," the albino finally said, his voice sounding low and muted in the thick darkness. "Let it be done, then!"

"Very well," the ghost replied. "I shall work again the works which I did of old. You shall all be my witnesses."

With a sudden flourish, the ghost made a great upward stroke with his sword. It was done so quickly and neatly that Ernest hardly saw what the ghost had done, but then the Albino's lifeless body toppled to the ground next to Longfinch's corpse, leaving only the pale, white-haired head in the ghost's hand.

Ernest drew back in horror as the ghost raised up the Albino's head for all to see, a gloating gleam in his eye. Throwing back his head, the ghost let out a great wail, something between the keening of an injured beast, and a cry of victory. Killjelly leapt to his feet, sudden terror filling his face.

Throwing the Albino's head to the side, the ghost let out a sinister laugh. "Who did you think I was? What works did you think I would do for you?"

The pirates scrambled backwards as the ghost now advanced to the edge of the dais. Killjelly dashed down from the dais, joining his men on the ground before it, though he never took his eyes off the ghost.

"Do you think I *ruled* the Gwambi people? No, I only endured them — for their living was odious to me. I raised them like cattle and made them sacrifice their sons and daughters on this altar for sheer dread of me. I was their god, not their king. I drank the blood of their offerings, and I devoured their flesh. Nothing pleased me so well as their death and suffering. Why should it be otherwise? Was I not given the body of a mortal, and now, from the careless angelic body, I must care for this mortal frame? I must feel every pain, every hunger, every want that you mortals feel, and yet I may never die.

"Oh! How I wished that they too would feel my suffering! But they could always die and bring that suffering to an end. And so I worked among them, year after year, decade after decade, century after century. I threatened, ravaged, and devoured, till there was none left but the priests. And then it was I who did the sacrificing. I slaughtered them on this very altar. I ate their flesh while the blood was yet hot.

"So now you summon me again. Do you wish me to work the works which I did of old? Very well, so I shall. I will again gorge myself on the flesh of man and become drunk with blood — your blood. You all will be my sacrifices, for you have offered yourselves to me. You say I shall do with you as I please? Very well. It pleases me to inflict suffering, to kill, and to eat."

Suddenly, Killjelly raised his pistol and fired upon the ghost. Ernest could tell that the shot struck the ghost directly in the chest. That should kill it if it really was a physical thing. But did Killjelly really think he could kill such a dreadful monster so easily?

To Ernest's surprise, the ghost toppled back at the shot, screwing up its face in pain and clawing at the hole in its body as if it were in the very throes of death. Yet, as quickly as that, it was on its feet again. There was no blood coming from the wound in its chest, but Ernest could see the dreadful hole in the armor where Killjelly's bullet had struck.

"Curse you!" the ghost shrieked, raising his sword high above his head.

"Kill it!" Killjelly cried, motioning frantically towards the other pirates. "Kill the thing, anoint it! Fire! Fire!"

The pirates answered for the first time, woken from a trance at Killjelly's cry. Even in their dreadful terror, they were a unit of fighting men again. As Killjelly quickly backed away from the ghost, the pirates raised their muskets and fired. Gunpowder smoke now filled the little area before the dais. The ghost collapsed to the ground, writhing in agony as every charge ripped through its body. One shot must have struck the ghost's sword, for it shattered into a million pieces, leaving only the hilt in the ghost's hand. The ghost's face twitched in torment, as if it were dying repeatedly. Yet still it moved, as if death were not the end for it, but merely a state of the ghost's existence. Perhaps the ghost had died a thousand times already.

Ernest clasped an arm protectively around Ella, but she suddenly shook him free, gasping in terror.

"Wun!"

Ernest blinked. "What!"

"*Run!*" Ella practically screamed.

Again the ghost rose to its feet, seething hatred flashing from his golden eyes. "It would have been better to endure me without resistance. You do not know the pain that is to die and yet live. Not yet. But you will feel it soon enough, in the torment of Tartarus — or wherever the Judge may send you!"

With that, the ghost let out an ear-piercing wail, flexing out its hands like claws. The ground trembled, and there was a terrible groaning noise, as of great stones grinding against each other. At that moment a thick smoke, or else a fog, filled the whole room, seeming to almost emanate in rippling waves from the ghost itself.

In an instant, Ernest could see nothing but that thick fog — not Ella, not Killjelly, not the ghost. All he could hear was the shrill wail of the ghost.

"Hell awaits!"

# 42

# KATABASIS

aeli took a deep breath and then plunged forward, following Martyn into the blackness of this new entrance into the Gwambi's city. She could just see Martyn's silhouette in front of her, standing out against the blackness as his lantern cast a halo all around him.

Haeli descended the first several steps quickly before looking back to see that Tiya-Aenji was close behind her, with Titus taking up the rear. As the big Slyzwirian man descended the spiral staircase, he reached for the handle of the trapdoor to close it behind them. Then he drew his hand back and shook his head, mumbling to himself.

"It's, eh, black enough as it is."

Haeli couldn't help but sigh. It certainly felt better to know that the door was open behind them, that there was a way of escape if they needed it.

As they continued their descent, the light of the trapdoor behind them quickly vanished. The staircase continued on in front of them, spiraling down and around itself repeatedly. Though the whole stairway was rather wide, it was also decently steep. Haeli guessed they must be descending into the mountain rather quickly, even at their cautious pace.

All Haeli could now see was the light of Martyn's lantern bobbing up and down in front of her and the pale glow of Titus' lantern casting strange shadows on the wall behind her. She shivered.

Tiya-Aenji plodded down the steps behind her, muttering under her breath with each step, "O Lord Almighty, be with your children. Guide and protect us as we descend into the realms of hell…"

Haeli took a deep breath. This was certainly a very sinister place. She could understand why Tiya-Aenji believed it was haunted. She might be tempted to believe that this stairway was haunted herself, if she didn't know already that such things could not be. These were just Elderian superstitions. There was nothing to be so terrified of. It was just dark, that was all.

Each step that Haeli took sounded close and heavy in her ears. She could hear Martyn's and Titus' footsteps too, their heavy boots sounding almost blasphemous in the stillness of that stairway. Behind her, Haeli could hear the slapping of Tiya-Aenji's bare, webbed feet against the stone and her continued muttered prayers.

"O Lord Almighty…"

And yet the stairway went on and on, continuing to spiral down, down, in utter blackness. Haeli did not know how much time they spent, or how many stairs they descended at this same steady pace.

After what seemed like an eternity, Martyn broke the silence. "Well, now, here's something new." He hurried forward down the stairs.

Haeli followed and soon saw what had piqued Martyn's interest. The stairs finally ended, and Haeli found herself in a long, narrow hallway. A strange, pungent, and very unpleasant smell wafted all around Haeli.

Martyn held out his lantern, shining it in all directions, and Haeli caught her breath in disgust. Skulls lined the walls on either side of the hall as far as the lantern light reached. Their bleached-white surfaces gleamed in the lantern-light. Haeli shivered. There were thousands of these skulls on either side of her. Where had they all come from? They simply sat there, their eyeless sockets staring, and their voiceless mouths leering.

Had this been a graveyard? It must have been. Why else would there be so many skulls in one room like this?

Behind her, Haeli could hear Tiya-Aenji catch her breath. "O Lord Almighty, be with your children..."

"What is this place?" Martyn asked, turning back towards Tiya-Aenji with a sickened expression on his face.

Tiya-Aenji shuddered. "It is the Hall of the Faces of Death."

"Heaven preserve us!" Titus gasped, now entering the narrow hallway himself.

Tiya-Aenji only shook her head. "Beware! You will see many things in these tunnels — strange and terrible things! There is the Hall of Etchings, and the Great Lower Hall, and the Seven Pillars of Sacrifice..."

Titus shuddered, pointing to the skulls that lined the walls. "Are those, eh, are those... skulls?"

"Do you see the painted ones?" Tiya-Aenji continued, ignoring Titus' question.

Haeli looked closely at the sickening lines of skulls all around her, and she noticed for the first time that some of the skulls were indeed painted a deep ebony. These painted skulls were all grouped together, so that as Haeli looked at the larger racks of skulls on the walls, the painted skulls seemed almost to form shapes, or perhaps lettering of some kind.

"Is it..." Haeli began, hardly knowing how to phrase her question. What a stench of death there was in this hallway!

Tiya-Aenji trembled. "It is writing, in the alphabet and language of the Gwambi. It is a message for any who enters these halls: Let those who enter face us. For we have faced death. And in facing, we are overcome."

Titus trembled all over.

Martyn, however, let out a great laugh. Haeli couldn't help but imagine all of those toothy skulls laughing, too. Were they laughing with Martyn, or at him?

Martyn's voice rose clear and strong as he turned to look at the thousands of lifeless faces which stared down on him.

"'Well, then, I tain some news fer you! You say that you ha' faced death, an' I cen see that you ha', and you ha' perished, never to live again. Yet I tain a Savior who ha' faced death Himself, yet He triumphed over it!"

Martyn turned back to Tiya-Aenji now. "But my question is, where does this lead? I cen keep on forward as I may, but what must I do if there is a fork?"

Tiya-Aenji only shook her head. "There is but one way from here to the Lower Hall."

Martyn shrugged. "Alright then, shall we go forward again?"

But he didn't wait for a reply. Martyn plunged forward, walking confidently between the two walls of skulls. Haeli swallowed. This was certainly very unsettling, but she had no other alternative. She had to follow Martyn.

Martyn began to sing now, and Haeli recognized the words as coming from one of the hymns that she would sing at kirk:

"Where death is your sting upon me?

Where grave is your dread victory?

For all is submitted to the Christ."

So they plodded on. Haeli tried as hard as she could not to look at the lines of skulls on either side. It was too sickening. The further they went, the greater that terrible stench became. Haeli could hardly let herself breathe. The smell of death was so potent.

Finally, after they had walked for some distance, the hall widened a little, and another stairway stood before them. This stairway, however, was straight, very wide, and not steep at all. Martyn did not even pause as he came to this new stairway, but immediately descended it. As Haeli followed, she could still hear Tiya-Aenji muttering her prayer behind her,

"O Lord Almighty, be with Your children..."

It was a rather long stairway, but they came to the bottom of it soon enough. Here, the passageway narrowed again to form another narrow hallway. That same disgusting stench clung to this air, too. Martyn lifted his lantern and shook his head.

"What is this now?"

Haeli felt as if she would vomit. Lining these walls were row on row of backbone vertebrae.

"More bones?" Titus moaned.

"Is it a graveyard?" Haeli finally asked, turning to look at Tiya-Aenji. "Did not you say these were catacombs?"

"It is the sacrificial victims," the little nymph replied solemnly.

But Martyn took no time to look around in this hall. He continued to walk forward. He no longer seemed so mockingly jovial as he had been in the Hall of the Faces of Death; his face was now set hard with determination.

So now they passed between these walls of bones. Haeli gagged at the oppressive stench. Finally, this hallway too ended, widening out as the hall above had, and ending in another wide, gradual staircase.

As they descended this staircase, Haeli had a brief reprieve from the horrid smell, but she choked again when they reached a third narrow hallway at the bottom of this staircase. Ribs and whole rib cages lined the walls of this hall from floor to ceiling.

"Another?" Titus howled, his voice rising to a pitch in excitement. "How many men died here?"

Tiya-Aenji shook her head, trembling all over. "Did I not tell you to beware of the strange and dreadful sights you would see down here? This is only the third of the Seven Halls of Death."

"Seven?" Titus said, "There's seven of these halls?"

"Come now!" Martyn cried. "Do no ye see that these halls were *meant* to make ye go mad with terror an' horror? Steel yourself then! We cen no fall prey to its devices."

Haeli nodded. Her heart was stone. She would not let herself feel fear.

And so Martyn went on. Haeli and the others followed reluctantly.

They passed now from this third hall, down another wide and gradual staircase, into the fourth hall, this one lined with the bones of arms. From here, they passed into a fifth hall, with row upon row of pelvises lining its walls. From here, they descended to the sixth hall, which was similarly adorned with leg bones. Finally, they reached the seventh hall.

Haeli could feel her stomach churning within her, and she felt that at any moment she might vomit. The stench of death that filled those halls had so permeated her that even when she reached the relatively fresh air of the staircases, she still felt the smell of death in her lungs. Even so, Haeli plodded on. Tiya-Aenji had said there were seven halls, so they *must* be coming to an end of it all.

Finally, they reached the end of this seventh hall, passing by hideous rows of skeletal hands and feet. But here again was another wide stairway, like the stairs which had separated all of those seven halls. Martyn did not hesitate when he reached this stairway, but continued forward and downward. Haeli, however, paused.

Surely this would not lead them to an eighth hall, would it? She could not think of any other part of the skeleton which had not been gruesomely displayed in these halls. Then what awaited her at the bottom of this seventh stairway?

Slowly and cautiously, Haeli followed Martyn. This staircase felt longer than any of the others had been, but when she reached the bottom, Haeli again found herself in a narrow hallway. Haeli hardly dared to look around her at what new apparition might be displayed along the walls of this hallway, but she could not stop herself from looking around.

To her great relief, Haeli saw that the walls in this hallway were nothing more than perfectly planed granite, such as she had seen in other Gwambi constructions. Tiya-Aenji came up behind Haeli and paused. Haeli looked back to see that Tiya-Aenji was still quite pale.

"It is the Hall of Blood," Tiya-Aenji spoke softly, almost fearfully. "The Hall of the Torment of Dying. See the ground?"

Haeli looked at her feet and could see — even in the dim light — that the stone which made up the floor of the hallway was definitely much darker. Was it that way naturally, or had it been stained?

Tiya-Aenji continued, "It is where the blood of the sacrificial victims was poured out as libations for their god of the grave."

Haeli shivered. "I wish I could believe you were making all of this up."

"Hush now!" Martyn whispered. "Is that a light I see ahead?"

And they all grew silent.

Haeli peered ahead in the darkness. She could just make out the end of the narrow hallway, maybe five yards in front of them. The hallway seemed to lead into a very large and expansive room beyond. She could not see — as she had expected from what Martyn said — a concentrated light as of a lantern or a torch. However, she thought whatever room this hallway opened into was lighted somehow, if dimly.

Slowly, the entire group crept forward. As they reached the end of the hallway, Martyn entered first into the room beyond, stepping down a few wide steps and pausing for a moment at the bottom. After holding up his lantern and looking all around, he motioned for the others to follow him.

As Haeli came up to Martyn, she looked all around this new room. It was certainly very extensive; she could not make out any walls or ceiling from where she stood. At great distances from one another in the room stood the bases of immense columns, stretching up higher than the lantern-light would shine. Those, then, must be the pillars that supported the roof of this great room.

What had been the light which they saw from the passageway?

She had hardly looked to discover the source of the light when Martyn let out a hiss in warning and dashed behind one of the great columns, blowing out his lantern hurriedly.

"What are you...?" Titus asked.

Martyn cut him off, putting his finger to his lips earnestly.

"Blow out the lantern!" he whispered in such a low tone that he practically only mouthed the words.

Titus obeyed. To Haeli's astonishment, she could still see. All four of them seemed to be illuminated, albeit dimly, by some other light. Martyn pointed around the corner of the column that he was hiding behind.

Haeli looked in the direction, when suddenly she heard a voice sounding loudly and clearly in the darkness of that hall: "Do you answer me?"

Haeli peered closely ahead in the dim light. Illuminated by a few flickering lanterns, seven pillars stood at a distance from where Haeli crouched. Amid these pillars, or else just before these pillars, she could see a group of perhaps ten people. Two of these people stood out to Haeli; they seemed taller than the rest, or perhaps they were standing on a dais of some sort. Had Haeli seen two? But there were three men standing up above the others. Haeli didn't know how she had missed the third figure at her first glance. She trembled as she looked upon him. Even at this great distance, there was something hideously wrong with that third figure.

"Lord have mercy on us!" Tiya-Aenji gasped, trembling all over. "It is *him*! Have they summoned him?"

Haeli looked at the group of people closely. Who were they? Certainly they had to be the pirates, but Haeli couldn't tell for certain. Was Ella among them?

"We have to get closer," Martyn breathed, shaking his head.

So saying, Martyn crept out from behind this column. Swiftly and noiselessly, he scampered across to the next column.

Haeli, Titus, and Tiya-Aenji followed Martyn closely, each one trying to remain as quiet as Martyn had been. As Tiya-Aenji followed, she muttered under her breath again,

"O Lord Almighty, be with Your children..."

Haeli looked back to see the entrance to the narrow hallway behind them. That was the way they knew to get out of this great room. No matter what happened now, Haeli knew she had better keep that exit in sight so that if the need arose, she could get back out to the Gwambi Tower.

Martyn crept forward again until he had reached the vantage point of the next column. Again, the others followed him. Haeli guessed they were close enough now to that strange group of seven pillars that she might be able to make out some features of the people standing there.

Just before she peered around the corner of the column to confirm her suspicions, a gunshot rang out in that massive room, followed by another voice — Haeli recognized it immediately as the voice of that hooked leprechaun who had attacked her father's trading fort.

"Kill it! Kill the thing, anoint it! Fire! Fire!"

Haeli cautiously looked out from behind the column and was dumbstruck at the scene before her. There were the seven columns which she had seen from a distance, yet now she could see that there was a dais in the middle of these pillars. Before this dais, a group of people stood — pirates, certainly. Yet on the dais itself, Haeli could see two corpses, and above them both stood a sinister-looking person.

The word 'person' did not seem wholly true, for it looked so much more like a creature, although it wore a person's shape. Its fingers were long, bony, and claw-like; its entire frame was wizened and ashen in complexion. Even its head seemed no head at all, but only a skull mounted on its shoulders.

As Haeli watched, the pirates standing before the dais fired a fusillade of muskets upon the hideous person, and he collapsed in a heap before the barrage. Haeli quickly scanned the group of pirates who stood before the dais. She immediately recognized the hooked leprechaun, who stood foremost among the pirates. Where was their renowned Captain Longfinch? Then Haeli saw another form; it was that coward, Ernest. Was he among this group? But no, he looked as if he were being held prisoner with that blonde-haired pirate clinging to him. But no, that was not a pirate at all — that was Ella!

Haeli pointed across the great room excitedly. "Martyn!" she whispered excitedly.

"I see!" Martyn cried, leaping to his feet. "It is Miss Ella. We ha' best be quick!"

"Ella?" Titus asked, getting to his feet himself. "My Ella?"

Martyn did not respond, but only drew out his tomahawk as he rushed forward, paying no heed to caution now. He charged headlong towards the group of pirates.

Haeli watched breathlessly. Did Martyn really think he was going to take down all of those pirates himself? Then Haeli saw that hideous creature-person rising back to its feet on the dais. How had it survived the musket shots?

The creature leapt to the edge of the dais, throwing its claw-like hands forward and letting out a great wail. Haeli looked on in terror as the whole ground shook, and a thick fog curled up as if from nowhere. Was this really black magic, then? Was she seeing an act of sorcery? But sorcery was dead! She could not be seeing what she thought she saw.

The ground continued to tremble beneath her, and Haeli suddenly wondered if the entire roof of this room was about to collapse on them. Suddenly, she heard a grinding noise and then a terrific crash behind her. Turning around, Haeli looked to see what had caused the crash, and her mouth went dry. The entrance to the narrow hallway — their only exit from this dreadful place — had collapsed, leaving nothing there, but a jumbled pile of rocks.

Haeli stared in disbelief. No sooner had she seen this than a great, thick fog rolled over her, and she could see nothing more.

43

# THEOPHANY

*E*rnest stumbled backwards in horror. For a moment he saw the terrifying sight of the ghost poised at the edge of the dais, its hands extended like the talons of a bird of prey about to snatch up its victims. Then a wave of fog rolled over him, and Ernest could see nothing. The fog seemed to absorb the light from the lanterns, as if the fog itself glowed, making everything that it enveloped seem to be only a shadow.

Ernest could make out nothing in the thick fog, but all around him he could hear screams of agony and pleas for mercy. As if coming from the fog itself, Ernest could hear the ghost simultaneously laughing and wailing. Now and then, Ernest could see a ripple or an eddy in the surrounding fog, and in it the shape of a pirate. But almost as soon as he could see one, the eddy would disappear.

Terror filled Ernest, and he stood, looking around wildly in great confusion. What was he to do? Should he run? Suddenly, a shape loomed up before Ernest in the fog. He let out a startled cry, but then saw that it was Ella. Her face was wild with fright, and her eyes stood out wide.

"E'nest!" she gasped. "I need a savio'h; but I only have you!"

She threw herself at Ernest's feet, clinging tightly to his ankles. Strangely, her words seemed to comfort Ernest. He had Ella. She was looking to him for protection. Well, then, he would protect her. His confused thoughts seemed to clear.

He was Ernest, a former pirate. These pirates here had captured him and killed his messmate. They were his enemies. If they were all slaughtered by some supernatural-yet-natural, immortal-yet-mortal, demon-yet-man — what was that to him? His only role now was to get out of here and take Ella with him. He would save her from all of this.

These thoughts had hardly come to Ernest when he saw another something looming up in the fog before him. Ella must have seen it too, for sheer terror spread across her face.

"God help us!" Ella cried, and then she sank down in a dead faint.

Of a sudden, the fog drew back. Had Ella's words caused this? Ernest could now see clearly in front of him through the retreating fog. A dark shape stood before him. It was the ghost. It stood very close, with its hands outstretched as if about to take Ernest by the throat. Yet, as the fog fled away from Ella and Ernest, the ghost too paused, as if unsure of itself. Ernest could see blood running down from the ghost's mouth and smearing the strange, woven armor. Was that all that was left of the pirates?

A sickening smile spread over the ghost's face. "You are not of Longfinch's crew, now are you?"

"How did you know Longfinch's name?" Ernest gasped, surprising himself that he should talk to such a dread phantom.

The ghost only smiled again, and Ernest could not help but think how that smile looked rather like Longfinch's smile. "What do I *not* know? I know you are called Ernest, and that girl with you is called Ella. Her I have haunted for a long time, as I did her father."

The ghost cackled. "Did you really think you were rid of me when you evaded me in the Hall of Etchings? Did I not say you could not avoid me forever?"

Drawing himself forward again, the ghost reached out towards Ernest's throat. "You will know what true suffering is when I am done with you."

At that moment, something came between the ghost and Ernest. It was a man, leaping upon the ghost with the ferocity of a tiger. Ernest gasped in surprise. It was the God of War — what was his name? Martyn, wasn't it? What was he doing here?

Ernest could just see the flash of a tomahawk blade in the eerie light of the fog as Martyn struck at the ghost. Letting out a pained howl, the ghost tumbled backwards.

"May God Almighty judge ye!" Martyn roared, "Be ye phantom or whatever else ye'll might be."

At these words, the ghost fell to its knees, letting out a long hiss, like water in a skillet of oil. Drawing out a long horse-pistol, Martyn leveled it and fired directly into the ghost's head. At the flash of fire from the barrel and the sudden burst of gunpowder smoke, the strange fog curled back, and the ghost collapsed in a bony heap on the ground.

Ernest's heart leaped inside him. So that was it! The ghost was dead! Yet the thought had hardly come to him when the ghost let out another wail and scrambled back to its feet. Its eyes burned like glowing coals. As the ghost turned again to face them, Ernest drew back in horror. He could clearly see the great gash in the ghost's shoulder from Martyn's tomahawk, and he could see the hole where Martyn's shot had penetrated the ghost's skull — but there was no blood, only two hideous wounds which had already begun to fester in the ghost's ashen skin.

The rage written on the ghost's face seemed beyond words, and indeed the ghost — who had been so loquacious thus far — had nothing to say now. Instead, he let out another unearthly howl and threw his clawed hands forward, as if he were heaving something at Martyn.

Martyn flew backwards, hurtling through the air and then striking head-first into one of the great columns which held up the hall. Martyn crumpled forward and then lay still. With a sudden fury, the ghost faced Ernest again.

"You men always struggle," the ghost winced as he passed one of his long claws along the wound in his shoulder. "But what is the point? It is always better for you when you simply accept your fate."

The ghost drew himself forward. In a moment, Ernest knew that those long, hideous claws would be around his neck, and then those dreadful, blood-stained teeth would sink into his flesh. At that moment, a sudden thought came upon Ernest like a flash of light in that dark hall.

Before the ghost could extend his fingers around Ernest's throat, Ernest pointed his finger in the ghost's face with the same authority he had seen that massive satyr use against the albino. A boldness came over him, and he cried out,

"I rebuke you by the authority of the Almighty God!"

The ghost recoiled, as if Ernest had smashed him in the face with a sledgehammer. The Almighty God — it worked! Just like it had for the satyr, and for Ella in the Hall of Etchings, and then for Martyn. That must be it then. No gun, sword, or tomahawk would halt this terrifying menace; only the Almighty God would.

And why wouldn't it? Was not this ghost a spiritual thing first, and was not the Almighty God the ruler of all the spiritual beings? That's what Lewis had said, at any rate. Besides, the authority of the Almighty God had made even the albino cower like a child. Surely there was a great power in that name — a power that even transcended the horror of this ghost.

"You would use that name?" the ghost said, hissing and rasping like a great serpent. "You, a pirate? What are you?"

The question was hardly out of the ghost's mouth before Ernest found himself answering it with the catechism answer that the father of that nice Llaedhwythi family had taught him;

"I am a sinner, justly deserving the wrath and damnation of God."

The ghost cackled in laughter at this statement. "That you certainly are. Who would save you from me? You have no hope."

But even as the ghost laughed, Ernest could see a hint of doubt crossing its ghastly face. Ernest felt a surge of courage flooding over him. It was a feeling he had never experienced before. His hair tingled, and his heart pounded heavily against his chest. The ghost was afraid. The catechism, then, must have a power in it too. But of course, it had power — it was a spiritual weapon. It was well-suited to a spiritual foe.

As the ghost raised itself up again, Ernest again pointed his finger in its face, blurting out all the answers to the catechism questions he knew.

"My only hope for salvation is in the Christ, the Son of God, who died in my place as my sacrificial atonement of sin, that I could inherit the glories of God. I must repent from my sins and look to the Almighty God alone for grace and forgiveness, for only He can save. I must make Him the Lord of my life and submit to His rules."

Each word seemed to cut the ghost like the edge of a knife. It flinched back into the darkness. A wave of triumph washed over Ernest. He stood up with his head held high and would have almost stepped forward, pursuing the ghost as he used this newfound weapon of the catechism. He was yelling — nearly screaming — the last catechism answer. The words he spoke were true, but more than that, they were the truth.

"By the grace of God alone, through faith in Him, which is gifted of His Holy Ghost, and not by any deed of myself."

The ghost had collapsed to the ground under this barrage of words, but as soon as Ernest had finished, it looked up with wild, hate-filled, golden eyes. The triumph in Ernest's heart suddenly died as he looked into those eyes. A sinking feeling of dread now sprang up inside of him. There was then great power in those words — but they were just like the bullets which the pirates had fired on the ghost. They were painful to the ghost, but in the end, they only sent him into a worse fury.

The ghost leapt to his feet with a sudden scream. "Who are you to use those words here? I will not allow you. *He* is not to be reverenced here."

The ghost sprang forward at Ernest. He tried to back away, but Ella still hung about his ankles, even in her state of unconsciousness. Ernest could not move. The ghost would strangle him in a moment. Maybe it had been useless to struggle after all.

"God help me!" Ernest said. He spoke with very little conviction now, but only out of desperation. There was nothing else he knew to do or say.

The ghost gurgled like a boiling pot, but halted with his claw-like fingers still stretched out towards Ernest's throat. The darkness swirled around the ghost. In that instant, Ernest realized he was not standing in darkness. There seemed to be a great lightness just behind him, as if he were standing right on the edge. The darkness, though, did not dissolve in the presence of the light like normal darkness would, but it swarmed up to the light, and the two seemed almost to clash right before Ernest's nose, like the crashing of waves against a cliff's face. As the darkness threw itself against the edge of the light, it fell away like the rolling waves of the sea.

With sudden clarity, Ernest realized that the ghost itself was nothing more than darkness — great hideous darkness that had bound itself together into that dreadful creature. Even as it reached out its clawed hand towards Ernest, it hesitated, for to touch Ernest would mean to force its hand into the light, and Ernest was quite certain that if the ghost at once touched the light, it would be destroyed. Ernest felt a little of his courage returning to him now. He was safe then, for he was in the light.

Now the darkness surged forward, throwing itself against the edge of the lightness. The ghost leered up at Ernest, bringing its face up as close to him as it could without touching the light. The foul stench of death wafted over Ernest, and he nearly gagged.

"He has no place here! These are my halls — mine! Do you hear?"

But what was the ghost saying? Who was he talking about? But even as these questions came to Ernest, a thought — an answer of sorts — dawned on him. If there was this dreadful fiend of the darkness — an embodiment of the darkness — might there also be a great embodiment of the lightness?

And then Ernest felt a grand and regal presence. It was almost as if it stood beside him, but he felt more as if this presence had suddenly come upon him — over, around, and within him. A great power and majesty seemed to surge through the air, and the very darkness bowed down in fear. Could it be the Almighty God? Had he answered to the call of His name as the ghost had answered to the call of its name?

A look of wide-eyed horror came over the ghost's face. "What is this you have done? You foolish man, you act as if you have nothing to fear. But surely He will damn you, too. You are not clean. What place do you have in the light? You are a *man* — unclean and a sinner. So you have said yourself! You are a son of the darkness, like me."

Ernest was looking the ghost directly in the eye, and he felt his heart sink inside of him. That was true. Looking down at his hands, he could see that they were as black as pitch compared to the lightness that danced around him. What place did he have in the light? He was a pirate, after all, no matter how much he claimed to be something different. He was an evil man. He had killed, pillaged, lied, and cursed. What sin was there that he had not committed?

The ghost was reaching towards him again, and Ernest realized that the wall of light was fading away, falling back before the vicious onslaught of the darkness. Soon he would be in the darkness again, and he would be at the ghost's mercy. But wasn't that where he belonged, after all?

"What right have you to invoke His name?" the ghost was saying. "You are not one of his children."

Ernest flinched at this. He was the child of a drunkard and a wife-beater. How could he aspire to be anything more himself? It was in his bones.

Then Ernest felt — as it were — a hand resting on his shoulder. It was strong, tender, and warm; the very touch seemed to send a thrill down Ernest's spine and warm his whole body. A voice spoke in his ear. The lightness swarmed all around Ernest, folding around him like wings.

"You are my son. Today I have begotten you. What I have called clean, let no one call unclean."

At that moment, something fell upon him. It felt almost like a rush of water pouring over his head, but it burned and tingled like fire. A great strength and courage previously unknown to him throbbed in Ernest's veins, and a wave of power coursed through him. Looking the ghost steadily in the face, he spoke, but the words did not come from his own mind. He was relaying a message from another Being.

"You are a liar. Be gone."

The ghost drew in a sharp breath. "You can not make me. I am spirit. I do not answer to the words of man."

*Today I have begotten you*

Ernest raised his hand, pointing at the ghost with authority. As he did so, he could see that his hand was no longer dark. It had transfigured into a clean and brilliant hand. The surrounding light danced like a flame against the darkness; it almost seemed to blaze forth from Ernest's own hand.

"By the authority of the Almighty God, the Christ who is my savior, I command you to leave." Ernest felt as if the voice was hardly his own. It was so mighty and authoritative.

"These are my halls. You have no authority here," the ghost replied, almost whining.

"He claims them now for His own. I am His son; you will no longer call me unclean. I belong in the light with Him. And His power — which is in me — reigns over all things. Now, by the power of the Christ, begone!"

The light suddenly leapt forward, and the darkness dissolved as if it had not been a living thing at all but only the normal darkness, which is easily overcome by light. The ghost let out a great wail and leaped at Ernest with its claws open wide. Ernest did not flinch, but only continued to hold out his hand. As he and the ghost touched, there was a surge of light and a loud hiss as of steam erupting from a geyser. With another wail, the ghost vanished in the spreading light.

There was now no longer any heaviness or foreboding in the air, but only the gentle stillness that one might expect in an underground hall. For a moment more, the brilliant and other-worldly lightness lit up the hall. Ernest could see the massive, vaulted ceiling towering above him and the hundreds of great columns that held it up. There must have been quartz or some other crystal in the granite of those vaults, for the ceiling flashed and sparkled like so many stars above his head. Then the light slowly faded until Ernest stood there again in the dim hall with only the earthly lights of the lanterns to illuminate it.

For a long time, Ernest felt the hand resting on his shoulder.

Ernest breathed a great sigh. It was over then. He felt strangely new and happy, as if he had just stepped from a hot bath and put on soft, clean clothing.

One thought kept repeating itself in his mind; he was a pirate no longer. Now he was a son of the Light.

# 44

# CONVICTION

With every step he took, Clerans could see more clearly into the fog. Yes, there certainly was a structure in front of him. Clerans could make out the outlines of two or three brick walls rising from the embers on the ground. This must be all that was left of the shops on this street. What a pity! These shops had all been the modern shops. But then again, that was probably the very reason the pirates burned them; the shops in the Upper Village were the old granite construction and would not burn so easily.

Before too long, Clerans and the others reached the near side of this burned-out shop. Clerans crouched behind the wall near a scorched doorway. They were concealed from the pirates' view for now. Peering around the corner of the doorway, Clerans could make out a long, black shape lying all across the ground on the far side of this burnt area. That was certainly a barricade. But how tall was it, and how heavily guarded?

Clerans guessed that if they could only get through that barricade, they would have little trouble avoiding the pirates inside and getting through to the Lower Court (with the fog and darkness and all). Getting over the barricade, then, was his chief concern.

He had to wait only for a moment before Halfdan returned, alighting on the charred rubble which lay all about.

"Well?" Clerans whispered, "How does our chance gard like? Do ye think we'll cen make it through?"

Halfdan ruffled up his feathers. "With the help of God Almighty, we shall."

"Ay then," Clerans nodded. "We could certainly use His help. How many sentries are there, then?"

"I counted ten in total," Halfdan replied. "They are pacing up and down the entire length of the barricade, though, and therefore I think it is likely that we could slip between them without them noticing."

Clerans nodded slowly. "An' ye think we will be able to get up to the barricade without being noticed?"

Halfdan glanced around. "God has sent you this fog for concealment. I believe we may be confident that He is with us."

Clerans nodded, peering back at the dark mass of the barricade. "Right then, I guess we'll will jist ha' to move forward and trust His providence, then."

Clerans took a deep breath. "Be our guard, O Lord," he prayed softly. "Guide us an' hide us from the eyes o' our enemies."

Halfdan ruffled up his feathers, whistling softly in affirmation.

"Amen," Clerans said, breathing deeply again. He could feel his heart beginning to pound in his chest. The gravity of this mission sank in on Clerans. He was about to enter the enemy's lines. He, Yohni, Halfdan, or Nōli might not make it out of this alive.

Clerans' mind strayed back to the dreadful events of the previous night. In his mind's eye, he could see the crumpled form of Meriwedhr as he collapsed under the Eagle Griffin's weight. He could see Mr. Gingrich falling on his face to the cobblestone street as his lifeblood left him. He could see the pale, wan face of Chaerls dying slowly in Mr. Fflemin's shop.

Oh! How much death he had seen! How many of his friends and fellow villagers were now dead? Now he was about to face the pirates again. Would he survive this time? Or was he even now living out his last few hours on this earth?

And supposing he got to Laendon and the others. What then? Who would he find there? He knew Laendon was alive, but what about Da? Was his Da alive, or had he too fallen before the awful piratical onslaught? Even as this thought came to him, he remembered the sound of his father's voice as it rose above the cannon fire the night the pirates breached the dikes.

> *"Though we are crushed, we are not slain,*
> *Though we are vexed, 'tis not in vain,*
> *For Thou wilt save when we're dismayed,*
> *And Thou, O Lord, wilt give us aid,*
> *We praise Thee, knowing thou wilt stand,*
> *For us Thou wilt lay bare Thy hand!"*

Clerans clenched his fists. *Yes,* he thought. *God will see us through. God will destroy these pirates. God will protect us.*

"Lord," he prayed aloud, feeling a wave of determination flood over him, "guide our hands to war."

Clerans motioned for Yohni and Nōli to follow him. Not daring to stand up, in case one of the pirate sentries saw him, Clerans crept forward on his hands and knees. He breathed steadily, his pulse pounding in his ears. He had to relax. They would be just fine. They would reach the barricade and get over it. They would successfully deliver their provisions to Laendon and the rest of the survivors. Halfdan was right. God had sent them this fog as cover. Surely God would see them through.

It was very difficult going crawling through that waste of

ashes and rubble. Now and then, Clerans (despite his best efforts) would set his bare hand on a live coal, and it was all he could do to keep silent at the sudden pain. Clerans clenched his jaw tightly. He just had to keep moving forward. Adding to the suspense, every few minutes the far-off bombardments of the cannons rumbled in the air, answered now and then by the sharp fusillade of muskets.

Slowly, inch by inch, Clerans, Yohni, and Nōli crept towards the barricade. Clerans tried to focus his attention on the ground so as not to put his hand on another live ember, but now and then he would look up at the dark line of the barricade on the far end of this waste of wet ashes and rubble. The first several times that Clerans looked out through the fog at the barricade, he thought they were no closer to it than they had been before. Gradually, he saw they were making progress. Soon, he could make out the shape of the barricade distinctly enough to see that it was made of hastily scraped together pieces of burnt lumber, stray bricks, chunks of cobblestone, and an assortment of furniture.

Only once did Clerans hear boots tramping on the far side of the barricade; otherwise, there was no evidence of the pirate sentries. More importantly, no one challenged their approach or fired a shot at them through the thickening fog.

Finally, Clerans, Yohni, and Nōli reached the near side of the barricade. Here Clerans paused, still crouched on his hands and knees, while he looked up and down this make-shift embankment. It was only about five feet high; they should easily be able to scramble over — but how could he be sure that there was no pirate on the other side?

As if in answer to Clerans' unspoken question, Halfdan fluttered down from out of the drizzly fog. "There is another sentry coming," the harrier whispered. "Wait until you hear him pass; then it will be clear."

Clerans, Yohni, and Nōli waited perfectly still and perfectly silent. Clerans breathed deeply, trying to calm himself down. He had to stay relaxed. He had to keep himself under control. Of course, he hoped to make it to the Lower Court without a fight, but if it came to a fight, he had to be relaxed. He could not let himself get excited.

Now Clerans heard the steady *tramp, tramp* of boots on the other side of the barricade. Now and then, the tramping would pause, as the sentry looked out over the barricade before marching a little further down the line. Clerans, Yohni, and Nōli remained motionless.

Gradually, Clerans could hear the sentry come level with them and then slowly move on, his footsteps dying away in the opposite direction from which they came.

Clerans now sprang. Still trying to move quietly, he scrambled up the barricade and then leapt down to the other side. Hardly had his feet touched the cobblestones on the other side of the barricade, when a voice hailed him out of the darkness.

"Hold it right there!"

Clerans could see nothing in the fog as he looked towards the voice. Had he been spotted? But no, if he could not see the pirate who challenged him, then the pirate could not see him. Clerans snatched off his tricorne hat and ruffled up his hair so that his silhouette would not look like that of a Pistosian.

"Who's there, eh?" the voice spoke again. A dark shape loomed out of the fog towards Clerans. Still, Clerans could not make out more than the outline of the speaker.

Standing up confidently, Clerans tried his best to imitate a thick seaman's accent, "Here now, lad, there isn't no reason to be so jumpy now — we've getted enough enemies as it is without turning on each other, now."

The shape before him snickered. "A good try, lad, but you willn't ever pass yourself off as a one on us."

At that moment, a blurred shape appeared in the fog, streaking over the barricade and tackling the sentry like a wildcat. Clerans thought he heard the faint noise of a blade sinking into human flesh, and the sentry collapsed to the ground without even a cry of pain. Yohni now appeared in the fog before Clerans, holding a bloody *karambit* knife in one of his hands.

"Well done," Clerans whispered.

Yohni only looked back at Clerans soberly.

There was a sound of grunting from the other side of the barricade, and in a moment Nōli tumbled down to Clerans' feet, rolling end over end, with the heavy pack seeming to drag him down the entire way. The little nymph collapsed onto the cobblestones with a loud clatter.

Clerans winced. Perhaps Halfdan had been right about not taking the little nymph with them.

Out of the fog on either side of them, came the shared cries of the pirate sentries.

"Who's there now?"

"Ay, don't move an inch!"

Clerans motioned for Yohni and Nōli to follow as he dashed away from the barricade down a road that led further into pirate-held territory. Just behind him, Clerans could hear a musket discharge from his left. Clerans waited, expecting to hear a bullet whizzing through the air nearby or clattering against the cobblestones, yet the shot was answered by a strangled cry from the pirates on his right.

"Return fire!" a voice was yelling out of the fog.

"We've been breached!"

Clerans couldn't help but smile to himself. Hopefully, the two groups of sentries would stay busy fighting each other for long enough that Clerans and the two nymphs could get away.

*Thank ye, Lord,* Clerans prayed. *I know that Ye will see us through!*

45

# REUNION

Slowly, the daze of her stupor fell off of Ella. She felt two hands pulling her to her feet. Ernest's voice was speaking in the air above her.

"Ella, Ella, it's over now. You can get up. It's all over."

Ella's legs felt like jelly, and her heart was pounding in her chest. What had happened? The last thing she remembered was that dreadful *thing* — that ghost — pursuing her with its dreadful claws. Had she fainted? Perhaps it had caught her and devoured her, and she was just now entering heaven.

But that was Ernest talking to her. Would Ernest be in heaven? Wasn't it one of the apostles who was supposed to bring people into heaven? Or was it an archangel?

"Ella," Ernest was still saying. "Ella, it's over."

Ella shook her head. "I'm dead then?"

"Thank God, no!" Ernest replied.

Well then, Ella thought, maybe Ernest wasn't so much of a heathen. Ella opened her eyes — had she been closing them this whole time? Slowly, she got her feet under her, and — with Ernest's help — she stood up.

Looking around, she could see the dark hall lit by the light of a few lanterns, which lay scattered about on the floor. Ella looked around quickly for that dreadful creature — the ghost — which the pirates had summoned. Where was it? There were those seven sickening pillars and the dais — Ella could just make out the still forms of Longfinch and the white-haired man in the dim light. Again, she scanned the room. She noted a few more obscure shapes on the ground, but there was no ghost in sight.

She felt comforted at this, though her mind told her that if she could not see the ghost, then it must be lurking nearby, ready to pounce on her. Somehow, though, the air no longer felt tense and sinister. She could not hear drums in her ears — though her heart was still racing. Darkness still surrounded her, but it was not thick and palpable as it had been before. The air was still cool, but it was soft and comforting, like the cool of a mountain spring on a hot summer's day.

"Whe'e is it?" Ella finally asked, looking back at Ernest.

"The ghost?" Ernest asked. "It's gone."

Ella furrowed her brow. "Gone? What do you mean, gone?"

"I mean..." Ernest was clearly searching for the right word, but he came up empty. "Gone. That's what I mean."

Ella shook her head. "What happened then?"

This question seemed even harder for Ernest to answer. He opened his mouth as if about to speak, but then closed it, clearly thinking about how to reply. He tried three or four times in this way, but did not seem able to answer.

"Is it still out the'e?" Ella asked. "Is it still hiding in the da'kness?"

Ernest shook his head. "No, he's... gone... or... eh... drived away?"

"Then who d'ove him away?" Ella asked.

Ernest swallowed, clearly unsure how to answer. "There was... eh... wings, or the lightness, or... no, but it was Him."

Ella peered at Ernest closely. "Him? But who is he, Ernest?"

Ernest let in a great breath. "The Almighty God." And he seemed unable to say more.

Ella continued to stare at Ernest for quite a while. What was he saying? What did God have to do with this? "A'e you saying," Ella finally said, "that God d'ove away the ghost?"

Ernest nodded enthusiastically. "That's exactly it. He answered to His name."

Ella couldn't help but notice that Ernest had a new light in his eye, a look of boldness and triumph that she had never seen there before. He was standing very straight and tall — though he was still a head shorter than her. And too, as Ella looked at him, she felt a deep sense of camaraderie with him.

Before now, she had appreciated his kindness to her and enjoyed his company in the darkness of those halls as a solace from the dread of the place. But in all of that, he had been nothing more than a fellow fugitive running from the pirates. What she felt now seemed more like she was looking into the eyes of a brother whom she had lost many years ago. There was a spark of emotion that could not be kindled from simply common experience. Ella's heart was telling her that she and Ernest had the same father.

But perhaps that was more true than she knew. Had they not both grown up without a father? What wounds did they both have that should have been comforted by their fathers, yet never were? And then Pastor Daerl's words came back to her — about a relational wound needing a relational cure. God himself was the Father who had healed her and been with her. By the look on Ernest's face, Ella was certain that Ernest had found that same cure. They did have the same Father then.

"God saved you then?" Ella said.

"That He did." And a bright smile spread all over Ernest's face.

Ella felt a great surge of joy come over her, and she threw

her arms around Ernest in a hug. The poor little gnome tried to return the embrace awkwardly.

"Now, now, Ella, we'd best look around."

"At what?" Ella asked, letting Ernest go.

Ernest motioned to a crumpled form that lay at the base of one of the immense columns. "Well, I'd like to know if'n he's alive, or dead."

Ella shuddered, and she looked around at the other obscure forms in the lantern light. "Is that all that's left of them? Longfinch's c'ew, I mean?"

Ernest nodded. "That remains to be seed. I'd best set my mind at ease. I'd want to know if'n there are any pirates left alive. Besides," Ernest again motioned to the form at the base of the column. "He nearly saved our lives — or he would have if'n he could have."

So saying, Ernest stepped over to a lantern. It was lying on its side, and the flame was spluttering and smoking badly. As Ernest picked it up, the flame righted itself and now flickered and flared, its homey light in the darkness.

Ernest walked over to the column and held the lantern directly over the crumpled form. Ella followed cautiously, but gasped when the light revealed the face. It was Martyn Blaeith! What was he doing down here?

"Ma'tyn!" Ella exclaimed. "But how?"

Ernest shrugged. "I wondered that myself."

Ella quickly knelt next to Martyn and felt for his pulse. "He's still alive. Goodness! He must be out cold."

"Here then," Ernest said, handing her the lantern. "You take this and look after him. I'll see to the pirates."

With that, Ernest hurried away, picking up another lantern from the ground.

Ella set her lantern down where it would cast its light directly over Martyn. Then she grabbed him by the feet and — with an effort — pulled him out straight.

There! He was no longer crumpled up in a heap. Hopefully, that would help him. At least he should be able to breathe more easily. Bending over him, she could feel his shallow breathing against her cheek. She could see that he had an alarming bruise on his forehead, but he seemed to have no other injury.

Ella sighed, and she sat back on her heels. What was she to do now? Oh, how much she wished that she had read some medical books in all of her studies! Then she could do something for Martyn. Ah, well, it couldn't be helped. Thankfully, Martyn did not seem to be badly hurt. But how would she wake him? She might have splashed some cold water on his face, but she had no water with her.

Oh, water!

At that thought, Ella suddenly realized that she was very thirsty. How long had she been in these dark halls? And she hadn't had anything to eat or drink that whole time. Ella's stomach growled painfully. Bother! Why'd she have to think of this now? What good would it do for Martyn if she were sitting there reveling in her thirst and hunger?

But what could she do for Martyn, anyway? Perhaps it might be a good idea to see if he was responsive, even in his sleep. Ella brought the light up close to Martyn's face, and then — feeling rather silly for doing it — she poked him on the cheek. He flinched and turned away. Good, so he wasn't *that* unconscious. But that single poke must have been all that Martyn needed, for he stirred now and groaned.

At that moment, Ernest came hurrying back, holding one of the pirates' pistols in his hand and shaking his head. "All the pirates are there, and they're dead, sure. But not Killjelly. I can't find him. He must still be around here somewhere." Ernest sighed wearily. "I don't like it one bit. Of all on the pirates to get away, it haved to be Killjelly. Ay, and he's the one what's most likely to give us trouble."

But then Ernest paused and perked up his ears. Ella did the same. She thought she could hear footsteps in the darkness.

Ernest held his lantern up high and pointed his newfound pistol towards the sound. "Here now, who's there? You'd best show yourself and come along nicely, or it'll be worse for you!"

"You again?" a voice replied from the darkness.

Ella leapt to her feet in surprise and joy. "Haeli, is that you?"

And the next moment, Haeli came bounding out of the darkness, her coiled hair dancing in the lantern light as she threw her arms around Ella.

"Ella! Ella, we have found you at long last!"

"But Haeli," Ella replied, her mind a blur of confusion. "How did... I mean... you and Ma'tyn... but where...?"

Her question died on her lips as she saw two more forms enter the lantern light. The first was one of the small savages — not unlike that little savage boy whom she had met the day she washed up on the beach. But it was the second form that made Ella pause.

"Fathe'h?" Ella stared in disbelief. It was Titus Donne. How could it be? How could her stepfather be here now?

"Fathe'h?" she said again, but she could say no more. A wave of emotion fell on her. She was weeping now, and her stepfather's strong and tender arms wrapped around her. She didn't know hardly what to say, or think, or do. She only leaned close against him and wept.

"Hush, now, Ella, my girl. Hush," her step-father was saying. "You'll be... er... It's alright. It's alright."

Ella hardly knew how long she wept, but finally she drew herself away and looked her step-father in the face. Yes, it was him. There was no denying that. But how had he gotten here? Out of the corner of her eye, Ella noticed that Martyn was standing on his feet now, blinking like an owl and leaning against the column heavily. Ernest was at his ear, talking excitedly. Was he trying to explain what had just happened?

Suddenly, a thought came to Ella, and she burst out in tears again. "O Fathe'h!" she cried, burying herself in her step-father's arms again, "oh Fathe'h, I've seen Papa! He was here. He was alive."

"Er, eh, what now?" her step-father replied, alarm on his face.

"He was he'e," Ella said again. "My Papa. Don't you understand?"

Titus held Ella out at arm's reach and looked her closely in the eye. "Your Papa? You mean Silas?"

Ella nodded. "He was alive! I saw him, befo'e the pi'ates shot him."

Her stepfather looked at her blankly. For a moment, a familiar revulsion came over Ella. Of course, he didn't understand. Why did he have to be so slow? He couldn't hardly finish a sentence once he had started it.

"Silas Pickering... er. Oh! I see. You think... eh, I mean... in the basement? You saw him in the basement?"

Ella nodded. "Just befo'e he died. He talked to me. He said that he was Silas Pickering. Can you believe it?"

Her stepfather nodded. "Ah, yes, it was quite a coincidence. Er, another man, with the same name as, er... well, your father."

Ella shook her head. "What eve'h a'e you talking about? It was *my* Papa. He said so!"

Titus looked confused. "No, er... eh, I should know your father. I was... eh, that is... we were good friends for years. I should know."

"But don't you see?" Ella said, growing angry now. "I've seen my Papa. He's been alive this whole time!"

Titus shook his head emphatically. "Oh no, Ella. It was... eh... it was some coincidence that they had the same name — I should know your papa."

Ella pushing herself away from her stepfather, standing a few feet away and regarding him closely. "What a'e you saying?"

Titus nodded. "I'm... eh... I'm saying that the man in the basement who, er, claimed to be Silas Pickering, was not, eh, *the* Silas Pickering."

Ella looked at Titus closely. "But..."

Titus shook his head. "No, Ella... eh... I should know. Your father and I were best friends."

"But..." Ella cried.

Titus waved his hand to cut her off. "Your father had blue eyes, like you. That man in the basement had brown eyes. He was *not* your Papa."

Ella took a step back, thinking back to that picture of her Papa in Mama's locket — those bright blue eyes. But Titus was right. The man who died in the basement — the man who had sacrificed his life to save her — his eyes had been brown.

46

# PREDESTINATED

The fog seemed even thicker on this side of the barricade. Clerans could hardly see two feet in front of him as he rushed down the street. He had a pretty good idea of where he was in the Lower Village, but couldn't tell for certain what street he was on by the little he could make out in the darkness. Finally, he saw a small alley just to his right. Darting into it, Clerans crouched low, taking cover. Yohni crouched mutely beside Clerans, and Nōli stumbled into the alleyway just behind them, panting heavily.

Clerans tried to catch his breath while he waited, straining his ears for any evidence of pursuit. He could hear several more sharp reports from the direction of the barricade, followed by loud cursing. Then a loud whistle sounded in the thick air. Clerans recognized it at once as the sound of a boatswain's whistle.

"We're breached!" he heard a voice crying loudly while the whistle continued to screech.

Though Clerans was not familiar with the boatswain's whistle signals, he guessed that the pirates at the barricade were raising an alarm. Clerans bit the inside of his cheek. He may have made it past the barricade, then, but the pirates would be on high alert now.

Clerans moved to continue down the street when he heard many boots rushing across the cobblestones. Clerans ducked back into the alleyway and crouched low. The group of reinforcements rushed past the alleyway, taking no notice of it.

After waiting for another moment, Clerans slunk out of the alleyway and continued down the street, keeping close to the shop fronts on the right side. The entire street was in equal darkness now, and the fog was still thick. Clerans hoped that if another group of pirates rushed down the street, they would not see him, Yohni, or Nōli.

Avoiding detection, however, was only one of Clerans' concerns; he also had to find the Lower Court. After crossing the burnt section of the village, Clerans was no longer certain what street he was on. Taking careful note of each of the shop fronts that he passed, Clerans guessed that he was on Efynson Street, which would run directly into the north-western corner of the Lower Court. If this were true, however, then they would run into Jetty Road shortly, just south of the old stone jetty.

Clerans had only just come to this conclusion when the line of shops on his right came to an abrupt end. Here Clerans paused, pressing himself up against the outside of a shop. Yohni and Nōli followed his example. Nōli was still panting heavily behind him.

Bother that little nymph! Even if they could escape being seen in this fog, any pirate who passed by would be certain to hear Nōli.

Clerans turned back to Nōli and could see the little Twengoli boy still struggling to stand up under the weight of the pack. Clerans shook his head.

"Here, Nōli," he whispered, "this will never do. Give me the pack, now."

Nōli looked at him in some confusion.

Clerans bit the inside of his cheek. Of course, the boy couldn't understand the common tongue. Clerans tried to think how he could repeat his sentence with the little Tylweni that he knew.

"Give thou unto me," Clerans said haltingly in Tylweni, painfully aware of the fact that he was using the familiar voice instead of the formal voice. But what was the formal voice for 'to give?' "Give thou unto me the... thing of carrying of thee."

Nōli still looked at Clerans in confusion.

"Of thine," Clerans corrected. "Give thou unto me the thing of carrying things of thine."

Nōli blinked.

Clerans clenched his teeth together. This was useless.

Just then, Clerans heard more pirates marching down the street in front of them. Clerans stood stock-still, pressing himself up against the outside wall of the last shop. There was no time to hide. Clerans could only hope that the fog would conceal him from the pirates' sight.

"Dear Lord," Clerans breathed, "keep us hidden!"

To his great relief, Nōli held his breath — at least, Clerans could no longer hear the little Twengoli boy's panting. Clerans could hear (but not see) the group of pirates marching with some haste down the road. Even as the sound passed them, Clerans could see no more of the pirates than a few vague shadows.

As the sound of this latest group of pirates faded away towards the barricade, Clerans focused his attention ahead of him again. If he was right about being on Efynson Street, then they had just reached the intersection with Jetty Road. Yet he could be sure of nothing in this thick fog. Really, though, Clerans had no other option but to trust his guess about where he was.

After another moment, Clerans motioned for Yohni and

Nōli to follow him, and he started out from the cover of the shop across Jetty Road — as he presumed it to be.

He could see the dark shapes of the shops on the other side of the street looming above him in the fog as he approached, and he hurried towards them. But now he could see a space between the shops directly in front of him. That had to be Efynson Street then. Now Clerans was certain that his guess was right. They were on track. In two more blocks, they would reach the Lower Court.

Clerans rushed forward, trying to cross Jetty Road as quickly as he could. Even in this dense fog, he felt exposed in the open street. At that moment, a figure materialized in the fog before him, standing directly in his way.

"Who's there?"

Clerans wasted no time, drawing out his tomahawk and throwing himself violently on the pirate before him. The pirate leveled his musket at Clerans, but they were too close now for that. Clerans turned the barrel aside with a deft stroke of his tomahawk, then, catching the man by the wrist before he could draw out his sword, Clerans delivered a fatal blow to the man's throat. The man collapsed before Clerans with a strangled yell.

Clerans' blood pounded in his ears, yet he still felt remarkably calm. He breathed deeply with his stomach and exhaled to calm himself. Surely the pirates' cry would raise the alarm now. It was only a matter of time before reinforcements would arrive. They were so close to the Lower Court! Maybe it was time to throw stealth aside and make a dash for it.

Clerans motioned at the dark forms of Yohni and Nōli. "Forward then: we are almost to the square!"

With that, Clerans plunged through the fog directly along Efynson Street. He could barely make out the shops along the road as he rushed by. He passed Trinity Street on his right; just one more block to go. They'd be in the Lower Court in no time. But would it be guarded?

The answer to these questions came to Clerans as three dark shapes directly in front of him. Clerans bit his lip. The plan had not misfired yet. God would guard them and see them through. He would give them the victory.

Three bright flashes lit up the thick fog, followed by three sharp reports. Clerans could hear the charges cut through the air a few inches away from his head before skittering across the cobblestone behind him.

There was nothing for it now. They would just have to fight their way through. As long as there were only three pirates before him, Clerans felt sure that he and Yohni could finish them before any more reinforcements arrived. They would reach Laendon and the rest of the survivors in no time now. They were almost there.

"Lord, guide my hands to war."

Clerans let his pack fall from his shoulders as he unslung his rifle. He would pick the pack back up after he had finished these three pirates. He had to be able to move freely. An electric energy flowed through him. He was ready. By God's strength, he would destroy any pirate that stood in his way. They would succeed.

The shape of a pirate appeared before him in the fog. Clerans deftly leveled his rifle and pulled the trigger. The flint struck against the steel as it was supposed to, but the rifle did not fire. Clerans was, for the moment, stunned. What had happened? His gun should have fired, and he should have already killed the first of these three assailants.

With a sinking dismay, Clerans realized that the drizzle must have ruined the powder in his rifle. He should have been keeping better care to see that his gunpowder was still dry! How could he be so careless?

Clerans had no time to berate himself, for this first pirate, sword in hand, was upon him in an instant. Clerans parried the first sword stroke with the barrel of his rifle and then struck the pirate forcefully in the knee with the butt of his gun. The pirate fell back with a scream of pain, but before he could back up more than a step, Clerans had turned his rifle back around and thrust his bayonet into the pirate's chest.

Clerans suddenly saw the dark shape of a pirate on his right, yet before he had time to draw his bayonet back, something slammed into the side of his head. Stars burst upon Clerans' vision. He was reeling and for a moment could not think what was happening. He felt his left side strike the wet, uneven surface of the cobblestone street.

His head still throbbed with pain, but he struggled to get to his feet. He could see the dark shape of a pirate looming over him in the fog, and he knew he had only a moment to act before the pirate struck him again.

Desperately, and as a last resort, Clerans drew out his pistol, praying as he did so that the powder was not wet. He pulled the trigger.

"God, be with me now!"

To his horror, all he heard was the mocking *click* of the flint striking the steel, but his pistol would not fire.

Now the dim outline of a musket butt broke through the fog, and then Clerans felt the jarring shock as it struck him in the forehead. His whole body recoiled at the blow, and the back of his head slammed into the cobblestones.

For a moment, he could see nothing but blackness and dancing stars. Dimly, he realized that he was lying on his face. His mind swam in confusion, and he expected any moment to feel the sharp prick of a bayonet between his shoulder blades. What would it feel like to be run through with cold steel?

"Alive!" Clerans heard a voice yelling, but it sounded muffled and far away.

"Alive!" the voice repeated. "Bloodrummer said 'alive.'"

"I was, I was," a second voice protested.

Something struck Clerans savagely in the side, and he let out an involuntary groan.

"See!" the second voice said. "He's alive."

"Good," the first voice replied, "because he wouldn't be any fun to us dead, now would he?"

Two hands grabbed Clerans by the shoulder, dragging him forcefully to his feet again. His vision swam, yet he could just make out the leering face of a gnome quite close to him; everything else in his sight seemed to be rapidly turning black.

"Oh, and he's a young one, too. All the better! They always have more pity on their young ones — especially when they hear them screaming."

The other voice chuckled. "Ay, and he'll scream when we're done with him, willn't he?"

Both voices joined in ribald laughter. The dark edges of Clerans' vision seemed to be closing in on themselves, and Clerans knew he was about to lose consciousness again.

"O Lord!" he mumbled. "Help me! It is not too late... Save me..."

The hideous features of the gnome swam in front of Clerans' vision again, and a sinister smile spread across his face.

"Eh, now what's that?"

Clerans felt like lead. His vision was rapidly going black.

"It *is* too late," the gnome hissed. "No one can save you now."

# PRONUNCIATION KEY

Most of the proper nouns in this book are transliterations from Llaedhwythi Tylwen, except for a couple from Helfenic. The following is a guide to the pronunciation of Llaedhwythi Tylwen:

***Consonants** – as in English with a few exceptions:*

- **c** - always hard as in *c*lub, never as in *c*ertain.
- **ch** - as in Ba*ch* never as in *ch*urch. Strictly not used in pure Llaedhwythi Tylwen, but often in other forms of Tylweni and foreign words.
- **dh** - like the *th* sound in *the*n, never as in *th*istle.
- **f** - v as in of.
- **ff** - f as in off.
- **g** - always hard like *g*irl, never as in *g*entle.
- **ll** - sounds almost like *dl*, in technical terms, a voiceless alveolar lateral fricative.
- **r** - flapped, as in Spanish.
- **rr** - trilled, as in Spanish.
- **th** - as in *th*istle, never as in *the*n.

*Vowels:*

- **a** - short as in Ell*a*. This vowel can never take the accent.
- **e** - short as in f*e*d.
- **i** - long as in sk*i*.
- **o** - short as in p*o*t, or long as in h*o*me.
- **u** - short as in p*u*t.
- **y** - short as in h*y*t. When followed directly by a vowel becomes a consonant, as in *y*olk.
- **w** - long as in pl*w*me. When followed directly by a vowel becomes a consonant as in *w*alk.

*Diphthongs:*

- **ae** - short as in *a*pple.
- **ei** - long as in h*ay*.
- **aei** - long as in sk*y*.
- **aey** - similar to *aei* but ending farther back in the mouth.

*Subjunctive*: the subjunctive case represents uncertainty or doubt, and is signified by the ending *'ll*. Example "They'll will eat," means "They might (or might not) eat."

# PISTOSIAN WORD GLOSSARY

**'ll** – subjunctive suffix used to denote uncertainty

**cede** – to go, or to yield (as in con*cede*)

**ceive** – take, hold (as in re*ceive*)

**celer** – fast, quick (as in ac*celer*ate)

**cern** – separate (as in dis*cern*)

**clude** – close, shut, end (as in ex*clude*)

**cognize** – know in a relational sense (as in re*cognize*)

**duce** – to lead (as in de*duce*)

**fiscate** – buy

**gard** – look, watch (as in re*gard*)

**kye** – cattle

**legate** – send, especially as a messenger

**lieve** – lift, raise (as in re*lieve*)

**llifsa** – interjection of general surprise or consternation

**merri** – much, very, lot

**maugre** – instead of

**petticoat** – a crude, derogatory term for a woman

**plete** – fill (as in com*plete*)

**pose** – put (as in inter*pose*)

**prehend** – grasp (as in *prehen*sile)

**prive** – rob, steal (as in de*prive*)
**priver** – petty thief, pickpocket
**quire** – ask (as in in*quire*)
**ruth** – pity (as in *ruth*less)
**scend** – climb, rise (as in a*scend*)
**spire** – breathe (as in con*spire*)
**sault** – leap, jump (as in as*sault*)
**tain** – have (as in con*tain*, or ob*tain*)
**trive** – find (as in re*trieve*)
**tryst** – as a verb: to have a romantic meeting. As a noun: a beau
**vail** – power (as in pre*vail*)
**vene** – to come
**vert** – turn (as in a*vert*)
**voke** – call, yell, cry (as in *vo*cal)
**ween** – imagine
**ye** – second person singular pronoun
**you** – second person plural pronoun
**younker** – youth

# ABOUT THE AUTHOR

Amos Christian Wilson is a history enthusiast, bagpipe player, fantasy cartographer, theology nerd, home-school graduate, and award-winning storyteller. His inspirations come from his love of nature and history, as well as his experience across a wide range of blue-collar trades, including carpentry and piano tuning. Amos currently lives with his wife and children in the scenic Flint Hills of Kansas.

Sign up for A. C. Wilson's newsletter to receive updates on upcoming books, and receive a free e-book prequel to *My Father's Land*!

**www.ACWilson.net**

*and*

**acwilson.substack.com**

# ALSO IN THE GWAMBI TETRALOGY

This series draws as much from J. R. R. Tolkien and Indiana Jones as it does from Charles Dickens. With a focus on immersive world-building that features fully developed fantasy races, deeply religious colonists, and labor riots, "The Gwambi Tetralogy" is black-powder, epic low fantasy, bordering on magical realism, with a faith-based, and character-driven plot.

### Book 1 - *My Father's Land*

☞ https://wisepathbooks.com/products/my-fathers-land

These pirates who just kidnapped Ella seem to think that she knows the location of the Gwambi's Lost City of Gold. Sure, her father died looking for the Gwambi city, but that doesn't mean she knows anything about it. Her mother wouldn't even let her read the one book they owned on the lost Gwambi city. Mind you, she read every other book in the house—every other book in the parish—so she knows a thing or two. The question is, can she do anything with all that head knowledge? I mean, does it matter if she can positively identify the difference between a gnome, a leprechaun, and a nymph, if she can't defend herself when they are trying to stab her in the gut? And let's not even start talking about the sorcerer...

With a focus on immersive world-building that features fully developed fantasy races, deeply religious colonists, and labor riots, *My Father's Land* draws as much from JRR Tolkien and Indiana Jones as it does from Charles Dickens.

### Book 2 - *My Father's Ghost*

☞ https://wisepathbooks.com/products/my-fathers-ghost

Her father taught Haeli everything she needs to know to get along in the world, everything from breaking in stallions, to martial arts, to negotiating with the Indigenous nymphs of the coast. But then her father gives her the ancient Gwambi keys... and tells her to run.

With pirates, a sorcerer, and a griffin hunting for her and her family, Haeli must rely on all her will and wits to keep the keys safe. Is it even worth giving Ella the keys, or is she too preoccupied with the labor strikes devolving into violence, and the indigenous people taking revenge on the rural populous? Oh, and then there is the ghost...

**Book 4 - *My Father's Will* - coming soon**

After finding God, things couldn't be better for Ernest. I mean, it would probably be better if he wasn't trapped in the ancient Gwambi catacombs, with no food or water to speak of. It would also be better if Clerans wasn't about to be skinned alive by the pirates, or if Martyn wasn't slowly bleeding to death from a traumatic head injury. But no fear, there *is* someone else trapped in the catacombs with them, someone who — if he doesn't kill them — has the medical knowledge necessary to save Martyn's life: Killjelly…

www.ingramcontent.com/pod-product-compliance
Lightning Source LLC
Chambersburg PA
CBHW060608300726
48975CB00005B/1495